ALTAR OF ASHES

Library of Congress Control Number: 2023944350

ISBN (paperback): 978-1-956450-83-5
ISBN (Ebook): 978-1-956450-84-2

Thousand Acres is an imprint of Armin Lear Press, Inc.
Armin Lear Press, Inc.
215 W Riverside Drive, #4362
Estes Park, CO 80517

ALTAR OF ASHES

Bruce Westrate

THOUSAND
ACRES

For my Father

PART I

November 1, 1996
4:30 a.m.

Ted Polanski poured himself another glass of milk. 4:30 a.m., and he'd been up since 3:00 preparing for the hunt, gathering his gear, cleaning his rifle...and waiting. *Tim's always late.*

This was an important occasion, after all. Because they were finally seniors, ready to blow their little town. Next fall, he'd be in Ann Arbor without a firearm, or a forest, or the deer he loved to hunt. Since he had begun hunting at twelve, it was all about a successful outing. But this year, for some reason, it seemed more about relishing the experience. Give themselves something to remember years later when they took their own sons hunting.

An hour ago, Ted had been furious; now he was just irritated. *Perspective, that's what I need.* He could work himself up to a foot-stomping, spittle-flying rage, or he could try not to let it spoil his day.

At last, the beam from a pair of headlights arced across Ted's dimly lit kitchen. The garage door hummed and clacked.

"Hey. All set?" Tim Scanlan, laden with an enormous box of donuts—a peace offering—looked apprehensive.

"I've been set for over an hour," Ted grumbled. "Late night, y'know?"

"Oh right," Ted scoffed. "Sheila wouldn't let go. Tim offered in ribaldry, eyebrows arched in lame appeal. Ted could smell last night, strong on his buddy's breath. It seemed Tim always reserved his tardiness for the express aggravation of his closest friends. *Hell, maybe in its way it's even a compliment.* "Forget it," Ted said.

Ten minutes later all the gear was packed into Ted's pickup. Beneath the star-splashed dome of November sky, the early morning air was bracing, tainted only by exhaust from the warming truck. Inside, the vehicle was suffused with reassuring aromas: strong java, dewy gravel, sodden leaves, the baked-in sweat of old hunting jackets, and a hint of bourbon. Mugs of coffee, balanced precariously on the dash, fogged the windshield. The now-endangered stash of donuts lay open between them.

Tension defused; Ted grinned at Tim. "Let's get on the goddamn road."

All forgiven, the two boys chattered like squirrels as the truck crunched down the slag driveway. Its low beams swung along a field of unharvested corn, reaching

4

through the morning mist. Minutes later, lulled to slumber by the highway, Tim began snoring.

On the back-road access to their favorite campsite it was still inky dark. Old man Stickle had graduated high school with Ted's grandpa and had always allowed him to stray onto his property after deer, just so long as he didn't abuse the privilege. He parked the truck as close as possible to the level spot where they usually pitched their tent and shook Tim's shoulder. Tim finally roused himself enough to un-rack his 30-06 rifle; then he nodded off again with the pickup door open. Purposefully, Ted started to unload by the light of the headlights, grousing to himself. *Tim, like always, could sleep through the Second Coming.*

Then, shining from somewhere deep in the forest, a glint of light caught Ted's peripheral eye. He returned to the truck and doused the lights. *There it is again.* He blinked, rubbing the corner of his right eye with a meaty fist. Presently, his vision cleared. The forest was thick, but not so dense as to blot out dancing wisps of what appeared to be flame. About 200 yards in the distance, a fire—or maybe even scores of fires—flickered like fireflies through a filigree of beech, maple, and oak. *Forest fire? Not likely during this wet season.* But neither did the many random movements he saw suggest campers.

Ted squinted hard. Shadows danced among the trees. *Torches? Lanterns?* He couldn't be certain.

"What the hell do you make of that?" He looked over at his friend, but Tim was still dozing, loosely embracing his rifle. Ted prodded him hard in the ribs.

Groggily, Tim brought his rifle to the ready, as if by instinct, scanning for a target.

"No, goddamn it!" Ted pointed, "Over there!"

"Christ Almighty!" Tim stretched as he yawned. "That ain't gonna help our chances much. Maybe we better move."

"Yeah?" Ted scowled. "Well, if I'm gonna be forced to leave our best spot, I want to know why."

"Whaddya mean?"

"What do you *think*?" Ted clambered out of the truck, grabbed his rifle from the window rack and heaved the backpack with the spare ammo out of the truck bed. Tim followed reluctantly. "Shit fire and save matches, Ted, forget it! Let's find another spot. Maybe just follow the ridge south."

Suddenly, the two boys froze. *Something very strange was going on in that glade. Eerie sounds.* Ted turned his ear toward the distant noises: Cymbals? Castanets? Mournful chants. Drums thumping out vaguely sinister tempos. He shivered despite himself and thought aloud: "What the hell could be going on over there this time of day?" Overwhelmed by curiosity, Ted signaled Tim toward the voices and bobbing lights. Clutching their guns with white knuckles, they closed to within

50 yards of the commotion and took cover behind two large oaks. In the wind, Ted got a passing whiff of something exotic, pungent. *Some sort of incense?* In the back of his mind, frames from the latest horror movie he'd seen danced for attention. *The Craft*, maybe.

Scores of torches lit the scene: maybe a hundred people milling in a clearing, muttering incantations Ted couldn't decipher, depositing nondescript bundles onto the bare earth. Robed women flitted, wailing eerie lamentations. In the center of a clearing stood an elevated stage festooned with flowers and overhung by a silk canopy, atop a pyramid of interlocked logs about seven feet high. *Some kinda ceremony.* Most striking of all, Ted noted as he sat hunched, shivering: *The crowd was almost… captive, hypnotized, transfixed*—chanting, pulsating as if by one will.

From the west, where the wooded path opened onto another expanse of corn stubble, some sort of procession wended its way toward the crude platform, led by dark figures decked in long lace robes beneath headdresses like Ted had never seen.

A young girl, perhaps 10-12 years of age, seemed to be the focus of the crowd's fixation. She was clad in a flowing red robe embroidered with gold; a decorative ornament gathered her black, silken hair; her ears, ankles and wrists were adorned with an assortment of gold earrings, jewels, anklets, and bangles, looking for all the world like a character from 'Aladdin'. Her lower face was obscured by a scarlet veil, her coal-dark eyes were clearly fixed straight ahead of her. Ted gaped in astonishment at the top of the structure where a man's body lay, wrapped in what he took to be a burial shroud, leaving only its waxen face exposed to the sky.

As the company approached, the chants grew louder, more distinct, cadenced. Ted made out the syllables: "*Sati... ki. Sati... ki;*

One by one, people approached the girl and genuflected before her. Ted picked up on a couple more utterances: "*Sati mata ki. Sati mata ki...*"

Individuals bent half-crouched, trembling as they approached, and deposited flowers, sheaves of grain and bolts of embroidered cloth at the girl's tiny feet, then scuttled back.

"Sati mata ki... Sati mata ki..."

The flow of the procession split into two pulsing channels on either side of the rude edifice, and the chanting changed. Ted detected two more words being repeated:

"*Job... Roop... Job... Roop.*"

Slowly, as if deliberately, the girl turned toward the platform. She removed her jewels and gold ornaments, handed them to a slight matron, and stood utterly still. A stocky man in a red headdress emerged from the crowd and leaned close to her, prompting movement suggestive of juvenile ballet: Once, twice, three times she circled the structure. The priestly figures poured something over her hands. She clambered up the ascending tiers of logs to the top, where the body lay, placed herself on it "Indian style" and gently rested the corpse's head at her immature left breast.

Ted looked at Tim who, like himself, was staring, stunned, terrified.

The child began to rotate her head on her slender shoulders. Her eyeballs disappeared under drooping lids. In a disconcerting monotone, she muttered, *"Ram, Ram, Ram, Ram…"*

Several men advanced from the crowd with firebrands and lit tinder bundles on the fringe of the structure; others poured a viscous fluid on the kindling. In seconds, the blaze whooshed into an inferno as eager tongues of flame lapped up the fuel. Still, the child chanted, louder and louder, and Ted heard above the droning throng: *"Om sati, om sati, om sati…"* The girl cradled the corpse as if she were a Madonna, succumbing to a rhythmic rocking, back and forth.

Smoke coiled into bluish columns that sometimes masked the bier from the hunters. Ted saw Tim signal him, visibly quaking; but with his attention riveted on the girl, Ted ignored him. Yet the huge tree that shielded him from view afforded little real comfort.

Abruptly, amid the searing heat and choking smoke, the child's seeming trance gave way to something else:

first, mounting awareness then, finally, panic. She flung aside her macabre companion, rising to tear at the veil, her face now contorted by stark, looming terror. Stumbling, she scurried frantically across the top of the pile, flailing at the canopy, grasping for escape.

But what had seemed a worshipful host below, now soured into a clamoring mob. Dark, menacing, it screamed unintelligibly and raised clenched fists aloft, throbbing in unison. The girl whimpered, pressed her palms together as if to implore mercy, then tripped over the body to sprawl piteously over the corpse. Now, a forest of knotted arms stretched from below, pinning her to the pile with long staves of bamboo. Then, just as suddenly, the pyre collapsed into the conflagration beneath. The girl's hideous shrieks diminished to dull wails, which were soon lost amid the ululations of the enraptured throng.

As if on cue, the stupefied boys turned at once to stare, saucer-eyed, at each other, struggling to process the events unfolding before them. "We gotta do something," Ted mouthed inaudibly, pointing first at his rifle, then at the fire. Tim responded only with a mute, wide-eyed, but definitive, shake of his head, then a gesture hinting at immediate retreat. They were armed, it was true, but badly outnumbered for all that. Unbidden, an old saying popped into Ted's head having to do with valor's link to discretion, as he tried to backtrack slowly from the glade. His legs felt rubbery, unresponsive, hampered by the disconcerting dread that he would be nailed by fear to that tree.

Ted's paralysis was broken when Tim grabbed his arm, and crouching, tripping, inching backwards, they dumbly, gingerly picked their way through the edge of the forest. Then a loud snap as Tim stepped on a tinder dry limb of Jack Pine. At once, the boys heard shouts behind them, then the unmistakable commotion of panic. They picked up their pace, breaking into a dead run toward their campsite once they emerged from the concealment of the woods. Ted couldn't help but steal one last backward glance at the glade. *Crackling fire, but no torches, no shadowy forms, no frenzied movement. Did I hallucinate all that?* Tim's panicked gait suggested otherwise.

The boys shot through the boggy brush on the other side of the clearing and into their camp. "Leave the gear!" Ted shouted, his pulse racing like an Indy car pulling out of the pit. Through the undergrowth the boys careened toward the pickup and scrambled into the cab, not even bothering to fasten their guns to the window rack. Slamming and hurriedly locking the doors, Ted gunned the engine to life. The groaning vehicle lurched forward, squealed into a U-turn, spat gravel from the shoulder, and sped off down the asphalt in a blue fog of oily exhaust.

November 1
5:20 a.m.
Allen Southworth's home, town of Principia, Indiana

Allen Southworth sat in his dimly lit kitchen, drinking his first cup of coffee. His wife Jan and his two small children were upstairs still snug in their beds and would be for a couple of hours yet.

He was contemplating the large changes that had recently taken place in his life. Though he and Jan had been married for fifteen years, they'd only recently had the children, a boy, and a girl. Once the babies arrived, Jan insisted Allen find a way to cut back his practice and spend more time with the family. Now District Attorney for Pope County, up until a year ago he'd been a high-powered attorney in private practice with a partner, working 80 hours a week and bringing in the kind of money such devoted labor could accrue.

And it hadn't been for nothing. Glamorous romantic getaways to Ann Arbor, Chicago and New York whenever their busy schedules permitted. They'd been to Europe. Allen had learned much from her over the years whether in the spiral of the Pantheon or the endless corridors of the Louvre. He never would have looked twice at the Winged Victory had it not been for the animated narration of his brilliant wife.

But once the children arrived, his preoccupation with work became an issue for Jan, who wanted both help with the kids along with a father who'd be present. Not just for important events but for all the minutiae of daily family life. Yet, much as Allen loved his kids, he struggled to reconcile himself to this new, duller routine. His wife was well-acquainted with the feeling.

She'd abandoned her life as a globe-trotting graduate student in cultural anthropology for the unanticipated confinement of small-town domesticity. Their shared passion for golf didn't quite compensate for those forays into the Argentine Andes trailing San Juan peasants and cranky llamas. And while her serious work had begun in Argentina, Jan had crossed Europe in all directions sandwiched between a year of philosophy at the Sorbonne, easily picking up passing Italian and French with which to complement her Spanish. She'd always had a facility for languages. A fat lot of good all that did her now, she often groused, as she pondered her domestic confinement with her adorable, but high-maintenance children. As Allen sat brooding, he heard footsteps on the stairs. Jan had risen early. He cringed automatically, anticipating the inevitable conversation. Already plotting an escape, he stood quickly.

Jan entered the kitchen, yawning, "You're up with the birds."

"Have to get to work early this morning," he deadpanned, avoiding her gaze. "I'll call if I'm going to be late."

"Uh-huh," Jan grunted.

Yeah, she'd heard that one before.

November 1
6:00 a.m.
Stickle's Farm, outside Principia, Indiana

"Aw-r-OOOOOoooo!"

Danged mutt! Abner Stickle grimaced, squinted, and slowly opened his right eyelid to the blackness of the farmhouse bedroom. Beside him, his wife Gertie seemed to be snoring contentedly. *But she's faking, for sure.* This was hardly the first time they'd played this game: one outwaiting the other to avoid bringing in Chance, Abner's aging Lab retriever.

"Aw-r-OOooo!"

Damned dog. Oughta shoot 'im.

Tossing the down comforter aside, Abner groped for his robe and slippers and stumbled downstairs in a fog. He shuffled toward the kitchen counter to start the coffee, in no hurry to silence the howling outside. *Serve her right to hear a little more of it,* he thought. As he absently rinsed and filled the pot, Abner tried to stare through his reflection in the still-dark window above the sink, he winced at the old man who stared back.

Then he saw what appeared to be fleeting movement in the woods on the other side of his bean field.

He'd sold the woodlot recently, in a rather strange transaction. Conducted through a local bank, the buyer had insisted on anonymity. Ordinarily, such a condition would've queered the deal for Abner. *But the money!* The old farmer marveled. *Ten grand an acre – for nothin' but marshy woods!* He supposed it had some development potential, what with the stream that converged from two rivulet branches near the edge of the trees. And the timber might bring in a few bucks. But none of those 20 acres was tillable. *Buyer obviously knows squat about land values.* The money, though, would ensure him and Gertie a comfortable retirement. Their one extravagance with the money so far had been a big-screen TV for Gertie. *Larger than bloody life, her soaps, the Oprahs, the Jerry Springers, her precious Regis and Kathy Lee—Gertie does love her TV.*

In a way, Abner was glad to be shuck of the piece of property; it'd always been a magnet to local teenagers in search of a good time, to guzzle beer, smoke pot, screw their girlfriends and vent adolescent emotions around a campfire. *But now it looked as if they'd made one hell of a blaze* last *night, bigger than usual.* He'd first noticed the flame from the bathroom window two hours before, when he got up for one of his ever-so-frequent visits to the toilet. *Damn prostate.*

Proprietary instincts die hard, though. *Sonuvabitchin' goddamn kids!* Even now, from inside the house he could hear a dozen or more cars roaring to life. *They'll have the access road all churned up into a bog...*

Something about this commotion didn't seem quite right, though. *Timing's wrong: Even teens rarely hang out till almost dawn.*

He opened the screen door and stepped onto the porch. *Strange.* The last of the string of vehicles was stopping intermittently to replace the logs and the brush Abner'd placed there to discourage such intrusions. *Not the way kids normally behave. Hell, kids letting me know they've been there by leaving a mess seems to be half their fun.*

It was awfully goddamn early, but the old farmer felt he'd better investigate the damage. And the fire. Old Chance was already way ahead of him, scrambling toward the intruders. The warped driver-side door of Abner's rusting Dodge pickup creaked tinnily as he swung it open. He carefully laid his shotgun and a flashlight on the mouse-eaten seat and tossed a shovel into the bed, followed by a clanking, rusty pitchfork.

With the small of his back screaming from a recent muscle pull, Abner winced, eased himself gingerly behind the wheel, shifted into first gear and chugged out the driveway onto Griffis Road. He strained to see through the clear crescent the Dodge's indifferent fan was melting into the hoarfrost on the windshield. The truck sounded like a Sherman tank, but the crumbling muffler and deafening exhaust were like allies to Stickle, enough to scare hell out of any stragglers.

The countryside around the Stickle's house beckoned

like a painter's canvas, splashed with a glorious impending dawn, the surrounding woods serving as backdrops to the recently clipped corn and bean fields. Well past their peak season, bronzed oaks still shone. Brazenly, given the season, whitetail deer nuzzled the fields for leftovers. Forgetting his irritation for a moment, Abner grew reflective: *Great to be up and about on such a fine day. Might as well enjoy it; probably won't arrive in time to catch anyone, anyhow.*

He pulled the truck into the grassy lane that separated two of his fields and stopped short of the first tangle of brush. *Useless.* Abner didn't feel up to removing all those debris piles. *Gotta build me a proper gate.* He grabbed his shotgun and cradled it in the crook of his right arm. Then, with the shovel slung onto his left shoulder, he began the quarter-mile trudge to the woods at lane's end, his progress signaled clearly by puffs of short breath in the tingling November morning.

As he'd figured, the lane—with which Abner shared an easement with the woods' buyers—was wrecked. Crisscrossed with deep, greasy ruts etched in the sod, it made for rough walking. He abandoned it for the corn-field edge. Wary of ambush, he laid his shovel at the woods' entrance, to free his hands for the shotgun.

Under the twisted sinews of beech that lined the field, he could see that both the earth and corn stubble on its surface had been tortured by scores of vehicles.

The area was littered with muddy flower petals, interspersed with what appeared to be burnt sparklers. *Great, something else to puncture his tires in the spring.*

His anger now tempered by caution; the old farmer penetrated the lingering darkness of the woods. To his surprise, he found the glade itself in a miraculous state. It almost had a pleasing, park-like aspect, belying the usual jetsam of beer cans left behind in the wake of partying kids. The forest floor was cleared and neatly tamped down; the usual slash of rotting trunks and grasping undergrowth had been swept away. Abner couldn't, at first, even glimpse the remains of the old farm dump. A jumble of rusty stoves, water heaters, batteries and pesticide cans. Begun decades ago, it now lay blanketed by brush pruned and gathered from the clearing. Abner sniffed the bracing air. A strange odor, sickeningly sweet, vaguely putrid, hung over the site.

The glade was eerily still, save for the chug of Abner's breath, his dog's snuff-snuffing, and the gurgling stream ahead. About midway between the vanishing cornfield and the steaming creek spread a circular glen, perhaps fifty feet in diameter, from which several large trees had been cut away, giving him a spectacular view of the brightening sky. They must have been cut by hand, for otherwise he certainly would have heard chainsaw screams, which could carry for miles in the country.

In the middle of the circle lay the obvious origin of the fire he'd seen: a large pit about 30 feet across, set off by stones and a skirt of golden straw. A smoldering heap of charred logs had collapsed in upon itself, teepee-like.

Satisfied that he and his dog were alone, Abner leaned his shotgun against a large oak, retrieved the shovel and returned to the pit. Instinctively, he began to turn the dirt—starting at the pit's edge and working in—scattering and burying whatever bits of fuel remained along the periphery. He made another trip to the truck for the large water jug he kept there to replenish a slow, time-to-time radiator leak. Carefully, he splashed the fringes of the pit, flinching from the smoky steam that occasionally spat back at him. Within twenty minutes he'd cooled all but the center of the charred circle, where the largest of the log remnants lay.

Chance inched forward near him to investigate, sniffing, whining. The dog circled the blackened ruin, hackles bristling, pawing and nuzzling the wreckage. He started to dig. Then, whining, he strained his haunches trying to snap off a branch from the edge of the heap. He ricocheted backwards as it gave way, and then began to chew on his prize.

"C'mon, Chance, goddamn it," the old farmer scolded. "You're gonna plug yourself up again." *The last thing I need, especially with a dog this long in the tooth, is another vet bill.*

Sullen, reluctant, the dog skulked over and submitted to having his muzzle groped by his master. Gingerly, the old man fingered the inside of the Lab's mouth, trying to pry his jaws apart. Nothing. Then, along the ridged roof of the dog's snout, Abner felt a stick tightly wedged between Chase's back teeth. Curling his index finger around it, Abner levered the piece loose and extracted it; Chance whimpered in protest.

Abner almost cast the stick back into the pile, but then noticed something odd about it. Halfway up it was a distinctly un-woody, metallic-like knot. He pushed his glasses further up his nose and peered more closely. *That's no stick!* Recoiling in disgust, he dropped the object into the powdery ash.

He squatted stiffly to confirm his find. The metallic object? *A ring. The stick? Could that thing be a severed human finger?* Concentrating his attention on the blackened heart of the pit, Abner recoiled at the charred, shrunken little head that stared back at him slack-jawed, as if in a frightful plea. Reflexively, he had dropped the finger, which landed portentously on its end in the ash, the encrusted, sooty nail tapered neatly, pointing upward to the hole in the forest canopy—and heaven.

"In you go, George." Sheriff Carl Peters slammed the cell door shut on George Foster, patriarch of a local clan of white-trash, inbred rednecks. Peters sighed. "With any luck at all, Lucifer himself will take this job from me one of these days."

"Hell's bells, Carl," George said, "I ain't done nothin' my own daddy didn't do." Then he added, "That is, *if* I really *done* it." He flashed a mouthful of stained gums and jaundiced teeth.

Foster was being charged yet again with statutory rape: in this case, of his 12-year-old niece.

"Just do me a favor," Carl growled. "At least show you're really sorry next time. Deep throat a shotgun. Aim your pick-up at a tree. Get plastered and take a snooze on the Grand Trunk. I don't much care, so long as the result's the same."

George spat, "I want my lawyer, Carl."

"Don't worry," Carl said. "Perry Mason'll be here *toot sweet.*"

"At least he understands my... problems," George whined.

Carl's stomach churned. "I can tell you what your problem is, George. And it won't cost the taxpayers a

21

goddamn dime." Carl always had to struggle to maintain his professional demeanor with this guy. And always failed. "You're a degenerate pervert. And an ugly one at that."

"Fuck you."

"No thanks, buddy." Carl chuckled, turning the key with satisfaction. "Maybe somebody else, some other time."

Carl paused as he turned the lock of the cell, unable to suppress a leonine yawn, as he casually scratched his backside. Following a late-night meltdown at the poker table, he had been called out early that morning for an 11-50—car wreck. Some deer hunter, from Illinois of course, couldn't manage to snag his quarry in the traditional manner, at the appointed time. Yet his aim proved better behind the wheel than with the crosshairs of his scope. The width of Highway 26 lay splattered with what was left of the doe, entangled with the grill of the Wrangler's front-end. After Carl cleaned the mess up, he had to check on another report of mailbox vandalism in Hochunk township. That made ten of those in two weeks.

Finally, he could get to the office, and the very dubious company of George Foster.

The Sheriff strode down the cellblock and buzzed through the heavy steel door to the anteroom. The broad back of his longtime deputy, Jonas Clevenger, loomed before him, all shirt, sweat and love handles.

The deputy turned as his boss entered the room and cradled the telephone receiver under his fleshy cheek. One sec." Jonas punched the "hold" button. "Candy Spencer," he told Carl, "up at the elementary school."

Carl groaned. "Not another civics class tour." Jonas shook his head. "Somethin' about a kid. Sounds worried. Want me to handle it?"

Carl knew the fourth-grade teacher was a dedicated, democracy-in-action type, and no alarmist. "I'll take it in my office." He settled his girth at his desk and got a pen and notepad handy. "Miz Spencer?"

Professional and personable, the woman apologized for taking up his time. "I wouldn't trouble you, except this child has always had perfect attendance. And I'm not getting satisfactory answers from her parents."

"How so?"

"On Friday when I called, her father was very evasive," the teacher said. "Today—" she paused and then said, "I'm afraid I might have put words in his mouth. When I asked if she was sick, he seized on it, almost gratefully: He said, 'Sick! Yes, she is very sick!'"

Amateurs. Carl shook his head a little. "Tell me about her."

The child's name was Roop Kumar. She was only

ten and had only been in Candy's class for three months, a late transfer. Despite the fact that her father spoke heavily accented English and her mother little at all, the girl had extraordinary diction, especially for one so young, "With a cultured accent, Candy said, "almost a class apart." Roop was a wonderful student—bright, even precocious—and advanced compared to the rest of the class. Otherwise, she was a normal kid in most ways and got along well with the other children.

Carl said, "When did you last see her?"

"Tuesday, but she wasn't at all herself. She was uncharacteristically quiet and inattentive to her work. She kept staring out the windows at one place: toward the woods on the other side of the ball field.

"We were having a Halloween party and she didn't have a costume, and at first I thought that might account for her aloofness." So, Candy dug out items for Roop from the cache of tramp hats, fake cigars, and Groucho glasses she kept in reserve, for just those kids whose parents were too busy or apathetic to care whether their children were left out of the fun. The effect on the child seemed electric: She jumped into the sweet stuff and revelry the way any child her age might. At the end of the day, as the other kids lined up for the bus, Candy poured extra caramel corn into a plastic pumpkin and handed it to Roop, who rewarded her teacher with a clutching hug and a toothy smile that lit up her dark little face like a beacon. Then, her glistening braid flouncing down her back, Roop dashed out the door for the bike rack.

Candy said, "None of us have seen her since. The principal's office had no more luck with her parents than I have. It just doesn't feel right. So, I called you."

"Trusting your instincts," Carl nodded. "Anything special about the bike?"

"Oh, yes; I watched her ride away. So proud! Roop loves that bike; it's quite exotic: the basket is ornately decorated – woven straw, with colored raffia flowers embroidered on it. Green streamers…"

"From the handlebars?" Carl scribbled down details.

"*And* the seat."

He underlined a word: *Gaudy.* "Roop's address?"

The teacher gave it, then said: "It might be just a failure to communicate with immigrant parents… I-I'd hate to waste your time on a kid with the flu."

The Sheriff thanked the woman for her concern and promised to check into it. "Believe me, I hope it does turn out to be just a kid with the flu." He hung up the phone and tore the address from his notepad.

Carl got up and passed through the office; Jonas looked up; Carl said, "Going out." He gave his destination, 'Victory Park', a low-rent subdivision on the south edge of town. Carl detoured through the cell block and saw George Foster was dozing on his bunk. "George!"

Carl rattled the bars on his way by. "You better be able to account for your whereabouts last weekend!"

Foster jumped up, clearly startled. *Frightened for a change,* Carl noted. Whatever his pathologies, the scum-sucking maggot-muncher tended to reserve them for his own family. *Cold comfort,* he thought.

Roop Kumar's home was a small ranch house on a large lot. An old Chevy truck and a rusting Ford Escort were parked in the driveway. The hulk of a Camaro lay visible in the backyard, on cinder blocks; a mongrel dog cowered underneath it. As Carl awaited response from within, he scanned the porch and noted the dwelling's general state of disrepair.

A chubby, 50-ish man, to all appearances of Asian descent, opened the door dressed in a stained white tunic and loose-fitting pants, his head wrapped in what looked to be a red headdress beneath which wisps of graying hair struggled to reveal themselves. His face was mustachioed, salt-and-pepper.

Carl said: "Good afternoon."

"Good day to you, sir," the man replied softly.

Carl looked at his notepad. "Are you Sirkar Swaraj?" The man nodded. "I'm the County Sheriff, Mr. Swaraj. My name is Carl Peters." Without asking, he advanced casually through the doorway, eyes scanning laterally. "I don't mean to bother you, but I'm here to inquire about your daughter, Roop."

Swaraj backed away. "I... I... hope there is n-no t-trouble, Sheriff..."

Carl noted the thick, distinctive, almost sing-song-cadenced accent Candy Spencer had mentioned and tried to wrap his ear around it. He said, "It may simply be a misunderstanding, sir. Is she sick? She's been absent from school for close to a week and calls from the principal haven't been returned."

"Oh, yes, Sheriff." The man seemed suddenly agitated. "I-I was going to call you today, to help me. My daughter went to the market several days ago. But she never came home. Her mother and I are very, very worried. We have notified all the neighbors and have searched all around. But no Roop!" He threw up his hands. "So, that you have come, is a *blessing* indeed." He seemed much calmer.

"Well, that is surely a coincidence, Mr. Swaraj." Carl edged out of the vestibule, craning his neck into the living room as he spoke. "Is her mother here?"

"No...ugh...Yes," Swaraj said. "She is here but very, very upset. She is very, very worried about little Roop. But I am looking for her, *very* hard."

"Why didn't you call us sooner, Mr. Swaraj?" Carl's tone telegraphed skepticism.

"I greatly apologize, Mr. Sheriff. But I thought our

friends would help me find Roop-Roop. They have been helping me look very hard. We have looked everywhere." *Civilians, thundering around the neighborhood, destroying whatever evidence there might be…* Carl suppressed his irritation. "Do you have any photographs we might use, Mr. Swaraj? Perhaps a worn piece of her clothing? Socks are best. A toothbrush would also be helpful. We'll bring in a tracker dog and our own search team as soon as we can." *Now that the scent's old. And the rain!* Carl cursed silently.

"Oh, yes-yes, Sheriff." The man seemed eager to accommodate. "Just a moment, please." He padded toward a back bedroom.

The living room was in shadows, the drapes pulled tight. Swaraj's new, outward serenity was a bit unnerving; his shift to equanimity, his carefully scripted concern, the conspicuous apparent absence of panic or fear.

Geez! Carl started as a shadow shifted in his peripheral vision. Focusing his eyes, he realized an old man was sitting in the midday gloom—legs crossed, impeccably dressed, the butt of an unfiltered cigarette glowing between his fingers—staring at him. *A grandparent, maybe?* "Excuse me, sir; I didn't see you there."

The old man volunteered neither information nor introduction, nor even any sign that he'd heard and understood the Sheriff's greeting. Rather, he lit another cigarette from the embers of the one he'd been smoking.

Carl then spied an older woman in a sari, peeking from behind what he assumed to be a bedroom door. He doffed his hat and nodded deferentially. "Afternoon, ma'am. Would you be Mrs. Swaraj? There was no reply. Swaraj returned with a photograph and a lightly soiled pair of pink socks. Immediately, he noticed the exchange, and beckoned for the woman to come out of the room. "Please for you to meet my wife Sushmita, Sheriff. She is also very glad that you have come."

Tentatively, her head slightly bowed, the woman emerged, and smiled guardedly at Carl. She had the appearance of a matron who'd been beautiful once, and still of striking visage. Then she shot a glance at the old man on the couch, as if anticipating rebuke. "Good day sir," she replied, limply shaking his proffered hand, her gaze directed downward.

"I'm sorry about all of this ma'am," Carl offered. But you have no idea where your daughter may have gone?"

"No, Sir," she whispered, shaking her head determinedly. "My fault," she pointed at her bosom. "I should have gone to the chemist."

"Chemist?" Carl asked.

Her husband broke in. "She means a pharmacist, Sheriff. It is how the British say it."

Carl cocked an eyebrow. "But I thought she had been sent to the market."

"There is a pharmacy at the Martin's supermarket

down the road," he clarified. "That is why she was confused."

Carl donned his hat again. "I see," he said, scratching the back of his neck absently. Then he bagged the socks, exchanged a perfunctory good-bye and left the house. Striding past an open garage at the end of the driveway, he glanced inside. There, on the north wall, leaning against a sawhorse, he saw a child's bicycle, just like the one Candy Spencer had described: ornately decorated basket, green streamers...

Troubled, Carl brooded all the way back to his office. Have to strategize a more thorough *search...*

The Sheriff belched from the sausage McMuffin with egg he'd wolfed down on the way back to the office. That had been a mistake. Didn't want his diverticulitis to flare-up again. Especially now.

A sheaf of pink message slips impaled on his desk spike greeted the Sheriff. Jonas, on the phone again, looked up at Carl. "You'd better get this one, boss."

Is the man incapable of acting on his own? Carl sighed and grabbed the phone from his deputy. "Peters."

"Sheriff? That you, Sheriff?"

The high voice was urgent, and Carl sensed both youth and terror in it. "This is the Sheriff. Who'm I talking to?"

"I... uh. That is, me an' my buddy... We might be in real trouble."

Carl tried to sound businesslike and reassuring. "Why don't you let me be the judge of that..."

"But... oh, man, you see, I think somebody may be after us. We saw a ceremony or somethin' last night. A... *sacrifice*, sort of. I think."

"Of *what*, sir?" Carl leaned forward, frowning. "What do you think you saw?"

The voice sounded more panicky. "Listen, maybe we should just—"

"No!" Carl realized he'd sounded harsh. "I'm sorry. Would you please try to be more specific? Why don't you start at the beginning? Where did this event take place?" He drew out and clicked open his pen.

He heard mumbling at the other end of the line, background argument and whispered expletives. "It was in the woods. *Way* out in the woods. We were hunting. God, it was awful."

"Listen, slow down." Carl motioned to Jonas to check the caller ID. "Let's take this one step at a time. Give me your name. Then you and your friend can come down here to the department, where it's safe, so we can talk, OK?" The line went dead. "Hello?"

"Sorry," Jonas shrugged. "It was from the mini-mart out on Division. Want me to check it out?"

"I suppose," Carl muttered, "for all the good it'll do. But maybe somebody saw someone on the phone."

"A prank, you think?" the deputy asked.

"Hell, I don't know. Maybe. It's just past Halloween and the moon's full." Carl drew his palms down his face in frustration. "Any other reports of trouble?"

"Nope."

"Then file it and keep your eyes peeled for a couple of days. And just in case we don't hear from this joker again, keep it to *yourself.*" Carl handed Jonas the photo of Roop Kumar and issued preliminary orders for the search of her suburban neighborhood. But something niggled at his consciousness. "That guy at the mini mart. Did he say where they'd been hunting – maybe off that public access road into Palmer Forest?"

"Maybe," Jonas replied. "If you don't have anywhere else to go, it's better than nothing."

Carl left the office for the parking garage. He'd no sooner started his car than the radio squawked. *Christ, some days you can't even leave the building.* "WHAT?"

Jonas' voice crackled: "Abner Stickle just called. Been some weird kind of disturbance in the woods behind his house…"

"You mean right now?"

"No, the other night. He said his phone had been knocked out by the thunderstorm."

Carl's pulse revved. *Stickle's farm backs onto Palmer Forest.* "Check it out Jonas…NOW!"

Carl and Howie kept their thoughts to themselves as the black-and-white crunched down the gravel surface of Griffis Road. Perfunctorily, the Sheriff groaned as he eased his torso out of the passenger's side and hitched-up his trousers. Then the two men addressed the rutted path through the beanfield leading to the distant glade. They split up, each man taking a circuitous route through the field, lest they disturb any residual clues on the path itself. The sucking of their boots in the thawing mud provided the only ambient sound. Carl made note of the time. It was 2:00 p.m.

He and Howie entered the glade from opposite sides at about the same instant, having reflexively fixed their gaze on the ground as they progressed, scanning for clues. Having told the old farmer to stay put at the house, the Sheriff didn't wish to be disturbed before he could have a look.

Wisps of smoke wended their way up toward the aperture above the trees, undisturbed by the windless morning. The two men stepped around the pit from opposite directions, taking note and carefully photographing the detritus: garment remnants, charred stakes lying across the scorched physical remains, lotus blossoms and dead or smoldering torches. The putridly sweet miasma lingering over the pit made Carl want to retch. Abruptly covering his mouth in time, he forced himself to swallow back. Had to avoid setting a bad example.

Gingerly, Howie donned gloves and bagged as much as possible himself, pending the arrival of larger evidence vessels. He was careful about keeping items separately, in molded plastic containers, or paper bindles for any organic items. The remains would have to wait on the Medical Examiner. Then he and Carl began wrapping crime-scene tape around the entire glade to ward-off the inescapably curious onlookers to follow.

The rutted path from the road was given the same treatment, meticulously photographed and set aside with crime scene tape in anticipation of technicians who would form tire molds on the tracks.

Then, Carl phoned the Indiana State Police for backup.

November 3
4:30 p.m.

If Abner Stickle had been bothered by the damage done to his farm the night of the disturbance, he was horrified now. He'd argued for hours with Gertie over whether to call the cops and risk trouble from whoever was responsible for that fire. *Hell, this is Principia,* he kept reminding himself. *There had to be some reasonable explanation for that damn fire pit, maybe a gang initiation or somethin'.* His stomach roiled as he struggled to keep breakfast down as he recollected. But Abner couldn't shake the image in his mind's eye: the charred skull beyond the finger, the gaping mouth locked in an eternally silent scream.

Eventually, Gertie Stickle's gossip-meter over-loaded. Unable to contain herself any longer, she took to the telephone to inform the neighbors, leaving Abner no choice but to call Carl Peters.

Rumors had spread from Gertie like corn borer over the countryside, and now both cornfields swarmed with law enforcement activity: squad cars, ambulances, satellite vans and various other locals' vehicles.

Gertie, drawn irresistibly to the hubbub, stalked the woods surrounding the fire pit. A matronly Columbo in tattered housecoat and black rubber boots, her gray hair sprouted randomly from her scalp like dandelion fluff. She'd appointed herself unofficial liaison with the neighbors, though she knew nothing beyond Abner's breathless initial description of his bizarre discovery. With no option but to improvise, she spun lurid speculation involving satanic sacrifice and teenage cults. They'd do for her gossip, that is until actual facts turned up to contradict her.

Carl Peters brooded over the spectacle. In just a few hours, his job had gone from the mundanely predictable to this weird, un-Principia-like fever: a media circus in the woods and a couple of search teams with tracking dogs deployed across town, looking for a lost kid.

He glowered as the medical examiner's assistants moved gingerly, painstakingly picking through the ashes for clues, plucking out remnants of clothing, bone, and charred flesh. Meanwhile, deputies combed the woodlot. Meticulously, they isolated footprints and tire tracks, shot still photos and made relief impressions. Carl congratulated himself on having secured search warrants: on the Swaraj house, their two cars. Nothing found would be excluded. He'd also got Jonas to track down the child's medical and dental records.

Tom Stivers, Carl's chief detective ambled over, his London Fog trench coat buttoned up to his neck. His sartorial profile was deliberate, often drawing affectionate drollery from his colleagues. "Helluva thing here, isn't it? Any leads yet? I've been ramping up the search for the Kumar girl."

"Hard to say, Bogie" Carl answered laconically, then with a knowing grin, "at least until the ME does his thing. We have some tire molds to go on, but that's about it. Nothing new on the girl?"

"I'm headed over to interview the parents this afternoon. Hoping to get some clarification on when and where she disappeared. They seemed all over the place from your initial interview."

"Good," Carl said. "Something's giving me the

creeps about them. Then there's this mess on top of it. Goddam papers are going to be all over this."

"Comes with the territory, Carl," Stivers toed the dirt with this shoe. "But I'll try my best not to make things worse for you. Mum's the word until we've got a grip on things." Then he strode languidly toward his town car, clutching his fedora against the gusting afternoon breeze.

To avoid talking with reporters, Carl exerted what authority he could. He folded muscular arms over his ample middle; his tree-trunk legs straddled a small stump. *All for show.*

Medical Examiner Rick Jaansen edged his way around the pit to Carl, handed a plastic bag to one of his assistants and then peeled off his latex gloves.

Carl said, "What've you got that I can use?"

Deftly, the ME popped a cigarette into his mouth, opened a matchbook one-handed and lit up. "Won't know much for sure till I get back to the lab." He sighed in smoky exhalation. "About all I can tell you is, we've got some human remains here, probably male, judging from a partial femur and skull. At least there's a medial ridge present on the backside of the latter."

"Probably *male?*" Carl asked. *Not much to go on.* But Jaansen was a pro and had bailed him out of tight spots before. If there was evidence to be found, he'd find it.

Clutches of reporters and gawkers had sprouted

like mushrooms just beyond the squad cars at the far edge of the field, emitting a detectable buzz. Carl set his jaw. *Jesus, I hate this part of the job, dealing with the press. Rumors must've spread wide already. Best hope to squelch the wackiest of 'em and shift attention from the rest.*

Determined, Carl jammed three sticks of Juicy Fruit gum into his mouth and repositioned his sunglasses on the bridge of his dripping nose. Then, with all the enthusiasm of a condemned prisoner trodding his last mile, he futilely sucked in his gut and stepped behind a thicket of microphones on a small open trailer near the entrance to the glade. Two black-and-whites flashed like pinball machines nearby. The trail entrance behind him was a sinister portal to mystery: a great backdrop for the six o'clock news.

He opened: "Good afternoon, ladies and gentlemen," and relaxed a little. His intestines roiled from the stress, but at least his bulk was concealed by the podium his deputies had erected. "I have a short statement to make regarding the circumstances that have brought us all here today. I don't expect it will satisfy you completely. But as my own curiosity has yet to be satisfied, that should come as no surprise."

Anxious laughter coursed through the crowd of about 150 people: local farmers, reporters, a smattering of the cryptically ghoulish and the simply curious.

The Sheriff squirmed and went on. "In any case, I'll

tell you all we know definitively, at least at this initial stage of the investigation." With emphasis, he added: "Beyond that qualification, I will not go. Once the statement's been read, I'll answer a few questions on *it*, and *it alone*. Now then, let's proceed."

With a well-timed shirttail adjustment, he snuck a quick scratch of his backside. Then he held forth. "What we know for sure at this point, is that there was quite a bonfire in these woods last night, and it was set and attended by an as yet undetermined number of people. And it appears that a... cremation of some sort took place as well."

An anonymous voice rang out: "What do you mean by a *cremation*, Carl? Like a secret rite?"

Before he could reply, more scattershot questions peppered the Sheriff: "What kind of cremation takes place in the woods in the middle of the night? Is some sort of satanic cult involved?"

Carl continued warily, "Preliminary indications suggest human remains were among the ashes of the fire."

"Are you sure, Carl? Couldn'ta been a pig or calf, or somethin'...?"

"Of course, I'm *sure*," he snapped, "I wouldn't've told you if I *wasn't*." Under his breath, but loud enough for the microphone to pick up, he muttered to Jonas, "sons of bitches..."

"What was that, Carl? Did you say *witches*? You

know for sure there were *witches* mixed up in this? How do you mean...?"

"I didn't say that!" *The usefulness of this exercise is evaporating,* Carl thought, as he preempted the reporter's dopey thought. Eager to end it, he took a deep breath. "Let me assure you, and all the citizens of Pope County, that forensic experts are checking the site to determine whether a crime has been committed, here or elsewhere. But as in all cases involving fire, painstaking analysis will be required. Therefore, the patience of the press, at this time, would be greatly appreciated. Thank you very much."

"Hey, Carl! What about Q-and-A? Can't we ask questions?"

Carl stepped down from the trailer. "You've asked some already. I don't have anything else to give you. Besides, I've got a job to do." He made a beeline for a squad car.

"But you didn't give us any answers! What about suspects? What about reports of satanic cults in the schools? Mrs. Stickle told us kids party in these woods all the time. Any truth to that?"

Carl brushed away three camcorders with his beefy fist, leaned back toward the mic and reminded them that the Stickles didn't even own the property. Not that it helped.

With touching fidelity, Jonas interposed himself

between his boss and the mob of reporters long enough for the Sheriff to squeeze into the cruiser. Carl slammed the door, at some risk to the grasping fingers of his tormentors.

The deputy backed around the car and shoehorned his massive body inside. "Get the hell out of the way!" Flashguns and live cams blanketed the windshield.

Christ." Carl patted his shirt for a smoke. "Thanks a million, Jonas; I owe you one."

"No problem, boss." The deputy smiled broadly; then he jammed the car into reverse, pulled a 90-degree turn, and peeled off through the bean stubble—spattering his pursuers with loam flung from the spinning Michelins.

"Beautiful, Jonas." Carl adjusted the seat to conform to his bulk, then finally relaxed with a deep draw of his Kool as he turned to watch the scattering reporters. "Freakin' beautiful."

The local press harpies next swooped down next on Gertie Stickle who, oblivious to taste or prudence, was holding court next to a vintage manure spreader, giving her rendition of events. Yes, come to think of it, she'd noticed animal carcasses in unusual numbers lately, mostly near the woods. There'd been possums, raccoons, woodchucks, the occasional muskrat—and yes, some appeared to have been savagely mutilated, as if from some ghoulish rite. And now that you mention it, she'd heard eerie satanic music emanating from the glade at unusual hours.

Abner leaned against the old truck, sucking on his pipe. He'd had quite enough. If these idiots wanted to waste their time listening to Gertie, he guessed he couldn't stop them. That so many of his neighbors could be gulled by stories of eviscerated varmints astonished him, especially since the real culprit for those 'atrocities' watched from the truck, his muzzle resting on Abner's shoulder. Mightily bored by this point, Chance was hankering for his favorite spot: curled around the wood stove in the kitchen, absorbing the convective heat of the warm tile. Abner smiled. Gertie was an old warhorse, but she sure had her moments.

"Come on, Chance, let's go get some dinner," Abner said. He shoved the dog over, eased himself behind the wheel and slammed the rusting door hard. As he bounced down the lane on lifeless shocks, he could still see Gertie in the rearview mirror, channeling Ma Kettle, seizing her moment on a manure spreader, ready for prime time.

Well before he'd puffed it all, Carl Peters threw his cigarette down into the slush pile of the large parking lot. In the old days, when doctors and most nurses all smoked like chimneys, the atmosphere had been more convivial between medical personnel and law enforcement officers when they came to Heartland Hospital on a case. These days, by contrast, it was almost like entering hostile territory. Even the smell of tobacco on one's clothes could elicit icy stares and cold shoulders.

But the morgue was different. Maybe the people at work in the bowels of this old Depression-era building clung to a more fatalistic conception of mortality, which enabled them to do their jobs routinely, professionally. In any case, Rick Jaansen smoked and didn't give a shit who knew. Perhaps one of those twig-eating, asphalt-slapping joggers, who hankered to live forever, would judge him unworthy and try to have him fired. Somehow Carl didn't think so. They mostly left Rick alone.

Rick's curious call to Carl earlier that afternoon had caught the Sheriff at the makeshift command post he'd set up in the missing girl's neighborhood, from which to oversee the search. Mentally, he re-traced all the steps he'd already taken: registering Roop in the Law Enforcement Education Network database of missing persons; notifying the local media of her disappearance and last known whereabouts; signaling surrounding jurisdictions for logistical support.

Within eight hours, the small development had become a hive of activity: mounted deputies fanned out into the local farm fields. Teams of civilians had mustered, along with canine units from the state police; search and rescue teams had deployed from surrounding fire departments; even a helicopter flew in from Grissom Air Force Base in Kokomo, equipped with thermal imaging scanners. Little Roop's movements could be traced to school last Tuesday morning, and to the school yard that afternoon, but not beyond. After that, she'd simply vanished.

Efforts had concentrated, so far, on the area between the school and her home, with especial scrutiny paid to the derelict pickle factory next to the rail line—a sometime flophouse for transients. Tips were coming in steadily, as they always did in this sort of case: from assorted psychos, law enforcement wannabes and local eccentrics. Madame Cleo, a radio psychic from Gary, had even charted the child's astral movements. Nothing usable, but they all had to be checked out and eliminated. The Sheriff was hopeful that implementation of the new 'Amber Alert' would bring in more useful leads as well.

Carl felt discouraged. The girl's abduction—for he'd resigned himself to that description—was already "officially" 48 hours old and unofficially, a lot older than that. This cremation thing was an unwelcome diversion; Carl hoped Rick had news that would put that to bed at least, so the Sheriff could concentrate on the kidnapping. From the frosted glass door to Rick's office, Carl could see the ME's silhouette, feet up on the desk, phone mashed between hairy cheek and shoulder—flipping through papers on a clipboard. He entered without knocking, as always.

Jaansen motioned for Carl to sit down. A cigarette, mostly ash, dangled tenuously from the M.E.'s lips, bobbing as he spoke, then tumbled onto his stained smock. A glass of vodka sat in a glistening ring on his once-expensive oak desk. Rick's restless fingers tapped the lip of the glass, his eyes seeking assent. At Carl's nod, he reached around to grab a tumbler from the cabinet on the wall behind and poured a hefty measure. Impatient to end the call, he made yakking motions with his hand, finally succeeded with goodbyes and hung up.

The ME turned his full attention to Carl. "Well, old buddy, I've got some good news and some bad news. Which do you want first?"

"It's been a long day; I'm dead on my feet." Carl tapped out a Kool, inserted it into the corner of his mouth and reflexively sheltered the flame of his butane lighter from a nonexistent draft. "So, give me the most interesting news first."

"It looks like," Rick began, picking up his clipboard and riffling through the pages, "we have a homicide on our hands here." He flicked his cigarette into what was left of his drink.

"Just my luck." Carl cursed and spat. "Now every crazy sonofabitchin' reporter within a hundred miles is gonna be riding my ass about satanic cults. And just when I've got more pressing matters on my mind."

Jaansen's eyebrows lifted. "You mean the little girl? Well, you can call off your search."

Carl came to full attention.

"I think I may have found her for you." Jaansen grimaced. "Or, at least what's left of her."

"Goddamn it, Jaansen," Carl said. "Don't screw with my head."

"You found her the other day, Carl; you just didn't know it." Rick let the clipboard drop to his side. "She was in the fire pit."

"What? Are you sure?"

"I sent the remains up to Indy's chief forensic pathologist. He quick-matched some of the girl's dental pulp with a toothbrush from her house. I knew how busy you were, so I just asked Jonas whether you'd picked one up from the girl's house." Rick picked his cigarette butt from his tumbler, refilled it and shook the ash fragments around. "And an odontologist has matched her jaw with dental records."

"That's not good news." Carl slumped in his chair. It was never good news when a missing person turned up as a corpse. His stomach gurgled the mounting tension.

The ME was somber. "I didn't say it was."

With an edge of accusation in his voice Carl persisted. "But you told me on Monday the remains were *male*." As if the girl could possibly be resurrected by reverse logic.

"She was there, all right, directly on top of the John Doe, almost melted to him by the heat. Luckily, the body wasn't completely incinerated." The ME directed smoke rings at Carl. "Maybe something, or somebody interrupted the proceedings. I suspected as much at the time, but the media circus seemed stressful enough. I didn't want to add to it with my own speculation, so I decided to wait on the lab work."

"Thanks." Fighting nausea, Carl mopped his brow with his handkerchief. "Who the hell was the John Doe?" he asked.

"Working on that," Jaansen replied. "But the remains were probably also South Asian; I can tell you that much."

"Asian, huh?" Carl shook his head. Forensics. Never ceased to amaze him. "How in hell do you know that?"

"Like I said," Jaansen took another long drag and exhaled, "at this point, it's only a guess. But it looks like the corpse was wearing a turban. Or what's left of one."

"A turban? No shit." Carl's eyebrows arched. "So, what've we got—double homicide? Suicide? What?"

"Nope." Rick's fingers thrummed the desk. "The male was already dead when the fire began—from what, I can't say conclusively. Not enough tissue left. But the child was killed by the fire and smoke. Residue from her lungs and nasal membranes were saturated. Besides that, the carbon monoxide level in her blood was off the chart: near 90%."

"Jesus." Carl belched.

"And that's not all," Rick added. "We got a little break with the remains of one of the girl's fingers. Enough was left to test her blood. She was drugged. Looks like an opiate, apparently a dose insufficient to knock her out. Adrenaline trumped it."

"How's that?"

Jaansen threw back his head and downed what was left of the booze and ashes. "Judging from the rib fractures she sustained, I'd say she was restrained—pinned to the corpse—probably by those poles we saw at the site. The kid was murdered, Carl. I'd stake my reputation on it."

Carl rested his head against a cradle of knit fingers, eyes transfixed on the yellowed ceiling tiles. Fantastic as Rick's assessment seemed, it made a perverse kind of sense. Carl rose from the chair and grabbed for his coat. "Fine job, as usual, Doc. I owe you another one. And thank the Quincys down in Indy for me."

"That's what I'm here for, Carl." Jaansen leaned over his desk and looked up intently. "I just hope it helps you nail the bastards."

"A goddamn little girl. Who in the hell would do that? And in that way? Got something I can take to the prosecutor?"

Jaansen tossed him a stapled set of papers. "Here's a copy of my preliminary notes. I'll try to wrap up my report in the next couple of hours and fax it to you right away. If something dramatic comes up in the meantime, I'll give you a ring."

A ring. The word sent a sudden reflexive shudder up Carl's spine. "Christ Almighty," he gasped. At once, he remembered the weird phone call he and Howie had gotten at the department on Monday afternoon. The trajectories of these two unusual cases had converged. And while he was no nearer a solution, at least it seemed not all the alleys were blind ones.

November 3
6:15 p.m.

Is this day never gonna end? Carl let out a weary sigh as he left the hospital morgue. Much as he wanted to wait until morning with the news, he'd rather break the news to the prosecutor that night than wait until morning. Southworth had an inviolable early morning ritual involving coffee, *The New York Times,* and a bran muffin that nothing short of a nuclear blast could break. This rite unfolded in Southworth's private office, which had an extra phone line installed in it, with a number given to only a select few in his life. Carl had the number, but no inclination to justify an early-morning intrusion; he hated to be on defense when talking in person to his boss.

Carl dialed the prosecutor's direct line, praying—despite his fatigue—that Southworth was working late. The prosecutor answered on the second ring.

Carl said, "I'm on my way over with important news."

The prosecutor offered no argument.

The receptionist and paralegals had long since departed by the time Carl arrived at Southworth's office. Allen looked up from a sheaf of papers and pointed Carl to a chair.

Carl said, "Hey, Allen, sorry to keep you away from another family dinner."

A faint flush showed in the prosecutor's long lean face. "I already called Jan and told her to put a plate in the oven and go ahead without me."

Carl inwardly winced at his own runaway mouth. He'd momentarily forgotten the local rumor that Jan Southworth had threatened to leave Allen over the amount of time he spent at the office, away from her and their children. He looked away for a second, then returned to the matter at hand. "Listen, before I tell you what I suspect, you gotta know that I'll need some extra help on this one."

"You're the professional, Carl," Allen yawned. "Just make sure that your paperwork is in order. But what's up here?"

"Not sure," Carl answered. "I almost feel like I'm

following a trail of breadcrumbs…like someone is leading me to a particular conclusion."

"I'm confused," confessed Allen. "Looks pretty straight-forward to me. Gotta be some connection between the perpetrators of whatever this was and a cult of some sort, right?"

"That's been my suspicion too," Carl said. "But this is too pat for comfort. The father couldn't lie his way out of a wet paper bag and the crime scene was just abandoned in a hurry, almost like they wanted it to be discovered."

"And the parents are either the worst liars in creation or baiting us toward a conclusion." Carl took a gulp of coffee.

"Cults, particularly the satanic variety, typically don't want to draw attention to themselves. That's how they manage to survive on the margins. You sound as if someone's trying to get caught." Allen looked quizzically at the Sheriff.

"Nevertheless," Carl deadpanned. "Trouble is, Allen, that I don't know much about the world outside of this part of Indiana. Anything east of Detroit may as well be the dark side of the moon. Might have to talk to someone out at the College."

"You mean intellectuals, don't you?" the prosecutor corrected, absently riffling papers on his desk before looking up. "What could those eggheads teach an old sweat like you?"

"Maybe plenty." Carl tossed the ME's draft report onto the desk and recapped its contents, his initial interviews with family members and the telephone call he'd failed to give any credence. The events seemed to defy mere coincidence.

Allen slumped and massaged his forehead, the fingers of his right hand making circular kneading motions. At last, he looked at Carl with concentrated intent. "Isn't cremation preferred to burial in places like India? Something to do with reincarnation, isn't it?"

Carl shrugged. "No clue."

"Mmmm, funeral sacrifice of women—strikes a vaguely familiar chord," Allen said. "Out of some novel I read... somewhere." He paged absently through the ME's report, then started suddenly. "First and foremost, I want *discretion*, Sheriff." He tapped his desk hard. "That's all we need: the notoriety of a satanic cult case. Have you shared any of this with your people?"

"Not the sacrificial angle, no." Carl shook his head. "It's beyond what little they might know from that circus the other day in the woods. I have a couple of men still on the kid's disappearance. Sort of a misdirection play."

"What about the ME's office? Can they be trusted to keep this to themselves for now?"

"Jaansen's never let me down before, and I've already

given him a heads-up," Carl said. "Anyhow, aside from those policing the crime scene, he anticipated the problem and limited his help on the remains to one assistant he swears can be trusted."

"Good. Let's keep it that way." Allen made a few quick notes. "What about Magdalene?"

Carl stroked his chin as if to summon a strategy. *Need a shave,* he decided. "There's this woman," he read from his notepad, "a Dr. Lata Besant. Got her name from the head of security over there who used to work for me. She's chairman of the Women's Studies Program there. And she's Indian, so there's that." He winced reflexively. "Magdalene is a pretty small college," Carl added. "Not a whole lot to choose from, at least with experts on India there's not. But she seems to have published quite a bit, mostly on women's stuff."

Allen grunted as he jotted notes. "Anything else?"

"Well, there is another guy who, at least the students say, knows his onions. But he's kind of a weirdo, I guess. Odd duck. Who knows with these types anyhow?"

"Good," Allen nodded grimly. "I care more about his expertise than his savoir-faire. We could probably use his input anyhow."

He tapped his desk again sharply with the blunt end of his pen. He felt uncomfortable dealing with intellectuals, whatever their métier. "Meet me here mid-morning to talk strategy. I'll check out that fellow at Magdalene and bring him along. He's bound to know more than we do. Say, eleven-thirty."

"Right." Carl stood. "I'll be here."

Allen reached for the ME's report as the Sheriff let himself out. He put his feet up on his cluttered desk, propped the report against his knees and began reading.

Speeding through the five-page summary, he soon grew troubled: The first problem he saw was *motive*. Why would anyone want to murder a little girl *this* way? The whole thing was obviously too ritualistic for your run-of-the-mill child abuse. *Some financial incentive, insurance perhaps? But then, why risk discovery by doing something conspicuous like this?*

Less mundane explanations were also unsatisfying. If this girl had been offered as some sort of sacrifice, why not kill her first to avoid resistance? Or if that somehow wasn't enough to propitiate whatever deity the perpetrators were trying to appease, why not drug her into unconsciousness? Then again, maybe that was the point: *for the victim to be both conscious and tormented?* Perhaps that was the object after all: a requirement... some sort of catharsis.

And what was the connection between the victim and the adult corpse? *Was the adult a brother?* The ME's report set the man's age at around 32, the girl, ten. *What should the next move involving the family be? And why did Roop have a different surname?*

Whatever was going on here, Allen sensed it was big—and he had a nose for big cases. He'd developed it while growing rich as a prominent local law firm's 'King of Malpractice', winning huge settlements for victims of medical negligence. Principia's modest size had proved no hindrance at all to the consequent growth of his reputation. Now, just a year into his role of public prosecutor—underpaid champion of justice and due process—he was smelling another variety of 'mega-case' in the wind.

The irony was too delicious to miss. A spectacular performer at 45, on the verge of premature flame-out of retirement, Allen was suddenly in no frame of mind for either. At almost precisely the time when he'd decided to abandon the fast track for his family, here he was, thrust into prosecuting a case that might be at least sensational and at worst a media happening: a feeding frenzy, with all the publicity, fame and opportunity that went with it. His antennae rose-up and tingled, savoring the possibilities, from the financial to (dare he think it?) the political.

Jan would howl bloody murder, of course; she'd accuse him of relapsing into old ways. But wasn't it she who'd wanted him to take this godforsaken job instead of continuing to torment medical malefactors? Trouble was, now that he felt in predatory mode, Allen was too superstitious to abandon the mind-set that had attended his greatest courtroom triumphs. Asking him to change his modus operandi now would be like commanding a bloodhound to forsake his quarry. And while Allen Southworth was no canine, nothing short of an unforgiving fate would command him now.

November 4
8:45 a.m.

Magdalene College lay just south of Elkhart, within easy partying distance from South Bend. It had the appearance of an Ivy League oasis, despite its geographical remoteness from the rarified East, and the bucolic setting. A massive stone archway stood as a portal to wisdom with the graven inscription *Libertas Affert Felicitatem*— "Liberty Brings Happiness"—etched in curved Latin script along the top. He'd been ready to summon the expert he was visiting here to his office but thought it better to evaluate the guy in his own element, to determine whether he'd be of any use to the case at hand.

Allen couldn't help feeling conspicuous as he strode toward the Smythe Building, less for his demographic misplacement here (after all, he was old enough to be a professor) than for his Armani suit and sleek briefcase. The tweedy faculty and scruffy students dodging him on the sidewalk kindled twinges of nostalgia that recalled his years at the University of Michigan in Ann Arbor: lying with a beer under the majestic oak trees on the Diag, passing along a joint to his girlfriend, in an effort to make a sunny autumn afternoon even more sublime... Nominally, Allen now professed a more conservative outlook than he'd had then, less with an intent to convert others than to place peer pressure on himself, to calibrate his own misbehavior. While most might employ religion as a buffer against natural inclinations, he preferred a more terrestrial realm he might better understand... such as politics perhaps. Community "standards"—even arbitrary, bourgeois ones—might help encourage and enforce a caliber of deportment that no single person could sustain alone. He'd resurrected within himself some of those same old Yankee chestnuts that he and his running-buddies had once found such fun mocking, His life had taught him that they actually paid off in the respect tendered by one's family, neighbors and peers. He even found himself craving such status, perhaps now more than ever. Yet how might that weighty virtue be coupled to an aging, not to say conflicted, lawyer? That was the question.

Walking up to the Smythe, Allen suppressed a shudder. The newest building on campus, it was stolidly utilitarian, white, blocky, and contrasting incompatibly with the stately, heavily ivied halls surrounding it. In its entryway was a bas-relief of Oscar and Harriet Smythe, whose generosity had given rise to the monstrosity. They sat rigidly, side by side, unctuous grins frozen for posterity, as students milled about, unheeding, oblivious of their beneficence. Allen mused that the couple must have anticipated far more respectful, or at least appreciative, treatment.

Allen rode the elevator up to the third floor and asked the History Department secretary for Dr. Mark McCorkle.

She looked surprised, perhaps even suspicious. "Uh, he's down the hall in 3266. But we hardly see him. He pretty much stays inside his office when he's here."

"Is he in class now?"

"Oh, I doubt it." She grabbed a catalog to check the class schedule. "He's only part-time, you know."

A sudden cramp seized Allen's neck; he winced. *Goddamn Peters didn't tell me that! Here I've blown off an entire morning to interview some part-time journeyman lecturer?*

Mark McCorkle, the object of Allen's quest, fidgeted as he read the article in *Scientific American* on the Mad Cow disease scare of the 80s. He glanced warily at the half-eaten burger on the corner of his desk, balanced precariously atop a mound of beige file folders. Gingerly, he picked up a magic marker and prodded the abandoned snack into the overflowing trash can below it on the floor. It was two days old anyhow, he shuddered. He'd been absorbed in the writing of a book review for the *American Historical Association Journal* on Saturday and simply forgotten it was there. His nose often failed him like that: an olfactory sentinel asleep at its post.

McCorkle's office was an utterly nondescript, windowless cell with a Doonesbury comic strip taped to the door. Allen rapped three times.

"Come in," a voice called. "It's open."

Allen turned the knob and peered in. In front of a computer screen, a burly man sat transfixed. His bushy beard and unruly hair reminded the District Attorney of Bert Lahr's cowardly lion.

"Dr. McCorkle?" Allen stepped into the cubicle. "I'm Allen Southworth. I believe the Sheriff mentioned I'd be calling on you."

McCorkle turned and stared, unblinking, for a moment and then said, "Oh, yes. Mr. Prosecutor, I presume." He rose from his chair and pumped Allen's hand vigorously.

"Very nice to meet you, Sir."

Allen's shoulder shook in its socket, and he dodged a spray of saliva. "Thank you, Professor. That *is* your title, am I right?"

McCorkle reached into a brown paper sack, grabbed an apple and began to munch. "Well, actually, I'm an *adjunct associate* professor, which means I do the same job as a full prof, but for almost no money. But at least I'm in the classroom."

The moment when McCorkle might have perfunctorily invited Allen to sit down had long since passed. Allen decided to wait it out; the guy really looked the part of the absent-minded professor. But he was pleased that McCorkle hadn't tried to dissemble about his status... or lack of it.

At last, increasing physical discomfort seemed to nudge McCorkle toward social convention. "Please, sit," he said, motioning at a small chair in the corner of this glorified broom closet.

"Thank you, Dr. McCorkle. I'm here because I was hoping you might help us out with a rather unusual case..."

"Wouldn't be that fire in the woods the other night, would it?" McCorkle chuckled, mouth full of apple chunks.

Allen was a bit unnerved. *How did he know that?* "I'm afraid you're way ahead of me, Professor; yes, that's the one. But at the risk of indiscretion, I have to ask: Does the college have any scholars on the faculty especially qualified to address Indian history and customs?"

"That depends on what you mean by 'scholar'," Mark air-quoted. "We have sociologists and anthropologists and gender studies people who *claim* to know something about those areas."

"But..."

"But I'm the only historian who teaches any non-Western subjects, so I guess you're stuck with me."

"And your field is?"

"The British Empire. Which pretty much covers the globe, except for South America."

McCorkle showed him a book he'd written, a page of wonderful reviews of it, source citations and a sheaf of articles. There seemed to be no connection between the man's obvious underemployment and his abilities as a scholar. Despite his lack of social skills, Allen couldn't help but like the guy—as a one-dimensional history geek, uncomplicated by awkward political agendas toward which Allen was a little leery. Surely, this was evidence enough to call McCorkle in. But Allen would hold off on the more lurid details of the case until they got together downtown.

The two men chatted amiably as they descended the stairwell to the parking lot. Allen asked, "Can I give you a lift? The Sheriff can bring you back later."

McCorkle waved away the offer. "I have my own car."

Allen watched as the heavy man hoisted himself into a small, decrepit, rusting Ford Maverick. They left the parking lot almost in tandem; yet when Allen pulled his Lexus into his reserved spot at the courthouse, McCorkle was nowhere to be seen.

November 4
1:05 p.m.

Carl Peters was waiting in Allen's office.

Shaking his head in disbelief, Allen growled, "God-damn it, McCorkle was right behind me."

"Want me to put out an APB?" Carl chuckled. "Quite the eccentric, isn't he?"

"Yeah, a real foul ball, so to speak," Allen quipped, casting an annoyed glance at his wristwatch. "One wonders if he has a life. A queer bird, as my dear, departed father used to say."

The intercom buzzed on his desk. "Show him in," he cracked into the receiver, and to Carl he said, "Go fetch him yourself, will you? Just so he doesn't get *lost*."

The two men smirked at each other.

McCorkle shambled into the room. "Sorry, I… made a wrong turn."

Carl and Allen exchanged knowing glances. "Please." Allen saw him comfortably settled and offered coffee all around. McCorkle drank his with peculiar tentativeness, as if he were being offered a potentially poisonous brew— which, Allen admitted to himself, at certain times of the day the office coffee did seem to resemble.

Then, suddenly, McCorkle began slurping his gulps noisily, just as Allen began. "We'd greatly appreciate any help you might be able to give us."

For the next 40 minutes, Allen recapitulated the case, punctuating his narrative with occasional asides to Carl, relating what they knew for sure, along with the questions that remained regarding other evidence at the site: the hunting gear found abandoned nearby, and the anonymous witnesses to the ritual who might conceivably be traced. Unfortunately, aside from the fire pit and the human remains, precious little else had been recovered. Stacked in teepee fashion around the site had been the charred remnants of eight staves of what looked to be stout bamboo. Some 50 small rods were scattered about the clearing; these appeared to be incense sticks. Lotus blossoms lay scattered on the ground and aligned along a path that must have been significant to the event. Allen said, "Cast molds of the numerous tire tracks rutting the site might prove useful in implicating a suspect – in the event we identify one."

Other than this trace of evidence, all they had were a few items of half-melted jewelry scattered about the clearing and small scraps of clothing that had somehow escaped the flames.

After this introduction, Allen directed his attention to Carl, mainly for McCorkle's benefit, barking a question to which he already knew the answer: "Sheriff, has the identity of the victim been established?"

Carl was ready. "Yep. We knew our only hope of immediate identification was through dental records, so we requested them from the family. Her father was no help. Said she had excellent teeth and had never been to a dentist—what a crock! Yet we didn't want to arouse suspicion, so I went through the school and found out which dentist the girl had been seeing. He forked over the x-rays, and Rick Jaansen, our Medical Examiner, matched them. We've since also secured a DNA match from the girl's toothbrush. We haven't yet notified the family of this, however."

"Why do you think the father lied, Carl?" Allen asked.

"Obviously, it doesn't look good for him," he replied. "But I've been spooked by the family's attitude from the beginning. The father seemed *not* to *want* to know the missing girl's whereabouts. It's as if they don't give a shit one way or another. They're just impossible to read. Blank. They certainly want as little to do with *me* as possible. Strange, isn't it?"

Allen smiled. "Wanting little to do with *you*? Hardly." Then he glanced at McCorkle and saw that, as he'd intended, his exchange with Carl had captured the educator's undivided attention.

Allen went on: "When the time comes, we'll no doubt have to crossmatch the family cars with the tire molds we've got." Glancing at the Sheriff, he gave instructions face down, fixated on the desk, his arms locked in concentration. "Ok, well, keep a low-profile surveillance on the place, but don't use anyone you can't trust, or who's likely to be seen. What about the family's citizenship status?"

"We're checking with the INS," Carl said. "The

school doesn't know anything definite about the girl's status, and to tell the truth, they're not particularly curious. They don't consider it part of their 'mission,'" (he air-quoted) "especially if the government is involved."

Allen started, head up now: "What about those possible witnesses who called you?"

Carl said, "Jonas is monitoring the phone traffic. We'll find them if they call again."

Allen turned to McCorkle. "Well, Professor, might you be able to tell us anything helpful on the subject of human sacrifice?"

At first McCorkle just stared ahead, unblinking; then he shook his head. "From what I've gleaned so far, this doesn't seem like a *sacrificial* rite, per se."

"What's your best read?" Allen stretched his arms behind his neck, preparing his restless body for a long explanation. "I'll ask questions if I need to once you've finished."

McCorkle said, "May I ask one important question first?"

"Sure."

"Was the victim married, by any chance?"

Carl burst out, "The victim was ten years old!"

Allen clarified: "No legal marriage is permitted in this state before age sixteen. And, even then, marriage can only be with parental consent."

McCorkle harrumphed. "You said the family's

citizenship status is in question. I asked because it is possible she was married *extra*-legally, which is hardly unheard-of in India. In fact, in rural areas, the level of poverty almost encourages it."

"Come again?" Carl sputtered.

"Oh, yes." McCorkle's eyes brightened. "In some regions, an unmarried girl beyond the age of fifteen may never be wed, or she might have to wait around for a widower to become available. Marrying-off an underage daughter costs less, for one thing, smaller bangles and anklets—which are traditional, but very expensive. And the sooner these children become wives, the sooner they become a burden on someone else's household. Many traditions in rural society reinforce this custom."

"How and why?" Allen's brow furrowed.

McCorkle arched his back, as if starting a long disquisition. "For instance, an unmarried child who is raped will likely become a spinster, whereas a child *bride* who suffers the same fate will still be accepted by her husband's family. Our notions about childhood and a woman's full potential are, for the most part, Western constructions: outgrowths of modernity."

"I suppose it's possible," Allen conceded. "But if so, it would have to have happened in India."

"Then," McCorkle went on, "this begins to sound like an Indian custom known as '*sati*.'"

"What's that?" Carl asked.

"The British abolished it in India over a hundred-fifty years ago." McCorkle glanced sharply at the Sheriff. "But it's still rumored to exist there in isolated pockets. The word refers to the burning of widows on the pyres of their deceased husbands."

That's it!! Allen bolted upright in his chair. That's the memory he'd been rifling his brain for. "Go on, Professor; we're all ears."

"Sati," McCorkle said, "—or s-u-t-t-e-e-as the British anglicized it – is a Sanskrit word for the exalted state a widow achieves by performing this rite. It's a Hindu practice, sometimes Sikh as well, with very ancient roots."

Both Allen and Carl both leaned forward, eyes narrowed.

"While its origins remain obscure," McCorkle continued, "there have been persistent attempts over the centuries to incorporate sati into the sacred Hindu religious texts. Yet despite its persistence as a tradition, it's generally regarded by most scholars as a *corruption* of Hindu scripture. More of a cultural than a religious practice, really."

Allen nodded.

Encouraged, McCorkle focused intently, intertwining his fingers in front of his face as if talking to himself. "So, in its way it was an aberrant, parochial phenomenon that was rejected by most Hindus, even at its height. Today, the vestiges that remain are restricted to portions of Bengal in East India and Rajasthan in the west. It's also traditionally confined to the upper castes."

"Rich folks, you mean?" Carl asked.

"Yes." McCorkle's voice now deepened in its monotone. "By 1829, so many women were taking their lives, perhaps thousands each year, that the British decided—against some of their most astute political instincts—to abolish the practice. I believe what really provoked them to action was the age of some of the brides choosing to commit sati, some as young as eight or ten.

"But" he went on, "they also were able to use the issue to leverage further Westernization into India. The British needed Westernized Indian collaborators to help rule the place. Few better ways than an issue like this that could be used to discredit indigenous culture and advance an alien one, even if most of the widows involved had chosen that course."

Allen put in: "'Chosen' seems a peculiar turn of phrase in this context, if you don't mind my saying so."

"Nonetheless," McCorkle nodded, "in Hindu society, sati is perceived by some, especially in rural areas, as a voluntary, even virtuous act. That was why it appalled the British so much. Even so, given the servile status of widows in India, death might reasonably be preferred. Not much has changed."

"Servile status?" Allen raised an eyebrow.

"Many Hindu women, at least in India, are regarded

as persons only as they're adjuncts to their husbands. This status descends from a high Hindu ideal known as *pativrata*, which dictates a wife's total devotion to her husband—the highest manifestation being self-immolation at his funeral. When the husband dies, the widow may be held to be, at least indirectly, responsible for his death. So, she becomes a non-person, unable to remarry. "She may be compelled to sleep on the ground; eating just one spare meal a day; and she's forbidden to wear ornaments, perfume or brightly colored clothing of any kind. She's consigned, because of her unclean status, to the most menial and demeaning jobs in her deceased husband's household. She's forbidden to speak or to be spoken to.

"She becomes, in effect, an ascetic, living only to pray for the salvation of her husband's soul." With more drama than Allen thought the man capable of, McCorkle said: "Her existence becomes a living death – though that's not to say such attitudes haven't evolved rapidly in India."

Allen felt the hairs prickle at the nape of his expensive haircut, as he reached behind to rub with his hand. "Grim."

McCorkle pressed on: "But sati offers another option, don't you see? For, others also have much to gain from the widow's 'heroic' sacrifice. Her in-laws are relieved of the burden of her support. Inheritance problems are simplified. Her family gains a saint, and thereby, enhanced prestige. The sati widow is assured eternal happiness with her dead husband, along with a leg up on the next incarnation. Even the locals profit from the traffic of pilgrims if a shrine is established in her honor. And, one must admit, such a grim prospect gives a woman one heck of a stake in the well-being of her mate."

"I'll say!" Carl sputtered on his smoke. "But what about the widow herself? What does *she* have to gain, besides escaping a life sentence?"

McCorkle raised and waved a single finger. "I'd be careful about disparaging the family's motive here, Sheriff. If the child in question had lived to be sent back to India after her husband's death, sacrifice in some form might well have been her fate anyway."

Carl frowned. "So, you're telling me this ten-year-old *voluntarily* climbed into that fire?"

McCorkle paused for a moment. "You misunderstand, Sheriff. I'm saying no such thing. I've merely been trying to explain the ideal of the practice, along with its possible motivations. The reason it so bothered the British was that many women *did* appear to participate freely. Others refused and ended up drugged or forcibly placed on the bier. Others thought they could do it, but changed their minds once the flames were lit, and so had to be held down, or retrieved after attempting to escape."

"Christ on a crutch," Carl muttered.

"You see," said McCorkle, "after a few attempts to intervene in the ritual itself, the British finally effected an abolition by punishing participants after the fact. Even then, prosecution was difficult unless the ceremony had been carried out in the open. This prohibition led to the more clandestine gatherings, of which this may have been a type." Then to Allen he said, "At the risk of intruding on your investigation, may I ask a few more questions?"

"Fire away." Allen drained the last of his coffee.

"Was there a stream—or even a confluence of streams—near the site of the event?"

Carl sat bolt upright. "How did you know that?"

McCorkle said, "Because those sites are considered sacred, and so ideal for such ceremonies. It would tend to confirm my hunch that it was a sati. And what about drugs? Was the girl drugged?"

"Bingo, Professor," Carl said. "Hydrocodone."

Use of drugs to induce compliance has historical precedent," said McCorkle.

Allen said, "And you say this sort of thing still occurs in India?"

"No," McCorkle said. "Well, not commonly, at least. There have been a few score perhaps since Independence, at least of this spectacle variety."

Allen said, "By which you mean...?"

"By which I mean in such a way as to deliberately attract attention. There are many ways to kill oneself, after all, if one is determined to do so, without drawing a crowd. Hard numbers are hard to come by. But don't misunderstand; most Hindus would deeply disapprove of sati, if pressed."

Allen said, "What do you mean, 'if pressed?'"

McCorkle cleared his throat. "Indian-born Hindus living in the United States, are well-educated, law-abiding, very accomplished, modern-thinking people. And sati has been illegal since well before Independence from Britain. But there are still fringe religious groups mobilizing politically in India, as elsewhere. They're prone to celebrate their traditions and to dismiss Western judgments passed on them by outsiders as wicked.

"For those reasons, many may at least give lip service to tradition as a cultural defense mechanism, without an unqualified embrace of it."

"You mean," Allen said, "kind of like describing cannibalism without actually condemning it?"

"If you like, yes," McCorkle nodded. "In 1987, there was a sati in Rajasthan, witnessed by thousands of people. Yet the debate over its legitimacy, as opposed to the rule of 'British-inspired' law, spawned fierce debate throughout India—despite police reports suggesting that the girl was coerced." McCorkle shrugged. "Of course, none of the bystanders would go on record for a prosecution. It was a conspiracy of silence from which all benefited financially…or politically…" – he paused – "…except the poor bride, of course."

Allen said, "And you think that's what's happened in this case?"

"In my opinion, McCorkle said, "—and it is only that, an opinion—this appears to be an atavistic event."

Carl's brow furrowed in frustration.

Allen asked: "To any possible purpose, beyond what you've described?"

McCorkle squirmed in his seat, folded his hands and bowed over them. Then he looked directly at Allen and sighed, "I'm sorry to say, I have no clue about that beyond the rituals I've described."

Allen digested the academic's admission; a prosecutor's success depended heavily on mastery of the facts. *And so far, even total revelation of the facts is insufficient to understand what happened to that girl. McCorkle's aroused more questions than he's answered.*

Carl Peters kneaded his brow with all ten fingers. "Anyone got an aspirin? I've got a headache to beat hell."

November 9
12:15 p.m.

After the confab at his office that morning, Allen headed back to the courthouse, taking the long way, just so he could swing by the war memorial, which was set in a small park right at the heart of Principia. The site aroused a lot of nostalgia in him. He knew that the love of country he felt so keenly at times was probably tied to the Rockwellian childhood he'd enjoyed in the 1950s—when the country seemed more anchored than now—and that his wistfulness originated from the memories of long-gone boyhood heroes. Hero worship was uncomplicated then.

He still had a soft spot in his heart for the limestone column flanked by graven sentries, erected to commemorate Principia's Civil War dead, particularly three local heroes who'd fallen at Gettysburg. An irreplaceable town landmark, it was a thing of beauty artistically, especially at night when bathed in the soft, caressing shafts of moonlight.

Sadly, local punks had lately grown fond of defacing the monument. The prosecutor took such affronts personally, but he nonetheless felt a little sorry for the vandals with their paint cans. They didn't seem to have much in the way of heroes to emulate, or talk to, these days... not even limestone ones.

What with the world now just some goddamn social media-village, who can the kids admire, other than athletes and entertainers? Hell, even Presidential stature doesn't seem to mean as much as it used to.

Once, there'd been real heroes living across the street, down the block—even in Allen's own house—and he'd been lucky enough to know them. For a few moments, he lost himself in recollections of his father, wounded in the Battle of the Bulge, lying crippled for hours in a damp, manured field before he was brought to an aid station. Last year, the Memorial Day parade had been canceled for lack of interest. Still, a pitiful remnant of the town's veterans had gathered quietly at the cemetery to lay wreaths and kibbitz with each other. *What must they think?* A chill coursed down Allen's back.

His tires crunched on the gravel of the road's shoulder. On a whim, Allen veered off alongside the shore of Lake Constance. Then he stepped out to take in the view. He tapped out a cigarette against his palm, lit it, then jammed his fists into the deep welcoming pockets of his trench coat. Trying to quit a two-pack habit, he rationed himself to half-a-dozen a day and reserved them for reflective moments. As he took a drag on his Marlboro lite, another compromise from the preferred menthol, he scanned the leaden skies embracing the lake below. Memories rushed back.

Once upon a time, Principia was a world unto itself, a place where it was possible to procure anything one might need in life within the limits of the little town. The community hit demographic pay-dirt in 1960 with the baby boom population of 2,346 souls and its old school, Clisbee High, long abandoned now, filled to bursting.

The town had two main thoroughfares: Broadway and Main Street. They intersected beneath the village's only traffic light; a junction dominated by the looming Pope County Courthouse on its northeastern corner. Its distinctive, red-roofed clock tower tolled every hour of every day, reinforced by a screaming siren daily at noon, and provided a comforting predictability that never failed to reassure. And while he didn't really know it then, that anchor was an important component of Allen's childhood. Amid the news of race riots, communism and far-off war, Principia had seemed blissfully immune to the turbulence of the time. Maybe, he speculated, that's what the founders had intended all along: a mathematical constant in a sea of variables.

Whether he wished it or not, the village's fabric was interwoven with his cultural DNA, his history unfolding alongside Principia's. At least for the foreseeable future.

Allen tossed down the cigarette butt and crushed it with his shoe. Time to head home. He turned, gave one, last, appreciative nod to the ducks, and settled back into the warmth of his car.

Even though it was the long way home, Allen's chosen route was almost totemic to him, a reaffirmation of sorts that his soul was where it ought properly to be— deeply rooted in the small town in which he'd grown up. Yet the ritual exacted a price. At the courthouse, he turned right onto Main Street. This was the most depressing part of his route; its name seemed ludicrous now given all the vacant storefronts. Twenty years before, there'd been three banks, two drug stores, two hardware stores, two clothing stores, a grocery store, two taverns and a pet shop on that one bustling block. Of course, that was back when all the factories were humming in Elkhart and Mishawaka, offering what many assumed would be lifelong employment and lucrative pensions for Principia's mostly World War veteran fathers. The surrounding small farms were mainstays of the town as well, bankrolling one of the better country fairs in the state.

It was before the jobs fled, before all the children had begun to disappear, before Studebaker shut its doors. By the 1990s, most of the businesses were gone, save for thrift shops, a charity warehouse, a tattoo parlor, a karate "academy" and—most appropriately, Allen thought—four law practices attracted by proximity to the county courthouse. Bankruptcies, disability claims and domestic disputes represented their stock-in-trade. Principia was slowly suffocating amid the coils of drugs, delinquency, and divorce. What little wealth she did generate was siphoned off now by the Walmart down the road, and the sundry shopping malls sprouting across the landscape like the weeds that now blanketed the once-pristine garden of the local Presbyterian Church.

Same story in villages and towns all over the region,

Allen knew. And while he understood that the forces behind the decline were likely inexorable, he grieved a little with each day's commute. And seethed a little, too. "Sonofabitch," he sighed as he pulled into the parking lot of his office. "I hate progress."

Behind his battered oak desk, Carl Peters removed a black pen from his breast pocket and began to write on a yellow legal pad. Allen had directed him to compose one press release on the incident in Stickle's woods and another, for same-day release, related to the girl's disappearance. The prosecutor hoped the conjunction of the two stories might, just might, jog the conscience of the anonymous, jumpy tipster who'd called the office.

Carl sighed and then belched. Heartburn shot volcanically up his esophagus. "*Christ,*" he bitched to himself, "*goddamn Allen's coffee.*"

As he started to scratch absently on the paper, the door opened, and Jonas stumbled in, pointing in panic at his phone. Carl had little trouble translating his deputy's facial contortions: *The guy!* As if cradling a live grenade, Carl picked up the telephone, inhaling deeply as he did so.

"Sheriff Peters here," he began, nervous despite his best efforts. He winced, annoyed at himself.

"We gotta meet, Sheriff." The voice on the line

sounded frenzied, almost teary. "That fire in the woods the other day—it had more than a man in it. I know. I—that is, me and my buddy—saw a *kid* burn in that fire, too."

An awkward silence followed; Carl held his breath; the voice went on: "And I'll tell you somethin' else..." Carl winced, trying his best to decipher the breathless, profane and very confused exchange between the caller and another voice. "It was like they was devil worshipers or somethin'. The crowd chanted and shouted and screamed, but we couldn't understand a word of it."

"We?" Carl interjected. "You had company then..."

"Goddammit! I didn't say that...I mean...Christ, I don't know what I mean..."

Jonas motioned with thumbs up that he had the trace and raised his eyebrows to ask if Carl wanted him to head down to the site. Carl scrawled furiously on the pad to go in an unmarked car, but not to apprehend the caller unless he tried to flee. Carl wanted a cooperative witness.

"Listen," Carl croaked into the phone, "you seem like a good kid, who just wants to do the right thing. Sure, you're a little scared, but that's understandable. You really have nothing to worry about, at least once we arrest those responsible."

"*But what'll I tell my Dad?*", the disembodied voice sounded desperate. "He didn't know we were ditching school during senior year! And I left his binoculars behind! He won't believe any of this! Besides, I don't want those cats after us too!"

"How do you know that whoever did this didn't see you at the scene? You're probably in far more danger alone than if you cooperate with us."

"*Son of a bitch!*"

"I mean it." Carl sensed vulnerability now. "Do you want to live like this the rest of your life—scared out of your wits, looking over your shoulder, with your conscience torturing you?"

Carl heard muffled voices, argument, whispered epithets.

"All right, all right," the voice conceded, as if all resistance had been wrung out of him. "But we got to come in on our own. We'll meet you at the station in an hour, okay?"

"You're making the right decision," Carl tried reassurance. "We'll do all we can to work with you and meet every concern you might have. Will you both be coming?"

The conversation ended abruptly with a click and a dial tone. Carl waited a few seconds before radioing Jonas, who'd arrived at the Quik-Mart payphone, which was just two blocks from the department. The deputy said he'd seen two young men depart the scene nervously. Carl directed him to follow the witnesses only if he could avoid detection. Jonas, who tended to overstate his surveillance skills, responded with a decisive, speedy "Ten-four!"

A little too speedy for Carl's comfort. "Don't blow this, Jonas!"

"Not a chance, boss," and he signed off.

November 9
2:15 p.m.

Roughly 90 minutes later, two boys, looking no older than seventeen, walked into the glass entryway of the Sheriff's department. One was sandy-haired, burly, with an alert look to him despite the Oshkosh B'Gosh bib overalls he wore. The second was taller, bespectacled, gaunt. Maybe it was his duck-footed walk that made him look like the dimmer of the two. One thing for sure, with his hands trembling and his eyes darting about, he appeared petrified.

Deputy Brenda Hughes had been told to expect two young men, but nothing beyond that. Accordingly, Carl noticed from near the cellblock that she welcomed them in her naturally flirtatious way, doing her best, he supposed, to allay their obvious discomfort. It didn't work, so she didn't usher them into one of the regular interrogation rooms. Instead, she buzzed the Sheriff to come immediately.

Thirty seconds later, Carl sped toward them, and

out of the corner of his eye, he saw Jonas guarding the door the boys had come through, as if to make sure they wouldn't bolt.

"Afternoon, guys," Carl began in his most avuncular voice. "Thank you so much for coming in. Want some coffee, pop, or anything?"

"Nothing for me, thanks."

Carl recognized immediately the voice he'd heard on the phone; the youth introduced himself as Ted Polanski, along with his buddy, Tim Scanlan.

"I'll have a glass of milk," Scanlan ventured with a twang.

Carl said, "Milk it is. Brenda?"

She trotted off, and Carl led the two young men through a back hallway to a block of offices and other rooms. Ted and Tim stared wide-eyed and anxious at the unfamiliar surroundings. Finally, at the end of a long corridor, the party entered a large room, sparsely furnished with a long Formica table, eight chairs, a blackboard on one wall and a large mirror on the other. A beverage machine in the corner completed the Spartan decor.

Carl pulled out the chair at the head of the table and motioned for the two men to sit. Jonas stood sentry at the door. Before they could begin, the door handle turned, and Tom Stivers looked in. The Sheriff waved him over and made introductions.

Stivers has become something of a legend in the

department over the years, owing to his interrogatory skills. He had a subtle knack of insinuating himself into the subconscious mind of a suspect and morphing into a friend, even a confidante. On one occasion, he'd reputedly taken a felon to dinner and extracted a confession before the entrée was served. Such tales, two decades of service, plus special training by the FBI, had generated enormous respect for him among his peers and the locals.

But above and beyond these virtues, was Stivers' cool demeanor. Carl had never heard Tom raise his voice, nor seen him betray an untoward emotion. He seemed to possess such an even temper, that most people naturally let their guard down around him. Invariably, that was a mistake. In the jailhouse game of chance, his was the poker face at the table: A royal flush, or a pair of twos, his visage stayed the same. Just a brief conversation with Tom Stivers, so his colleagues joked, was the restorative equivalent of catnap.

Carl had kept Stivers up in his briefing with McCorkle and had tried to filter out all the political aspects of the case so that the detective might focus solely on the material facts. After all, politics was more in the ambit of prosecutors than cops.

"Now then," Carl addressed the two men who'd come in. "Everyone's been introduced, and we have at least an idea what this is all about. So maybe we can clear some things up for you. And you can do the same for us." He motioned toward the two camcorders mounted strategically in opposite corners of the room. "I want you to know, for the record, that these proceedings will be taped for our mutual protection and safety, as well as for accuracy."

Carl waived his hand, as if to banish the boys' anxiety. "You guys are under no suspicion at all, otherwise I'd be reading you your rights. The cameras are for your protection. But you probably know that...from TV."

"Oh, yeah....right," snuffed Scanlan. But my Dad can't find out about this at all. It could go on my permanent record that I skipped school."

Carl was reassuring. "No need for him to know at this point. The purpose of this meeting is to acquire information about an incident in which a crime may have been committed. After all, *you* boys contacted *us*, remember?"

The men looked at one another, then nodded in unison without a word. At last Ted Polanski said, "I'll tell you what we know..."

For the next hour, the friends related their story in what detail they could, from the moment they'd left Ted's house, until their getaway in the pickup.

Knowing full well that the pair's gear, blankets, a camp stove, and a pair of binoculars, had turned up in the routine search of the area, Carl knew that this was enough to verify their presence, if not their whole account of the episode. Still, he proceeded gingerly. "Is there anything to place you at the scene?"

Ted nodded, "We left our stuff, just dropped it right there. If you do find it, is there any chance we can get it back?"

"Eventually," Carl deadpanned.

Carl and Tom peppered the two boys with questions, occasionally scribbling notes: *What sort of people were in the crowd? More women? Men? Any particular ethnicity or manner of dress? What did they smell, exactly? Did the girl's demeanor change in any way, both during the procession and after the fire was lit? Did she seem sober? How many people did they think were there? What was the ratio of men to women? Did anyone interfere with the girl's efforts to save herself? How many did so? By what means did they do so?*

From their initial glimpse of the scene, the boys' attention had been riveted, first by the corpse, then by the girl. And though they recalled some sharp details about the ceremony itself, they offered little else of use, transfixed as they had been on the blazing horror.

Stivers pressed them: "Did any of the participants stand out to you? Was anyone there you might recognize again, given the chance?"

The available light was poor, and they'd been scared half out of their minds, they said. But then Ted spoke up: "There *was* one man..." He turned to Tim. "The one who forced the kid hardest back onto the fire?"

"Yeah!" Tim said. "The guy in the red turban."

Carl urged: "Can you describe him a bit more?"

"About fifty?" said Tim.

Between them, they began to clarify their picture of the man who'd most caught their attention: "Handlebar mustache... Big nose!"

Sirkar Swaraj! Carl hoped the two friends might be able to pick Swaraj out of a lineup, if it came to that. *Might be enough.* Both men were certain that the girl, while she seemed initially willing, had changed her mind and tried to escape the death trap. She was prevented from doing so by others who, as Rick Jaansen had surmised, assisted Swaraj in pinning her down. The implication? Conspiracy, at very least – at most, premeditated murder.

After the boys had recalled all they could, Carl took the time to assure them that they and their families would be in no danger from whatever cult lay at the bottom of this horror. Yet, despite such reassurances to the boys, Carl found it hard to dismiss those anxieties as easily from his own mind. Notwithstanding the exposure achieved up to now; he didn't know yet precisely what he was dealing with, and until he did, he felt he'd need to assign a couple of his deputies to witness protection duty. Secretly, he wished he could have assigned more.

After the teenagers left, Carl held an informal strategy session, Jonas joining him and Stivers at the table, along with Allen Southworth and Mark McCorkle, who came from behind the interrogation room mirror.

Allen began: "I should tell you that I've been in contact with the INS. The 'father'", he air-quoted, "whoever he really is, appears to be here legally, but not Roop."

"Interesting." Carl reached for a smoke. "Except that her being in school and at the dentist's office *are* matters of *record*."

"And the adult corpse is evidently related," Allen leafed through a file, "identified as a student at Magdalene, here on a student visa. His name was Rishi Swaraj. He was evidently very active in the Ganges Mission out on Route Six. Has some connection with Theo Carver's Diversity League outfit, too."

Carl knew about Carver, all right: a local political activist. "I still don't get it," he said. "Are we assuming this Swaraj was a pedophile or something? I mean, *marriage*?" He cast an accusing glance at McCorkle, as if it was somehow his doing.

Allen snapped, "It's more complicated than that! We've got to stop thinking about this as an ordinary crime. It's a foreign custom that happens to be criminal *here*." He jammed his pen on the desk for emphasis. "That's what McCorkle's driving at." He waved his right hand in the air for emphasis as he rose.

McCorkle nodded agreement.

"Aw, shit!" Carl spat. "You think too goddamn much, you know that Allen? This isn't India, it's *Indiana!* Should be a crime *anywhere, anyway.* It's not rocket science, for Chrissake!" His face flushed and he hitched-up his trousers.

"Listen, Carl," Allen warned, "I know that. But a case like this has, well... *political* ramifications that are going to affect the way we do our jobs, at least a little. And we'd be morons not to expect some trouble."

The lawyer leaned back and stretched out his suspenders. "At least now we've got some eyewitnesses to the father's involvement, so I think it's time to move. We'll need tire molds from the family cars and to search the home. But first, let's bring Swaraj in for an interrogation. Maybe if we handle him gently enough, we'll get some more names before he lawyers-up. And we've got to prepare for publicity. Lots of it."

"Here?" Jonas asked in a high-pitched voice. "In Principia?"

"You bet." Allen draped his rolled-up sleeve over the empty chair next to his own, grinned broadly and winked at the deputy.

Carl leaned forward, elbows on his knees, massaging his temples. "My headache's back," he moaned. "Too damned much thinkin', I guess. Too damn much thinkin'..."

November 9
4:30 p.m.

Allen eased his Lexus onto the entrance ramp of I-20 for the quick four-mile jaunt home, not knowing whether to praise fickle fortune for this case or curse his rotten luck. *Retribution for a murdered child. What better target could I ask for?* On the one hand, this situation had everything fifteen years as an attorney had conditioned him to long for, including an inescapable opportunity to enhance his profile out of all proportion to his surroundings. On the other, any carefully considered plans to reconfigure his frenetic lifestyle were about to be scuttled. All his instincts told him so.

Jan would greet the news as enthusiastically as she might a county bar outing. What was in it for her? Cold dinners, boozy late-night arrivals and innumerable evenings in bed alone watching Letterman. He could just hear it: "There you go again, placing your ego and ambition over the *family*…"

The family. The kids were young, both still pre-school. Born—boom-boom!—a year apart, after he and Jan had been married almost 15 years. They'd planned for and anticipated children, but they hadn't been "blessed" until they were both practically too old for them. Jan had adapted quickly enough, even though she'd largely written off the possibility after all those years.

But Allen had become so set in his ways that he

hadn't yet adjusted. *Damn her domestic fantasies anyway.* He dreaded her hectoring and his own guilt, dreaded going home. Not that it was Jan's *fault.* Familiarity and complacency were byproducts of time, and, not paradoxically, of a rather good marriage.

Yet they'd been married long enough for all the stereotypes to apply. No more New York Times crosswords together in bed on Sunday morning. No more watching Jeopardy together in the evening. Their lovemaking had become infrequent. They'd each heard each other's jokes and perspectives *ad nauseam.* Monotony suffused their intimacy. Jan's stalwart fidelity and her stifling *predictability* had become his proverbial ball and chain – an inescapable burden.

Allen approached his long, serpentine driveway and pressed the garage door opener. As the door clacked its way upward, he pulled the Lexus in, bracing for the evening ahead.

His daughter Angela poked her head into the garage, grinning impishly. "Daddy's home!" she shouted over her shoulder. "What did you bring me, Daddy?" she cried, grabbing for his pockets as she raced to his side, nearly bowling him over with acquisitive affection.

Jan stepped into the open doorway behind her. Allen caught a flicker of something that might have been hope in her face, but then it flared and died. She crossed her arms under her breasts. "Yes, do tell," she said. "Why *are* you home so early, Daddy?"

His gut response? *You don't want to know; you just don't want to know.*

November 10
10:30 a.m.

Theo Carver paused before the full-length mirror to study his reflection. He had, he decided, reason to respect, even admire, the man who stared back at him. He'd come so far, he reminded himself, though there was still so much to do. His mission had been both his salvation and his reward, and it remained, stubbornly, unfinished.

Carver thought he'd seen it all along the way. Raised in a family of 13 children in the Mississippi Delta, he'd migrated with his parents to Indiana in the 1950s, the family finally settling in Principia. Unusually, a rather large black population was scattered about the countryside surrounding the town, descendants of Underground Railroad fugitives who'd "jumped off the train" there. The Carvers opted to join their descendants.

The surrounding prairie had originally been settled

by gentle Quakers in the decades before the Civil War, who offered plots of land to the runaways as an alternative to Canadian exodus. Not a few fugitives had taken them up on the offer. Over the intervening century, successive waves of new migrants arrived from the South, driven away by Jim Crow and the Great Flood of 1927. The word got out about Principia, so much so that many arrivals from Dixie forsook the bustle and din of Chicago for this little town that was so much closer to their own recollections of home.

Young Theo grew up, then, in a village far more integrated than most in Northern Indiana, though for the 1950s that wasn't saying much. For all of its diminutive virtues, Theo's Principia was unevenly prosperous. And the racial divide was hard to miss. Still, in some ways it was an exceptional little place. His school was to all appearances integrated for its time, his black teachers were extraordinary, especially for such a small town. This was largely due to the fact that many highly educated black citizens found themselves encumbered by limited professional options elsewhere and simply remained where they were. In a twist of ironic misfortune for Theo, however, most of these departed once their career vistas broadened with the civil rights legislation of the mid-1960s. Principia's black students were left behind as equally qualified teachers were impossible to find and mediocrity replaced the academic rigor of earlier years.

Even this tiny burg felt the myriad cultural shocks of the 1960s, but young Theo noticed they hit black folks a bit harder than everyone else.

Against the backdrop of social polarity that dominated the early 1960s, however, Theo remembered that the diverse oases of kids in town got along rather well. His friends joined Boy Scouts and Girl Scouts, swimming and camping together in other venues. Theo also played Little League every summer. It was, after its fashion, an improbably intimate place, where everyone at least claimed to know everyone else and kept watch on one another's children with the same seemingly solicitous care. Black or white, he recalled, any stranger in town attracted the same condign scrutiny.

Sadly, however, other cultural signals in the region were impossible for Theo to ignore. 'Black' and 'White' barber shops co-existed on the same block. There was the white tavern and the black tavern, and interracial dating was still very rare, if not taboo.

Still, a restrained but unmistakable air of communal civility prevailed, born of the village's unique origins, which in some ways allowed it to stand out as an island of comparative enlightenment in the 'Michiana' region. And Principians of all stripes had proven themselves capable of circling the wagons around their own when the occasion demanded it. Chief among their athletic rivals were the "Raiders", down the road in Jonesburg, who contemptuously dismissed Principia Public as "Congo High." Mostly blue collar, redneck families, employed across the county line in South Bend, their insult was returned in kind. Theo and his friends referenced "Jo-burg" as if their bigoted neighbor was populated by the crudest sort of latter-day Boers.

So, Theo didn't grow up *chronically* angry. Just *sometimes* bothered.

His friends, Theo knew, saw no bigotry in themselves, though subtle hints of it hovered over their personal interactions and reflected the culture in which they were raised. Black men 40 years old could still be called "boys" by the town's older men, though derivative more from lifelong habit than deliberate malice. Still, Theo bristled when he heard the slights.

When confronted with seeming anomalies, Theo suppressed the obvious explanations as best he could. These were his friends; he'd known them all his life. They weren't anything like those maniacal crowds frothing and screaming at students in Little Rock or Selma; of that he was certain. They couldn't be. Mustn't be.

Yet he recalled that the armor of his own self-denial began to corrode during his sophomore year, in the spring of 1968.

After a particularly grueling track practice, the banker's son offered to take him water skiing on Sapphire Lake, home to a fabulously wealthy enclave and about a mile from the village. Theo spent the entire afternoon turning his considerable athletic prowess to something he'd only dreamt of attempting. After a tentative start, he stood up on his skis. A couple of falls later, he ventured beyond the wake. He even managed to drop a ski and slalom a bit before their gas began to run out, forcing a return to the dock. To Theo, it was the most fun he'd ever had in his life.

Then came the blowback. The banker's phone rang off the hook: hysterical neighbors threatening to withdraw their accounts for the banker's effrontery in allowing a *black* teen to ski in *their* lake. The estimable banker would have none of it, informing his detractors plainly what they might do with their 'business'. Theo was asked back, of course, but never again went skiing.

Theo's dad was a farmer, not very prosperous, who lived in perpetual dread of the IRS, because he hadn't filed a tax return in 20 years. Former heavyweight Joe Louis' fate weighed on his mind like a mighty stone; he feared that he, too, might be mercilessly harassed and eventually driven to destitution. So, going to college seemed out of the question for Theo.

But times were changing, and sympathetic counselors found money for him. Everyone nagged him about not wasting his "potential," a word he came to dread because he never was able to figure out precisely what it meant. Then fate took his hand.

It seemed as if eighteen-year-old Theo couldn't turn on the television at night without the day's horrors unfolding before his eyes. The Freedom Rides, James Meredith, Rosa Parks and the Edmund Pettus Bridge all took their places among his lifetime mile-markers. First President JFK was assassinated, then Malcolm, then Dr. King, then Bobby. It seemed that every night a new city went up in flames. The Vietnam War was in full spate and generating ferocious resistance across the land. By his senior year, all Theo knew was that *he had to become part of it*, to become a player in the epic drama that was washing over the country and galvanizing his people.

Theo went off to Marquette University, which generously offered a scholarship, but he soon became so swept up in "the struggle" that his studies went begging. Police brutality mandated a response. Protests, mass meetings, student strikes and political demonstrations consumed his life. And while he managed to stay in school long enough to escape the draft, authorities finally asked him to leave.

Seething at his core now, Theo Carver smoldered with shame and indignation. It seemed clear now that a structural conspiracy undermined his chances at success. Sporadic arrests for disturbing the peace, along with a couple of busts for marijuana possession, underscored Theo's frustration at finding just the right place in the world. And as the roiling '60s gave way to the rudderless '70s, he found the market for political activists of his stripe less promising than it had been.

Nonetheless, Theo persevered, embracing the latter-day activism that took off like a rocket in the aftermath of the Rodney King riots of the early 1990s. Ensconced now in Milwaukee, he organized protests around the death of an immigrant from Guinea, shot by Milwaukee PD officers, who was clearly the victim of police brutality and racial profiling. Theo persuaded the aggrieved family not to despair; he would assist them in filing a massive civil suit against the city. Yet in the end, the officers were acquitted, and the family accepted a modest settlement, against Carver's earnest counsel. He understood their grief and exhaustion, but the failure of justice that he perceived burned in his heart.

Opportunities beckoned anew shortly after Theo Carver arrived back in Principia five years later, broke, homeless, and fleeing a clutch of adverse court decrees. Just after entering the town limits, his attention was drawn to a crowd outside Principia's high school, which was demanding recognition for Martin Luther King's birthday. He decided to stay in town awhile, and after investigating the racial situation further, began meeting with local black leaders of the *Citizens Coalition*, gradually growing accustomed to the prospect of his 'return'. The *Coalition's* leaders were much impressed by Theo's smooth, erudite mien, burnished by his life-long familiarity with the locals. Many of the demonstrators were old acquaintances, who'd followed their old friend's collegiate exploits. He sensed his sail filling with the wind of a nascent Afrocentric movement here, fueled by publication of Martin Bernal's *Black Athena*, which included a curriculum endorsed by several national civil rights organizations. This confrontation, he mused, had destiny written all over it.

Mastering the rhetoric to make himself useful to this movement hadn't proven difficult. Nor was situational passion, which came easily to him. A demonstration here, a school board meeting there, and Theo had a platform from which he could advocate for Afrocentric erudition through what he called a Diversity League. Grants soon followed his efforts, mostly from sundry government educational departments and local businesses in search of favorable publicity and positive civic profiles. These soon found themselves recipients of Carver's appeals. Who, after all, could be opposed to *Diversity*? He found himself formulating a multicultural "gospel," at the heart of which were twin objectives: decentralization of Eurocentric traditions and elevation of other cultures that had a claim to America's future—as well as its soul.

No longer would people of color be marginalized through sole study of the standard

Anglo-American-Eurocentric literary canon. Theo even began to fashion tracts of his own, propounding Afrocentric and multicultural themes and local educators made quick use of anything he offered that might qualify as diversity fare.

In short, Theo held that traditional history was a carefully crafted confection of half-truths and calumnies designed to exaggerate the role of Europe in the march toward civilization. Egypt, not Greece and Rome, he insisted, had been the font from which mankind had imbibed the flood of scientific, philosophic, artistic and mathematical knowledge requisite to Western civilizational progress. And since the tenets of Afrocentrism dictated that ancient Egyptians were indistinguishable from the rest of Africa's population, the legacy of 'White' Europe was essentially derived from unacknowledged African sources.

Theo understood the power of the prevailing narrative; he, like generations of students down the centuries, had been deceived by it. He remembered his own shock when he began to discover that other narratives were not only possible, but, historically, more plausible. Knowingly or not, legions of scholars, from Oxford to the Sorbonne and on to Harvard had helped fashion a falsehood that denied Africa due credit to justify the debasement and enslavement of its people and the usurpation of its cultural patrimony.

The time had come to set things right. Theo Carver had embraced a new mission, one that perfectly suited his principled, long-delayed pursuit of cultural justice and redress.

November 10
1:00 p.m.

The picture of confidence, Theo strode into the office of Professor Lata Besant, Chairperson of Women's Studies at Magdalene College.

He'd known Besant for most of the time he'd been in Principia. And since she was, in his estimation, both a colleague and fellow traveler, their relationship had proven useful. It helped to have someone with an academic pedigree associated with his work.

Besides, he was useful to Professor Besant as well. After all, their association reinforced her solidarity with the "other," as she often referred collectively to the victims of Western oppression. Through Carver, she might weave a feminist strand into the local movement, thereby enhancing her role as a soldier in a common struggle for ethnic dignity and political justice.

And this morning she was particularly anxious to please. "Good morning, Theo. How are you?"

She sounds almost chirpy, he thought, but replied aloud, "I am well, Professor. And you?"

"Well as one might expect during finals week," she sighed. "The work is unbelievable this time of year."

"Indeed, we are all grateful for your labors," he said.

"You are too kind."

To business. He began: "You must wonder what brings me to Magdalene today. I don't wish to sound alarmist, but as you may be aware, the Diversity League has become concerned by the mood on this campus, what with Republican assaults on affirmative action and the general principle of diversity."

"I understand. Hard to fathom, isn't it?"

He nodded. "In fact, we are so concerned that this may adversely affect students of color, we feel a dramatic statement is in order."

"I have tried my best to bring such matters to the attention of both the faculty and student body," she reassured him. "But you must remember that I am not the Chancellor, only a department chair."

Carver frowned. "Any initiative from on high is unlikely, I admit. But as you know, neither is it required to get our project off the ground."

Besant pushed her glasses closer to her eyes. "And the nature of your project?"

He shifted his backside, which was beginning to fall asleep in the fiberglass chair. "I wish to organize a campus-wide event – a major Diversity Day, with roundtable discussions, prominent speakers, ethnic cuisine, multicultural demonstrations and historical symposia." He paused, then added: "There'll be no need for you to provide anything other than the use of Magdalene's facilities. My people will organize everything, including the publicity. And of course, we will ask you to speak at the opening convocation." He smiled, most charmingly she thought.

The professor was clearly flattered. "Of course, I would be honored to participate in such a worthy event. And if we frame the proposal as you have just done, I don't know how the administration can object to it. I'll run it past the Office of Campus Climate. They're always in the market for events which emphasize inclusion, but some security will have to be provided. And is there any-thing else I can do to facilitate matters?"

"Please, no!" Her visitor waved her off gently and rose to leave. "You have done far more than you know already."

**November 10
2:30 p.m.**

"Aw-r-OOOOOO!" Chance howled, prompting Abner Stickle to look out from the side of his vintage Farmall tractor, at which he'd been cursing magnificently while working to repair a hydraulic hose.

He peered out toward the field, his vision obscured

slightly by a silver radiator cap. *Goddamn. Sonsabitchin gawkers!* A dark pickup truck, green ford maybe, bumped over the cornstalks in the field, around the piles of tree limbs he'd so naively reconstructed in the lane after his grim discovery in the glade. These were obviously irrelevant, now that the cold weather had arrived and frozen the field.

Abner recalled the Sheriff's warnings not to return to the fire pit under any circumstances. So, he deposited his hydraulic hoses on a nearby cultivator, wiped his oily hands on a rag draped over one of the tractor's tires and strode to the house to call Carl Peters.

Gertie met him on the porch, her eyes fixed on the distant lane. The dog still howled, his tail as rigid as a flagpole, hackles bristling. Gertie was clearly in an investigative mood. Her heavy coat bulged with the flashlight she'd tucked there. She'd pulled a stocking cap down over her ears, jamming her baggy blue jeans carelessly into her high rubber boots.

Now grown a mite weary of her fondness for local celebrity, Abner hacked, "Where the hell do you think you're going?"

"Come on, Ab." She fidgeted as if she might wet her pants any moment. "They could be doing it again, Ab. We need to check it out while there's still time!"

"What we're going to do," he shot back, "is obey the Sheriff and keep the hell out of there, Gert." He hacked, spat and added, "Hell, it ain't even our land anymore, or did you forget? We ain't gonna trespass again, just so you can be a star with the neighbors."

"But the neighbors depend on me, Ab," she whined. "They're scared close to death! First Methodist Church was filled to the brim on Sunday, they're so scared. You'd know that if you *ever went*. Flossy Bailey says we should get an exercise-ist to cleanse the clearing."

"You mean ex*or*cist." Abner spat. "Flossy Bailey's nuts, and a Baptist to boot."

"So?"

"So, we ain't gonna disobey the Sheriff by mucking around down there, you understand? Sooner this business is done the better, as far as I'm concerned." Abner meant to end the conversation there.

"But Flossy says—"

"I don't care what Flossy says!" Abner growled. "Now, get into the house before I have *you* committed!"

A short time later, a black-and-white pulled into the lane and stopped. Abner saw Carl Peters and Jonas Clevenger get out of the car, fall to their knees and finger the dirt. Then, as Carl flicked a cigarette into the cornstalks, they climbed back into the squad car and eased slowly down the lane, circumventing the brush piles on the left side, a route opposite the one taken by the most recent visitor to the site. The yellow crime scene tape which had united the beech trees in grim purpose around the clearing had been cut.

Several minutes later, Carl and Jonas reached the woods, exited the squad car and stepped into the darkening gloom of late afternoon. Tension seized Carl's shoulders.

"What are we looking for?" Jonas asked quietly.

Good question. "We'll know it when we see it. Anything different from the way it was the last time we were here?"

"What the—?"

There! Next to the cremation site, a stone about three feet high had seemingly sprouted from the cold, damp earth.

"A grave marker?" Jonas asked.

Carl shuddered. "Doesn't look like any tombstone I've ever seen."

The stone was engraved with strange likenesses, separated into two panels. A yellow garment, edged with silver, was tied around it. In front was a small mound of carefully situated items: coconuts, stalks of wheat and grass, and what looked like red grains of rice. And on several beech trees surrounding the clearing, an even more bizarre adornment could be seen: *swastikas,* carefully molded from mud, or maybe manure, clearly visible on the trunks.

Jonas sang out in his best Tony Orlando impression: "'Tie a yellow ribbon round the old gravestone!' At least if somebody's gonna make swastikas, they're using the right stuff! Somethin' is wrong, though," he cocked his eye. "Looks backwards, doesn't it?"

"Shut up, Jonas." Carl could hear the distinctive engine noise of a squad car approaching just beyond the glade. He turned and yelled to a pair of deputies who came into sight: "Go back and get on the radio. I want McCorkle from Magdalene out here, pronto! Go pick him up, will you?" To Jonas, he said, "That guy couldn't find his ass with both hands."

Next, he directed Jonas to remain at the site to divert the curious. "Find a good spot where you can watch that lane entrance – I want to know if anyone else tries to get in here. And keep out any goddamned reporters. And Gertie Stickle, too!"

Carl spent about an hour combing the area for other signs of disturbance. His CSI team had arrived just behind him, and quickly began dusting the stone for usable prints as he watched.

Then he turned to scan another squad car entering the field. "Here comes McCorkle," Jonas hollered. Carl took a last drag on his cigarette, chucked it onto the greasy mud and ground it with his boot-toe. Leaning with their backsides against the squad car's fender, he and Jonas watched the other black-and-white make its way tortuously across the rutted field, bean stubble rustling beneath its undercarriage.

Mark McCorkle greeted Carl somberly. "Hello, Sheriff."

When Carl extended his hand, McCorkle gazed at it blankly for a moment—as if suddenly a handshake were some alien ritual to which he didn't subscribe—then absently offered Carl his own.

"I was hoping you might be able to tell me what we've got here," Carl said. "The Stickles spotted a truck leaving the woods a few hours ago and called us to investigate." He steered McCorkle toward the stone object. "Is this a grave marker, you think?"

"Hindus don't use cemeteries," McCorkle said, "so I doubt it." He hunkered down on his haunches, peering intently at the engraving. "It's not a grave marker so much as a sort of totem, a shrine. The materials scattered around would suggest that."

Carl was skeptical. "I need a better answer than that, Prof. Suggestions don't get us very far in this business."

"You can call in someone else to help," McCorkle said, seemingly unoffended—as if he were used to having his expertise dismissed. "An anthropologist, if you want. I wouldn't be put-off or anything."

Last thing I need's a pack of consultants on this case. Pointing to the swastikas on the trees, he asked as deferentially as he could: "What do you make of those? What are we dealing with here?"

McCorkle shook his shaggy head. "Fact is, the swastika symbol was unfamiliar to most Westerners until the nineteen-thirties. It used to mean good fortune, that is until Hitler hijacked and defamed it, likely beyond all redemption. It originated in Asia, not Europe, as most people think. It's an Eastern symbol, representing the universality of the cosmos, among Hindus and Buddhists chiefly. Ironically, its literal meaning, in Sanskrit I think, is 'to be good.'"

Cosmos? Universality? Carl shook his head. *Jesus!*

"What's your take on the stone then – a commemorative item of some sort?"

McCorkle spoke more assuredly: "I think it's a chhatri stone, erected to celebrate the event. They're found all over India."

"Vonderbar," Carl snorted. "What does it mean? Or don't you have a clue?"

Mark was unfazed. "You see how the stone is divided into two panels, each engraved with a picture? The lower panel depicts a rural cremation, with the husband and wife laid out on the pyre." He pointed at the left of the object. "That's a post, with an arm projecting from it, to represent the arm of the sati widow. The ornaments are bangles, symbolizing her married state. Widows normally break their bangles to signal their entry into widowhood."

"But these aren't broken," Carl noted.

"Exactly," McCorkle said. "That these are unbroken verifies the *sati mata*—the sati-mother—reaffirming her continuing wifely state and denying separation from her husband. The hand gesture itself is generic to Hindu icons, intended to dispel fear and defy the terror and finality of death."

Carl nodded as if he understood and Hindu icons were generic to his town. "What about the top panel?"

"That depicts an afterlife where gods, ancestors and the happy couple now dwell together peacefully by dint of the widow's sacrifice, her sati. They stand before a Vedic fire, surrounded by singing celebrants."

"And the tied cloth?"

"It's called an *udni*." McCorkle said "In some Brahmin sub-castes, it's worn only by married women with living children. Placing one around the stone is an act of homage—meaning that the pilgrim, or supplicant, regards the sati mata as his or her spiritual mother. The various articles of flora are simply offered in tribute... respect if you like."

"Christ," Carl spat. "Can you write that up for Southworth?"

"Certainly. I'm done with classes for the week, so I'll

get right on it." He pointed to the stone. "Do you have a camera? I'd like some good quality close-ups of this."

Jonas promptly stepped forward with half-a-dozen Polaroid snapshots. "These okay?"

"Perfect," McCorkle nodded. "See you tomorrow." He lumbered off toward the squad car; the big engine roared to life.

As the vehicle drove away from the site, past Stickle's farmyard, the deputy tooted the horn in farewell. Abner waved.

Chance whined; so did Gertie. "A-aaaabbb!" She somehow managed to make two syllables of the one.

At last, Abner revved up the old truck and flung open the passenger door. It was obvious to him that the clearing was the focus of attention again, with forensic technicians policing the site, swiping fingerprints off the stone, carefully examining recent tire tracks.

His wife practically sprinted across the lawn and catapulted herself in, chattering like a ten-year-old on a scavenger hunt. Abner, silent, puffed on his pipe and headed out to join Peters, hoping to Christ he hadn't troubled them all over nothing, and that Gertie hadn't squealed to her cronies.

At the tree line, they approached the scene of the fire. There Carl and Jonas stood like sentries, hands on hips, puzzling over a stone about three feet high.

Conversing in hushed tones, the two men quickly turned, reluctantly greeting the elderly couple.

Abner approached while Gertie lurked behind, craning her neck to peer at the mysterious object. "Sheriff?" Abner nodded, his pipe was still clenched firmly in his teeth.

"Afternoon, Ab." Carl nodded. "Thanks for the call."

"Appears it wasn't for nothing."

Jonas nodded toward the farmer.

"What do you make of that?" Abner removed the pipe and wagged the stem at the stone. "Grave marker?"

Carl shrugged. "While I want to thank you for your help—" these words brought a look of rapture to Gertie's face "—I'm trusting both of you to keep this development to yourselves. You wouldn't want to jeopardize the investigation or any testimony you might be called on to give later, would you?" Please, just lie low and keep quiet for now so we can use you in our investigation later."

"Oh, I *will*, Sheriff," she gushed. "You *know* I will."

Abner lit his pipe, winked, and led his wife back to the truck.

Carl groped his shirt pocket for a last roll of Tums, peeled off four and popped them into his mouth. *Damned stomach.* For a moment, as he chewed the powdery tablets, he regarded the small stone, embraced by the fluttering garment. It all seemed vaguely occult. And since he had little acquaintance with the metaphysical realm, if that was indeed what he was dealing with, he couldn't help but feel a tad ineffectual. He was just at a loss. Suddenly, as the cold chill shot down his spine, he suspected that it hadn't originated solely with the mournful late autumn wind.

November 10
5:45 p.m.
South Bend, Indiana

Fifteen minutes from airtime, Janey Jermane ensconced herself behind her desk on the set of WEKT television, thumbing through the airy news copy she'd soon be reading "for the folks!" as the station's theme trumpeted ceaselessly.

Of course, by then, the script would be only a prop. She and her gorgeously coiffed co-anchor, Mickey Marshall (the producer loved alliteration) would dutifully rustle their papers, while scarcely consulting them, to lend the impression that their contents had been fully committed to memory. They would relate the day's events as if caught in a genuine conversation with one another, one on which "the folks" were permitted to eavesdrop. Meanwhile, the invisible teleprompter would scroll along.

If one concentrated deeply, Janey mused, one might detect three or four minutes of hard news sandwiched between the "love those kids" segment, the "doggone report," health and beauty tips, financial gurus, "Kenny's Kitchen," a yuck-it-up weather girl and a self-proclaimed "dean of sports." The two anchors' roles had been reduced, effectively, to transceivers of the prepackaged, campy fluff that had become the six o'clock news, but she was effervescent, sexy and, most important of all, on top of the ratings heap in her market. Let the purists rant about the decline of standards.

Janey smiled.

A production assistant tapped her on the shoulder, handing her a cell phone. Placing her palm over the receiver, she mouthed "Who?" but got only a non-committal shake-of-the-head from her producer in return. "Christ." In as saccharine a voice as the hectic circumstances permitted, she answered, "This is Janey Jermane."

"Hello, Ms. Jermane, I've long been an admirer of yours." The male voice at the other end was deep, a little affected, a black guy, she thought, though she was unsure.

"Thank you very much." Janey was less annoyed by the gratuitous flattery than by its intrusion on her impending airtime. "And I would be speaking to—?"

"Let's just say I'm a citizen interested in social justice," the man answered, "as I'm sure you are."

"Of course," Janey said, incredulous that he had

somehow gotten through to her. "But I'm also interested in getting out a broadcast on time, so will you please get to the point?"

"There has been a significant development," the man said, "in the disappearance of a schoolgirl missing from Principia for over a week. There will be an arrest of a man named Swaraj."

"I've heard of a missing girl over there," Janey said, taken aback, "and it sure has generated a lot of publicity and a wide search. Always does..."

"Perhaps there'd be more—if the girl were not in the country illegally," the voice offered. "Surely, I don't need to remind you of how differently law enforcement treats crimes directed against people of color."

"Are you suggesting the authorities in Principia have been less energetic because of racism? Do you have any evidence?"

"I'm only making you aware of the facts." The disembodied voice sounded calm, almost instructive. "The answers to such questions will be for the press to ask and answer. I trust I've come to the right person."

"You have." Janey scrawled furiously on a notepad while assistants worked to perfect her hair and make-up. "Where may I contact you? What's your name?" The line went dead. "Hello? Hello? Shit!" She waved off her minions and issued rapid-fire orders. Much as she wanted to run with the story, she needed something more to hang it on.

Without missing a beat, she swiveled, focused on the red camera light near the teleprompter as it began scrolling and commenced her usual rat-a-tat delivery. *For the Folks!"*

November 11
8:45 a.m.

The Porsche Boxster pulled into the parking lot in front of Madison Fulbright's office building in downtown Principia, and as the large man driving it swung open the door. He shut off the ignition, then eased his frame onto the asphalt.

Fulbright cut an impressive figure, all six-foot-six of him. He wore an extra-long leather trench coat with an expensive scarf tied as an ascot around his neck. On his head was a black fedora with a small feather in the left-side band.

It was Saturday. He normally used weekend mornings to catch his breath and attend to any unfinished business. It was usually quiet; he answered no telephones and ignored knocks at the office door. This was *his* time: a few hours to read *Sports Illustrated*, do the *New York Times* crossword puzzle, unwind within the familiar confines of his office with no demands except those self-imposed. The best dividend of devoted bachelorhood, he'd found, lay in his ability to distinguish family diversions from his own.

Since Allen Southworth had left the firm the year before, Fulbright had prospered, profiting handsomely from some of the practice's cash cows and keeping a much larger percentage of the fees than ever before. Not that these rewards weren't richly deserved, he continually reminded himself. Allen had brought in most of the high rollers, it was true. But Fulbright had retained them following his departure, as he labored to maintain the viability of the practice.

But the imposing attorney had much more going for him than mere work ethic. Not only did he resemble a youngish Morgan Freeman, but he was also built like a latter-day Jim Brown. His imposing frame was belied only by his own awareness of prematurely arthritic knees and a painful disc in his lower back. Moreover, he was a prideful man. After all, he had clawed his way to the top of the cutthroat county bar through guile, iron discipline, dogged perseverance and 12-hour workdays. And he always carried with him a rugged integrity that had, at least up to this point, stood up rather well.

He hoped the rain would hold off, so that he might get a round in at the Montpelier Country Club. Despite the lateness of the year, the weather was just warm enough to enjoy an autumnal eighteen in his cardigan sweater, just cold enough to see his breath in the breeze. Yeah, he knew that he was the only African American member, but at least he was inside the citadel. He'd had too many doors closed to him in his life, to disdain this proffered portal to privilege.

Fulbright jangled the wad of keys deep in his pants pocket, fingering to separate them from the jumble of change that was his coffee fund. Finally finding the right one, he slipped it into the glass door to the anteroom. Striding through the entrance hall, sleek leather briefcase at his side, he opened the door to his sumptuous office. Unlike Allen's workspace, his was immaculate. Invitingly overstuffed chairs lined the cherry-paneled walls. At the front of the room sat a giant teak desk dominating the scene. Yet the plush surroundings were only partly the product of personal indulgence; for he believed deeply in the necessity of the presentation, both to overawe clients and to intimidate rivals.

He'd doffed his hat and coat, brewed a cup of strong, steaming coffee and settled into the morning when, abruptly, his concentration was shattered by a fist knocking on the louvered window along the top of his office wall. However high he and Allen had made them, Fulbright thought, they weren't high enough.

"Bullshit." He flung the newspapers to the desk and stalked to the back door, where he knew the owner of the fist would be waiting. Any number of clients knew the emergency entrance routine. But he was mildly surprised to see the beaming face of Theo Carver—an old acquaintance he'd made years before within the African American community of Principia.

"Hey T.C.', what's up? How long's it been?" At least eight months, he thought, but Fulbright preferred long intervals between their meetings. He wasn't much of a "joiner," whatever the professed cause. Still, Carver's local standing wasn't lost on him. *Hard not to give him his props.*

"What's happening?" Carver opened. "The usual shit." Fulbright stepped aside and offered Carver a chair at the office library table. "And to what do I owe this honor?"

"Do I need a reason to say hello to an old friend?"

Fulbright tensed a bit but managed a smile. He wasn't sure he appreciated the presumed familiarity.

"Yet this time," Carver continued, "I do happen to have a concern; one which, I am confident, you will share with me and with our people."

Carver seemed to end every other sentence with "our people," Fulbright had noticed, and he winced, suddenly wishing he hadn't come in this morning. He shrugged. "You know I always do what I can. But I have a lot on my plate, so spill it, okay?"

Carver grimaced. "You read the morning paper?"

"I was just about to when you knocked on the window." Fulbright held up a palm to halt the proceedings and then dashed into his office and retrieved a stack of newsprint. On his return he sighed, "I presume you're referring to the *Dispatch*, South Bend's only daily?"

He plucked the paper from others in the pile, hurriedly scanning the banner headline. *"HUMAN SACRIFICE: MISSING GIRL FOUND AMONG FUNERAL PYRE ASHES. ONE SUSPECT IN CUSTODY.* Scanning the grim article revealed the victim's ancestry. He looked up; across the table, Theo Carver appeared to be alertly tense, hanging on his reaction.

"Lord." Fulbright gulped from his coffee mug without first testing the brew. *Too hot.* "Allen's going to have his hands full on this one. And the publicity. Oh, man, the publicity…" For that he could almost envy the prosecuting attorney.

"Precisely!" Carver leaned forward, as if recruiting a conspirator. "Which brings me to the purpose of my visit."

"Why've you come to me?" the lawyer replied. "From what I see here, the girl was Indian, not one of 'our people.' And, while that doesn't lessen the crime any, it hardly explains *your* special interest in it."

Carver shook his head, disappointed.

"My interest is in *all* humanity. Besides, you might consider whether this may be an 'incident' that *appears* more unacceptable than it actually *is*."

"Says here the girl was ten years old. What are you

suggesting? That she barbecued *herself*? She wasn't of age. She had no agency."

Carver sat back and knit his fingers together on the broad expanse of his stomach. "Is that really so unbelievable? Especially when *religion* is involved?"

"Come again?"

Carver waved his hand dismissively. "You read about things like this all the time. Some Christian Science or Pentecostal family's into faith healing and refuses to get help for a child's sore throat. The kid gets pneumonia and buys it. Not unprecedented. It's a *spiritual* thing. Very personal."

Fulbright felt a touch of scorn. "Give it up, man; defendants like that are raw meat for prosecutors. And that kind of case is a lot different from what we've got here, at least, as far as we know."

Carver looked away, clearly agitated, one knee shaking an end table with its jiggling.

Fulbright tried to explain: "Those are crimes of *omission*. Neglect, stupidity, if you want, but not *murder*. Faith-healing may not be effective, but its followers aren't usually considered criminals. Not many people would give the same benefit of the doubt to the people involved in this sort of thing, whoever they are. Hell, what kind of religion does stuff like this, anyway?"

"Maybe you're right," Carver shrugged, then winked.

"Then again, maybe you're not. Anyhow, you're missing the *Big Picture*."

"Which is?" The attorney folded his massive arms.

Carver's brow knit grimly. "Shouldn't it be up to the community to determine what 'religion' means? And shouldn't there be a right and duty to *resist* if followers of a religion are denied the freedom to practice it?"

"Resist *what*?" Fulbright glared.

"How about cultural genocide?"

Fulbright sat silently, annoyed but vaguely amused, trying to size Carver up. He'd heard this riff so many times over the past few years, it was like fingernails on a chalkboard to him.

He said aloud: "I don't think that's a proper coupling, but okay, I'll bite. What's in it for you really?"

"That's a cynical outlook," Carver replied, wounded. "Tell me: why do some religions get respect in this country and others not?"

Fulbright decided to change his tack. "Remember Mr. Perry from high school? He preached that people have only themselves to blame for their fate. And he was black as we are! Crazy is crazy, and I know crazy when I see it. I can't see that all religions deserve equal respect. The same is true with people. Morality and character trump culture alone."

"Even when people have been brutalized?"

"Especially then." Fulbright leaned forward, his eyes brightening with both recollection and resolve. "Perry always drilled into us that people generally don't rise above their own expectations."

Carver's voice deepened. "I think you need to re-examine the "coupling" you just mentioned. Mr. Perry wanted us all to climb up by ourselves. But onto what? A platform built out of another culture's expectations that determine what morality means, and automatically dismiss and denigrate any other cultural point of view. That kind of generational trauma leaves no room for *social justice*."

Fulbright's eyes narrowed and probed Carver's face. "And you think this *ritual*, or whatever you call it, has something to do with social justice? We only deserve the social justice standard we demand of ourselves as well as others. That's what Mr. Perry would say."

Carver shot back: "The assumption being that there is one valid standard of social justice and 'we', meaning Western civilization, determine what that is. We are the judges eager to pronounce a verdict on people and customs we not only don't understand but believe we have no obligation to understand." He sighed heavily. "You're quite right though; our Mr. Perry would probably disapprove of me and my African perspective."

Fulbright blew a slight groan of exasperation out with a billowing cloud of cigarette smoke. "Regardless of 'cultural' context, T.C., it's not cool to incinerate a child."

"That's because you only see what you *want* to see. Is a child bride's *willing* sacrifice any worse than Catholic nuns cloistering till they croak? I thought feminism was all about women having control of their own bodies. Besides, what law permits certain cultures to set global standards while they command others to obey?"

"Ah," the lawyer nodded. "Now I think I'm beginning to see where you're coming from. You want me to represent someone having to do with this case, is that right?"

"Now at least you have a sense of my *mission*," Carver smiled, "if not of the sincerity of my *motives*." He crossed his forearms on his chest, plainly waiting for Fulbright's immediate decision.

The lawyer drummed his fingers on his desk for a moment, then said: "I can't possibly give you an answer now, you know that." But I promise to chew on it for a while, ok?"

"Later, my brother." Carver sang, as he rose. "Don't be a stranger."

"My causes, you'll be reassured to know," Fulbright said, "are Justice, Porsche and Armani, in that order."

Carver grinned as if well satisfied. "You sound like a capitalist. But with God's help and inspiration, all ends pursued here may be served."

"Shit." Madison Fulbright stood at the open back door, watching Carver disappear down the alley into the Saturday morning mist like a phantom. The big lawyer sighed. "Jesus, I hate rain."

November 11
10:00 a.m.

As they waited around the Formica table for their guest to arrive, Allen Southworth, Tom Stivers, Carl Peters and Jonas Clevenger sat quietly, anxious. The Sheriff and his deputy tapped ashes from cigarettes, while the others fidgeted with pencils.

On the verge of arresting Roop Kumar's father, Sirkar Swaraj, and bringing him in for questioning, Allen had flinched after receiving word about the stone at the immolation site. Instead, he'd opted to give McCorkle a little more time to investigate that development. But not too much. Once the guts of this case were laid out, the press would be on it – and them – like a pack of jackals.

Some ten minutes later the professor stepped into the spare little room, apologizing for his late arrival.

"Never mind, Mark," Allen said. "I've read your description of the stone. What are we dealing with?"

McCorkle dealt the Polaroid shots of the stone onto the table like a deck of cards and began: "This is what's called a *satigal*. It's a sati stone which confirms my original suspicion that what we have here is indeed a sati."

"Go on." Allen waved his hand impatiently.

"Well," McCorkle went on, with calm deliberation, "as I've said before, the word 'sati' does not denote the *act* of self-immolation. Rather, it's the name of the exalted *status* the widow achieves by her sacrifice, which means that she becomes a deity herself, elevating the social station of her family in the process and evoking reverence and supplication among those in need of divine intervention of some sort. As such, she becomes deserving of a shrine. That's what the stone is for."

Allen recalled a possible European parallel. "You mean, kind of like Lourdes is for Roman Catholics?"

"In a way," Mark said. "The widow has become *sati mata* or sati-mother. Now she may be called on to assist with any number of problems: healing, curing infertility, even passing examinations." He cleared his throat. "And there may be another problem down the road."

"Which is?" Allen raised his eyebrows.

"The glade has now become sati *sthal*, that is, the *abode* of sati. These stones are all over parts of India apparently, but some have morphed into more elaborate shrines or temples in which pilgrims may pay homage.

The family is honored, even enriched. Local merchants love the appeal; because they become holy sites, popularly sought out."

Carl put in: "That's neither here-nor-there. Aside from the growing number of families who come from great distances to the Ganges Mission, there's no constituency for that sort of nonsense around here. I realize that the demographics are changing. The country clerk puts the local south Asian population at 1,134 but that's up 30% in the last five years. Still, this is *Indiana, for Chrissake*! And I don't think many of our *local* merchants want this kind of publicity for Principia."

"No doubt that's true now," McCorkle nodded, "but remember, at one time no one had heard of Lourdes either. Now, what have you learned about the Mission that's associated with all this?"

Allen stroked his chin absently, "Not much. Tom?"

"They pretty much keep to themselves," Tom said. "Very leery of the curious passer-by, as a rule. I do know they've been buying up a lot of property out that way east of town. Still, their publicized ceremonies are open to the public. The Mission's head," he said looking down at his notebook, "is one Pandit Savarkar."

Carl started in recognition, then piped in. "Wouldn't be surprised if that's the old gent I ran into at Swaraj's place. He wasn't too enthusiastic about meeting me either. But I'll tell you this: from the traffic going in and out of the Mission, I'd say they're putting up something like a city out there."

McCorkle said, "I can't say I agree with your *scale*, Sheriff; but I know some Magdalene students who live out on that compound, and from what they say it's pretty self-contained: temples, agricultural plots, a library, a clinic, the whole nine yards. It's at least two-thousand acres and attracts good crowds on Hindu festival days. The Asian population of Pope County has tripled in the last ten years—most of them from India."

After a brief, Alan grimaced. "So, what's the point, Doctor?"

"Well," McCorkle said, "assuming that those behind that set-up are also behind the sati, I wonder why they didn't do it *there*? I mean, why did they use Stickle's place, where they were more apt to be noticed?"

Allen tapped his pen on the desk. "You tell *me*." "Honestly, I don't know."

"Jesus Christ," Carl sighed, scratching behind his left ear.

McCorkle sat up straight. "You know, your word choice is intriguing, Sheriff. When you stop to think about it, this whole thing has certain theological parallels with Christianity. Christ, after all, sacrificed himself—to expiate sin and reunite with his Father in the process.

And he's been the object of veneration and supplication ever since. His sacrifice is regarded as selfless, laudatory, exemplary—just like the sati widow's. And haven't you read about the martyrdoms of some Catholic saints? Bone-chilling…"

"Yeah, sure," Carl sputtered. "Except that Jesus was over thirty and had it *done to him*; he didn't nail himself onto a cross."

"Aha!" McCorkle's eyes widened. "But he *knew* what his fate would be and did *nothing* to escape it; and the Church itself has always regarded his death as a self-sacrifice."

Carl shot back, "But the boys said that *she did try to escape, right?*"

Allen raised a hand. "Come on, you guys, this isn't a theology seminar."

McCorkle turned toward him. "Don't get me wrong; I'm merely playing devil's advocate here, trying to give you some insight into the thought processes of those responsible. I'm trying my best to be neither an advocate nor an excuse-monger for sati."

"Fine," Tom Stivers said. "But how do you know this 'sacrifice' wasn't coerced? I mean, are you telling me these events are always voluntary?"

"Not at all." McCorkle shook his head. "In fact, given the age of the girl, I'd bank on its *not* having been, especially given those remaining bamboo poles. And the history books are full of witness accounts of coerced sati—women and girls drugged to mount their dead husband's funeral pyres and/or dragged and held there, screaming."

"And", Allen said, "is that what you believe happened here?"

"You gentlemen are the detectives, not I. But my instincts tell me that probably is what happened. Not that the question of volition even matters, insofar as I'm concerned."

Allen pressed further: "What do you mean by that?"

"This may not be my place…" McCorkle said slowly, "so, if I'm out of line, please let me know. I only mean that, given the state of our politics, I'm surprised something like this hasn't happened before." The others stared at him in silence.

"Look." McCorkle shifted into what Allen thought was likely his classroom demeanor. "Our entire system of law has its own cultural context. It is not, nor has it ever been, pristinely neutral where religion or culture are concerned, any more than our Constitution is. But then," he shrugged, "that's just my opinion."

Carl pushed his chair back impatiently. "This is all very interesting, Professor, but I don't see the connection. Murder's murder in any religion."

"True enough," McCorkle nodded, "but not all unnaturally caused death is murder. Our definition of murder *isn't* universal and, as in this case, it may depend a great deal on one's cultural baggage. The principles that underlie Western law are Judeo-Christian, not Hindu."

Carl huffed smoke through his nose. "When in Rome…"

"I agree personally, Sheriff," McCorkle said. "But many in the academic world today would not. The trend now is to avoid any assertion of a Judeo-Christian basis as a starting point for debates about crime or justice, and reinforcement of our nation's debt to Western political and philosophical traditions is shunned, even denounced in those circles."

Surprisingly assertive for a change, McCorkle got up and began pacing heavily around the conference table, as if he were in a lecture hall, gesticulating to himself. "A new emphasis on what's known as *multiculturalism* seeks to blur that Euro-Western legacy and refocus on universal respect for *all* cultural traditions. And that sounds really good—until you're faced with a case like this."

"Excuse me, Professor," Allen interjected, "but are you seriously suggesting that America *isn't* multicultural?"

"That depends on your perspective," Mark clarified. "America is multi-*ethnic*, it's true. But it also has a culture of its own, synthesized from all its varied sources – one that's sweeping the world, in fact, even as we speak." He scratched his scruffy beard. "But multiculturalists see their mission as rebutting that view and replacing our single, unified culture with a pastiche of separate cultures—each with adherents identifying with its own ethnic and political constituency."

Allen shifted in his seat. "And you see this as bad because—?"

McCorkle blinked behind his owlish glasses. "Well, because it disconnects Americans from their common bonds and therefore, from each other. And the farther America's citizens drift from their philosophic moorings, the greater the likelihood that other philosophies will displace them with ideas less hospitable to our traditional notions of ethics, morality and public policy." He paused for breath. "Sorry. I don't mean to go on."

"Not at all," Allen said.

"It's just that, if current intellectual trends continue, the most scurrilous epithet in the future may well come to be 'Western.' It's already used as an insult within the academy, a euphemism for 'racist' or 'ethnocentric'." Absently, he smoothed a cowlick on the back of his head. "Odd as this may sound, someday it may be generally considered 'un-American' as well.

So, what will it all mean in the end? I don't know any more than you do. But I do worry about this, if only because I'm not fond of societal chaos, which may devolve from this process. If we find ourselves unable to defend the very principles upon which our laws are based, then it may prove impossible to draw any boundaries at all—except for those on which all can agree. And the prospect of all agreeing grows less likely, because multicultural thinking discourages assimilation and celebrates difference. Unanimity on anything becomes impossible, paving the way to discord."

Then he stared at Allen. "Look, millions of people arrive in this country every year, from all corners of the globe. And since cultures tend to have more differences than similarities between them in the ways they define and affirm human dignity—as we may be seeing with this sati—the product may be incoherent. So, we shouldn't be surprised if we find that whoever may have allowed, abetted or orchestrated that sati doesn't share the Eurocentric premises on which our laws are based."

Allen felt tense. He tapped out and lit a cigarette with a slightly trembling hand.

McCorkle added: "If my suspicions are correct, you may well have a precedent-setting case shaping up here, Mr. Prosecutor. Because whoever is behind this may actually be *seeking* a confrontation, a prosecution if you like. And you may well find yourself in the role of de facto *defense* counsel..."

"Really," Allen took a long drag, then spoke with serious purpose. "And just who or what would *I* be defending?"

"That much is obvious," McCorkle said: "Western Civilization."

November 11
10:30 a.m.

Tom Stivers wheeled his seasoned Mustang onto the forested access road to the Ganges Mission, curious as to what awaited him there. The secretary for Pandit Savarkar, with whom he had arranged an interview, gave him to understand that his subject might be working on other things during the exchange.

After about a half-mile drive up the rutted road, Tom could see the parting of the trees up ahead. As his car crossed the edge of the woods, a rolling meadow spread before his view, a considerable acreage dotted with distant pole buildings gathered around a squat brick edifice sprawling around a stone tower ending in a notched stone disc. Hundreds of people, dressed in south Asian garb scurried about, engaged in myriad chores one might see on any large farm, yet with a notable absence of heavy equipment.

Tom turned into a large parking lot and was met by an attendant, who informed him that Pandit Savarkar was "in the field." He was deliberately routed around the main building, over which the central tower loomed much larger now. This stroll gave him a much better sense of the layout, which included steel-roofed schools, dispensaries, several garages and what seemed a low-budget fire station, in addition to rows of manufactured housing units flanking dirt tracks teeming with women and children, dressed in colorful saris, which seemed improbably immaculate given the dusty surroundings.

After walking a quarter of a mile in a circuitous route beyond the dormitories, Tom reached a sloping expanse of conifers, planted in precise blocks of ten rows apiece. The ground was immaculate, well-groomed. Before he noticed, his attendant had gone, leaving him alone, arms akimbo gazing at the attractive field.

"You seem impressed, Detective," came a voice from behind. He quickly turned around.

A gaunt, almost emaciated man grinned at him, his head slightly atilt. He was dressed all in white, long sleeves and pants, sandals on his feet, a shovel on his shoulder and a cigarette dangling from his lips.

Tom smiled back, absently rubbing the back of his neck. "I must confess," he answered, "I never would have expected a field of Christmas trees. What do you do with them?"

"Why, we sell them," Savarkar said, stepping his shovel head into the loose dirt. "What did you think we might do with them? It is a very lucrative market. These are Fraser Fir trees, sir. Much of the Mission's income derives from these trees, not to speak of the local good will. We Hindus revere all religions you know. Our harvest will begin in about a week, during which most will be trucked to the South Bend area. Some as far as Chicago." Tom noted a prideful timbre in the old man's voice.

"May we find a place to talk?"

Savarkar inhaled deeply on his cigarette, then motioned Tom toward a bench next to a nearby tool shed. The two men sat down, the old man's arms locked, hands clutching his knees. "I assume you are here to ask about the sati," he finished Tom's thought.

"You acknowledge that's what we're talking about, is that it?" Tom asked.

"Of course," Savarkar agreed. "I have seen them before….in India."

"Were you there?" Tom pressed.

The old man gazed through him, then smiled enigmatically. "I did not say that Detective. But word of such things does tend to spread."

Tom's brow furrowed. "Do you know the family?"

"I do, yes. We tend to help each other as all new arrivals must. They have been out here several times to participate in festivals. That is not to say I knew what was afoot."

Tom delved more deeply. "Then why were you at the family's home before Roop's body was discovered? You had no idea something had happened to the girl?"

Savarkar's smile disappeared. "As I've said, the Mission did outreach to the family, and will continue to do so as they require it. Am I to be placed under arrest, Detective?"

"No sir," Tom answered, "that's not why I asked to see you. I'd hoped you might have some notion as to who may have put the child up to this."

"Put her up to this?" Savarkar's eyebrows rose in ill-concealed mockery. "You are referring to an age-old sacrament of Indian culture, sir. As such, it speaks for itself."

Tom's eyes narrowed. "In Indiana what happened was a homicide. The child was ten years old."

"I am aware, detective," Savarkar replied, "which in no way alters the substance of my statement." The old man picked up his shovel and hugged it against his knobby shoulder. "You cannot define what you do not understand. Good day, sir."

A bit flummoxed, but irresistibly intrigued, Tom's scrutiny followed Savarkar as he strode toward the trees. As he approached a small out-building, its door was opened to greet him. And despite the distance, Tom recognized the figure of Theo Carver extending his left hand, holding an envelope in his right. Savarkar looked back over his shoulder at him, then pushed inside and closed the door. At that, the detective turned around purposefully and loped toward his car.

November 11
12:15 p.m.

Samantha Desai flipped her phone down as she entered the restaurant, having just chatted with her father in Birmingham about a trip he was planning to the Sacriston Cricket Club in the cathedral city of Durham. Her eyes rolled a bit despite her best efforts. "You can take the man out of the Raj," she mused, but..."

She had just wrapped up a pro bono case that she had been working on for over a year—a case of three Muslim women from the Balkans seeking asylum on the grounds of religious persecution after suffering a vicious mass rape at the hands of Bosnian Serb forces near Srebrenica. Their detailed account made her nauseous, but also determined to redouble her efforts to seek, if not fitting punishment for the perpetrators from their neo-fascist sponsors in Belgrade, then at least some acknowledgement of and reparation for the crime. But of course, asylum would have to come first.

That is what got Sam out of bed these days. It lent meaning and purpose to her life. And while her firm's partners raised bloody Caine about her alleged 'crusades', and the grisly publicity surrounding them, she had been able to convince them that they might enhance their public profile by placing themselves "on the right side of history" or, to enlist a trendy cliché, to be warriors for social justice.

Still, after the final hearing tomorrow afternoon, Sam would look forward to a day off—a nice long workout followed by a trek to the art museum, before dinner in the evening with her friend Meagan at the Nepal House, which had the best curry this side of the Atlantic. She needed something to banish the professional malaise which had oppressed her lately, hovering like a dampening fog. She was growing so weary of the stifling atmosphere at WWC/ *Whitmore, Wenner and Casey* in Chicago. Each time she opened the doors to the executive suite, Sam could feel the air thinning, less from the altitude 42 stories up, than from the stultifying want of creativity, daring, empathy and courage that lurked within.

Then she got the call beckoning her to South Bend, Indiana.

Allen Southworth watched her enter *Monique's* and was immediately transfixed. Maybe it was the shimmering straightness of the hair draped over her left shoulder. Or the studied self-confidence she exuded as she scanned the room before the host led her to his table.

He'd gotten her name from a colleague and—at least judging from the vita she'd faxed him—she seemed a promising legal find. University of Wisconsin, Law Review, with expertise in immigration. Her Indian ancestry was merely icing on the cake.

"Ms. Desai, I presume?" Allen rose and withdrew her chair from the table. "Thank you so much for coming."

"Thank you for having me, Mr. Southworth," she smiled. "Although I must confess, I'm rather in the dark as to your purpose."

We've plenty of time for that," Allen waved dismissively. "Would you like a cocktail?"

Samantha Desai addressed the waiter who hovered nearby: "A glass of your house Chablis, please." Then she delicately deposited her purse, and with a graceful swish of both hands, brushed her hair back from her bejeweled ears.

Impressed with her poise, Allen said, "I didn't mean for my intentions to sound particularly mysterious, Ms. Desai. It's just that the case we're working on is at a rather sensitive stage just now."

She nodded her understanding.

He said, "Maybe the best way to start is for you to tell me a little about yourself. I mean, other than the raw data."

Samantha adjusted her blouse on her shoulders. "Actually," she said smiling, "I never planned to become an attorney at all."

"No?" Allen lifted his eyebrows.

"My first love is archeology." She sipped delicately from her glass. "But my father wouldn't hear of an academic career." She let her voice drop several octaves, obviously mimicking her old man: "I can still hear him snorting, 'They're all a bunch of fairies, and if I let you do that, you might marry one of them. *Then* where would the family be? Follow the law and make some real money!'"

Allen laughed. "A hard-bitten sort, eh?"

"You have no idea how hard."

She continued cheerily, "So after we moved to the States, I went off to Northwestern to poke through the ALR instead of ancient ruins." She shrugged. "Not as interesting, but my dad was right; the pay is better."

"Any regrets?"

"Not really. My father means well. And he does know the academy. He worked for years as Chair of Oriental Studies at Oxford, after leaving the consular service and before entering the law. He teaches now at the University of Wisconsin Law School. My mom is half-English, and an attorney. The real trouble is that neither of them can shake all the old traditions—one of which is the duty to choreograph a daughter's life for her. Both English and Indian fathers seem in concert on that one."

Allen sipped at his glass of bourbon. "So, I guess that explains your presence in Chicago," he asked without asking.

"Is it that obvious?" she asked. "Yes, close enough to see them in Madison, every so often, but far enough away to evade the directives. Still, it's a lot closer than Portsmouth, that's for sure."

"Well," Allen said, "I hope you won't find my orders as burdensome as that. That is, if you sign on with me."

Samantha's chin reposed atop her interlaced fingers as she considered this man. "That depends on what I would be signing on *for*."

As comprehensively as possible, Allen related the particulars of the presumed sati, as far as he understood them, leavening the narrative with a few cursory insights and speculative conclusions. He also bounced Mark McCorkle's political and metaphysical slants off her. She remained impassive throughout.

He finished and paused; then said, "Any first impressions?"

"Sounds positively hideous," she began, with a contemplative sip of her newly arrived glass of wine. "Of course, I've read accounts of widow-burning. But a sati, *here*? Now? I mean, it seems so incredible in this day-and-age, especially here in the States. There must be some other explanation."

"The only other explanation is a double suicide, but he would have to have been alive, too, for that to fly. Jaansen's certain she was *not* and that he *was*... dead, I mean. Besides, we have eyewitnesses."

"Eyewitnesses to what?" she came back. "For all they knew, it was a bunch of Satan-worshipers. Your witnesses sound plenty impeachable to me, I'm afraid."

"Thanks," Allen said, "I needed that."

She smiled. "Oh, don't mind me, Mr. Southworth. I was just playing devil's advocate. It's what I do, after all."

"Call me Allen." He looked down at his drink. "Which is why I asked you here, Ms. Desai." "Please. Call me Sam."

"If you like." Allen paused as the waiter delivered the appetizers they'd ordered. "Sam." He tasted the nickname, savored its simplicity. "This case is taking on dimensions I hadn't foreseen and with which I'm not familiar. I need trustworthy advice from someone with a sense of those dimensions, as they might affect my professional obligations."

"It sounds as if your Professor – McCorkle, is it? – has a good sense of the historical context. And his take on the philosophical ramifications also seems right on the mark. You'll need to focus on those eventually, I think."

"Yeah. I kind of got that idea from the Prof," he said. "But he's hard to follow sometimes. I mean—he seems to live for the esoteric. All this business with multiculturalism…"

"One thing must remain absolutely clear at the outset, Allen." Sam's gaze was disconcertingly direct. "I don't subscribe to any specific cultural agenda. And though I am a firm believer in the transcendence of ideas, I don't believe they're the property of any particular culture or civilization."

"Why is that?" Allen asked.

"Because that would play into the hands of bigots: those who think certain people are inherently superior or inferior to other people. It's a circular argument anyway, since all successful civilizations have contributed to progress over time.

Allen arched his eyebrows. "But don't specific civilizations get most of the credit for progress?"

"Well, that depends," she adjusted the pearls. "Sometimes spectacular advances descend from a particular design or singular genius. More often, though, they don't. Mere chance plays the biggest part, I think."

"Chance? Civilizations are just accidents? What do you mean by 'chance'?"

"Lots of things," she said. "Geography, natural resources, commerce, one's enemies—or lack of them – even desperation. All play a role in determining the way a culture responds to challenges."

She took another sip of wine, then looked away. "On the other hand, such factors *may* play a key role in giving rise to genuinely superior intellectual streams, which in time birth genuinely superior institutions, be they political, intellectual or economic."

Feeling his two bourbons and something else he couldn't quite pinpoint, Allen pressed further: "But Sam, don't you think McCorkle's half-a-bubble off plumb? I mean, given what you've just suggested, American culture isn't as fragile as he makes it out to be, is it?"

"Perhaps not," she shrugged. "But what he's trying to say is this, I think: that if this country were ever faced with a political crisis that required a broad philosophic solution, we might be in for tough sledding. It's kind of strange." She plucked at her stuffed mushrooms. "In a way, we're the victims of our own political and techno-logical triumphs, aren't we?"

"I don't think I follow you," he said.

"What I mean is that science has enabled us increas-ingly to allow certainty to displace uncertainty. Not only that, but it's also begun to eclipse humankind's more ancient approach to the hypothetical, the unknown and the unknowable: philosophy, coupled with the morality that evolved from its derivative: religion."

Sam stared, eyes half-closed, at the rafters for an instant, then cradled her chin on her interlaced fingers. She continued, "Even the most cynical atheist must admit that morality didn't just materialize out of the ether; it descended from religious philosophy. Yet now, the word 'morality' has been excised from the culture, almost to the extent that it's disappeared as an expres-sion of popular judgment. People may feel they know what they *feel* about a given moral question, without really knowing *why* they feel that way. Do you under-stand now?"

Allen ventured a slim smile. "I'm not sure, but it sounds an awful lot like you're defending the sati."

Her head shook slightly. "Don't misunderstand. I merely said that the processes by which civilizations advance may be more random than you may think, and not necessarily indicative of intrinsic sophistication. That's hardly the same as saying all civilizations are equally advanced or moral—at least by the most accepted international definitions of such things. And neither are all religions. Equally moral, that is. Understand? I don't shrink from employing that word, in its accepted context, of course."

She took up her napkin, dabbed her sensuous mouth. "For you to argue that the law has a moral right to judge another culture's religion, you need a mode of critique. You need a philosophic way to reassert the moral sense that's supposed to ground any legal standard. The trouble with trying to do that these days is that the American public seems uncomfortable with that word morality. To most people, I think, it just seems too arbitrary, too pat, too restrictive, too *judgmental*. But that's largely because we seem to have lost all the old presumptions we once worked from and orbited around."

"I think I get it," said Allen. "Though murder's forbidden everywhere, its moral definition isn't uniform everywhere."

"Something like that," she continued. "But it's aggravated by the way in which much of the world looks at the West: with the resentment and suspicion of a prey toward a ruthless predator, a voracious assimilator. America's image is consequently resented by many abroad. So, rejection of Western notions of morality and the revival of traditional practices are logically defensible to many immigrants."

Allen smiled indulgently, "You can't really believe that Sam."

"You aren't listening, Allen," she said. "Look at the world about you. At this moment in time, international law condemns slavery, totalitarianism, female circumcision, human sacrifice, and sati. Why?"

She paused and then answered herself: "Because, truth to tell, Britain *did impose* its philosophic superstructure on much of the world. And after the Empire died, America assumed the mantle, taking up the philosophic slack. Like it or not, the West proselytized and bullied much of the planet into its own variant of progress.

Whether that was a good or a bad thing really doesn't get us very far, does it? The more salient question is: does anyone really suggest going back to the old ways?"

She went on: "Some do. Especially, I believe, those who romanticize the past. This enables a practice like sati to re-emerge, and, ironically, its advocates will likely now claim protection under the very system they are working to dismantle. In response, our own bureaucrats may just go along with hare-brained educators.. So too, may judges and politicians and, if they become convinced, the trend is irresistible."

Allen watched, delighted, her delicate, yet emphatic, gestures; and he saw several of the wait-staff pause to watch her performance. He could imagine her in a courtroom, with *that* venue at her disposal...

"Now," she added, "multiculturalists love to spin metaphors about America not being a melting pot at all, but a salad bowl in which ingredients may remain separate, yet somehow all enrich the collective flavor of the whole."

She leaned over the table and pointed a tapered nail at Allen. "But that analogy is fatally flawed, because human beings, unlike vegetable matter, do not tend to remain that way for long. Inert, I mean."

"But America is multicultural, or at least multi-ethnic, isn't it?" Allen said. "That's what makes this case so damned difficult."

Samantha lowered her gaze, sighed with a hint of exasperation. "People are dynamic, contentious, combative. Discord tends to seek its own level. Within a society that prides itself on making allowances for difference, conflict is not only inevitable, but also enriching, stimulating, even catalytic. But without America's unique system and its legal protections to broker the process, the product will spiral into conflict."

Allen was unconvinced. "Sam, I'll tell you, that

sounds a little arrogant, even reactionary. Kind of a crabbed view of diversity, isn't it?"

"Not at all."

The waiter delivered the entrees; Sam virtually ignored them.

"Let's take my parents' homeland, for example. Talk about diversity! India is the most ethnically, religiously, economically, socially, linguistically, and politically diverse piece of real estate on the planet. It never enjoyed anything close to modern political unity until relatively recently. And look at the institutions which now knit it together, however imperfectly: democracy, a secular judiciary, a civil service, common law, and the English language. Together these helped forge an independence movement against their imperial rulers. Few Indians would ever admit it outright, but they have the British Raj to thank for those institutions, notwithstanding Britain's colossal blunders."

At last, she sampled the rapidly cooling escargot. "You see, I'm willing to bet that those behind this sati, if that's indeed what it is, aren't your typical Indian immigrants; they're fanatics, the sort of political opportunists with whom compromise is probably impossible. It's to those sorts that I'd look for keys to this case."

Suddenly, Sam became aware of the gathered audience. She looked around and fidgeted with her napkin. Several employees and patrons clapped appreciatively in her direction. "I apologize, Allen," she said. "I do tend to go on."

Allen grinned. "It wasn't only the staff you've impressed, Sam. Maybe you should do my closing."

Samantha smiled appreciatively.

Allen sighed, then rubbed the back of his neck absently. "Jesus Christ, this is a mess. I'm damn good when it comes to arguing statutes and case law. But this one has precious little of that. Could be we're just out of our depth and looking at a bloody circus."

Looking measurably calmer than he, Sam added, "I'm sorry to say, but you do seem about to be thrown to the wolves on this one. So, you'd better be prepared to give as good as you get.

For my money, they won't be above ambushing you with something like this, hoping you'll be too confused, guilt-ridden and conflicted to do anything but knuck-le-under to the zeitgeist. You have your work cut out for you, Allen." She paused and lifted her gaze and her glass to meet his. "As, it seems, have I."

Allen couldn't suppress his delight altogether.

"Then you agree to be the second chair?"

"In whatever way I might be the most useful," she smiled back at him. "When do we start?"

PART II

**November 12
5:52 p.m.**

Jan had that *we-need-to-talk* look on her face. "The kids are buzzing around you, I'm about to serve Sunday dinner." She handed Allen a drink and slipped onto the couch at his side. "But you're a million miles away."

How can I translate that, but as an accusation? He sighed, "This case belongs a million miles away, not in Principia." And as he tried to explain to her some of its broader ramifications, she asked a few probing questions and made a couple of arresting observations.

"We used to talk like this," she smiled gently. "Remember? Back in the courting days on campus. Philosophy? History?" Then, looking into the distance, she said, "The good old days, before I entered the great child-rearing debates, the differences in philosophy between Dr. Spock and T. Berry Brazelton. Before Barbara Coloroso started reminding us that *Kids Are Worth It*."

Who the hell is Barbara Coloroso? Allen took a swig from his glass. "Of course, kids are worth it. You're doing wonderful job." He squeezed her arm. "You *are*." She was; he was at least sincere about that.

But she was so much more. She'd have been more than happy to enlist Rousseau's *Emile* to argue for the kids to enter Montessori, if she'd detected any sign of Allen's interest in the subject. His bond to the children was so one-dimensional, abundant with play and goofy interaction but, at the same time, so intellectually feral. Their kids learned so little from Allen.

At that moment, his daughter Angela rocketed across the room, hugging his legs and smiling worshipfully up at him. He tousled her curly locks; she smiled in response. "It's Mountain Time, Daddy!" she exclaimed, grabbing his hand to pull him into the living room.

"Not now, Sweets, your mother and I are talking."

"Daddy!" she whined, "you didn't hear me, It's *Mountain* Time. Come on, Daddy, come on!"

Surrender.

Lying on the living room floor moments later, Allen gasped as the twins, Andy and Angela took turns jumping on "The Mountain" (as his corpus was known to them), after a running start of course. Once he gave in to their demands, he wondered why he'd been so reluctant. He so enjoyed their squeals and laughter, so utterly gleeful. His children's joy was intoxicating to him, invariably shoving the rubbish of his everyday concerns aside for a few minutes at least.

As Allen gasped for breath, he looked up to see Jan smiling down at him. She enjoyed seeing her husband revert to his playful self, even if only for a brief interlude. "See," she said coyly, "retirement wouldn't be so bad, would it?"

Allen's response was uninspired. Between the stomach-crushing leaps of his kids, he groaned, "Unfortunately, they don't stay this size forever. And come to think of it" (little Andy erupted in a spasm of giggling, as he lifted him into the air with his outstretched arms), "it's a good thing they don't." He looked up Jan's reaction, but she'd gone back to the kitchen. And Allen managed to stand up, a child under each arm.

"Tell me more about work," Jan asked perfunctorily from the kitchen.

She knows part of the answer already. "It's going to get busy." He tried to keep the defensive note out of his voice; he needed her on his side. "*Very* busy. None of us has ever seen a case like this."

"You're not in over your head, are you," she said half-smiling, "*The Great* Allen Southworth?"

"In truth, I think I just might be..."

"Then hire some experts!" She gestured broadly and leaned to uncork a bottle of red wine in the kitchen.

Her strained enthusiasm made him squirm. "I

already have," he admitted. *Best to get it out of the way early.* "They include a 'woman of color.' Fight fire with diversity, right?"

Jan nodded; her arms crossed under her bosom. Then she faced him directly: "Allen, I—we—"

He knew that look and hated it. Fill in the blanks: *Allen, I—have something to say. Allen, we—need to talk.* At that moment, he watched his wife's face contort through three different emotions. Jan couldn't do a poker-face the way he could. He set his expression in stone to give her no opening.

Instantly, she looked like she'd literally swallowed the words she was going to say, and decided on others to say instead: "What's her name?"

He loathed himself for a moment – but a moment only. "Samantha Desai."

Jan set her shoulders into the model-wife pose she usually wore: the help mate, the playfully bantering spouse, foil, and straight man to *The Great* Allen Southworth. "Why do I get the impression," she said, "that this 'woman of color' is something more than a colleague? Is she beautiful?"

Allen stared steadily at her. "Yes, she is, in fact. And she's absolutely brilliant at handling the sort of argument that's going to come our way."

Jan turned away silently, and Allen quickly said, "Where's the remote? Time for the news..."

November 12
6:00 p.m.
Pope County Courthouse

"Five, four, three, two, one."

The disembodied voice counted down in Janey Jermane's ear. She stood before the courthouse, ready to begin her first remote broadcast on the death of a young girl. She'd reassured her producer—and herself—that she had enough to go on, even though Carl Peters and Allen Southworth had both refused her requests for interviews.

At least she now knew it was a suspected homicide, concerning which the authorities were trying their best to keep the details under-wraps. But, just as her anonymous tipster had predicted, an arrest had taken place the previous afternoon. As for the rest of it—the illegal alien/people of color slant—she had nothing – *yet*. But the official reticence was suspicious enough for her to go with the story.

She had the lead tonight because this piece had all the elements of a blockbuster: under-age sex, graphic violence, ethnic conflict, religious fervor, a palpable exoticism. No wonder no one would go on the record with her or any other reporter. Anyhow, too little information was almost better for her, now that she'd been forced to acquire it through channels. She had the requisite cover to engage in her own speculation, or to bring in "experts" who weren't at all shy about doing the same.

She awaited the lead-in from Mickey Marshall at the studio. Then she said into the camera:

"Yes, Mickey, authorities are closed-mouthed about any details surrounding this case. Playing their cards very close to the vest, law enforcement officials are unwilling to deny or confirm rumors that both individuals perished in a blaze in the woods next to the farm of Abner and Gertrude Stickle.

That woods, News 8 has now learned, belongs to a religious organization closely connected to a local institution. The Hindu Mahasabha, as it's called, is politically active *and* controversial on the Indian subcontinent, and has close ties to the Ganges Mission, a South Asian cultural center located near Principia."

Janey glanced at her notes. For a change, she *needed* them. "According to our sources," she continued, "both individuals were recent immigrants from India, though the legality of their status is still to be determined. Whatever the outcome of that finding, however, this case is already assuming overtones of ethnic conflict. Local activists worry there will be a rush to judgment by authorities who are unfamiliar with diverse cultures." The camera's focus shifted. "Joining me here at the courthouse is one of those activists, Theo Carver, local spokesman for the Diversity League. Welcome Mr. Carver."

"Good evening to you."

Janey said, "In light of the most recent developments we know of, would you please share with our audience some of the concerns you have over the way this case has been handled thus far."

"Certainly," Carver replied. "The Diversity League is concerned that the Sheriff's department, if past performance provides any guide, is not philosophically equipped to evaluate this incident fairly. Nor is it sensitized to the kind of damage that may be done to the immigrant community through the spread of biased misimpressions?"

Janey sensed something familiar about Carver's voice – and she was experienced enough to be leery of anything that might smack of tactical misinformation. "Would you be a little more specific, Mr. Carver? What kinds of... *impressions* are you concerned about, exactly?"

"Well, it is undeniable that the images which have been conveyed to the public really don't reflect the rich diversity of cultures largely responsible for the founding of this nation, and especially of its multicultural mosaic. The authorities, and especially the prosecutor's office, ought to be very cautious about slandering the immigrant community and so exposing their own ignorance and insensitivity. The lack of hard information they've made available about this case so far, speaks volumes about the level of official objectivity. I, for one, have found the Sheriff's department's lack of candor troubling indeed."

Janey was momentarily stunned. "Are you suggesting there may have been no crime committed?"

"I did not say that. But we may have an issue here that lies beyond the ability of... say... the *traditional* authorities to judge accurately."

"And that would be—?"

"I think we all know, deep down, who is *empowered* here and who is not," Carver replied. "I merely say, let us be certain this is not a case of white men saving brown women from brown men. Do you understand?"

"I think I do," Janey lied. "Thank you for your speaking with us,

"One more thing," Carver interjected. "This Wednesday, public discussion of this case will be aired during our previously scheduled Diversity Day Dialogue at Magdalene College. I will have more to say on the subject at that time."

"Again, thank you so much," Janey said.

She turned from Carver to her left. "With me now to shed insight into the crime scene itself is Mrs. Gertrude Stickle, the neighbor who first reported strange events in the dark woods to local authorities."

The elderly matron standing next to Janey veritably

beamed, as the reporter began the interview. "Good evening, Mrs. Stickle."

"Good evening, Janey," cackled Gertie. "My husband Abner and I watch you every night. Can I say hi to my friend Flossy?" Before Janey could stop her, she was waving into the camera. "HI FLOSSY! I'M ON TV!" Then Gertie turned back to the reporter. "You're my hero, Janey. Mickey is so nice! And *so smart*! Are you two dating?"

"Now, now, Mrs. Stickle." Janey patted the woman's shoulder, trying not to grit her teeth. *Goddamn live interviews: loose cannons like this one can scuttle careers.* "There are people who say *you're* the hero. That more deaths might have been avoided due to *your* vigilance."

"Oh, no, Janey," Gertie shook her head. "I didn't do nothing any concerned citizen wouldn't have done. Specially to help a *child*. And I know you know what I'm talking about, Janey, 'cause I know how much you love kids. We're supposed to put kids first, just like you and Mickey say. So, this is just *wrong*, Janey. It's wrong to burn a little girl to death."

"Can you shed any light on whether or not there's some sort of shrine at the site, with strange engravings? There have been local rumors to this effect."

"Well, I can't really comment on *that*," Gertie said. She put a hand aside a cheek and added more quietly: "'Because the Sheriff – he told me not to mention it, 'specially to the press." Then she smiled proudly. "But I did find a lot of animal bones around the crime scene, and I pointed them out to the deputies. Sheriff Peters even said I could help in the investigation."

The reporter beamed. "Well, it sounds like the Sheriff should deputize *you*, Mrs. Stickle. Thank you so much for your time, and for being such a good neighbor and citizen."

Across town, his Sunday dinner forgotten, Allen Southworth grunted and reached for the telephone as the reporter wrapped up.

Janey Jermane intoned somberly: "Whatever the facts of this bizarre case, this much we know: An arrest has reportedly been made in the murder of ten-year-old Roop Kumar—a little girl who, by all accounts, loved poetry and cared conscientiously for the class hamster at school. Her remains lie for, now, in the county morgue, unable to tell us anything more, now. But one thing is certain: as the story behind her grisly fate unfolds, so too will the mystery of her untimely death. *For the Folks*, this is Janey Jermane. Now, back to you, Mickey."

November 13
6:00 a.m.

The next morning, Allen was out the door early, to avoid Jan's recriminations and his children's crestfallen faces. Far better to skirt such distractions; they might linger the whole day. Though the fridge was full of roast beef leftovers, he opted to wolf down a greasy, but filling sausage McMuffin with egg at a nearby McDonald's.

He'd scheduled yet another strategy session with Carl, Tom Stivers, Mark McCorkle and now, Samantha. This was essential, he felt, before questioning their suspect, Sirkar Swaraj. Though not yet under arrest (the reporter had that wrong, he noted with satisfaction), Swaraj had been detained for questioning and appearance in a lineup.

Samantha would bring a certain authenticity to the endeavor, he hoped, as to both ethnicity and gender. As he entered the conference room. Long since dubbed the "Formica Room" by the deputies, Allen saw he was late; the three principals sat waiting for him. Perhaps this was best; it made introductions unnecessary. McCorkle and Samantha were chattering away like old school chums – unsurprising, since Sam spoke McCorkle's language. But the professor was more agitated than Allen had expected, a fact that made him feel…well… vaguely jealous. *Jealous of McCorkle? Ludicrous!*

"Good morning." Allen tried to sound businesslike as he sat down. "Glad to see you're all getting acquainted."

Carl didn't look up from the yellow notepad on which he'd been furiously scribbling. "We've got a lot to go over," the Sheriff muttered. "New information's surfacing faster, I'm afraid, then we can absorb or verify it."

Allen sighed resignedly, then began the colloquy. "Why don't we begin with you, Tom," he said. "You've been out to the Mission, right?"

Tom leaned back in his swivel chair. "A couple of days ago. Very interesting, if frustrating."

"How so?" Allen said.

"Well," the detective began, "at first blush it looks very much like your preconceived notions of a commune: crafting cottages with a lot of basket-weaving and candle-making going on, interspersed with pole buildings with chickens and a dairy herd."

"Unremarkable so far," Allen remarked.

"But right behind the central temple-like building is an enormous file of *Christmas trees*, believe it or not. There were probably a hundred-odd acres of them in as pretty a layout as I've ever seen. I used to work on one of those farms as a kid. But from what I was able to see, everything was done by hand. Not a chainsaw or tractor to be seen anywhere. The trees were Fraser fir, I'm told."

"Told by whom?" Allen asked.

"I ran into Pandit Savarkar," Tom consulted his

notes. "He told me that they sell them to vendors in South Bend and Chicago. Hindus selling Christmas trees. When in Rome, I guess."

"What else did you learn, Tom?" Allen pressed.

"Savarkar was awfully cagey. He didn't deny knowing of Roop's family, or even knowing of the sati itself. Very matter of fact about it all. Yet he claims that his awareness stems from his knowledge of the Mission's outreach program. He's a very cool, very distant fellow, and extremely difficult to read."

"And his reaction to the sati?"

"That's the funny part. He seemed non-committal, agnostic...at least in his language."

Allen snuffed his cigarette. "By which you mean..."

"His expression," Tom shivered slightly, "was cold as sin."

"Well shit," the Sheriff turned to his notes. "At least we know a hell of a lot more about this family than we did before. Tom's been in contact with the Indian consulate in Chicago and has managed to extract, and I mean *extract*, some interesting tidbits. Not the least of which is that Sirkar Swaraj isn't the girl's father after all, but her *father-in-law*."

"What?" Allen looked up sharply.

"That's right." Tom took the floor and nodded at McCorkle. "The Prof's guess was definitely right. When we started to investigate the supposed father of the deceased, we discovered that he and her father-in-law were one and the same. The girl was married to his son and, as is apparently not unusual in India, living in the Swaraj house."

Stivers paused, then said, "That's not the worst of it."

Allen groaned. "Somehow, I knew it wouldn't be."

"Her 'husband,'" the detective air-quoted, "wasn't as desirable a marriage prospect as Roop's family had been led to believe. They were told he was about to enter medical school. But after some digging, I found out he performed miserably on the MCAT. So miserably, in fact, that unless he moved to the Caribbean, he wasn't ever likely to become a doctor. Not in *this* lifetime,"

Sam murmured, "Maybe he'll be more successful in his next."

McCorkle guffawed, his first-ever display of humor among this group.

"What's the joke?" Peters asked.

"Karma. Reincarnation." Sam chuckled, waving it off. "Sorry. Couldn't help myself."

Stivers resumed, "We managed to find a few lower-level officials at the consulate who didn't give us the bum's rush. They got in touch with the girl's family. Apparently, they were more shocked by that bit of news than by the deaths."

Allen relaxed and focused better now. "Anything else?"

"You bet." Carl picked up the ball. "Apparently—and

this is the kicker—we might have something less than a divine hand in this whole business. The girl's family, it seems, is not only uninformed, but loaded. And shy about 100K—which they sent as their daughter's dowry. Mr. Swaraj's family doesn't have a pot to piss in, excuse my French, Ms. Desai, comparatively speaking that is."

Sam waved it off.

"A whiff of motive?" Tom said.

"Not quite." Carl scratched his head. "I mean, the family already had its hands on the money. That's a wrinkle I haven't figured out yet."

Samantha raised her hand to speak. Allen said, "To you, Ms. Desai."

She said, "I make no claim to expertise in Indian family law, but I do know that the question of the dowry among Indians is very serious indeed. Women have been beaten, killed or abandoned because a promised dowry wasn't forthcoming. In this case, you have an amount of money significant by Western standards, but positively colossal by those of Rajputana."

Nods all around.

She went on: "Correct me if I'm wrong, Professor, but I believe that if a husband dies while his wife is still very young and childless, the widow is entitled to return to her father's household... *with her dowry intact*."

"That's right," McCorkle said. "That would surely

have spelled financial ruin for Mr. Swaraj, given his son's likely future ne'er-do-well status."

"Unless—" Sam added.

The three men craned their necks in her direction. "Go on," Allen prompted.

"Unless" Sam said, "the girl was induced, or *coerced*, to join her husband on the pyre that morning. Even if her family smelled a rat, to say so might impugn their daughter's motives ex post facto. Rather than return home as a disgraced widow-non-person, she would become a deity in the minds of many. This exalted status would redound, incidentally, to the stature of her family in India as well. That could take a lot of the sting out of the monetary loss."

Allen rubbed his chin thoughtfully. "What about the Indian authorities at the consulate? They certainly must have been in touch with their superiors by now. Have they expressed any interest in it?"

Stivers yawned, "I get the distinct impression that they want this whole thing to go away. Their silence has been deafening."

"Not surprising," McCorkle said. "They're wary of anything that might feed religious fanaticism. The Mahasabha appeals to forces that most incumbent politicians avoid like the plague. And while they're probably as shocked as we are, they can't openly denounce the act without looking Westernized and inauthentic, traits that extremists and opportunists would pounce on. Sad to say, politicians everywhere are moved by pressure..."

"And is this Mahasabha," Allen put in, "definitely mixed up with this thing, Tom?"

"To some extent, for sure," Tom said. "They bought that woodlot from Stickle, though I very much doubt we'll find a membership card on Swaraj: that is if they even have 'em. And there's something more."

"Go on," Allen said.

Tom flipped his notepad. "The Mahasabha, along with the aforementioned Pandit Savarkar, is bankrolling a lot of the construction on the Ganges Mission Farm."

"That's all?" Allen asked. "Doesn't seem so unusual." Tom smiled.

"Maybe not – but he's also been handing over some big checks to the Humanities Department at Magdalene too: over two-hundred-and-fifty grand last year alone." He glanced at McCorkle and grinned. "Why, he may just be puttin' food on your table, Doc."

McCorkle stared back, expressionless; then he got the innuendo and threw up his hands as if in surrender. He laughed loudly. "Hey, I just eat it, no questions asked!"

Sam broke in: "I'd like to add something here. We do know that the organization has become more active among the Indian 'Diaspora'—as its leaders refer to it—using members here in the States to raise funds, as well as to agitate politically against their government, far away from the scrutiny they might attract at home. But in India, causes like these are less the business of one organization than of a constellation of them, each professing a slightly different cause."

She tapped her yellow pad with her pencil eraser. "I suspect, for instance, that this one has close ties both to quasi-terrorist groups like the Rashtriya Swayamsevak Sangh—or, RSS—as well as to mainstream Hindu nationalist parties, like the Bharatiya Janata Party—the BJP."

"And there's something else," Sam added. "We must appreciate the psychological relationship between new immigrants and such organizations. Many of the new arrivals experience a cultural disconnect. While they may find much here that's familiar, and while they are drawn to all the trappings of modernity that *we* love so much, *they* often find themselves less comfortable with both the pace of change and the cultural context that often underlies it. Oddly enough, some become more spiritually needy over here than they ever were in India."

McCorkle nodded concurrence.

"They fret that their suddenly Americanized children," Sam said, "are more quickly and less superficially seduced by our culture. They're horrified at the ubiquity of crime, promiscuity and drugs here, and many parents regret the waning relevance of the old ways, which include respect for one's elders. Will their children, they wonder, remain sufficiently Indian enough—and Hindu enough—to respect their aged parents in the future? Many of these people really don't keep abreast of the viciousness of party politics back home and these organizations often reinvent themselves in an entirely new incarnation over here—cultural activities, charitable works and the like. It's no wonder they come off so appealing, both to immigrants and to American-born Hindus. In that context, gifts to places like Magdalene seem a good investment in its public image here in town."

"Remember," McCorkle suddenly chimed-in, "these groups are, at best, communal enthusiasts and, at worst, outright extremists dedicated to the establishment of a Hindu nation in South Asia. Their hostility toward Muslims and others whom they consider lapsed brethren is well-documented. They're prone to violence as well.

"So," Tom summarized, "we have a suspect with a motive to kill his daughter-in-law, who may also be somehow attached to the Mahasabha and the Mission. He may not have been overly fond of his son, either."

"Come again?" Allen asked.

Carl pointed his pencil. "Mr. Swaraj lived here in town, about thirty minutes from Hesburgh Hospital in South Bend, which happens to have a very fine surgical team. Yet rather than take his sick son there, his father drove him to Prairie View Hospital in Fort Wayne, which is over an hour away. Their facilities aren't nearly as good as Hesburgh's. And this, even though both he and the girl had seen a family physician here in South Bend half a dozen times over the last two years."

Allen said, "What did he die from, Carl?"

"According to the record? Burst appendix."

"What?" Allen's eyes bugged out. "No one 'dies' of a burst appendix! Peritonitis, most likely. What did the autopsy indicate?"

Carl said, "None was possible before the body was released. Only the post-mortem from Jaansen."

Allen was getting impatient. "Well, what did *it* say?" Carl flipped through the ME's report. "Inconclusive, due to the state of the charred remains."

Hardly a surprise. Allen cursed under his breath. "Nonetheless, it would've been something like 'intestinal gangrene and secondary peritonitis, occasioned by a ruptured appendix. In other words, it had to have taken the kid a good long time to die."

"What are you driving at.?" said Carl.

Tom grabbed at the baton. "Only that this guy Swaraj had everything to gain from the death of both his son and his new daughter-in-law. The boy was headed toward the under-employment line, and the girl was likely headed back to her family *with* her wad of dowry money. With this kind of death, he gets rid of one big financial liability while keeping the major asset: the girl's money. Still, he had to have been enabled in this by someone… perhaps several '*someones*'."

Allen barked, "Get hold of the medical records immediately – and send them over to Rick Jaansen on the double; we don't want 'em tampered with."

Carl yawned into his fist. "Already done and done."

Allen frowned in Tom's direction. "Next, talk to the nursing staff, will you? Quietly. See if any of them suspect neglect or malpractice."

"Right."

Allen might have left a lucrative partnership specializing in malpractice, but the specialty was still in his blood, and now his blood was up. He took a deep breath to calm himself and looked Sam's and McCorkle's way. "Now, about this Mahasabha outfit. Where does *it* come in?"

Glancing at McCorkle, Sam said, "*I'll* speculate on that one, if you don't mind." She riffled through her notepad and began:

"In India, sati, voluntary or not, is officially considered murder—even in Rajasthan, where remnants of it persist. But in fact, the criminal code doesn't give it special status as a crime. It's just lumped in with the rest of the homicides by authorities because they're hesitant even to accord it special distinction. In any case, it's seldom if ever prosecuted, because witnesses aren't forth-coming. Whether out of piety or fear, official, complicit winking is the usual game."

"So?" Allen probed.

"So, perhaps the main benefit to the Mahasabha *is* financial, or even political—memorials, endowments and so on. At home, after all, the festivals that would've been held and the temples that might've been constructed in times past to honor such practices are now officially outlawed as inducement or glorification of the sati. In fact, Indian feminists consider these laws among their greatest accomplishments. But this isn't India; it's America." Sam leaned over the table. "Maybe the Mahasabha thought that once the *ritual* had been pulled off—in the dead of night, in the middle of nowhere, and the remains scattered—a whispering campaign might begin to spread the word: those new communal attachments were being rekindled. In turn, that might translate into greater political sympathy and – more important – financial contributions, not to speak of an empowered ethnic network."

Stivers said, "The IRA's done the same thing for years among Irish Americans on the East Coast. Especially in South Boston."

"Exactly." Sam flashed her dark eyes. "Trouble is, everything didn't go according to script. No one counted on old man Stickle and his dog investigating, not to speak of the boys who witnessed the thing."

"Wait a second," Carl Peters said. "I know some Indian people. My own doctor's from Bombay I think, and he's a hell of a nice guy. And tradition can be a fine thing. Helps with the kids…"

"You're missing the point, Sheriff," Sam said. "If I'm right about this, the people who staged this event consider themselves mortal enemies of Indians like your physician. To them, he's a sellout. Or worse: an apostate."

"But I still don't get it," Carl said. "Why here?"

Sam said: "The Mahasabha may consider America an easier environment in which to lay down an organizational framework and conduct campaigns which will eventually be directed back at their homeland. Here, meanwhile, they're protected by free speech safeguards and the trendy gullibility of people ingesting the type of rhetoric I heard that Carver guy spout on the news last night."

Stivers growled, "I wouldn't be surprised if he were involved in this somehow anyway."

"That reminds me," Allen said. "Find out who's on the program for his Diversity Day rally."

"I can speak to that," McCorkle said. "The posters are all over campus. The main attractions will be Carver himself and Magdalene's own Professor Lata Besant, who is Indian herself."

Allen turned to Samantha. "Could you check her

out, please, Ms. Desai? Preferably incognito; I want to know what we're dealing with. What do you think their next move will be? Think they'll just lie low for a while?"

Sam shook her head. "Unlikely, now that the lid is off the press. They might as well go openly for what they were furtively after all along: publicity. I expect some sort of public demonstration, and soon."

Carl folded his arms. "What sort of demonstration? You mean like this Diversity Day thing? Christ, how many officers will I need to police *that*?"

McCorkle screeched his chair back from the table. "In India, particularly in Rajasthan, a great celebration is usually held thirteen days after a sati. It's called the *chunari mahotsav* and amounts to a public sanctification of the site and affirmation of the act. A trident is placed in the ground and draped with a red veil; pilgrims recount the 'miracle,' that is, the widow's bravery and grace. Rumors of miracles spread, lurid icons, memorabilia and refreshments are hawked, and new shrines are planned. The couple's bedroom often becomes a shrine as well."

"Christ on a crutch," the Sheriff groaned.

Sam added: "It might also be a good occasion to remind the faithful of their roots, their traditions and the debt they owe those safeguarding them. Understand, gentlemen?"

"One crisis at a time," Allen said. "*This* case comes

first, and I'm afraid it's pretty circumstantial." He leaned back and tapped his index finger against his chin. "But, hey, it's early. We have two witnesses, a possible motive, and tire molds from the scene that match Swaraj's Camry and his brother's green Ford truck.

By the way, where is the brother, Tom?"

"Hyderabad, I'm afraid," Tom said. "I doubt if he's involved anyway, at least directly."

Unsmiling, Allen turned to Samantha. "I have just one other question, Ms. Desai, if I may."

"Surely," she whisked her hair off her shoulder and shifted in her chair.

"This so-called 'marriage' – was it likely to have been *consummated?*"

Sam bowed her head, staring at her notes. "I very much doubt it. In such cases, the usual practice is for the bride to remain outside the husband's house until puberty. For a more definitive answer, you'd have to consult either the coroner or Mr. Swaraj. Not that you'd be likely to get one."

Allen rose decisively from his swivel chair. "Very good. Let's break for lunch before we interview the doting father-in-law, shall we?"

Wordlessly they stood-up and quietly dispersed. But Allen wasn't particularly hungry. He could make a meal of adrenalin any day of the week.

The group reassembled after lunch, minus the prosecutor who never participated in direct questioning of suspects. They sat apprehensively in the Formica room, awaiting the deputy and the suspect, Sirkar Swaraj.

At last, Jonas opened the door and stood aside, allowing the smallish man to enter ahead of him. Swaraj's graying mustache and temples seemed less well-groomed than the last time Carl had seen him; more hair than usual seemed to be springing from under his scarlet turban. This time, Carl also noted, he seemed frightened, even frazzled. His eyes darted about as if anticipating a blow from some unknown quarter; his head wagged reflexively from side to side, as if scanning for an unseen enemy.

Swaraj himself broke the strained silence. "I do not know *why* I have been arrested."

Carl thought panic was evident in the sing-song cadence, the thickened accent, the unfamiliar emphasis the suspect placed on his words. Carl would have to listen carefully to wrap his ear around the man's speech; he'd never been good with accents.

Swaraj sat at the head of the table, hands clasped tightly in front of him, nervously chewing on his drooping mustache with his lower lip. "This is the United

States of America. I have done nothing, *nothing* to warrant this intrusion on my rights."

Tom raised a calming hand. "Please try to relax, Mr. Swaraj. You are not yet formally charged with anything. And you may never be, if you just answer a few questions for us, OK?" The detective pointed to the corners of the room. "As you can see," he said, "this interrogation is being videotaped for your own protection."

"My *protection*, is it?" Swaraj's eyes flashed. "You must excuse me if I do not feel very *protected* at this moment!"

Samantha Desai spoke, softly but firmly, "Allow me, detective." She turned to Swaraj. "Sir, is there anything we might provide for your comfort before we begin?"

Up to now, the man seemed to have scarcely taken any notice of her, nor perhaps of her kindred ancestry. Almost at once he seemed calmer. "No, I am sorry. Thank you very much."

Samantha then said, "Mr. Swaraj, we are very sorry for your recent loss. To lose a child is never easy. But to lose a son is a very heavy burden. We all regret this intrusion at a time of such great stress and sorrow. And I assure you, Detective Stivers has no intention of prolonging this process beyond what he feels is necessary. Do you understand what I am saying?"

The man looked long and intently at Samantha.

Then he nodded. "Yes," he said. "I am very, very sorry. As you say, this has been a trying time for me and my family. I *do* not know *why* I am here."

Tom said gently, "When did you first notice your son was sick, Mr. Swaraj?"

"Several days before he died. He was vomiting and very, very sick to his belly, in much pain."

Tom said, "Did you call the doctor right away?"

"No, I *did* not," Swaraj replied. "I called my good friend, Mr. Savarkar. He is from the Ganges Mission and helped to bring my son's wife to the *United* States. He has instructed me to let him know if I have any problems at all."

Stivers scribbled on his notepad. "What did he tell you, Mr. Swaraj?"

"He told me to call the *doctor*," the man replied, "so I did that."

And whom did you call?"

"Dr. Tata at Prairie View Hospital," Swaraj said. "He took care of my son."

"Was Dr. Tata your family physician?"

"Yes, that is true, that is true." He looked more nervous. "Dr. Tata has taken *excellent* care of my family since we have been here."

Stivers said, "Now, Mr. Swaraj, did Dr. Tata say what killed your son?"

The red turban bobbed. "He told me that my son's

appendix broke, like a balloon—*boosh*! But I am not a highly educated man. I do not know more than that."

Stivers asked, "How do you plan to pay the medical expenses, Mr. Swaraj? You know that paying medical expenses is one of the biggest problems facing families in your situation."

Swaraj shook his head. "I do not know that, no, Mr. Detective. I did not care. I thought *only* of my son."

Stivers looked up from his notepad. "What about your daughter-in-law, Mr. Swaraj. Why did you lie to Sheriff Peters about your relationship to her?"

The prisoner's eyes widened as he began to tremble. "I know that I should have told the truth, but I did not think that he would understand."

"Understand what?" Stivers pressed. That you had played a part in her death?"

"You see? You see? I knew you would confuse everything! That you would not accept her marriage to my son." Swaraj's brow glistened with sweat.

"Then could you help us to understand the nature of her marriage to your son?" Tom persisted. "How else, after all, are we to judge these events?"

Swaraj's eyes widened, and one hand shook. "What is it you are asking me…"

Stivers cleared his throat. "Was she still a virgin, Mr. Swaraj?"

The man looked thunderstruck. "Why, of course

she was, Mr. Detective, she was not yet of proper *age*. That is a strange question, Mr. Detective. Roop was a *virtuous* maiden, not of *dis*-reputation!"

Stivers leaned forward, his face just inches from the suspect's. "Well, then, will you help us to understand how it is that Roop became sati?"

"Ah, Roop-Roop." Singh wrung his hands. "Who can know the ways of the gods? She was a *virtuous* bride who sacrificed herself to be with *my* son, to be with him always."

Tom furrowed his brow as if in empathy. "And whose idea was it to do that, Mr. Swaraj?"

As if incredulous that anyone would ask such a question, Swaraj cried out, "Why, it was her *own* idea! She went by herself to the *bier* and lay down *next* to my son, waiting to be with him in paradise. She was a brave and *virtuous* child!"

Stivers said, "Did anyone try to prevent her from killing herself?"

"*Prevent* her?" Swaraj's eyebrows lifted quickly. "I could *not* prevent such an act without bringing *damnation* on *my*self!"

"Well, then," Tom said, "who assisted this... work of God by lighting the fire?"

"No one lit the *fire*, Mr. Detective!" Swaraj protested. "*No* one lit the fire! No one *needed* to light the fire."

"Why was that?" Stivers said softly.

Suddenly the suspect burst into contemptuous-sounding laughter, as if he'd found himself in the presence of simpletons. "Because *she* lit the pyre, with the heat of her love and devotion, as she lay *next* to my son. It was a miracle from God, I say. Many people saw this miracle and knew they were in the presence of God."

Stivers said, "Was your daughter-in-law at any time *prevented* from leaving the pyre to save herself? Did anyone try to hold her there?"

Swaraj looked puzzled. "And why would that be, Mr. Detective? It was not necessary. She had chosen to become sati, and she did it for herself *and* for my son. There is nothing *more* I can say."

"Mr. Swaraj," Tom said, "we have reason to believe that this ceremony was witnessed by numerous people other than yourself, as you have already mentioned. Is that not true?"

"Yes, Mr. Detective," Swaraj replied. "As I said before, many people saw this event. They know the miracle of my son and his *holy* wife."

"In that case, will you share their identities with us, so that we may also be enlightened as to this miracle, so that we too may share in it?"

Swaraj's shoulders squared abruptly. "*Why* are you needing to *know* this? I have *told* you the truth. She *did* become *sati*! She will be remembered for *all* time!"

"Just the same, sir," Tom persisted, "we will need

to talk to other witnesses in order to verify what you've told us. In order to *verify* the miracle. It's for your own protection."

"I don't think so!" Swaraj shook his head vehemently. "I don't think so! You want to *punish* others for the *work* of God. It is *God's* work. You are trying to trick me, to profane me, just *like* he said."

"He? And who would that be, Mr. Swaraj?"

He pursed his lips. "I am finished talking to you people. I am *finished* answering these questions. I want to go home now."

Tom said quickly, "I'm afraid that will not be possible – unless you cooperate more fully."

Just then, the large handle of the metal door turned. Jonas swung it open to reveal a looming presence in the doorway. Madison Fulbright stepped in majestically, authoritatively.

The attorney's face expanded into a broad grin. "Gentlemen, I sense my arrival is timely." He set his briefcase on the table and tugged at the fingertips of his expensive leather gloves. "If you don't mind, gentlemen, I would like to speak to my client. *Alone.*"

Tom Stivers leaned back in the fiberglass chair, palms down and glared at his colleagues.

Carl sighed, resigned: *This case has just gotten a whole lot tougher.*

Samantha had requested permission to audit the class, "The Mute Subaltern: Gender Issues in Multicultural Perspective." She suspected its instructor, Professor Lata Besant, might be enlisted as an expert witness by Swaraj's defense.

As she entered the lecture hall, Samantha felt sudden surges of adrenalin and a shudder of déjà-vu, hangovers from her not-so-distant college days. Aside from the newness of her face, there was nothing to distinguish Sam from any other woman in the class, in such a way as to arouse suspicion anyhow. In any case, she approached the desk and deposited a note from the registrar stating that she was a high school teacher out to explore "consciousness-raising techniques." The professor unfolded the note and nodded Sam to find an open seat.

She scanned the room and made eye contact with a young woman who offered a half-smile in response. Sam took a seat next to her and introduced herself; the girl identified herself as Nadia.

"I'm auditing today," Sam whispered. "What do you think of the class?"

Nadia pointed to the syllabus and murmured, "Pretty much tells the whole story. We have been told to police our language for what she calls 'deferential sexism'. We are restricted to the approved lexicon, so watch yourself. The Prof's hinted that all references to gender be avoided altogether, even in questions directed to her. That applies to God too, by the way."

Dr. Lata Besant sat behind her desk like a graven Buddha, Sam noted: placid, seemingly inscrutable. Her sari was artfully draped over her left shoulder, partially concealing upper arms pinched by several colorful bracelets. Likely post-50-ish, her graying hair, gathered together with a red cord, hung down her back. She had full lips along with an ample bosom. Golden hoop ear-rings pulled at pendulous lobes. Her brow was deeply crevassed, perhaps by cerebral exertion. *Yet her olive complexion seemed very fair for an Indian woman,*

Sam thought. *Goan, perhaps.* Goa, she knew, had been home to Portuguese-Indian liaisons for centuries.

Sam scanned the classroom, noting that the class was all women. "Talk about gender imbalance," she whispered.

"Yeah," Nadia grinned. "Prof doesn't like to have guys in here: she claims that they talk too much, ask too many annoying questions and generally get in the way."

Sam smiled, "If one's exposing one's enemies, why admit them to the inner circle, right?"

"You've got it, sister."

Memories of Sam's own experiences, especially with white men, suddenly resurfaced unbidden. She'd had her share of love affairs in college and law school, but no one had seemed to her a suitable marriage prospect. She was fortunate that her parents weren't 'old world'. Sure, they'd prefer an Indian son-in-law, but modernity had Westernized them to the point that they were willing to consider alternatives, so long as their daughter didn't stray too far afield—to, say, a Muslim (they were lifelong Anglicans). She couldn't ignore the complexity of her own background.

Quite suddenly, she sought distraction in further conversation with Nadia. "I'm suppressing an old instinct," Sam confessed, "to duck behind someone's head and escape being called on."

"Oh, this row's safe enough," Nadia said. "She tends to direct her fury at the student nearest the center of the class, so no one has sat there twice running."

"Hmm." Sam craned her neck. Not surprisingly, perhaps, that "hot seat" was indeed unoccupied.

As students milled about, Besant sat rigidly, hands palms-down on her desk, fingers thrumming, awaiting a silence to descend that would command the class's attention. At last, all the students were sitting respectfully at their desks, their collective gaze riveted on Lata Besant, Ph.D., straining for her words.

"Today," she said, in an accent Sam couldn't quite place, "we commence examination of the pathology of colonialism, especially as it concerns the images of women, refracted through the prism of misogyny, the phenomenon of masculine imperialism and the disembodied females who were its chief, but not its only, victims.

"This is a narrative," Dr. Besant continued gravely, "of cultural genocide: the evisceration of the spiritual heart of the Indian people and the imposition of foreign constructs predicated on greed, violence, bigotry and vice, in which the subaltern was rendered mute, voiceless."

The Professor placed hands on her hips and began to pace. "Forget everything you may have been taught about these issues by the patriarchy in the so-called 'traditional canon', for it all has been filtered through the lens of the tainted scholarship of orientalism. It is laced with deceit, manipulation, condescension, sexism and racism."

Sam scanned the room. Judging by the expressions on the faces of those sitting around her, the students found Besant either enthralling or scary. Sam had heard such diatribes many times at Northwestern, of course, along with the healthy doses of cynicism with which most students digested them. No doubt, this woman was intimidating – yet she was also, to all appearances at least, sincere.

By this point, Samantha thought she'd seen all she probably needed to see and was not a little conflicted by the performance. Either Professor Besant was a cutting-edge champion of oppressed women every-where, or something considerably less than that.

Following the lecture, Sam waited for most of the classroom to empty out, before approaching Professor Besant, whose eyes seemed to track her movements as she approached. Sam extended her hand. "Thank you so much, Professor," she began. "That was certainly a thought-provoking session."

"You are most welcome," Besant replied, looking a little leery. "Have you matriculated?"

"Not exactly," Sam flashed a disarming smile. "Although I have enrolled in something else with which you may have more than a passing interest. Might you be free for coffee sometime this afternoon?"

Lata Besant was not used to being asked to chit-chat over coffee, but her curiosity was piqued. "I'm free at 2:00 if you are. Do you know the cafeteria?"

"Passed it on my way in here," Sam said. "I look forward to getting to know you better," she said, handing her a card and then headed to the door. The professor replied with an enigmatic grin.

1:05 p.m.
Rosa Parks Cafeteria, Magdalen College

After several hours of grading exams behind her desk, Lata Besant glanced at the clock on her office wall. The colors on the face mimicked the patterns of a Moroccan prayer rug, as she noted the fleeting time. Owing to chores in the copy room, she would have to leave in 20 minutes if she were to make her coffee date. 'Date,' she thought to herself. A strange word choice. But she had to admit curiosity about this obviously intelligent woman of color, with the colonial accent and stiletto heels.

The essays from her W460 class on the Psychology of Women had put her on simmer. Unlike the W301 offering on International Women's perspectives, or her W206 seminar on Eco-Feminist Politics, this one was over 50% male. As usual, they could usually be classed in two categories: 1) seniors looking for what they assumed to be an 'easy A' and 2) sexual neophytes hoping to bolster their sensitivity quotients in order to ferret-out receptive dates. While the latter were a tad more earnest, Besant found them just as insufferable. She had little patience for the kind of condescension they typically exuded.

Before the end of the first week, most usually dropped the class—once she'd clarified the nature of the subject matter: the psychological impact, social causes, treatment and cultural variations of domestic violence, sexual assault, and rape. If that failed, her initial lecture, a mandatory attendance policy, and massive syllabus, typically took care of the problem.

Yet, for some reason, this semester, a few hangers-on lingered.

"I must be losing my touch," the professor mused, as she took another sip of Chai.

She looked at the card she had been offered after this morning's W104 lecture and rubbed her thumb over the entwining WWC emblem. She pondered the title scrolled in a navy print: of Counsel, Human Rights Practice. This wasn't the first time she'd been called on by attorneys as an expert witness, which she assumed to be the reason for the introduction. That wasn't unusual for cases involving workplace discrimination. But human rights? This might be a different matter entirely and it inspired both her interest and a little suspicion.

She was leery of observers who happened upon her class ever since that huckster of a reporter popped up last year claiming Besant had plagiarized a portion of her dissertation. It turned out he had lost his job at the Indianapolis Star the year before for sexual harassment and had an axe to grind. A nasty business, she recalled.

November14
5:02 p.m.

Tom Stivers winced as he tasted the cup of hot coffee on his desk, then plopped into his swivel chair. Turning to grab a forensics journal off the shelf behind him, the indistinct waves of the surveillance screen and the kneeling man on it caught his eye.

Sirkar Swaraj had been on suicide watch since his

arrest three days before, a status that necessitated 24-hour surveillance. Distracted, Tom leaned back in the chair, blew on the coffee, regarding his unusual prisoner. Swaraj was on his knees at the bunk, the tops of his brown feet folded beneath him, revealing their whitish undersides. His palms were together, fingertips extended, just touching the front edge of his bowed brow. His body was rigid, still, but the turban nodded slightly from the animation of his unintelligible pleadings, eyes clenched shut in earnest piety. *Or,* Tom thought, *maybe fear.*

"*Om......Om......Om...* "A torrent of indecipherable plaints followed. At least they sounded plaintive to Tom.

The detective wheeled closer to the flickering screen, straining to glean a scrap of meaning from Swaraj's cryptic mutterings. And while he couldn't be certain, it seemed as if the man's face was twitching; his lower lip trembled, and tears oozed from his sealed eyes. Tom stood up and hitched his sagging trousers, folding brawny arms across his chest. Swaraj hardly looked like a man comfortable with his situation, let alone thankful over the fate of his daughter-in-law. Owing to the wall of silence set-up by Fulbright following his intrusion on the interrogation, Tom hadn't been able to probe with his usual thoroughness. *Now might be a good time to inspect the cell block.*

Less than an hour later, he stepped into the jail corridor, laden with an order of Indian take-out he'd driven all the way to Crestwood to pick-up. As he approached Swaraj's cell, he was relieved to see the occupant still genuflecting in prayer. The man's eyes opened, possibly in response to the pungent aromas rising from Stiver's sack. Swaraj stared blankly at Tom; his eyes were blood-shot, rheumy.

"Good day, Mr. Swaraj," Tom said.

"Good day, Mr. Detective,"

Stivers was astonished that the prisoner remembered his rank, given the brevity of their first encounter. He said, "I brought you lunch. Figured you might miss Indian food. It's a curry, I think."

The prisoner pushed himself up from his cot, smiling, respectful. "I must confess, it smells wonderful to me, Mr. Detective. You are very kind."

Tom jangled his wad of keys and opened the door. "Mind if I join you? I'm so busy, this is about the only time I have to eat. You want to call your lawyer, just in case we chat as we eat?"

"I would be honored by your company, sir." Swaraj said." Then he added, "there is no need to bother Mr. Fulbright."

Stivers sensed an opportunity as he reached in to remove the dinners, handing one to his prisoner. Then he sat down on a stool next to the cot and smiled, as if to sympathize. "Do you mind if I ask you a question?"

"Not at all." Swaraj ate a large spoonful. "This curry is very wonderful, thank you."

Tom cleared his throat and tried to look enthusiastic about the steaming portion balanced on his own lap. "Has anyone who's visited pressured you about your story? I noticed on the log that both your wife and brother came in yesterday."

"What do you mean, Mr. Detective?"

"Well, has anyone from the Mission tried to influence you with respect to your daughter-in-law's sati, or your answers to our questions?"

Swaraj's head drooped slightly. He looked about and began to rub his face and twist his mustache. "I have said all that I know. I cannot say more."

His body language is significant. Tom knew well that subconscious gestures around the mouth often signaled deception. "It just seems to me that you loved Roop so much. I mean, anyone can see that clearly."

"Oh, you are so right, Mr. Detective," said Swaraj. "She was a wonderful girl. She carried herself like a *rani*. As pure as mountain snow." His hands dropped instantly into his lap.

"So, it must have been difficult for you when Mr. Savarkar suggested the sati." Tom waited expectantly, hoping the leading inquiry led to revelation.

"You know about that?" The prisoner sat back,

wide-eyed, aghast. "How do you know about that? That is terrible. All is undone now!"

Tom's curry suddenly tasted better. He dabbed the corner of his mouth with a napkin. "Not necessarily, Mr. Swaraj. You see, I guessed some time ago that you had been talked into it. I just couldn't figure out why. But now I know you only wanted the best for Roop."

"You have no idea, Mr. Detective," Swaraj brushed spilled curry from his beard, "what kind of life she had awaiting her after my son died. But now she is a god. She is with my son in paradise forever." He pinched his nostrils nervously. "Still..."

"Yes, Mr. Swaraj?"

"I feel so guilty."

"What about?"

"That my son *could not* be saved." His hands dropped again. "That Roop *could not* be saved."

Seize the moment... "Is Savarkar to blame, then?" The prisoner lifted his gaze, and as if he was suddenly staring right through Tom, his passion seemed to dissipate eerily. He pulled the left tip of his mustache down and began to chew on it. Then he thrust the half-empty Styrofoam container at his interrogator.

"Take this away," he commanded. "I am no longer hungry. Please leave me alone now."

Tom watched with frustration, as Swaraj returned

to his cot and his knees, earnestly mumbling as before, oblivious now to his presence. Yet the detective noted that the prisoner's shoulders seemed to shudder slightly as he prayed, muttered and wept.

November 14
5:30 p.m.

After leaving the cafeteria, Sam went to Magdalene's undergraduate library to leaf through journal articles on sati, after which she decided to seek out Mark McCorkle in his natural element.

Allen had already regaled her with details of his recent excursion to Magdalene. *What an odd duck McCorkle is. How under-utilized the man's scholarship seems to be. How suspicious the department secretary was that anyone should seek out the Empire geek!* Samantha had decided that if a man was to be judged by the company he keeps, she'd do her part to raise McCorkle's profile; so, she made a big production of asking for him, and an even bigger production of closing the door to his cubicle after she entered it.

She found him hunched over his computer, typing furiously, still clothed in a heavy coat and scarf.

"Hello, Mark," she said. "I'm sorry to disturb you."

"G-g-g-g-good day, Ms. Desai." McCorkle seemed beyond flustered – rather, he looked something more like flummoxed – by her arrival.

She sat without being asked. "Please, Mark. Call me Sam."

McCorkle leapt to his feet, then sat again slowly and scrabbled at his unruly hair as if he might have fleas.

"Are you cold?" she asked gently.

"Cold?" He blinked repeatedly. "Your coat." She pointed.

He looked down at himself. "No... No, not cold. Just forgetful." He smiled as if by rote, having been told one must smile in such situations.

Sam felt a twinge of pity. She'd once known someone like Mark—Georgie, a neighbor of her family's, back in Birmingham, England. She'd read an article not long ago on Asperger's syndrome, a form of high-functioning autism, and she'd recognized behaviors in Georgie consistent with such a diagnosis. She'd read that people like these are often brilliant in one single-minded pursuit or obsession, while also being almost incapable of normal social functioning and relationships.

Sam said, "I've just come from Lata Besant's class; you were right about her: She *is* scary. Do you know which region of India she hails from? I can't place her accent."

"I've never heard where she's from," he said with a thin smile. "Or if I've heard, I can't recall."

"And what about you?" she asked solicitously. "How did you wind up in Principia? You're not from here in town, are you?"

He shook his head. "Chicago. I took my M.A. at Northwestern and did my Ph.D. at Cambridge."

"Why, you could have gotten a job anywhere!" Sam exclaimed unguardedly. Then she cursed herself... to herself.

"Well," Mark chased his glasses up his nose, "my cv gets me in the door, but..." he shrugged, "I guess I don't interview very well. Some people say job-hunting is just a game, and I seem never to have learned the rules well enough."

Again, Sam felt a knot of empathy in her gut.

He added: "And the subject of the British Empire has fallen from favor in most schools. Still, I'm able to teach courses in non-Western subjects that most of my colleagues cannot. And I do enjoy the anonymity of the arcane. I've heard it's coming back though – Empire studies, that is – what with Niall Ferguson and all."

He smiled again, this time with something approaching honest pleasure. She, too, had heard of Ferguson.

"I had quite a time finding a suitable apartment when I arrived. Do you live in town?" Sam asked.

"Um... nearby."

He was hedging, she could tell.

He shrugged, "*Quite* nearby, actually. I'm a proctor in the undergraduate dorm, so I live practically rent-free. All meals included, and I subscribe to the linen and maid service. Otherwise—"

Sam could just picture the *'otherwise'*. Academe had been McCorkle's salvation.

"Say," she said, suddenly inspired, "let me buy you lunch at the faculty lounge." The thought that she'd be making grist for the rumor mill there delighted her in an impish sort of way. Besides, she mused to herself, he could use the notoriety.

Mark politely declined.

November 14
1:40 p.m.

Sam clacked her way to the student cafeteria, wanting to arrive a little early for her meeting with Lata Besant, careful not to spill her half-caf skim latte. She was eager for the discussion, and to enlist the help of a fellow feminist in making the prosecution's case against barbaric practices perpetrated against women and girls. She was also confident that the professor would be eager to help. Throughout the hour she'd spent observing her class, Sam had been impressed by her passion for her subject, not to speak of her in-your-face lecturing style.

She took a sip of her latte, grateful that she'd taken the time to run to Starbucks, lest she be held hostage to the nameless, suspect, cafeteria brew, and picked a table in the corner, next to one of the floor-to-ceiling windows that lined the western wall, providing diners with a view of the back quad covered in brightly colored leaves. The trees were nearly bare now, with only a few orange and red stragglers clinging to their boughs, as if challenging their seasonal fate.

This table also afforded a good view of the steps leading to the front door of the Kathleen Bailey Center, so she could keep an eye out for Besant's impending arrival. It was after two o'clock now, so the ravenous hordes had dispersed for their afternoon classes. But a line of young men still queued at the ice cream machine, determined not to leave empty-handed. Sam took another sip and pulled a navy-blue leather portfolio from her shoulder bag. She opened it on the table, revealing a standard issue yellow legal pad affixed to the inside back cover. Then she reached into her bag once more, fumbling before pulling out a silver-plated Mont Blanc with the words *Veritas nunquam perit* (the truth never dies) engraved around the body. A law school graduation gift from her father, she took the pen from its holder, relishing its familiar heft, and began to jot down a few preliminary notes with which to guide the conversation.

She was engrossed in the effort when she heard a quick cough. "Ms. Desai?"

Sam looked up from her scribbling to see Dr. Lata Besant standing next to her. Her beak-like nose protruded from a round face. Her smile was welcoming, if a little curious, crinkled at the corners of bulbous blue eyes which conveyed an alert, almost owlish aspect. Hurriedly, she had changed into a more comfortable outfit for the encounter. A scarf highlighted by an intertwining color pattern of turquoise, gold and deepest purple, encircled her neck several times, popping against a backdrop of her black long-sleeved top and matching pants that seemed to billow beneath her sandaled feet. A curious choice for November, Sam thought, wiggling her toes unconsciously in the wool socks she wore underneath knee-high, black-heeled boots.

"Why hello, Professor," Sam replied, shaking the proffered hand. "Thanks so much for finding the time to chat with me. I appreciate how busy you must be. Are finals approaching?"

Besant shook back with a firm, short grip, smiling. "Not at all," she reassured, "finals don't begin for another six weeks, thank goodness. Lots of material yet to cover, I'm afraid. Besides," she continued, "I'm always happy to meet interested civilians. This place seems down-right institutional sometimes, if you understand my meaning."

"Not that different from a law office, really," Sam commiserated, "except in the quality of the consumers." The two women laughed comfortably. "Please, have a seat." Sam indicated the chair opposite. "Do you want to grab a coffee? I don't mind waiting."

Besant sat down. "Cafeteria sludge?" she asked

mockingly, shaking her head. "That stuff 'll kill you. I brought my own provisions, thank you." She reached into the brightly colored bag around her shoulder that mimicked the colors on her scarf and pulled out a gray metal thermos. As she unscrewed the lid, Sam's eyebrows raised in interest.

Sam held up her Starbucks cup with the green logo. "I was similarly cautious," she empathized.

Lata slurped at the milky, tan liquid she had poured into the thermos' multifunctional lid and sighed. "White Ayurvedic Chai," she answered the unspoken query in the sort of matter-of-fact tone that required no further explanation. "Now how may I help you, Ms. Desai?"

Sam glanced cursorily at her notes, taking a perfunctory swig before beginning. "I seem to have gotten myself involved in a rather unprecedented legal issue, I'm afraid, and knowing you to be a subject matter expert on the subjugation of women, along with your impressive resume, I wondered whether I might pick your brain, as it were, from a feminist perspective."

Besant's face remained impassive. "Are you not a feminist as well, my dear?" she queried.

"By all means," Sam reassured. "It may be the dawn of a new century, but law firms are still essentially boys' clubs, where women need to work twice as hard and be three times more brilliant than their male counterparts," she said with studied conviction.

Lata's face softened into a sympathetic smile. "I tell my students every day that the struggle against the patriarchy is a daily battle in which we all must engage," she said. "Please continue Ms. Desai, especially about your case. Are you a victim of sexual discrimination?"

"Me?" she started. "Not bloody likely. My colleagues all know better than that. The victim here is a little girl. A little Indian girl to be precise."

"Go on."

"It seems that a young girl died several nights ago in what appears to have been a sort of South Asian ritual. Perhaps a sati." Besant's smile disappeared, and her brown eyes flashed.

"Sati?" she said, eyebrows raised. "Yes, I am familiar with the practice. But what, may I ask, has led you to that determination, Ms. Desai? Such rites have long since disappeared from India and, to my knowledge, have never occurred outside the Punjab in independent India."

For the next fifteen minutes, Sam outlined the circumstances surrounding the death of the little girl to the extent she knew them, trying her best not to be too specific, lest she compromise the ongoing investigation, yet still projecting the most earnest transparency. Besant listened with rapt attention.

Finally, Samantha concluded with an overview of her conversation with Mark McCorkle.

Lata Besant crinkled her nose over a wry smile. "Ah yes, Mark McCorkle," she said. "Are you aware that he is only an untenured associate professor?"

Sam's eyebrows shot up, unable to contain her surprise at Besant's contempt for a colleague. "So, in your opinion, is he unqualified to render such opinions?" she asked.

Besant reached into her shoulder bag, this time for a Tupperware tub. She then opened it, revealing a tossed salad. Then she began picking at it with her plastic fork. "I'm saying no such thing," she replied, eyes averted, crunching her cucumber. "I merely asked whether you were aware of his... status or, more to the point, his *lack* of same."

Sam smiled. "Well, yes I am, but unless you have an objection to his conclusions, I am hoping to contextualize my understanding through your input as well, from a human rights and women's rights perspective. Like you, I have made a career out of defending the rights of women and children, and it is my opinion that this is a murderous violation of both. Furthermore, it is an egregious abuse against human rights if you take the child bride factor into account. But I leave it to you to tell me if I'm on the right path, since you are the tenured expert in such things here."

The tension dissipated as Besant made eye contact with the lawyer, noticing the authentic conviction in her eyes and manner. "Of course," she replied, "I'd be delighted to help." Then she folded her hands in front of her and began again. "But that is quite a theory. Have you any witnesses? Have you any motive? Are you certain that the child was, in fact, married?"

Sam opted not to mention the two hunters. "Not yet," she lied. "As to motive, we're hoping that you might assist us there."

"I think that the motive is obvious," Besant intoned, "at least if you can prove that this was actually a sati."

Sam leaned forward. "Go on," she encouraged, pen at the ready. "How might such a rite be rationally defended?"

"You may not like the answer, Ms. Desai," Besant said, "because it comes from another cultural reality."

"Come again?"

"In a multicultural perspective, this event is not deviant, nor even controversial. In other words,…"

Sam squinted in puzzlement. "Yes…?"

Besant stabbed a piece of radish. "She wished to do her wifely duty."

Sam almost choked, grasping at a napkin to receive a staccato of small coughs. "I'm sorry," she croaked. "I must have misheard you. Wifely duty?" she repeated. Clearly, she had blown her inquisitorial poker face.

"Ms. Desai," Besant sighed with a hint of exasperation. "You are of South Asian descent yourself, are you not? Why does that seem such a shocking conclusion?"

Sam struggled to maintain her composure and respectful tone. She had asked for the professor's opinion, after all. "Ethnically, you are correct. I am of Indian descent. My parents immigrated to Britain from Bombay back in the 60s, before coming to the States. However, I have never been there, and consider myself British. And I find your explanation a bit…startling, not least because the victim was a ten-year-old child, professor: *a ten-year-old*. Pardon me, but she was barely old enough to menstruate and, legally speaking, unable to give consent to either marriage or anything else. Considering that fact, how can you rationally argue that this child should be beholden to some ancient code of 'wifely duty'?"

Besant stared back fixedly. "I agree that the death of a child is undisputedly awful. However, you are ignoring the more salient fact that she was behaving as an Indian defined by the caste system, in the way demanded of her by her culture. Who am I or you or any other American to judge a Hindu religious practice? Using that logic, Hindus might rightly indict millions of Americans for unlawfully kidnapping their elderly parents and confining them to old-age homes. No Indian would condemn a parent to such a fate, nor would any other culture that reveres family and elders."

"But this isn't India," Sam protested, "it's Indiana! Besides," she continued, "India is a signatory to the Universal Declaration of Human Rights. How can such a practice still exist, let alone be rationalized? Surely, as a proponent of women's rights, you…"

"I what?" Besant finished the question, exhaling a sigh as she did so. "Of course, it enrages me when women are mistreated and subjugated at the hands of their male oppressors. But that is a manifestation of a Westernized perspective, which is grafted onto my consciousness. I must not ignore the distortions in perspective which it produces. I must be vigilant not to let my own cultural bias interfere with the religious beliefs and cultural practices of others. Remember, only about 15% of the world's population is considered 'Westernized'. How can a mere 15% of Earth's population dictate the rules by which the other 85% live and worship? After all, are Hindus to leave their religion at the water's edge? Does the first amendment only apply to Christians and Jews?"

Sam's frustration was surfacing now. 'But Professor, American culture does not permit…"

"Diversity?" Lata Besant parried preemptively. "American culture does not exist outside of a constellation which embraces the diversity of all cultures. Surely you must know that."

"Let me see if I understand you correctly, Professor Besant," Sam said, trying her best to keep a steady voice. "In your opinion, there is no such thing as American culture?"

"My dear," Besant insisted, "American culture is

nothing more than the sum of its parts, of course. If it were otherwise, all cultural diversity would simply vanish."

Sam mumbled into her tepid coffee, trying somehow to process the argument she'd just heard. "So how can we hope to fight for human rights and uphold the rule of law anywhere if these cultural extremists have carte blanche to behave as they wish and kill innocent children?" she asked.

Besant was in her rhetorical element now. "We must set an example and hold ourselves to a higher standard, rather than pointing the finger of cultural superiority at those whose views are different from our own. Our own communities must attempt to engage in a dialogue of empathy and acceptance which will educate the abusers. Until that change takes place," she continued, "we must strive to see the world through their eyes, and NOT through the distorting, existential lens of the oppressive West."

Besant's eyes searched the young woman's face for some sign of weakening, if not comprehension. Instead, she sensed Sam's confusion, shock. "I have published several articles on the subject of cultural relativism and its relation to the first amendment, Ms. Desai, if you care to read them. There are several copies in my office, in fact, if you'd care to stop by later," she offered as she rose from her chair and began stuffing her salad container and thermos back into her vibrant tote.

"Look at it this way, Ms. Desai. It's actually the rule of law aspect you find so troubling. The United States is supposed to have been based on political principles, and is the only nation, in fact, to make this claim. Principles, such as the unalienable rights of speech and religion, must be followed unvaryingly, or they cease to be principles at all, am I right?"

Sam shot back, "I noticed you omitted the right to life."

Besant gathered up her trash for the receptacle. "Murderers are released every day," she reminded her, "because of constitutional violations, irrespective of possible guilt, irrespective of that right to life. The exclusionary rule, barring the use of illegally obtained evidence, is a relentless taskmaster. And the reason for that? Because abandonment of the principle involved would be far worse for society than the release of one guilty man. As my male colleagues are so fond of saying, 'it's the principle of the thing.'"

"I'm sorry, I don't follow," Sam looked at her, her eyes narrowing with accusation. "Exactly what is the principle that is worth the life of a child?"

Besant picked up her fork from the table and pointed it at Sam, who couldn't help but detect a slight tremor in the utensil. "Cultural survival, counselor," she said, "and the diversity it will guarantee. That is the only hope for mankind's survival. I really must run. Hope that I've been helpful. Please come by for those articles when you have the chance. I think you'll find them quite enlightening."

She shuffled off. Sam, dumbfounded, sat at the table for another fifteen minutes.

November 15
1:42 a.m.

Allen Southworth fumbled for his keys, trying to be as quiet as possible. He'd spent the better part of the afternoon and evening poring over Tom Stivers report, striving mightily to get a handle on the real motive behind the sati of Roop Kumar. But for the last two hours he'd been in the old courthouse, drinking, alone.

By now, he should have been more accomplished at stealing into his own home during the wee hours. But he always seemed to stumble over the dog or trip on an action figure on his way to the living room couch, which was where he usually slept these days. *Easier this way.* Even at three in the morning, Jan was never deep enough in slumber to forego a groan when he came to bed. And even a groan, he'd come to learn, could convey unmistakable disgust.

Coming home wasn't really the worst part of an all-consuming case like this. Nor was the smell of alcohol on his breath. It was the guilt over time away from home, the lost connections with his family. And that had lately been aggravated by something else.

Deep down, he knew his interest in placing Samantha Desai on his team was more complicated than the simple need for augmented expertise. She was so beautiful, so brilliant, and so… inescapably intriguing.

Despite what passed for his best effort, Allen found himself fantasizing about her. *Sexually? Yeah, okay, sure.* He had to admit that was part of it. Her position as second chair would provide plenty of excuses for ostensibly innocent contact, those deliciously spontaneous, yet flirtatious, interactions. A giddy shudder climbed up his spine. But he'd worked with attractive women before and managed to keep the sexual tension caged, even if it growled low in his throat like a circus lion.

So, the erotic urge might be tamed. *But what about the intellectual… the creative urges?* Allen wasn't so sure of those.

He kicked off his shoes, yanked at his tie and draped it carelessly over a kitchen chair, then fixed himself a scotch and soda, swishing the ice cubes into the tendrils of alcohol, and ambled into the sitting room. In front of the gas log fire, the prosecutor plopped into the recliner and stared emptily at a flickering blue wisp dancing at the heart of the flame.

But the thoughts didn't stay away for long. Maybe it

had been the surging stock market of the roaring 1990s. Or maybe it had something to do with the end of the Cold War. Then again, maybe it was the generation of baby boomers finally facing its own mortality. Regardless, something had changed in Allen's America; all the old presuppositions about propriety, so long under siege, had begun to slump into doubt and irrelevance.

And just where did all this leave him?

He mourned the loss of all those old support systems: the friends who'd already defected, the parents who'd left him through their deaths, the disintegrating cultural totems. Still, their power over him lingered.

His current course, Allen reassured himself, was not so much determined by his own moral lapses as by bad luck, rotten timing. He hadn't asked for this case, or its need for Samantha's input. Did that mean he should give up the opportunity to seize whatever personal challenges were presented, or prizes proffered? It seemed hardly fair.

Still, he *was married*, with two children, a five-star mansion on Number-Three fairway, and a four-stall garage, amply filled. He was hugely wealthy by local standards and had stature in the community. He was an *example*. This was the payoff for a responsible life. It had been what he'd always wanted, despite the attendant downside: the lack of freedom gnawing at his soul.

Allen took a long, lingering swig from his glass,

savoring the fine scotch as he refocused his thoughts. He suddenly realized that he'd ignored the main issue, so much more consequential than his own trauma. His *moral* stake in this mess was huge—and growing daily. And that stake was as nothing when compared to the wider world.

So why was he so jazzed? Was it the opportunity to tap some vein in himself, some posturing sanctimony of moral outrage? The prospect of celebrity? Cultural voyeurism? The convenience of an excuse to escape his wife and collaborate with a sexy colleague?

He really couldn't say. But he feared he was impelled less by the rectitude he imagined within himself than by the basest ambition—a conceit that, over the long haul, might prove insufficient to the task. His father would disapprove, certainly; how unlike him Allen had become. He grimaced, then he leaned back, staring absently at the ceiling fan overhead. As his eyes grew heavier and the ice melted in his glass, his last conscious thought was of the sati's flame—crackling, rising. To consume him. Or to redeem him.

November 15
10:00 a.m.

Allen opened the door of his car for Sam for the short drive to Magdalene College for the Diversity Day conference. He had arrived three hours early to take her up on the Scrabble challenge she had offered on seeing the game box in his office.

He'd found very few serious competitors in that venerable board game, so when she told him of her addiction to it, he decided to pounce that morning before leaving for the conference. Two hours later, he thought better of it. For while their first game together was competitive, he was blown out spectacularly on the last play, when Sam had strung together the letters b-a-r-o-q-u-e along the bottom of the board, not only adding an 'r' to the perpendicular the word 'trade', but across a triple word score as well. Moreover, since she'd used all seven letters, she received 50 extra points, plus the 12 points left on Allen's remaining tiles. This had not only been just any battle on the Scrabble board; it was Cannae.

Moreover, it was that sort of whimsical humiliation with which the prosecutor was nakedly unfamiliar.

Sam didn't say a word. She just sat there at her kitchen table, hands folded in her lap, smiling sweetly, but expectantly, at her dumbfounded colleague. 'Baroque', Allen asked? Really? I'm speechless."

Matter-of-factly, she began putting the game away, pouring the tiles in the folded board into a saucepan. "Just a fluke," Sam reassured. "I really don't play much."

Allen's frown deepened. "That's cold comfort, I'm afraid," he said. "You're a Scrabble ringer, and a bit of a brat." Then he smiled broadly and grabbed for his coat.

Sam stepped into the Lexus, reaching back to lay her briefcase in the back seat. Then she asked *the question*. "This *event*...Are you sure it's a good idea?"

To spend time with *her*? To be seen with *her*? For a moment, he stared deeply into her bituminous eyes, then slightly shook his head] to refocus

"What do you mean, Sam?"

"I mean," she continued, businesslike, "that someone in the crowd's bound to recognize you. Aren't you at all concerned that you might be compromised? Could be awkward."

With a potential blockbuster like this one, risk

was implicit; Allen had considered the downsides to his attendance at the Diversity Day Celebrations but discounted them.

"When the case comes to trial," he said, "some of the folks attending this event will be in the jury pool. It's a good way to gain insight into their perspectives and susceptibilities." He sensed his effort to sound cosmically embracing felt forced.

But Sam added: "It won't hurt to know what the professional activists are up to, either, just in case they've got plans afoot to arouse local passions."

Passion... He mentally shook his head to clear his mind. "In my experience, these enthusiasts are fearsome to listen to, but most of it is bark." Allen had spent much of the previous afternoon going over a report Tom Stivers had prepared. "What do you make of Carver's dossier?"

Sam recapped the salient points: Carver had moved back to Principia via Milwaukee after concluding three semesters at Marquette, before flunking out. Following that, he drifted around for the better part of five years, getting arrested intermittently for shoplifting and assorted petty infractions. Yet he'd seemed more aimless than felonious.

She said, "He seems to have undergone quite a transformation since returning from Wisconsin in '84. He really is a force around here now, I think, and a highly regarded one at that."

As the pair walked from the parking lot to Abrams Hall, where the main event was being staged, Allen couldn't help feeling a little foolish. The crowd surge that carried them along was so young, it was impossible for him to appear inconspicuous. Sam wouldn't sense it, of course; being 15 years his junior, she hadn't yet lost touch with the popular youth culture.

He couldn't shake the feeling that all the indifferently dressed people pulsing around him suspected he'd robbed the cradle...with Sam in it.

As Allen and Sam shoehorned their way through the glass double doors of the hall and waited to click through the turnstile, she also felt vaguely uneasy. On one level, she was supremely confident in who she was, fully aware of her background, education, and self-appointed place in the cultural cosmos. Nonetheless, a twinge of unease was inescapable. With her tacit rejection of Hindu activism, juxtaposed against her parents' embrace of Western ways and even Christianity, Sam couldn't help feeling vaguely, indefinably, sad. Sort of like a Catholic forced by circumstance to attend an Episcopal church. While it might be better than no church at all, one might feel naughty, if not a little heretical.

Sam and Allen worked their way toward the middle of the crowd. The pervasive hum began to diminish as a short, stout woman—dressed in flowing saffron robes—shuffled to the mike.

"That's 'She, Who Must Be Obeyed,'" Sam murmured, channeling Ryder Haggard.

"Who's 'She'?" Allen hissed.

Sam shot him an impatient glare, then waved him off. A hush fell over the assembly as Professor Lata Besant stood motionless. Then she began to speak:

"On behalf of Magdalene College and its faculty, I welcome you all to Diversity Day, sponsored by the Diversity League of Principia. Our purpose in gathering here is to mobilize and empower supporters of inclusiveness and multiculturalism to *act*, so that the forces of *re*action, which seek to *suppress* the *hopes*, *dreams* and *aspirations* of the *masses* of Americans may be put *on notice!*"

An ovation erupted from the assembly. Besant raised her arms, palms outward, entreating silence. "… On notice that the *people* will no longer tolerate a climate of *exclusion*, either *here* at Magdalene *College* or—"

The assembly bellowed its assent.

—or *anywhere else* in our community, or *anywhere* in this *country* where fear of the 'other' results in oppression, injustice and de facto slavery!"

The hall pulsed with pounding applause and stomping feet.

Besant's voice rose a notch. "I am not here to talk about *theories*. Typologies intimidate me because of their nebulous schemas, for those serve only to exclude most of *us* and bolster the bastions of *privilege* and *prejudice*." Besant paused to mop her brow and draw breath. "People—the *real* people who make up most of humanity—are weary of mythical models that place the privileged, the male, the European *white*, atop the pyramid of power, wielding authority, restricting access, defining education just as they define success: self-interestedly. To them," she said, "fulfilling one's potential translates into playing the role you've been assigned from birth: a few of them are winners, most of us losers."

"We want that model to change," Besant went on. "We want those definitions to change. We want to explicate a new paradigm, inscribed by *new modalities* which are reflective of the perspective of the long-forgotten 'other,' the subaltern who has not *been allowed to speak*." Now Besant stood straight as any popular "champion of the masses" might and cried, "The history curriculum at this institution has been written by those forces of which I speak: by the *victors*! And it is a blueprint for domination and the perpetuation of political and social systems which do not deem the history of women or people-of-color worthy of study, unless practiced in a token, non-threatening way. *Our* power structure is judged *inferior*. What lip service is given *us* is in an archaic context, is the infuriating condescension of *noblesse oblige*."

"I am here," Besant was building toward a crescendo

now, "to expose this institution and the forces responsible for all those lies."

She wagged her finger now. "But our cultural appetites remain unsatisfied and our thirst for truth *unslaked*. Where are the tales of the sweating Africans who built Mount Vernon? Or of all the women who sweated through the ages on behalf of the pampered male literati so that they might labor to bring forth their precious canon?"

She nodded for emphasis, as her voice began to quaver: "The cult of American individuality is nothing more than a muddying myth designed to lull the 'savage' *other* into quiescence through internalization of racist and misogynist notions of inferiority."

As the Professor grew more impassioned, she swiped a handkerchief intermittently at her beaded brow. "The *people* must make the diversity of the world's cultures— the wisdom of our global anthropological mosaic—the normative, redemptive standard, *not* the mere problematic irritation, the nagging itch on the backside of the Western power structure that begs occasionally to be scratched. By submitting, we have been hoodwinked, exploited, degraded, and used as vehicles for racism, sexism, elitism and militarism."

Besant reached for the sky, as if entreating the heavens for succor. "We must resist the so-called canon and the deception on which it is based, in which the rich and the powerful are left to define religion and knowledge, as they place—not coincidentally—Western Civilization at the apex of human achievement. The canon serves *uniformity*, not diversity; *reaction*, not revolution; *exclusion*, not inclusion; *tyranny*, not justice."

"*Right on, Sister!*" Shouts echoed throughout the auditorium, and soon rhythmic secular incantations emerged: "*The people, united, will never be defeated!*" The crowd erupted thunderously now, affirming yells punctuating the applause. Lata Besant held both her fists in the air, as tears of thanksgiving coursed down her cheeks. Triumph, at least for the moment, was hers.

Three other speakers, reputed to be kindred small fry, were slated to follow Lata Besant before the keynote address by Theo Carver, so Allen and Sam stole away to a small restaurant across the street to have some lunch. There, they slipped into opposite sides of a window booth and ordered coffee.

"Well?" Allen thought he'd better not be too hasty in his judgment of the opening address; at least not till he'd solicited Sam's reaction.

"Well, what?"

Sensing a tease, he clasped his hands before him and looked directly into her eyes with a wry, impatient smile. "Your reaction to Besant's speech?"

"You mean, the official *woman of color* slant?"

"How inclusive of you," he chided gently, grinning. "I can't wait to hear."

"On one level, I'm in sympathy with much that she had to say."

Hmm. Empathy was the one thing he didn't *expect.*

Sam said, "I mean, it's not hard to argue that history has, at least to some extent, been written by the *winners,* right? There is such a thing as triumphal scholarship, you know."

She blew on her coffee thoughtfully. "But that doesn't mean I believe a deliberate conspiracy's the reason for that. We're talking centuries of accumulated thought and literature here. No supposed 'power structure' could have controlled the dynamism, not to speak of the chaos, required to sustain a consistent *conspiracy* of ideas, especially later, among Western democracies."

She sipped from her cup. "In fact, democratic cultures *must* be that way: dynamic and tensile, I mean, else evolution is impossible. It's in places like China—where dynasties have traditionally exercised rigid control over the population and its contact with foreigners—that those orthodoxies maintain themselves for hundreds of years at a time in cultural stasis. But no single group has ever succeeded in consolidating control over all of Europe, at least in the modern era. Perhaps that's the one beneficial by-product of chaos: dynamism."

Allen watched Sam rip open a sugar packet and dump it into her cup. He was momentarily captivated.

Sam put her hand on her hip and snapped, "Are you listening to me at all?"

"Of course."

Appearing almost sullen now, she looked down at the coffee, then gazed wide-eyed at him. "I'm making a serious point here."

"Sorry," he looked chastened. "Lost in the moment."

Unconvinced, Sam forged ahead. "I think a more plausible explanation for our popular culture is that people tend to cling to anything that meshes with their sense of place, and that can lead us to irrationality sometimes."

"What do you mean, Sam? What are you driving at?"

"That this is the predicate for unexplainable cultural institutions like slavery, foot-binding, female circumcision – or sati.

Certainly, organized religion isn't off the hook in this respect either, is it?"

Samantha licked her spoon, then wielded it with a mischievous grin, as if she held Excalibur. "But with modernity, with sweet reason—", she aimed the utensil at him for emphasis, "—we may compensate for our shortcomings."

Allen started, as if struck with a revelation. "I think I get it. But then aren't you just dismissing the professor's speech as demagoguery? I mean, history isn't moral or immoral, is it? It just *is*." Absently, he gnawed at a cuticle, then stared at it. "The verdict on a person or a culture can be rendered only in retrospect, right? No people can choreograph history preemptively, for Christ's sake."

"Of course not," Sam replied. "If Besant's sincere, then she's not only chasing phantoms, but asking others to join her. Aristotle, Newton, Shakespeare, Augustine, Gandhi, Leonardo, Lincoln, King, *et al* are revered *around the world*, not for their ethnicities, but for their transcendent *genius*. And I'm sure any university would leap to include an Aleut Voltaire in the canon, if one could be found. Besant fails to ask herself the more important—and, to me, the most obvious—question: What features of Western civilization helped give rise to such genius in the first place, and how are those traits best replicated and spread?"

Samantha lowered her cup as she shook her head. "To deny the intellectual facts of the matter, especially for an educator, is profoundly dishonest, even dangerous, because it deprives students of the philosophic critique they need to assess and contrast cultures, in order to contrive an acceptable, mutually agreed upon standard: the universal constellation of all these so-called 'human rights. Without that, all is Babel; everything must remain relative to one's own experience."

"Christ, I'm glad you're here to provide some context" Allen chuckled as he gnawed at a roll. "My eyes tend to glaze over after a point. I just assume it's bull-shit from the beginning." He scratched absently at his temple. "Still, I'm not so obtuse as to ignore the sheer power of this thing…this movement. A lot of people seem captivated by it."

"At its base, it's an illusion," she whispered, dabbing her chin with the napkin. "Their case will seem more compelling than it is – at first. They throw opponents off their stride by making them feel elitist. No rea-sonable person wants to appear intolerant or bigoted or chauvinistic, so the most obvious rebuttal is never used. The most compelling weapons history provides lie unexploited, unpacked in the arsenal."

"I think what you're saying is that the best defense," Allen said, arcing his eyebrows in an acknowledgement of mutual understanding. Sam nodded in return. He perused the check and slapped a ten-dollar bill on the table. "Forewarned is forearmed. Now let's go see what Carver has to say."

Amid a rumble of applause, Theo Carver strode to the dais, colorfully bedecked in a billowing robe. He smiled and nodded as he looked down at the crowd, which veritably pulsed with the celebratory indigna-tion of the multi-ethnic student body: white, black and brown young people, generously sprinkled with activists from myriad campus organizations, buttressed with a smattering of faculty members. He said nothing, allowing the rapturous clamor to wash over him like a Pacific wave. He felt reassured by the shouts and chants echoing from the mass below.

With a deliberate precision, Carver placed spectacles on the bridge of his nose and extended both arms outward from his body—ever so slightly flapping his palms, like a quarterback attempting to quiet a boisterous stadium so that the game might proceed.

"My sincere thanks," he began, "to sister Besant and those others who have preceded me and so ably outlined the challenges the progressive peoples of this community face—one of which, contrary to the 'voices of traditional reason,' is *not* to find more effective ways to *communicate* with our oppressors." What is going on in Principia is too damn much *miscommunication!*"

A roar of assent momentarily drowned his words, and he had no intention of discouraging it—at least, not before a sufficiently pregnant pause had elapsed.

"The *intellectual* culture that this institution represents not only controls the spread of knowledge, but the *production* of knowledge... Not that this is anything *new.*"

He paused and pointed to the ceiling. *"Noooo!* So-called *historians* of long ago set the pattern of *deceit!* *White* men seized the truth in the name of the *so-called canon*, without pangs of conscience, the *slightest pang* of guilt, or the slightest twinge of *humanity*."

Carver leaned forward as if seeking intimacy with the crowd. "We *all* know, *deep down*," he extended his arms, "how America achieved her *greatness*, her *wealth*, her *magnificence*, and *how* this was *acquired*. We *all* know that at the bottom of all *Western Civilization's accomplishments*, was a person of *color* doing the *real work!*"

People of *color*, if *truth* be told, are the *fathers* and the *mothers* of *humankind* and *human civilization*. Yet what has happened to *them*? Why, they have been turned into profane facsimiles of their *oppressors*. And the worldview of the *oppressors* is killing our *children*, our *traditions*, our *culture*, and our *minds!*

The Western patriarchy, having kneaded us into some *formless blob of cultural dough*, uses its power like a cookie-cutter, to turn out exact copies of itself – except in the one characteristic which they cannot change: *the color of our skin!*"

Once again, the assembly erupted in volcanic approbation.

Now his voice softened: "Every culture is sacred within its own system, united in an emotional and psychological oneness, both in the homeland and among those cruelly flung to the Diaspora."

His face clouded again. "*Eurocentrism* is rooted in the *oppression*, *domination* and *racist* traditions of that continent's sinful past. The Western World is built on the three Ds: *domination, destruction* and *death*. And so-called *western civilization* is neither *righteous* nor *moral* nor *fair*! It is *vulgar* and *revolting* and glorifies *one* segment of the people over *another*! And this *devil-spawn* armed Europeans with the *excuse* to expand and to spread their doctrines of *lies* and *hate* and senseless *violence! Oh, yeah!* They *talk* about *morality* and *objectivity* even while they *scheme* to destroy the *cultural 'other.'*"

Allen felt uneasy, unsure as to where the speaker was headed, beyond high dudgeon of course.

"Now, we all know that changing the power structure will take time, for we have not yet reached our revolutionary threshold. But we must battle injustice wherever we find it and resist cultural destruction wherever we can. And right here in Principia, within a mile of where we gather today, an immigrant from India, a descendant of *British slaves*, sits in a cell, mourning the deaths of his son and daughter-in-law who, in accord with *her grief and her traditions*, threw herself on his *funeral fire*! Torn with sadness, devastated by sorrow, she determined to join her precious husband in *eternal felicity!*

Of course, no one disputes that her deed was tragic. But this was her *custom*. This was her *choice*. This was the route to her *salvation*. Yet how do the *authorities* respond?"

Carver defiantly placed his fists on his hips. "Why, they arrest her father-in-law for *murder*, a foul accusation that *disrespects* her, disrespects her *culture* and disrespects Indian *civilization*! Of course, they *pretend*—" he threw his hands to the sky—"to be more *righteous*, more *humane*, more *civilized* than the bride's father-in-law."

Carver leaned over the lectern toward the crowd. "But brothers and sisters, I ask you: Do *they* have any claim to *righteousness*?"

"NO-NO-NO-NO-NO-NO!"

"Do they have any claim to *morality*?"

"NO-NO-NO-NO-NO-NO!"

"Do they have any claim to *civ-il-i-za-shun*?"

"NO-NO-NO-NO-NO-NO!"

Allen and Samantha had scarcely looked at one another since Carver had begun, both so caught up in his oratory that they lost track of passing time. But startled by the thumping cadence of the crowd's approval, Allen felt a sudden chill. He whispered to Sam, "I've seen enough. Let's get the hell out of here."

And while the hall continued to reverberate to the cheers and stomps of the multitude, the two began, gingerly, to thread their way toward the exit.

November 16
1:00 p.m.

The day dawned cold and misty. From the outside, the

Ganges Mission—wrapped in bucolic bustle, four miles outside of Principia—had the appearance of a large neo-Wrightish church, with a high glass ceiling and a conical center core, around which the rest of the building seemed, figuratively, to revolve. A black Lincoln Town Car pulled slowly into the parking lot, which was mostly empty except for a light Toyota pickup and a green Volvo sedan.

Theo Carver eased himself out from behind the wheel and proceeded up the walkway to the building.

Inside, the expansive structure was a rabbit warren of idols, alcoves and small mausoleum-like temples bedecked with Hindu iconography of every description, of whose meaning and provenance Carver hadn't a clue. A bearded giant guarding the entryway gave a knowing nod and directed him to a side office bearing a small sign on the door inscribed *Pandit Savarkar*.

Carver found the old man sitting at his desk, head bowed over the *New York Times*. Dressed in an immaculate Savile-row suit, a cigarette trembled in his palsied left hand; his index finger loomed above, as if ready to flick a long segment of ash. To his right sat a small, thin-stemmed glass of what might have been wine. Carver stood silently for a moment, awaiting acknowledgement.

Presently, Savarkar looked up and squinted through his black glasses, lips arcing into a thin smile. "Ah, Mr.

Carver, come in." He laid aside the newspaper. "Sit down, please."

"Thank you kindly, Panditji." Carver was relieved at the cordiality of the invitation.

"Cigarette?" Savarkar extended a silver-inlaid case.

"No, thank you. Blood pressure, you know?"

"Then I will not be so rude as to offer you some wine," Savarkar said, "unless you feel particularly venturesome today." He sipped from his glass. "Now then, what news of my request?" The old man sat back slightly in the large armchair, chewing on his cigarette holder, affecting an almost Rooseveltian air.

"It's all set," Carver said. "The Diversity League is organized and recruiting actively for group leaders to work with your people. The handbills are typeset and ready to go, once you give us a date. And we've contracted with several local companies to produce photo reproductions for placards, as well as for the souvenir icons you wanted. We're also going to have food and drink on site and some fruit and vegetables available for prayer offerings. I'll use motorhomes to carry and sell the stuff. With any luck, we'll make a profit."

"With God's blessing, a large one," Savarkar smiled.

"Perhaps," Carver grinned. "My Diversity League could surely use it."

"Now then, Mr. Carver," Savarkar said, "may I

ask what local sources of *political* support you have cultivated?"

"That's going great," Carver said. "We'll have delegations from the ACLU, Magdalene College Alliance for People of Color, Americans for a Democratic Future, Alliance Against Academic Racism, the Multicultural Union, even SPAWN."

"I'm sorry?"

"Society for Protection Against White Nationalism."

"I see."

"But as I see it, Panditji," Carver said, "we ought to wait a bit before politicizing this thing."

"And why is that?"

"Well, you understand, we don't want to *peak* too early. This trial could drag on for weeks, once it gets going. One thing I've discovered after years in this struggle is that a few demonstrations go a long way with the public. Timing will determine the flow of public opinion, so it's not the main thing right now. Move too vigorously too quickly, and you might as well pack up and head home."

Savarkar jabbed his cigarette in the direction of his guest. "Do not presume to instruct me, Mr. Carver.

"Sorry, man." Carver opted for tactical retreat.

"I have reason to suspect," Savarkar said, "that this case will come to trial more speedily than you anticipate. And when it does, we must be ready. The ground must be prepared, the narrative carefully crafted before we attempt to sell it. Enlightened accounts of the matter, giving the *true* facts, must be disseminated among all sympathetic groups. Those accounts, we will provide you in due course. Meanwhile, since the event will take place at the site, requisite permits and ample publicity must be arranged. Mr. Fulbright has assured me that there should be no insuperable obstacles, so I trust that I may feel comfortable leaving that in your capable hands?"

"You may indeed. Demonstrations are my specialty."

"Excellent." Slowly, Savarkar opened a desk drawer to his left and pulled from it a bulging manila envelope. He extended it toward his guest. "If any unexpected difficulties arise, you know how to contact me."

Carver grasped the envelope with a polite smile.

Then he exited the room.

November 16
1:30 p.m.

Huffing and puffing, hurriedly swiping at the crumbs that cascaded down his battered sweater, Mark McCorkle stumbled tardily into his survey course in Modern World History.

Immediately he was struck by the change in the students: Unlike the nonchalance that usually greeted him, the lecture hall was now like a hive, buzzing with chatter, murmurings, and the hushed tones of intense argument.

For an instant McCorkle deluded himself into thinking that his last lecture on Bismarckian diplomacy had been a hit—then reality snatched him back. It took much effort to galvanize this group to *interest*, let alone passion. Nonetheless, he smiled as he shuffled to the podium.

Oddly, his presence did nothing to quiet the assembly. The commotion became even louder than before. Yet he was still reluctant to stifle the uncharacteristic din. For several minutes Mark just stood there watching, straining to catch snippets of the discussion. The hubbub seemed in part to be about yesterday's Diversity League rally. Feeling out-of-place around his fellow academics, Mark had avoided the convocation, and now he felt awkward about joining the class's drift.

At last, a red-haired woman in the front row raised her hand and asked, "Professor McCorkle, what do you think about the Diversity Day rally?"

"I was not present, I regret to say." He replied softly and then spoke louder as the chatter diminished enough to hear him. "But if you would all enlighten me about the proceedings, I'll be happy to comment."

Suddenly the clamor began again, as over a hundred voices vied, almost riotously, he thought, for the chance to educate *him*.

He gestured for silence. "One at a time, please! One at a time! I'm willing to suspend our normal routine temporarily, *if* this discussion seems important to you. But we must all be able to hear one another." He called again on the redhead in the front row.

"What do you think of the Kumar case?" she asked. "Don't you think she was murdered?"

Taking care not to betray his insider's perspective on the incident, Mark knew he had to choose his words carefully. "Maybe," he said. "But what if she freely chose to commit suicide?"

"According to Janey Jermane, she was a *child!*" protested the redhead. "How could she be competent to make a decision like that?"

"Well, what if she had been older?" Mark asked. "Would that have made it more acceptable?"

The woman's brow knitted. "You mean like an adult?"

"I mean," McCorkle said, "if she'd been an adult and seen it as her obligation to die in that fire, and had done so voluntarily, would that change how you'd view her actions?"

A short black man dressed in fatigues called from the back of the hall, "Sure, it would make a difference! This is their *custom*, their *culture*, their *religion*. They have a *right* to it."

A heavy-set, older woman half-way back shot to her

feet, hands defiant on her ample hips. "Why should any woman, or worse yet *a child*, give up her life simply because she's become a widow? I'm asking, because I *am* one. What about *her* hopes and dreams? What about *her* rights? Doesn't anybody care about *those*?" She glared at the black man, her eyes welling with tears.

The black man shook his head. "Hey, she has a right to do whatever she *wants* to do with her own body. *And* we also have something called freedom of religion in this country. Does anyone tell *you* how to worship? Where do you get off telling *them*?"

Time to intervene, McCorkle thought. "Let me offer you a hypothetical situation," he said, "You are a district officer in the pay of the East India Company, circa 1820. You get wind of a sati – a religious, ritual self-sacrifice – of a ten-year-old widow. Now, knowing full well that this is a common practice in your district, how do you respond? Your superiors have dictated a hands-off policy regarding native customs. But what is the moral imperative? *Is* there a moral imperative? Should you follow your deepest ethical sense? Would it be barbaric to allow the ceremony to proceed? Or should you retreat before the knowledge that the people have—as you just put it, my friend—a *right* to their *religion*?"

The man laughed bitterly. "With all due respect, Dr. McCorkle, that's bullshit. Those British had no business being there in the first place. And they had no right to judge a culture they didn't understand. What if things had been reversed?"

"How so?" said McCorkle.

"What if Indians came over here and tried to tell us that abortion, capital punishment and thongs are barbaric. What would you say then?"

Guy has a point. "But where do you draw the line?" Mark asked. "Is the cultural defense the ultimate defense? What happens, then, to notions of *universal rights* on which our own founding principles are based? What would happen to American culture and America's Constitution? Or is the very *concept* of a common American culture in and of itself imperialistic?"

The black man sat down, chuckling to himself. Then he let fly: "Excuse me, Professor. By these 'universal truths,' do you mean the renowned 'life, liberty and the pursuit of happiness'? Because, if you do, then you owe people of color and a hell of a lot of aborted fetuses an explanation. Face it! Those so-called principles aren't universal and never have been. They mean whatever the people decide they should mean. And maybe *the people* are getting ready to redefine what freedom of religion *really* means."

A shaggy white youth shouted assent, then rose:

"Professor, you know he's right. American history is nothing more than the propaganda of, like, white men who imposed their sexist, racist, homophobic and patriarchal, like, ideas on those who, like, couldn't fight back. This country is getting, like, more sophisticated now. We're entering a, like, *global* society where more diverse people are, like, *empowered*. You know what I'm sayin? Those cats on top are gettin' nervous, and they *oughta be*."

Livid now, the redhead in the front row turned toward the black student. "I can't believe you said that! What about the freedom of women to live their own lives, not to be chained to a man? Not to have their fates tied-in totally with their husbands or boyfriends. That's medieval. What's next, chastity belts? You're a moron!"

"Civility, people, civility." Mark waved his arms.

How do I keep a lid on all this?

The student in fatigues rose again and shrilled at his adversary. "No, *you're* the moron! You want choice and freedom only so long as they're *your* choices, *your* ideas of freedom, right?" He pointed directly at her. "You want the freedom to kill your babies out of selfishness, and to kill yourselves if you're too weak to endure pain. But a girl chooses to fulfill her wedding vows and die with her husband, and somehow that's *barbaric*? What a joke!"

A bespectacled, self-effacing, nerd who always sat as far from the front as possible now rose quietly, and Mark acknowledged him. "Professor McCorkle," he began timorously, "this is the scariest thing I've ever seen. America is an incredibly diverse place, and we've always been told that's good. But at the same time, the reason we're strong is that we have laws and customs in common. The less we have in common, the more... diverse we'll become. I mean *serious* diversity: in our opinions about right and wrong; tolerance and intolerance; freedom, justice, even life and death.

"And if it comes down to living in a country where burning little girls—whatever the reason—becomes somehow OK, then turn out the lights, *the party's over*! I don't know how to say it exactly. But if we're not all on the same page for the important stuff, then we might as well burn the book."

A change swept over the lecture hall. Everyone fell suddenly, eerily still, as if some line had been silently drawn and banners slipped from their cases and unfurled, leaving little else for anyone to say.

November 17
7:00 a.m.

Gertie and Abner Stickle stood on the crumbling porch of their old Sears farmhouse in the vague light of pre-dawn, tightly gripping two steaming mugs of Maxwell House, mouths agape.

It had been almost two weeks since Abner's grim discovery. They'd expected the excitement to move into town, what with the impending murder trial and all. Abner had been pleased with the temporary peace and quiet, though Gertie was nettled by the sudden diminution in her celebrity status.

Griffis Road passed the entrance to what locals had dubbed, at Gertie's instigation, "The Devil's Way"—the rutted lane that led to the notorious glade where sati had occurred. Scarcely a dozen cars a day ever went down it. Yet this morning it was lined with motorhomes and vans for a quarter mile on either side, mobile command centers for ABC, CBS, CNN, and NBC, along with the logos of a host of regional TV stations, festooned with antennae or topped off with satellite dishes. Smaller vans, plastered with explanatory banners proclaimed myriad cultural affiliations.

The Sheriff's auxiliary posse was already there, majestically astride gorgeous palominos, trying to keep the road open and manage the flood of chartered buses and smaller cars converging on the rural ribbon of gravel. Already, clusters of spectators milled about, organizing themselves in formation, unfurling banners celebrating the sati of Roop Kumar. Clearly, a major happening was imminent.

As the Stickles stared open-mouthed, stupefied, trailer panels opened upwards to reveal the wares of vendors, which were drawing customers almost as fast as they disgorged themselves: for drinks, chapatis, head scarves, protest signs, incense, red-jeweled bindis for the adornment of Hindu women. Over the next two hours, the heretofore obscure tributary of gravel was transformed into a torrent of activism. The old farmer swore with exquisite futility as he watched it lap inexorably onto his winter wheat, then sweep away the twisted old fence that bordered his field. The sight was too much, even for Gertie. So, the couple opted to remain on their porch, where Gertie said she could better operate a command post for the locals who depended on her to speculate on the meaning and purpose of it all.

The late November weather was seasonally dreary, with a fine mist and a chill wind. Abner tamped his pipe and then relit it. Jamming his hands into his pockets, he shuddered under his heavy wool coat and tilted his head slightly to peer at the unfolding drama framed by the ragged brim of his Pioneer Seed hat.

Gertie was a fine woman, he mused, and a good wife, despite her eccentricities. Life was still a daily adventure for her and therefore, unfailingly fun. But as good a person as she was, she was a simple soul who seldom read a newspaper, let alone a book. Whatever reality lay beyond the pale of the village fell to Abner to assess and pass judgment on, and he couldn't resist doing so, even for an audience of one.

As he surveyed the spectacle from his porch, Abner was secretly glad the world was passing him by. *Not the same country I was reared in.* He was no Bible-thumper, but damn it, he figured he knew wickedness when he saw it. The old Ship of State seemed to be listing, headed toward a murky end on looming rocks. All the virtues he'd grown up with—pride in working the fields in the hot sun alongside his father; the solidity of the family unit branching unbroken toward the generational horizon; the value of personal integrity—in short, all the old

Yankee chestnuts that had defined masculinity, morality, propriety – were now fading to the quaintness of a cross-stitch sampler. No one seemed capable of speaking favorably of them at all anymore without provoking a knowing smirk or condescending sneer.

"Jesus," he sighed, as he tamped down his pipe, not only were fanatics taking to sacrificing children, but they were positively bragging about having done it.

The country could indeed become as bad as it wanted to be. And while Abner wasn't quite sure who to blame for depositing the idyllic land of his youth into a civic cesspit, he fervently hoped a special place in hell had been reserved for the perpetrators. *Just hope I go to meet my Maker long before the whole rotten thing collapses in on itself.*

November 17
9:00 a.m.

Carl Peters and Jonas Clevenger eased the squad car gingerly down the road with the mounted deputies, to coordinate crowd control.

Carl said, "I hope to Christ this situation doesn't get out of hand."

When Theo Carver officially applied to the Sheriff's office for the proper demonstration permits, neither Carl nor Allen anticipated anything on this scale. *Quite beyond the capacities of rural Pope County,* Carl thought.

Before seven o'clock, he'd notified the state police and requested assistance. Before ten, he'd been on the phone with the governor, concerned with the horde of media. Already, regional news crews from as far away as Indianapolis, Detroit, and Chicago, not to mention the major networks, had snapped up every hotel room within 50 miles of Principia.

Now, in a low voice, as if the crowd outside the squad car was straining to eavesdrop, Carl said, "Jesus Christ, Jonas, can you believe this shit?"

The broad scope of this event was simply striking. It seemed to be tapping political and religious fringe elements from all over the Midwest—Afrocentrists, advocates of multicultural education, South Asian immigrant organizations, Hindu revivalists, Native American groups, Spiritualists, Right-to-Die advocates, Libertarians, American Atheists and ironically (Carl thought), women's rights groups—along with a score of others he hadn't before known existed. He popped a handful of cashews and fondled his shirt pocket for a cigarette.

Despite the chill, Jonas wiped perspiration from his brow. "Never seen anything like it—no way, no how. Where in the hell did this all come from?"

Carl ran his fingers through his short wavy hair in lieu of a comb. "You know what? The more I think about this, the more I think Ms. Desai's right; this whole thing's beginning to look like a setup."

Jonas made no comment, and Carl added: "I mean, just think about it a goddamn minute. Everything starts with the purchase of this parcel here, by the Mission or the Mahasabha or whatever." He gestured toward the woods. "Shortly after, a bunch of Indians cremate one of their own, who's died, suspiciously, of a burst appendix. His child bride is sacrificed on the pyre, allowing her father-in-law to steal the dowry money he might've lost otherwise. And his son's incompetent medical care is arranged *and* paid for by the same outfit that bought the woods in the first place."

Carl shook his head. "Those are all coincidences? I doubt it. But one thing I can't figure is: What's in it for those Mahasabha folks? I mean, all this is putting them out of pocket a good chunk of change."

Jonas said, "I think you're forgetting the main objective, Boss, the one Ms. Desai was talking about."

"Oh, yeah? Enlighten me, Sherlock." Carl reached for a Tums.

"Well, look at all the shit you got here, the hawkers, the flyers, the banners, the pilgrims, the chanters, the rhymers: the show biz. *That's* the reason for it right there. Exposure. Publicity. Politics. *Real bad* politics, if you ask me."

Carl exhaled a long stream of smoke. Jonas was no brain surgeon, but he did have an intermittent sense of the obvious. This mayhem had a hell of a lot less to do with Principia per se than with its isolation and its usually reliable people being intimidated by strangers with political agendas. *Me, Jonas, Allen, Ms. Desai, McCorkle — we're all pawns about to be swept aside to make some larger point.*

The rural venue would guarantee the perfect foil, and that might be what the activists are really after. And Magdalene College was there as a conveniently sympathetic base. They—whoever "they" were—*wanted* a battle, a media event that might showcase their cultural perspective and mobilize political support, both here and at home in India. *Brilliant. Christ, I've been hangin' around McCorkle so much, I'm starting to think in egghead-ese myself...*

Carl's cell phone rang. Allen Southworth's voice crackled at the other end. "Carl? You there?"

"Wish I wasn't," Carl said.

"I've been on the phone all morning," Allen said. "How bad is it?"

"Bad as it gets," Carl replied, "though everyone seems pretty peaceful so far. Any way we can keep 'em out here on the road?"

"Nope. The woods belong to the Mission; we no longer have cause to deny them entry. "Believe me, I've tried, but Judge Thorndike was adamant."

"Vunderbar," Carl groaned. "Any more news from the Guv?"

"Only that we are not to *over*react," said the

prosecutor. "Said he'd send two state police cars. Guess that's to insure we won't. Overreact, I mean."

"Swell," Carl said. "Should've figured he'd do that when I asked. Guess my plan, then, is to open up the lane at noon and hope we can send them all home by five or so. Any further advice?"

"Yeah. I've notified McCorkle, and he's heading out to observe the demonstration. Long as he's there you might want to pick his brains – well, that is *if* he can find the place."

Carl choked back the rejoinder—*He's been here before!*—although he knew that was no guarantee the prof would be able to find it again. "Ten-four, Boss." Carl signed off. "See you back at the ranch."

As the car approached the lane entrance, Carl and Jonas saw McCorkle lumbering ahead. He was speaking earnestly to several demonstrators, but then disengaged and flagged down the cruiser.

"Give me a lift, gentlemen?" he asked. "I'm not sure I want to be in the middle of this circus once the show starts in the center ring."

Carl waved him into the back seat, then directed Jonas to park the car at a spot close enough to the lane's entrance to provide maximum surveillance potential and the possibility of a swift exit from the scene via Stickle's old equipment path. After all, everything was without precedent now, including any assumptions that the crowds would stay peaceful.

The professor spread his elbows on the front seat and hung his shaggy head between Carl and Jonas. He seemed eager, attentive—like a big dog allowed along for a car ride. Carl was briefly irritated; then he wondered, more charitably, how many days out with "the guys" McCorkle had ever experienced. The prof veritably panted with gratitude at having been included. All the business of the last few weeks was probably the most excitement the academic had ever experienced in his life.

At noon, the barricade blocking the lane was removed, and the procession began to funnel through, forming a noisy phalanx, four abreast, toward the fateful glade. As they did so, McCorkle began his running narrative: Today was the 13th day following the cremation. Tradition dictated this *chunari* ceremony of the veil, both to glorify the widow's sacrifice and to sanctify the site for future pilgrims.

"From what I've been able to gather," he said, "rumors about the girl's miraculous sati have been spreading."

Carl grunted. Then he gave a thumbs-up to Tom Stivers, who was snapping photographs of participants for his Ganges Mission dossier, close to the churned-up entrance.

Said McCorkle, "Witnesses attest to her ethereal appearance: smiling, unburned inside the pyre's flames, even that it was ignited telekinetically by the power of her virtue."

Carl snorted, "What a load of crap."

"Others say the girl was visible almost to the last, inside the flames, cradling her dead husband's head to her breast. Such accounts have been faxed and emailed all over the place." McCorkle handed the Sheriff a hand-bill glorifying the sati. "Also, thousands of *these* have been distributed."

The hordes of assembled vendors were hawking tacky memorabilia: ribbons, toys, posters, plastic icons, prayer offerings, incense sticks and assorted snacks. In the forefront of the mass were students, holding aloft placards bearing large photographs of the bride and groom, beaming, holding hands. At the flanks of the procession, large, turbaned youths marched, bran-dishing swords with which they evidently intended to protect the site from desecration. Those in front chanted unintelligible slogans—in Hindi, Mark guessed. They were followed by more familiar, decipherable chants, mostly by non-Indians who'd congregated toward the rear to protest the authorities' "persecution" of Mr. Swaraj and the intolerable oppression of the law.

Theo Carver led a large delegation from Magdalene College, who rhythmically chanted: "YOU KNOW OUR STRENGTH AND U-NI-TEE, DEPENDS ON OUR DI-VER-SI-TEEE!"

Like a bad hangover from the high, happy 1960s, Carl thought.

Telegenic placards abounded, libeling Prosecutor Southworth and the Sheriff's Department as fascistic instruments of cultural genocide—elitist, exclusionary, privileged, and Eurocentric.

Many in the crowds carried American flags turned upside down, or posters sporting revisionist twists on history.

Once the crowds reached the glade, the cultural tenor of the event became clearer. Those in front passed word that reverence was to be observed at the sati site. Cadenced slogans trailed off, conversations stilled, and hundreds of weary arms allowed their messages to descend from view. As the vanguard gathered around the site of the pyre, tridents were implanted around it, draped with red veils to sanctify the new ethereal state of Roop Kumar. Muscular youths, bare-chested despite the chilling temperature, stepped forward to begin a slow march around the pit, long swords held aloft.

Supplicants soon emerged from the crowd to leave tribute offerings to the *sati mata*: fruit, sheaves of grain, finely woven bolts of expensive cloth. A small commemorative blaze was kindled to a slow smolder with dry sticks and coconuts anointed with ghee.

Then, four young men from the Mission stepped forward to spread a gold-embroidered stole over the pit, incinerating it as mantra-chanting priests looked on. Once the cloth was completely consumed, the holy men doused the smoking pit with water and milk.

Then the assembled throng began, just as unexpectedly, to disperse. Long columns began the long trek back toward the road and into the arms of roving reporters in need of an emotive moment.

Mark McCorkle mused, "Almost makes you question your perspective, doesn't it?"

"Oh, *sure*," Carl huffed, unmoved. He snuffed out the butt of his Lucky Strike in the ashtray. "Let's get the hell out of here, Jonas, before McCorkle starts *thinking* again."

November 17
1:30 p.m.

Except for brief breaks to warm themselves and replenish their coffee, the Stickles had spent the entire morning on their porch.

Gertie, for once, sat silent. Even Abner was stunned by the mob of reporters in his own farmyard. A score of regional news outlets had also set up shop, all resolved to impress and not be intimidated by their more celebrated colleagues from national networks, the old farmer thought, whom they probably viewed with a mixture of grudging admiration and pure envy.

Just below the Stickles in the yard, Janey Jermane looked spectacular in her luxurious faux fox coat, better prepared for Indiana in late autumn than her rivals. Now thoroughly conversant with the details of the story, she looked poised to dazzle, waiting for Mickey Marshall's lead-in. Then the Stickles could hear her carefully cadenced delivery emanating from their big screen TV, which was tuned to WEKT in Elkhart. Despite the weather, they kept the inner door open so they could hear the real thing through the screen door:

JERMANE: *Thank you, Mickey. This is Janey Jermane, coming to you from Griffis Road in rural Tennyson Township, near the Abner Stickle farm where, just two weeks ago, a young Indian immigrant girl, Roop Kumar, was burned to death on the funeral pyre of her husband. Today, a very large demonstration has drawn marchers from throughout the Midwest. Many are protesting to express solidarity with Mr. Sirkar Swaraj, the girl's father-in-law, who was charged ten days ago with first degree murder in that death. With us today is Theo Carver of Principia's Diversity League, one of the organizers of this event. Thank you for taking the time to speak with me, Mr. Carver.*

CARVER: *Thank you, Janey. Nice to be with you.*

JERMANE: *Can you tell our viewers the purpose of
            today's demonstration?*

CARVER: *Certainly. Its main purpose is to honor the
            departed widow who, in accordance with
            her tradition and her faith, has sacrificed
            herself in order to be with her husband, to
            confer divine blessing on her family and that
            of her in-laws.*

JERMANE: *Some critics have suggested that Miss Kumar's
            age — ten — makes arguments like the one
            you've just made, impossible to defend.*

CARVER: *These sorts of marriages are not considered
            evil in the South Asian community. What
            right do prosecutors have to pass judgment?
            Indeed, with all the sexual promiscuity
            around today, we should not condemn such
            examples of fidelity, but honor them. Roop
            Kumar should not be slandered for entering
            what many in her country would consider a
            holy union.*

JERMANE: *But polls conducted among South Asians
            show 90% of people disapprove of this
            practice, Mr. Carver. How do you respond?*

CARVER: *Biased polling, of course, generates such
            reports. The people cry out for enlightenment on
            cultural matters.*

JERMAINE: *What about the argument that the sati ceremony is demeaning to women? Hasn't the victim simply become an extension of a man... her husband?*

CARVER: *Victim? Look about you, Janey. Look at the pictures of the widow and her husband. Do they not seem equally honored? Look at the offerings and the prayers. Do they appear to honor a non-person? These are scurrilous lies spread by cultural bigots who will see only one view: a Eurocentric one.*

JERMANE: *Thank you so much for speaking with me this afternoon, Mr. Carver.*

CARVER: *Thank you, Janey. Go with God.*

Meanwhile, media lesser lights approached, anxious to corral Carver for their own interviews, one after another in insubstantial succession, leaving little behind to distinguish one from the next.

Not far up the road, Abner had grown weary of the cold and damp. He reentered his house and eased his bones into his favorite recliner, to watch the proceedings in more comfort.

Meanwhile, Janey Jermane moved on, turning to an Indian college student who stood with a sign on the fringe of the woodlot, sartorially westernized in denim jeans and starter jacket. Gently, she drew him to her side. "Next, Mickey, we have one of the demonstrators from Magdalen College, right down the road. How do you do, sir?"

"Very well, thank you," the youth replied.

"Would you please explain to our television audience why you've come here today? There seem to be a lot of mixed feelings out there, both about the death of young Roop and about your community's reaction to it."

The student cleared his throat. "If there are, it stems from the falsehoods people have been led to believe because they're more compatible with their own cultural viewpoints. What we have going on here is a witch hunt, designed to satisfy America's bigoted judgment over an event they don't understand."

"Judgment…" Janey repeated pensively, carefully, as if turning it round and round in her brain.

"That's right," said the young man. "Europeans have a difficult time understanding both the piety and valor of our Indian women. Roop Kumar, has acquired enormous respect for her courageous act. She wasn't forced to do it. The whole thing would have lost its power if that had been the case. It took incredible courage. But during India's glorious past, when the gods willed it, the great warriors fought on, even when their heads had been cut off." His eyes grew wider, saucer-like.

"I see," Janey nodded.

"No, Miss Jermane," the man persisted, "I don't think you do. This is the age of *Kaliyug*, the age of Kali, the epoch of *disintegration...*"

Janey stood frozen for a moment in time, then turned to her cameraman drawing her index finger across her throat. How apt, she mused.

Mark McCorkle left the squad car to join the departing crowd on the road, which was a morass now. He'd enjoyed the stroll, the mix of demonstrators, the celebrity pundits and their eager acolytes. Most of the participants seemed to exhibit a curious detachment as the crowd began to disperse. Laughter, banter, the midway snack. People seemed to ditch their outrage as easily as they did their placards...

Half an hour after the ceremony in the glade ended, the first buses drove away. An hour later, Sheriff's deputies formed up their mounts and headed back to town. By late afternoon, the road was almost deserted, and the only remnant of the event was the carnival-bright mess: yogurt cups, muddy cardboard, Popsicle sticks and tram-pled blossoms. Even the ever-watchful guardians of the site were nowhere to be seen.

It was as quiet as the grave.

8

November 20
9:30 a.m.

If the scene outside the Pope County Courthouse was
a harbinger of the media attention the upcoming case
would command, it hardly looked good for the prosecution. A small encampment of reporters, satellite trucks
and motorhomes milled around the parking lot across
the street from the century-old granite structure. Its
occupants hoped to snatch a glimpse of the alleged per-
petrator, or perhaps glean a snippet or two from the lead
attorneys. Security, especially by Principia's standards,
was unprecedented. Jonas paced outside the glass double
doors, barking at the contingent of deputies, both on
foot and horseback, that he'd mustered for the occasion.
Portable radios and cell phones were ubiquitous.

About ten o'clock, a small caravan pulled up to the
back of the courthouse annex, using the impromptu
barricade erected at the entrance to the building's lot to

avoid scrutiny. A crowd of officers and jail attendants enveloped the vehicle, moving as one in a scrum up the sidewalk and through the annex entrance. Dozens of cameras clicked hopefully, but visual access to the defendant remained obscured.

Inside, participants in the hearing prepared their briefs before Judge Homer Thorndike. Although well-known in Principia, he lived 30 miles west, in the posh community of Twyckenham Hills. Something of a judicial legend, more for his tyrannical disposition than his scholarly reputation at the bar, Thorndike was known to run a tight ship. His long tenure bespoke a utilitarian ruthlessness in the way he presided over his courtroom. Without hesitation, he disabused lawyers on both sides of any illusions as to who was top dog: it was always Homer Thorndike. Lawyerly self-regard had no place here.

Though he usually liked nothing better than to showboat for the press, Thorndike didn't look forward to this case, mainly because someone's ox was bound to be gored. He'd be satisfied to emerge from it with his rather ambiguous reputation intact. And while this might mean walking a fine line between principle and pragmatism, those were skills with which he was well familiar.

He'd need them all here, too. For though Thorndike had always prided himself on his empathy, his compassion, his sympathy for the wretched of the earth, he'd never reckoned on a case like this. He'd tried but failed to kick it into another jurisdiction, owing to objections from the defense. Then he'd tried to recuse himself because his wife, a schoolteacher, knew the victim's family. But the public response was decidedly unreceptive. It might well be a compliment of sorts, Thorndike consoled himself.

So, he was stuck here, just 14 months from retirement, beset by group petitions, calls from *Oprah* and requests for interviews from the *New York Times* and the *Washington Post*. In his younger days, he'd have embraced all the attention eagerly. But, nearing retirement, he welcomed neither the controversy nor revelatory scrutiny. Since this initial uproar had been over a mere preliminary hearing, Thorndike was determined to get through it with dispatch and a minimum of prima donna grandstanding by either side.

Desiring nothing less at this stage, Allen Southworth proceeded to kick off the preliminary hearing with his usual efficiency, bringing forward various material witnesses to establish probable cause for Murder One. And though the evidence presented was circumstantial, the judge swiftly bound Sirkar Swaraj over for trial.

To no one's surprise, the defendant pleaded not guilty but requested no change of venue. The defense, however, moved to have evidence struck from the initial interview, notwithstanding Stivers' usual meticulous protocol. The motion was denied, and the hearing speedily adjourned. The whole business took less than an hour and a half.

Directly following the proceeding, Allen reached across the aisle to grasp the hand of his old friend, Madison Fulbright, at the defense table. Then the two men drew together in intense, hushed, discussion. Shortly thereafter they parted, having arranged an immediate meeting in the prosecutor's office.

Madison Fulbright reached down, swept his hand along the trough of the candy machine, and grasped for the invisible package. He tore at the wrapper and jammed the Bazooka bubble gum into his mouth. Then he retreated to the concrete balcony overlooking the street, hoping to escape those voracious ants below, not to mention the bedlam issuing from the courtroom.

Anyone leaving the building by the front entrance was immediately swarmed by a frenetic cohort of reporters and photographers. This meant less attention was directed toward him as he perched on the balcony, despite his impressive physique and the symbolic ascendancy he assumed as he grasped the rail, inscrutably regarding the buzzing throng below. Whatever misgivings he may have had at the outset about serving at this trial had been shunted aside by the proffered opportunity.

Damn! He was spotted: Whirring camcorders swiveled skyward, flashbulbs popping as randomly as corn kernels. A few of the more brazen newshawks even attempted to shout questions. Fulbright merely smiled, extended his arm as if in benediction, and withdrew inside to cross swords with the prosecutor.

As Fulbright entered Southworth's office, Allen sat behind his desk, feet up on an indifferently stacked pile of briefs, talking on the phone to Tom Stivers. The detective had just discovered some interesting anomalies in the medical procedure followed in the Rishi Swaraj appendicitis case that might signal gross negligence, if not outright malpractice. Not wishing to give his opponent any unnecessary information, Allen ended the conversation abruptly and waved opposing counsel toward a stuffed chair in front of his desk.

"Thanks for coming, Mad-Dog," he said. "Some circus out there, eh?"

"You got that right," Fulbright groaned. "But Thorndike handled it all well. I was pleasantly surprised."

"Me, too," Allen said. "And I hope we can cooperate to keep this trial on task and avoid any unnecessary theatrics that could hurt your client's chances for a fair hearing."

Fulbright grinned knowingly. "I'm sure my client's interests are paramount in your consideration, Allen."

Allen wasn't amused. After an uncomfortable pause: "Shall we cut the bullshit and talk business?"

"That's why I am here." Fulbright popped a gum bubble.

"I hope you know I'm pleased that you're opposing counsel in this case, Mad-Dog. I mean that. This is the sort of case a… less scrupulous attorney might attempt to turn to his advantage."

Fulbright frowned.

"To me," Allen continued, "this is a murder trial, pure but not necessarily simple. It's so full of potential…" he paused momentarily "… ambiguity. I am convinced, in fact, that many more people are guilty here than might reasonably be charged. But you know what, Mad-Dog? I don't think this was your client's idea. I don't even think he's insincere in his version of events, no matter how implausible it seems. I think there's a larger story to tell here that might turn to your client's advantage. He may have been a pawn in this whole thing. You may have a diminished capacity argument working in your favor, as well."

Fulbright sat, expressionless as an idol.

"For example," Allen went on, "since we've ascertained that your client has few financial resources on which to draw, it seems curious to me that he's managed to acquire such august representation as you, my friend."

Fulbright glowered. "By what means my client compensates his attorney is no concern of yours, Allen, unless of course you believe it derives from illegal sources. And I believe you know me better than to assume that."

"Of course," Allen smiled. "Please don't misinterpret my point. I'm not accusing you of anything. But I am curious as to the source of your retainer. Could Theo Carver or the Ganges Mission have anything to do with this?"

"Again, Counselor," Fulbright said, "unless you're bringing charges against my firm, that remains none of your affair. And what have these questions to do with the business at hand?"

"They may have a great deal to do with your client," Allen said, "especially if he's simply a footnote to a larger agenda. Perhaps he was coerced, or somehow became a foil for a political movement that has some... interest... in widow-burning..."

"Don't blow smoke at me, Allen," Fulbright shot back. "My client's sincerity is the primary issue here...

his religious conviction. His guilt or innocence goes to his state of mind. And I believe him when he tells me Roop Kumar's death was not only voluntary but, at least in his mind, spiritual."

"Is that what you're prepared to argue, Counselor?"

Fulbright smiled, inscrutable.

"Because, if you are," Allen leaned back on his chair, "you'll have a very tough row to hoe, I guarantee you that. There may be *demonstrably* darker motives at play here."

"Mr. Prosecutor," Fulbright replied, "religion is a powerful agent of the mind. And you know nothing about his religion. You know nothing of his perspective. You know nothing of his state of mind."

"I know all I *need* to know," Allen said. "And we're not in India; we're in Indiana, where what your client did was both criminal and horrific."

Fulbright smirked, "We're not going to argue the case here, Counselor. I'm a busy man, so *get* to the *point*."

Allen lit another cigarette. "I have reason to suspect there are bigger fish than your client mixed up in this, and you'll be apprised of those reasons in discovery. I just wanted you to know that my stance *is* somewhat flexible. If you find that Swaraj was put up to this somehow—duped into taking a fall—I might be willing to consider leniency in exchange for certain...

testimony – prearranged, of course. Think of your client's interest first."

Fulbright bristled. "Know what I think, Allen? I not only think you got squat to back up your suspicions, but you're desperate to avoid a trial."

"More than that," he said, "you know this case is not only going to be hard to *prove*, it'll also be very hard to *win*. People are more culturally sensitive than they used to be, more open to—shall we say—*unorthodox* perspectives that might, even in a relatively unsophisticated community like this one, acknowledge some interaction with the global society."

Allen sneered. "C'mon, Mad-Dog. What do you take me for, some kind of rookie? This is no sensitivity seminar; get serious."

"*You* get serious!" Fulbright grabbed his trench coat and rose to leave. "And I'll take that remark as a compliment."

"Funny," Allen clasped his hands behind his head, "I sure didn't mean it that way."

Defense counsel clenched his jaw and glared at his old friend, who could see clearly for the first time the width of the chasm that was yawning between them.

"See you in court, Counselor," Fulbright said over his shoulder, hand on Southworth's office door. "I'll be there – with bells on."

November 20
1:30 p.m.

Jan Southworth sat stock-still in her car, eyes filling, fixated on the yellow slot marks striping the parking lot. Although the sun shone brightly through the windshield, she didn't shade her brow from the glare.

She'd almost not made it from the medical annex in nearby Granger, so stunned was she by the news. Jan had first noticed the lump in the shower that Sunday when Allen had last been home for dinner—what, only a week ago? She'd tried to talk with him about it then, hoping that he might allay her fears, help her decide. She'd wanted to believe she was a partner in a marriage of equals.

Stricken with fear, she'd put off seeing the doctor for a few days, hoping it would just go away. Classic denial—*Ha, ha, silly me, a little premenstrual fluid retention.* She visited her doctor on Wednesday and was whisked off for a mammogram. On Thursday, she had a biopsy performed. Now, here it was Monday and already the fateful judgment: cancer, rather far advanced, necessitating an immediate mastectomy, to be followed by a grisly regimen of radiation and chemotherapy. Even with all that, the prognosis wasn't good.

All the awful media-implanted images marched through her tortured mind during the intervening days: hair loss, incessant retching, thickets of tubes, backless gowns and cavernous syringes. She was only forty-one and had felt in better health than ever in her life—that is, before being seized by a bout of galloping hypochondria that had paralyzed her days and haunted her nights as she lay alone in her huge bed, open eyes transfixed on the plaster ceiling, searching for answers, blessed relief.

All the new and indispensable questions: should she tell Allen? What should she tell her children? They were surely too young to understand. Should she even risk the impending medical torture, given the grim prognosis she'd been handed? Her odds, if the oncologist was to be believed, were one in three, at best.

Her life with Allen had lately gone sterile, it was true. She felt alienated from him, perhaps beyond reclamation. She loved him. But his behavior—his indifference toward the family; the absences; the sometimes out-of-control drinking; the volcanic fits of profane temper—had persisted, despite his having left the law firm for the prosecutor's office. It was ironic, really, because he continued to insist that he'd made the change for her, for the good of the family. Far as she could see, it was "same shit, different day"—except now he could take the moral high ground again, as noble 'Defender of the People,' while being paid considerably less for his trouble.

Then, there was this new case. The tremendous pressure building and the constant publicity it was already generating seemed to offer cold comfort for her future.

Still, Allen was her husband; they had children together and had once been the closest of friends. Maybe she'd been too quick to judge his behavior and too slow to appreciate the anxieties that came with his job. His lawyering had, after all, given her the palatial home, the country club memberships, her brand-new Lexus, her rarefied status in such a middling town.

Vacillating now, she was uncertain whether two good people had simply "grown apart" or whether she'd been engaged in a Faustian bargain from the very beginning, unconsciously forsaking genuine love for mammon. She'd have to tell him; she had no choice. Besides, she might be surprised. Surely this was a matter that would finally refocus his attention. They would join hands to face the crisis. And with all that to live for, she couldn't die. *I* won't *die! Reason? Or simply another self-generated fantasy... this time to compensate for the terror?*

Suspended on a pendulum swinging between hope and despair, Jan drove to the courthouse, oblivious of oncoming traffic, stop signs, other drivers. The car must have been on autopilot, perhaps driven by a guardian angel? After parking, she finally collapsed, sobbing uncontrollably. For ten minutes, maybe 20, she wept inconsolably, yet without catharsis.

The car radio was on, as it always was, and she gradually became aware of it again: Herman's Hermits' "There's a Kind of Hush." The music transported her back to when she and Allen had first met, dated, and explored each other's mysteries in the privacy of lonely beaches, forest glades, drive-in theaters and parked cars in cornfields or along remote gravel roads. She recalled things only the two of them could know: Memories so sweet—so deliciously, wonderfully, magically intimate—they even now instilled a resolve, a renewed faith in the foundation of their love, ever strengthened by the curing of time and the rearing of their children.

Inhaling deeply, she dried her eyes, swept her auburn hair behind her ears, and began to fix her face—both to conceal her mood and to resurrect some facsimile of the confident teenager she'd once been. Then she flung open the car door and stepped out, anxious to proceed to the encounter before her nerves failed her.

Jan strode to the door of the courthouse annex, smiling as best she might at the employees she knew, even at the jail trustee she didn't know. She took the elevator to the second floor, turned left, and marched down the hall to the prosecutor's office, where she greeted Allen's secretary, Joanie Carter, as if she'd not a care in the world.

Jan complimented her on her sweater, which she'd been given for a birthday present the month before. Trying to put Joanie at her ease she lied, "You must be frazzled over this Kumar case. Allen talks about little else." In truth, after their initial conversation, they'd scarcely spoken about it.

The secretary couldn't have looked more flummoxed. "Oh, yeah, uh-huh. It's been so... *hectic* around here lately. You know, people of all sorts coming and going. Unbelievably busy. Allen seems to be in meetings all the time," she rambled. "I mean, every time I make another appointment, I'm amazed at the number of people involved. I mean experts, *Indian* experts and the like."

"Is Allen in?"

Joanie's face reddened. "Oh, yes," she replied. "But he warned me I was not to disturb him, no matter what." She looked down at her desk and shook her head as if to convince herself of the words she'd just uttered. Then she looked up again, a forced smile etched on her face. "He's very involved, I mean, you know. Busy. *Extremely* busy. But I'll be glad to give him a message." She raised her eyebrows as if in a plea, imploring Jan to take up her offer.

Jan's intuitive antennae sensed oblique deception. Joanie was acting more like a gatekeeper than an old friend. "That's fine, Joanie," she replied icily, "I'll just surprise him."

Joanie knew that further resistance was futile, though she met Jan's stare stoically. As Jan stepped toward the door of Allen's suite, it opened. Laughter—male (Allen's) and female—spilled into the corridor, and a stunning woman emerged: doe-eyed, lithe, disconcertingly youthful, in a leather skirt and tight argyle sweater. She stood in the doorway a moment, concluding the conversation in stunning profile. The words seemed entirely professional, yet the woman was so intense, and Allen's responses were so animated, Jan felt as if she were eavesdropping on an intimate exchange.

The distracted woman glanced up from a sheaf of papers. "Good afternoon," she smiled, and glided from the office.

Joanie busied herself at her desk.

Jan remained behind the half-opened door. She could hear Allen talking on the phone mere feet away. Stunned, like someone who had just received a punch to the solar plexus, she looked back at the secretary, who offered only a weak smile of futile reassurance.

Joanie sees it; Joanie knows. *She tried to protect me from it. It's not all just in my overactive imagination.*

It didn't matter that Allen and that woman—Samantha, was it?—might not be having an actual affair; in fact, the level of intellectual tension between them was so high, Jan was certain they were *not*. Or at least not *yet*. It was the passion—political, professional, personal—that was so telling. They were literally playing with fire and probably didn't even know it.

Desiccated by the backdraft of this revelation, Jan turned and stumbled from the office, before Allen even knew she'd been there.

Madison Fulbright paused briefly on the sidewalk outside the granite courthouse to consume another candy bar before heading for the county jail to speak with his client.

Professional contretemps between egotistical attorneys were hardly unusual; in fact, they were an integral part of the business, the thrust-and-parry. Yet he was uneasy over the dust-up with Allen, his old partner and—more difficult to admit—his mentor. Fulbright also had the sense that his client was indeed an unwitting fall guy. Swaraj's motivations seemed so byzantine: spiritual, political, or financial, perhaps an admixture of all three...

Defense counsel was upbeat about his chances, though. Southworth's case was circumstantial at best and bound to be porous. Eyewitnesses, particularly terrified ones, were notoriously unreliable—Asians no doubt 'all looked alike', to adolescent Hoosier boys, anyway. And what else did the prosecutor have? For Swaraj to have known of the upcoming rite was one thing. But mere knowledge hardly proved his client was even at the scene. And given the political overtones of the case, it would be difficult for Allen to establish a motive for murder.

Fulbright was not without weapons in his own

arsenal, because Allen had no lock on the slipperiest intangible of all: the *girl's* motive. She was conveniently unavailable for interrogation. The defense was prepared to defend the question of volition to the last barricade. No one was capable of crawling into the mind of that dead girl, especially since she might have been emotionally trapped in another time, another place. This was hardly a case of rank pedophilia, after all, but was rather an ancient custom. And even if some overpaid shrink should try to suggest otherwise, Fulbright could always counter with shrinks of his own.

But all this speculation would be moot if the prosecution failed in its primary mission, to prove that his client had not only lit the pyre but had *coerced* that little girl to climb up on it and then forcibly *kept* her there. Still and all, this was lurid fare for a trial. It might be best not to let the jury think too much about the raw evidence, lest they concentrate disproportionately on the mere forensics, rather than the existential facts of the matter.

Gunning his Porsche into the entryway of the large new county jail complex, he found an unusually convenient parking place and, after locking his car, the attorney shrugged the shoulders of his leather trench coat to ensure the proper hang and adjusted his fedora and sunglasses for intimidation mode. Then he walked casually toward the bank of glass doors at the entrance.

Through his own approaching reflection, he saw Carl Peters discussing something intently with Tom Stivers. Peters looked up at the attorney's approach.

Stivers opened the door for Fulbright on his way out. "Good morning, Counselor." Tom saluted with exaggerated formality.

"Good morning, Detective." Fulbright tipped his hat. "You aren't, I hope, departing on *my* account."

Stivers grinned, "No rest for the wicked, as my momma used to say. So, I guess there's none for me, either. But don't worry. The boss is here."

"I hate to settle for second-banana, Tom, but if I have no choice…" He smiled toothily, drawing a chuckle from the detective.

Clutching his monogrammed attaché case, Fulbright shoved through the revolving door into the entryway and grasped the Sheriff's outstretched paw.

"Mad-Dog." The Sheriff smiled affectionately. "How's your poker fund? Haven't had the pleasure of extracting contributions for my retirement lately," he said, referring to their occasional smokers. "I've been eying a big screen TV for the hunting lodge."

"In your dreams, my man, in your dreams." Fulbright's grin widened. "Carl, I'm here to see my client. That is, if you don't mind. Come to think of it, even if you *do.*"

"Touché, Counselor," Carl laughed. "I'll take you back myself."

The defense attorney waited patiently in the small conference room, noting that it was taking an inordinate amount of time to retrieve Swaraj. He scratched a few talking points on his legal pad, sipping the jailhouse coffee Brenda Hughes had brought in.

Another ten minutes elapsed, and Fulbright rose to expedite the process. Just then his client was ushered in, dressed in an orange jump-suit, manacled, followed by Jonas Clevenger and an older Asian gentleman with whom Fulbright was not yet acquainted.

Fulbright said testily, "This is supposed to be a private consultation, Jonas."

"Sorry, Mr. Fulbright," the deputy answered, pointing at the older man, "but your client insists on having Mr. Savarkar here, so you can take that up with him. I'll be right outside if you need me." Then he departed, locking the heavy steel door behind him.

"Mr. Savarkar?" Fulbright extended his hand and introduced himself. "I'm Madison Fulbright. I've been retained to represent Mr. Swaraj."

The man replied, "I am fully aware of that fact, Counselor, since it is *I* who happened to retain you."

"I don't understand." Fulbright hated surprises.

"I said, I am the one responsible for your retainer," Savarkar repeated.

Since receiving his $10,000 retainer in a courier-delivered envelope, Fulbright had assumed the source was Theo Carver and his Diversity League. He now realized he didn't really know with whom he was dealing. Worse, the whole setup had an unpleasant odor about it.

The man before him was Indian, he guessed, about 70; he wore a white Nehru hat and jacket. His skin was the tone of sallow leather, deeply crevassed, possibly contributing to an erroneous estimate of his age. He was short—about five-and-a-half feet—and cadaverously thin. His eyes were hidden from view behind the opaque lenses of dark glasses. His manner seemed enigmatic, to be sure; even a little sinister, and difficult to read. Fulbright felt instinctively repelled by this Savarkar, though he would labor not to let it show.

Fulbright said, "So you're my mysterious benefactor? Whom do you represent, and what, if any, is your connection with Carver's organization?"

"I represent sympathetic members of the Ganges Mission," Savarkar said. "You have heard of it, I trust. As for Mr. Carver, suffice it to say he and I have, for lack of a more precise word… a *collegial* relationship."

Indeed, the lawyer was well-aware of the Ganges Mission. It was, as far as he knew, a cultural gathering place for the small Indian community of Pope County. Beyond that he knew little, as its practices and activities seemed hopelessly mysterious to most of the locals, despite rumors as to its growing topographical footprint on the landscape. Most were aware that the mission had also become something of a sub-cultural cynosure, drawing pilgrims from all over northwest Indiana for special events. Yet its just-revealed link to Carver made the connection between the two seem vaguely illicit to Fulbright. Never one to relish an ambush, he stiffened.

He said, "As much as I appreciate your trust in my legal skills, I must be alone to speak with my client."

"I'm afraid that will not be possible," Savarkar smiled.

"Excuse me? The fact that you claim responsibility for my retainer does not *entitle* you to be here."

"That is true enough," the old man said. "But you see, your client *wants* me to be here, both to act as his advisor, and yours as well. But if you don't believe *me*, why don't you ask *him*."

Swaraj nodded his head twice and wrung his hands. "*YES! YES! It is true!*" he wailed, shaking his head. "I *want* Mr. Savarkar here to guide me. I *cannot* proceed *without* him. I *cannot!*"

Dumbstruck, Fulbright stared at the man as if he'd just blurted out a confession.

"Now then, Counselor," Savarkar cast an opaque

smile, "shall we proceed? First, in your opinion, how stands the case for Mr. Swaraj?"

The lawyer knew few details yet. Discovery had barely begun; the Sheriff's department's investigation was ongoing. He informed Savarkar that tire molds had been made, and that several eyewitnesses had apparently identified Swaraj from a lineup. Credit card receipts connected the accused to the purchase of 20 long rods of bamboo from a local lumberyard. Most damning of all, perhaps, his client's fingerprints had been lifted from the *sati* stone itself. Then there was Swaraj's irregular choice of hospitals, the questionable medical care given to his ailing son, and the defendant's suspicious appropriation of the girl's dowry.

Fulbright turned to address the prisoner himself, finding his demeanor very different from that he'd earlier displayed. At that time, Swaraj had seemed disoriented, fearful. Today, despite the initial discomfort and outburst, he seemed calmer, more collected, perhaps even… rehearsed.

Of course, he'd been present at the rite, Swaraj said; he was the father of the deceased. Bamboo was traditionally used to help the pyre hold its form and assist in incineration. He didn't deny placing the stone, which was, after all, a memorial to the dead couple. Retention of the dowry was customary for widowed households, he explained, notwithstanding the duration of the union or the youth of the widow. Yes, it was true that the choice of hospital and doctor for his son might seem unusual, but Mr. Savarkar had been in America longer; Swaraj presumed he was more knowledgeable in this regard, and he had taken Mr. Savarkar's direction in the matter.

Savarkar was silent during the exchange, though he listened intently. Once the attorney finished, the old man spoke again. "I hope this has been helpful to you, Mr. Fulbright. Now may I ask about your strategy?"

Fulbright explained that the evidence in the case was, at best, circumstantial, and the eyewitnesses could probably be nullified in cross examination. And since Swaraj hadn't denied the allegation that he'd been present, the prosecution might be neutralized.

The evidence as to motive, while potentially troublesome, required assumptions that would be difficult to substantiate. Had the defendant willfully killed his own son through neglect? In the pursuit of monetary gain, had he sacrificed a young girl afterward? If so, had it been willful? Was it any more credible to suppose that a grief-stricken widow, of any age, might choose to join her husband in death? Finally, and perhaps most importantly, if Swaraj were guilty, why weren't the girl's parents pressing the matter and demanding his head? Considering all this speculation, Fulbright didn't think it necessary to confide his backup strategies to his client's *eminence grise*.

Savarkar sat perfectly still, peering at the attorney, legs crossed, hands clasped in his lap. Then he said abruptly: "So, judging from your synopsis, Mr. Fulbright, one might conclude that our prospects are rather good."

"I think so," the counselor replied. "They're certainly good enough to implant reasonable doubt in the minds of most jurors. And at the risk of seeming immodest, I will tell you that my rapport with juries is well known."

"That is gratifying to hear, Counselor," the old man smiled enigmatically, "for you see, Mr. Swaraj wishes to mount rather a… different defense from the one you seem to have in mind."

Fulbright was confused. "I'm afraid I don't understand. I just told you: our ground is solid, with every prospect for success."

"I didn't misunderstand you, sir," the man said. "But this provides even more reason to attempt a more ambitious defense stratagem, one that will also free Mr. Swaraj, along with our community, from any *stigma* associated with the sati. Our desire—that is, Mr. *Swaraj's* desire—is that you stipulate to most of the evidence— except any which suggests the murder of Roop, as that was a volitional, sacrificial act of ritual suicide."

"*Excuse* me?"

"As many of us at the Mission, along with those in our underrepresented communities, see it," the old man expanded, "the reaction of the authorities to this issue is not only arbitrary and bigoted, but we believe *unconstitutional* as well." Savarkar leaned back and fumbled in his jacket pocket. "Whether or not Westerners approve of ancient Hindu religious traditions is immaterial to the more pertinent question, to wit: did this young woman possess the inherent right to practice her religion as she saw fit? And what right has the government to interfere with her free exercise thereof?"

"You can't *do that*, Mr. Swaraj!" Fulbright faced his silent client full on. "If we stipulate in any way that you had prior knowledge of Roop's intent, and the prosecution can demonstrate a solid financial motive for you to have done so, you may well be convicted."

"And if it is the *truth*?" Swaraj asked. "Then I must stand before God and declare it so. I cannot condemn my *faith*, my ancestors."

"Listen," Fulbright tried again, "what Mr. Savarkar is saying is *madness*. We will, in effect, be doing the prosecutor's work *for* him. Whether the act itself was good or evil needn't even become an issue, unless we're forced to make it one."

Savarkar now injected himself into the exchange: "Mr. Swaraj is not ashamed of what happened. In fact, he was laboring under the impression—mistakenly, as it happens—that America is a free country, where the authorities stay out of religious matters. The legal system has a right to punish murder. But as Mr. Swaraj perceives it, this was not *murder*. This was an act of love, an act of sanctification. An *apotheosis*, as it were." He inserted a cigarette into a long holder and lit it.

Trying to conceal his intense agitation, Fulbright said, "If we adopt this strategy, this case will turn from a murder trial into a political circus. Mr. Swaraj will be vilified as a freak, a scoundrel, and a barbarian besides. He will be ruined, personally and financially."

Savarkar's smugness drained from his face. Grimacing, he enunciated each syllable that followed with particular care: "The Mission shall assist Mr. Swaraj with his financial burden. As for accusations of 'barbarity,' let me remind you that Indians were building palatial monuments in an age when most Europeans were living with their swine in straw hovels. Indians were unraveling the mysteries of the cosmos while Europeans fretted, they might topple from the earth if they traveled too far west."

He leaned provocatively toward Fulbright. "Do not, I repeat, *do not* patronize me. If you do your job half as well as I have been assured you can do it, then the label 'barbarian' just might actually – and properly – be reassigned to the prosecution. Now, let us have done with this tactical drivel. Do the job you have been paid to do."

With that Savarkar rose and rapped on the steel door. Jonas opened it wide.

Savarkar said, "We will talk again soon, Mr. Fulbright. Please keep me apprised of any future developments." Then, with his arm around the waist of the suffering Mr. Swaraj, he left.

PART III

Winter

"Is this it?" the little girl asked, wide-eyed. "Is this Roop's bedroom?"

"Yes, my child," the young woman said. "Just think of her last days here, knowing she would soon be in heaven with her beloved."

"But wasn't she awfully afraid?"

"I suppose, little one, but holiness has its price, and she was the *sati mata*."

Tears welled in the child's eyes as she was led away to make room for those in line behind her, queuing to take it all in as she had: the small bed, bedecked daily with fresh flowers, Roop's beaming face staring back from photographs on the walls. Candles and incense burned around the clock in the nascent shrine.

As he stood with the Sheriff watching the house from a squad car, Allen knew that the *chunari* ceremony was the beginning, not the end, of the spectacle: Clamorous parades choked the narrow streets of Principia now; tacky floats covered with spray-painted Kleenex in lieu of flowers depicted the putative rapture and dignity of the sati mata.

Theo Carver had been busy. He'd enlisted local school children in the campaign to globalize perspectives and "deconstruct Western thresholds of injustice." Young girls Roop's age toted signs and mouthed slogans in support of the dead child's right to "new expressions of spiritual love." Allen made it clear that all this rankled his conservative disposition, and that he found this aspect of things especially hard to take.

He had also never been so focused – or so annoyed – in his life. His secretaries trod carefully these days, wary of swings of temperament coinciding with the stress of the marathon protests.

Meanwhile, it appeared that his wife needed space: to think, to plan, to cope. Jan had grown up on a farm, where women always keep the books, and she still paid all the bills. So, she might be able to keep Allen ignorant of the added medical expense for now. This was critical for Jan, for the one thing worse than the cancer was the prospect of his pity. Pity would destroy any spirit to fight, or any chance at genuine communication with Allen. He would find out, in due course, she hoped, but on *her* schedule.

So, she swept up the children for an extended adventure, as she called it. Her parents wintered in Florida; where they would spend Christmas with them and at Disney World, see all the sights, stay on into the spring if necessary. Jan had already scouted a Cancer Treatment Center near Orlando.

She told Allen, "It's not good for the children to be exposed to this kind of constant, heavy media attention. None of us will have a private moment."

Allen spoke with them all intermittently now. He even missed them at times when he found himself knocking around the big empty house like a stone in a metal drum. Still, he agreed it was better this way. "Thank you," he kept telling Jan. "It's so much easier, knowing you and the kids are having a great time." The stress would have been intolerable with too much guilt added to his mix.

"You're a saint, Jan," he told her.

"Make me proud," she said fiercely. It seemed practically a command, he thought.

For Allen, everything now revolved around the case. He was mired in it, and while he wished he could say all the work was fueled by laudable motives, he knew better. At the best of times, he blazed with idealism. Dammit, this case *was* worth winning...on principle *alone*.

Nonetheless, a starkly cynical voice in his inner ear

kept reminding him of the rewards at the finish line: the money pot; the cushy consultant interviews; the book deals; the celebrity buzz. Or should that be notoriety? Judging from the attention this one-horse town was getting from the rest of the world, his golden fleece was real enough.

Allen couldn't afford to worry about his adversary. He knew that in Madison Fulbright he faced the very best. Allen had been close to his protégé, both as colleague and friend. Still, he couldn't ignore the sad truth that they hadn't spoken more than a few words since ending their partnership.

In any case, there'd be plenty of time for fence-mending once the verdict was in, and Allen's reputational payoff from it was guaranteed. All he had to do was prove, beyond a reasonable doubt, that Swaraj had both motive and opportunity to murder his daughter-in-law, and that he had, in fact, done it. The case for the prosecution had eyewitness testimony and considerable circumstantial evidence to prove the defendant had much to gain from the girl's demise. Mad-Dog would have his hands full rebutting it. Besides, the grisly nature of the crime was a prosecutor's dream. Somehow though, he struggled to keep overconfidence at bay. If the O.J. Simpson case had demonstrated anything; it was that—given the right jury—nothing was impossible. Still, all-in-all, his prospects looked good.

Once it began, the trial seemed almost anticlimactic. Thorndike banned TV cameras from his courtroom. The gaggle of journalists admitted in lieu of the cameras grew bored, and could be seen yawning, glancing at their watches, questioning their bosses' commitment of time and money to the Kumar affair.

A parade of witnesses came forth to implicate Swaraj in one way or another. Rick Jaansen confirmed the cause of death as well as the presence of indefinable quantities of opium in the child's scorched tissues. Tire mold experts tied the defendant's car to the scene. Dr. Tata from Prairie View Hospital testified as to the cause of Rishi Kumar's death and the impact of the added traveling time on the efficacy of treatment. Bank experts attested to Swaraj's swift appropriation of his son's bank account on the day of his death.

Fulbright's cross-examination was uncharacteristically lackluster. Essentially, he conceded the prosecution's reading of events, seemingly content to cast doubt on the inferences drawn from them. Of course, Mr. Swaraj had been in the glade that morning; it was his son's funeral. Yes, he probably could have and, perhaps, should have found a closer hospital. But his judgment had been clouded by the intensity of the moment. Yes, he'd withdrawn money, for he had no insurance, and

Indians, unlike many Americans, take debt as a serious matter. And though it was true that Dr. Tata had, rather mysteriously, neglected to bill him, Swaraj had had no way of anticipating that generosity in advance. Nor had he felt compelled to reinterpret the gracious gesture afterwards.

As for the girl, the autopsy results could in no way determine whether she had mounted the pyre voluntarily or had been placed upon it. Rick Jaansen had to admit as much but offered his own speculation as to the purpose of the bamboo staves that littered the site— speculation to which Fulbright promptly objected. His speculation was stricken from the record as insupportable. But given the state of Roop's remains, the coroner couldn't definitively contradict Swaraj's claim that the "marriage" hadn't been consummated.

Curiously, Allen observed, his opponent was making his job unexpectedly simple, even easy. All that remained for him to do was to put his eyewitness on the stand, place the case in a neat little box, tie a bow, and hand it to the judge and jury.

April 12
1:00 p.m.

Allen noticed that Ted Polanski had been on an unmistakable slide since the event. He'd gotten death threats, cryptic messages, and vague intimidation from, as yet unknown sources. Carl Peters had provided a police cruiser to guard the boy's home, but its deterrent effect had been minimal.

Reporters greeted the young man at school with flashbulbs and shouted queries. Demonstrations destined for the courthouse invariably wended their way first around his block and up his own Jefferson Street, reaching a crescendo as the marchers passed the Polanski place, all eyes riveted on the home. Ted's parents had listed it with a realtor.

But hard as things had been for Ted, they'd been even worse for his buddy. Tim Scanlan had moved in with relatives out of state, dropped out of school and avoided attention as best he could. He'd taken to drinking heavily, driving recklessly and gambling impulsively. And Ted hadn't spoken to his friend in months.

Not surprisingly, as Ted's other friends began to avoid him, he grew morose, then severely depressed. His parents provided professional therapy to prevent his buckling under the weight of criticism and public scrutiny. Yet he had little choice but to persevere, for to recant his testimony would mean forfeiting what self-respect remained, as well as liberating the criminal who'd murdered that little girl. "Unthinkable," he told Allen, especially, since he blamed himself and his buddy for failing to intervene. He had no excuse, save the obvious: the stark terror of the moment. And whatever the future held for him couldn't possibly be worse than what *she* had suffered. To give in now would have been to go against everything he'd ever been taught or believed in. So, when the day finally came to testify, Ted welcomed it—not only to see justice done, but to gain some blessed personal peace, he said. His plans to attend school in Ann Arbor now stillborn, he now planned to attend classes at a local community college in Michigan.

Allen had long ago decided against calling the more nervous, less predictable Scanlan. Ted Polanski was a solid, if above average, student: a good kid who would likely appeal to the jury. Finally, here was an average citizen with no political ax to grind, no agenda to pursue, just a harrowing story to tell.

The witness cleaned up well. He was clean shaven, his hair trimmed and brushed back. The effect was reassuring, both to himself and to the prosecution team. Calmly, with purpose, he strode to the dock. With great solemnity, he placed his right hand on the Bible, made a special effort to stand fully erect and professed his intention to tell the truth…whole and nothing but, so help him God.

Allen calmly walked Polanski through the events of that early morning in November. Everything had been painstakingly scripted in terms of the sequence of inquiry and the depth of his responses. Well-coached, the witness seemed to grow calmer in his role, reciting the lines much as Allen had hoped he would.

Allen had asked Samantha to note the highlights of the witness' testimony, Fulbright's objections and the emotional reactions of the judge. She had a fetish for thoroughness and dispassionate critique that might provide him needed perspective.

During a short recess, she went over her notes with Allen: "The young man set the scene very well, I think. The dimensions of the pyre, the sound (prayers drums, cymbals), scents (incense, lotus), approximate numbers of the crowd. He identified Roop from the poster without hesitation. He established her movements—three times around the mound. Then," she flipped several sheets on her steno pad, "he picked out Sirkar Swaraj from the defense table as the man who helped Roop onto the pyre."

"Sounds safe enough so far." Allen shrugged. "Nothing for Fulbright to challenge there."

"That's right," Sam agreed. "But he *did* object when you tried to establish her state of mind as calm and dreamy."

"Yeah," Allen said. "I knew that might be a problem, but I had to tie in the presence of opioids in her bloodstream somehow."

"And I noticed a pattern here, Allen," Sam said.

"Fulbright starts to challenge the moment the *emotional* stakes are raised. Look." She used her gold pen as a pointer, cross-referencing the notes she spread out in front of him: "Jurors one, three and five are already blowing their noses surreptitiously as the boy describes Swaraj lighting the pyre, the spectators applying accelerant—and *bang*! Objection—*liquid* into the flames. Spectators offer flowers and gifts, yada yada."

She waved her right hand and rushed on to the next thought. "By the time Roop panics amid the flames, Jurors one, three and five are weeping openly, and two and four have started to sniffle. Even the *Judge* is overcome and averts his eyes from the witness to paw his robes for a tissue."

Allen smashed his palm with his fist. "Priceless! Old Stoneface has a heart after all!"

"If only," Sam tapped his wrist gently, "*he* had a vote."

"Naturally," Allen shrugged. "After that point, Fulbright was up and down like a jack-in-the-box."

"Exactly," Sam confirmed. "Mob—*objection*—becomes *assembly*; ugly—*objection*—becomes *agitated*. The foreign shouting is understood by its tone—and again he challenges that as speculation."

"Should have seen those coming a mile away," Allen said. "We'll have to make sure we don't give him those sorts of openings with McCorkle; it disrupts our rhythm. Great job, Sam."

Samantha closed her pad, removed her glasses and flashed a stern admonition.

"No hubris, Counselor."

April 12
3:30 p.m.

After the recess, Madison Fulbright rose to cross-examine the witness. As usual, Allen thought, Fulbright was dressed to intimidate, and his flawless Armani suit hung perfectly on his imposing frame.

For the first few seconds, Fulbright merely gazed at Ted Polanski. At last, he asked: "Young man, why did you and your friend not try to *stop* the spectacle in the woods?"

The boy squirmed in the wooden chair. "Well, at first, we didn't know what we were looking at," he said. "I mean, it's not every day you see a... cremation... especially in the woods...in Indiana. It was... like... out of a horror movie. We didn't know how to react, or even whether we should do anything besides keep our mouths shut. We were scared."

Allen nodded to himself. *Scared*, as any sentient creature would be, given the circumstances.

"Uh-huh, so, then, you're telling this court—" Fulbright's voice grew louder, "—that you and your friend placed your own safety ahead of not only the life of Roop Kumar, but of justice itself, essentially allowing the perpetrators of this alleged atrocity to escape?" He cast a glowering glance at the jury. "Is that right?"

"Well, uh, no, I mean, not really," Ted said. "You're kind of twisting everything up. It was just that—you know—just that we'd never seen or heard anything like this before. We just didn't know *what* to do. There were two of us and a big bunch of them."

Again, a reasonable response. Allen offered an encouraging half-smile to the witness.

Then the boy added a thought he and Allen hadn't discussed before: "I mean... we had our families to think about."

Christ! Allen's throat tightened. How many times had he coached the man—*answer the question that's asked and that question only!*

"Your families?" Fulbright turned on the witness, his eyebrows arced in mock astonishment. "Do you mean that, in the middle of this hideous event, you had time to consider your *families?*" The cynicism in Fulbright's voice was scathing. "Do you mean that you would have been more comfortable knowing your community is home to what you thought might be a mysterious coven of Satan-worshipers roaming the woods *murdering little girls?*"

"Of course not!" Mack insisted. "But we didn't know *who* saw us, or *who* those people even *were.*"

"Then you thought you'd talk your folks into moving

304

out of town to avoid the danger…" the attorney stated matter-of-factly.

"No, not really," Mack replied sheepishly.

"How, then," Fulbright pursued the issue, "were you planning to protect yourself… and your *families*… from this… *menace,* if you were unwilling to go to the police *and* unwilling to warn your parents?"

"I don't know." Mack shook his head. "You see, uh, like, hindsight is twenty-twenty, you know? We were… like… planning to call the police, it was a matter of timing."

"By the way, Mr. Polanski," Fulbright asked, almost as an afterthought, "Where *is* your buddy, Tim Scanlan? Is he in this courtroom??

No. I don't think so."

"Is he in town?"

"I don't know."

"Is he even in the state?"

"I couldn't say." Ted folded his arms.

"Why is it, do you suppose," Defense Counsel continued, "that he hasn't come forward to testify?"

"He *did.*"

"Really!" Fulbright feigned surprise. "Then why is he not here to verify your account?"

"I guess you better ask Mr. Southworth about that," Ted said. He looked desperate to end the torment. But Fulbright wasn't finished.

Allen finally objected to the line of questioning, which involved issues beyond the ken of the witness. Judge Thorndike mercifully blocked that avenue of exploration.

"Now then, Mr. Polanski," Fulbright continued, "can you describe in detail the clothes Roop Kumar was wearing on the morning she died?" Allen took notice of the new formality in Fulbright's address to the witness. Blankly, the boy looked to the prosecutor like an actor hoping for a prompt. Allen gritted his teeth. *Come on, come on! The flowing red robe embroidered with gold; her lower face obscured by a scarlet veil*—he'd been over it so often with the witness he could recite it himself.

"I-I'm not really sure," Polanski said. "It was pretty dark and there was so much confusion…"

Allen fingered his own red silk tie, but the witness seemed possessed with the pure panic of a condemned prisoner fingering a hangman's noose.

"Come now, sir!" Fulbright pressed. "You have provided an account with some of the most lurid and remarkable detail, about the fire and the deceased's position on the bier, and the fluid spread by the spectators, even the nature of the girl's screams. It was a huge fire. There must have been plenty of light to illuminate the girl atop it. Surely you can tell us how she was dressed."

Allen objected. "The witness has answered the question and is being badgered."

Thorndike was unmoved. "The witness will answer the question."

"Well," Ted sighed, "I'm pretty sure her dress was all white, with silver or gold thread around the edges. It was tied at the waist… with a hood, I think."

Allen winced. "Really?"

"I think so."

"Well, you're *half*-right, Mr. Polanski," Fulbright said. "There was such a garment, but the girl wasn't wearing it that morning. It is, in fact, the dress in which the deceased appears in over twenty national magazines, as well as on national television."

He reached into a portfolio and withdrew the picture in question, much enlarged for effect, and placed it in evidence with the appropriate documentation as to its source and date of publication. "But the lady in question was wearing a red garment, not white. So much for your powers of observation, young man."

Ted glanced at Allen, who quickly broke off eye contact and looked down at the table, head shaking.

Still, defense counsel wasn't finished. "Are you aware," Fulbright said, "that the very garment you see in this picture still hangs in a closet at the home of the defendant? Now, how would you explain that?"

"She might have had two of them?" Ted offered weakly.

Fulbright pressed on: "Now, sir, will you please describe some of the other participants in this drama— for instance, the men who allegedly helped the defendant return the deceased to the pyre. Or perhaps, the men who held her down. Or maybe the person who handed the torch to the defendant, or—"

"Objection!" Allen stood up. "Counsel is badgering the witness!"

"Overruled."

"—or, even, those who splashed liquids onto the fire. Surely those fearsome sword-bearers are etched in your memory."

"I don't know if I can," Ted offered, almost as a whine.

Defense counsel grinned and lifted his eyebrows. "But if what you say is true, those people are at least as guilty as my client. You had no way of knowing at the time that Sirkar Swaraj, the one man you *can* identify, was the girl's father-in-law, did you? Then why is it that his face is the only face you can recall? Or—do most Asians all *look alike* to you, Mr. Polanski?"

"Objection, Your Honor!" Allen barked. "With no basis in fact, Mr. Fulbright is implying that the witness has a racial motivation to identify the defendant. That is contemptible."

Thorndike rubbed his glistening forehead. "Sustained, Mr. Southworth. The jury is instructed to

disregard the last question. You may proceed, Mr. Fulbright – it is to be hoped, in a more civil tone."

"Surely, Judge." Defense counsel leaned back against
his table as if relaxing. "I just have one more question,
Mr. Polanski. Why didn't you intervene in this affair?"

"Excuse me?" Ted shifted in the witness chair again.

"Objection!" cried Allen. "The witness has already
been asked and has answered this question."

"Overruled."

"Exception," Allen called out.

"Noted," the Judge averred. "The witness will answer
the question."

"I asked," said Fulbright, "why didn't you intervene?
I mean, there you were, two experienced hunters with
loaded firearms, witnesses to what you regarded as an
unforgettable *atrocity*, and you both just *stood there*?
Explain yourself, young man!"

"I-I don't know. I—"

"I repeat. *Why was that Mr. Polanski?*" Fulbright
bellowed.

I guess we were both just too scared," Ted's voice
cracked. "We just choked, I guess."

Virtually the same answer he'd given the first time
he'd been asked the question, Allen noted, but somehow
now—after holes had been punched in his credibility—
it seemed like a terrible admission of failure and weakness. It made Ted Polanski appear entirely in the wrong.

Madison Fulbright straightened himself to full height, once again hooked his thumbs in his vest and stared piercingly at Ted. Then, grinning like the Cheshire Cat, he wagged his huge head slowly and waved a hand gently. "I have no more questions of this… bystander, Your Honor." Then he turned on his heel and walked to the defense table.

Allen requested a recess; he knew he'd been badly bruised.

April 12
6:00 p.m.

The Pope County Prosecutor held open the door to *Monique's* and followed Samantha silently to their reserved table. Their usually playful banter was absent today, for he'd committed the cardinal sin of the over-ambitious attorney: reckless cockiness. And there'd be the devil to pay for it, he knew.

Once the appetizers had been ordered, the two fell to serious conversation.

"How bad was it?" Allen asked, though he knew the answer.

Sam minced no words: "Bad as it gets. On a scale of one to ten, I'd give it a bad eleven."

Allen frowned.

Sam said, "To prove Swaraj deliberately murdered that girl is going to be tough, now that your sole witness has been compromised. Any chance of Fulbright calling Scanlan?"

"After today, he doesn't really need him," Allen groaned.

Sam gently pounded an open palm with a clenched fist as she pondered alternatives. "In any case, you've got to shift the focus from whether the act was voluntary to the propriety of the ritual itself."

Allen shook his head balefully. "I've tried like hell to avoid the broader questions, because it's bound to politicize things even more than they are now. Then they'll have all the advantages, organizationally, politically—"

"Morally?" Sam finished his sentence with a quizzical right eyebrow raised.

"What's your point?" Allen picked at his salad.

"My point is what it's been all along," she said. "The only reason people like Carver operate with such impunity is that overly sensible attorneys like you choose the path of least resistance. You'd rather punt than go for the short yardage." She rolled her eyes. "God, it's come to this. I've been reduced to American football analogies. And it isn't even *real football.*"

"I'm glad *someone* feels like joking," Allen sighed. "But I'm uncomfortable with the morality argument in the first place. Hell, who isn't? Who's to say what's moral and what's not anymore? I mean, these people have their own reality, their own morality. And lord knows my own record on that score isn't perfect." He sawed absently at his steak, avoiding her eyes.

"You're not exactly an ax murderer," she teased.

"Maybe not. But as Robert Louis Stevenson once said, all men have thoughts that would shame hell."

"Would that make you Jekyll or Hyde?" she quipped, not even looking up. When she did so an instant later, their eyes met. A long moment passed. "Well, it *is* hard to control one's thoughts," she said. "Anyhow, I know whereof I speak."

Allen instantly picked-up on the opening, but how should he proceed?

"Sam, I have to tell you something..."

"Not now, Allen, please, this isn't the time or place," she forcefully whispered. "Anyhow, I'd hate to think you'd be ashamed. I'm certainly not." Then she offered an unconvincing smile, squeezed his hand, then let it go.

He said, "and moral high ground has to be held, doesn't it—even if at enormous cost to the troops. But sometimes the troops are *that* close—" he held a thumb and forefinger a micron apart – "to insubordination."

"Agreed," she said, eyes lowered. "But does that mean we operate from the same set of absolutes?" She looked up and caught his gaze. "Are our principles mere illusions to be redefined and trotted out in accord with personal morality swings? Or are there *no* absolutes—just ephemeral will-o-the-wisps that flee before the searing logic of your lawyerly bullshit."

Allen blinked, surprised.

"I'll make you a deal, Allen." She placed her fork on the plate with a trembling hand. "If you won't let some misplaced sense of shame interfere with your obligation to that little girl, I won't either."

A contract was implicit somewhere in her words, he realized. They smiled at each other across the table, Allen feeling something like regret, that they both were willing to step back from the precipice of seduction, back into the safer, more prosaic, yet blessedly diverting refuge of abstraction.

"So," she said, straightening her shoulders, "you'd better get with it, Mr. Prosecutor. Your eyewitness was well-nigh nuked this morning. You have no choice but to exploit your alternate strength: *fear*. You must make those jurors ask themselves what kind of country they want; you must convince them *their* future is at stake."

"You'll have to conjure up a world commanded by diversity zealots, who use their multicultural chain mail as shields." She looked him straight in the eyes. "Someone has to throw down the gauntlet in front of them, Allen, and it might as well be you."

April 6-8

Over the long Easter weekend, the prosecution team sequestered itself on the top floor of the courthouse, preparing to confront Fulbright's suddenly formidable defense case, so one had been surprised when they opted to abruptly rest their own. But there was little more to be gained from the forensic evidence that would sway the jury definitively toward conviction. Ted Polanski had been the only solid evidence of coercion, and he'd been damaged, perhaps irretrievably, by the defense cross.

Taking Sam's advice to heart, Allen now huddled with her and Mark McCorkle, trying to anticipate defense arguments and concoct a plausible counterattack. Allen had decided to keep McCorkle on for a variety of reasons. For one, he was local, familiar with the townspeople and, given the popular disdain in town for snooty ivy league types, his conspicuous underachievement presented a good look to the average citizen and, prospectively, to the average juror. On occasion, McCorkle even had an almost Jimmy Stewart-ish stammering earnestness about him.

Allen had already researched a few prominent iconoclastic scholars to use as witnesses and winnowed the list down to three, one of whom might be called upon in rebuttal. Mark had been indispensable in this task; he'd also been invaluable in shedding insight into the "expert" witnesses Fulbright was expected to call, including Lata Besant and Theo Carver.

By Sunday night Allen found himself, paradoxically, both exhausted and energized by the intellectual vibrancy of the experience. Samantha was a remarkable resource, schooled in the Great Books in a way he himself had never been. But he was a quick study; he absorbed her intense tutorials like a sponge and erected a framework for his attack, augmenting ground-level assaults on the credibility of the upcoming witnesses.

Somehow, they'd managed to ignore the incessant demonstrations outside the old courthouse, aggravated now by evangelical groups joining the battle against "godless paganism." The latter was an unwelcome development, as it threatened to transform the contest from a philosophic battle into a communal one: a context that the feckless press would more easily grasp, Allen thought—and therefore distort.

So, the three crammed to virtual collapse. Finally, Allen thought he could take at least an educated guess as to how Fulbright would proceed.

"Well, I don't get it." Sam said. "Fulbright certainly isn't going to waste time challenging facts he's already conceded."

Allen looked up from writing. "Which leads me to suspect that what he's really going to do is prove you right."

"Come again?"

"I mean," Allen said, "there must be a reason he

gave us so much rope at the beginning. I believe he's going to try to frame this case as being *culturally illegitimate*. Remember, that was your initial impression when I brought you up to speed at dinner."

Mark said, "And make you defend the American judicial system in the process – just like *I* said they might the other day. He's taking the cosmic path."

"That's right," Sam agreed. "It would suit their template exactly."

"And de-legitimize *us* in the process," Allen said.

"They'll say that the fact that we have a Western perspective somehow disqualifies us from forming a judgment, either on the defendant or the ritual."

"And that's not all, Allen," Sam added. "By the time they're through with their case, they plan to place us in a very uncomfortable position."

"Where's that?"

Sam looked down again at the document in front of her. "On the wrong side of history, as intellectual Luddites... rebels against the demographic future, so to speak."

Allen could now see how this case stood in stark relief, in the vanguard of forces demanding affirmation, respect, and credibility. Any failure along those lines would result in discord, even disaster. Allen suspected Theo Carver would be called upon to expound the diversity gospel. Lata Besant would explain sati and the ways in which the State had run afoul of a culturally righteous perspective. Moreover, she might try to explain the rationales for deconstructing Western thought: postmodernism, deconstructionism, and the multicultural movement those schools had generated.

With the help of Sam and McCorkle, Allen now felt much better prepared to joust with those witnesses. And notwithstanding his fatigue, he couldn't wait to have at them.

That was until the following day brought more anti-climax: Fulbright requested an adjournment, telegraphing the possibility that the defense wouldn't even offer its own case.

Thorndike was not amused. "Am I given to understand, counsel, that you do not plan a defense?"

"Perhaps not in the traditional sense of the word, Your Honor," Fulbright replied, with conspicuous deference.

Looking skeptically down over his spectacles, the Judge relented with a gavel whack. "Granted. Court will resume tomorrow at 9:30 a.m."

A short time later, Allen, Sam, and Tom Stivers retired to the oak-paneled library on the second floor of the courthouse. "This isn't right... it's not right," Allen muttered repeatedly to himself, staring blankly at the grounds at the bottom of his coffee cup as he paced the polished hardwood floor.

After draining his own cup, Tom Stivers looked puzzled. "What's not right, our case? Couldn't be going better from where I sit. Even with Polanski's meltdown, this sucker is wrapped up."

"That's exactly what I mean," the prosecutor shot back. "What's the point of their lying down for us? Our case sure wasn't perfect, but in the absence of defense opposition, conviction's a dead certainty. So, what's Fulbright's game?"

Then Samantha deadpanned one soft word almost inaudibly from the other side of the room: *"Mitigation."*

Staring out the window at the street, she'd been uncharacteristically quiet, twirling a pencil between index fingers. "Maybe they plan to make their case at sentencing – perhaps the case we've been suspecting they'd make all along."

Allen was nonplussed. Any lessening of sentence severity would be hugely controversial, especially in this case. "That'd be a tough-sell, Sam. Swaraj wasn't exactly father of the year, not to speak of father-in-*law* of the year. And it's hard to imagine old Thorndike being moved much by character witnesses…"

"You misunderstand, Allen," Sam sighed. "We've been preparing up to now for a politically driven case, so maybe that's exactly what Fulbright plans for the sentencing phase. They have a better chance for mitigation with this Judge than exoneration by that jury. They'd also have a perfect forum in which to showcase this multicultural enlightenment of theirs."

She knew that mitigation allowed a judge to consider any factors that might weigh on a defendant's culpability for a crime, once convicted. Moreover, the universe of consideration was inclusive of anything that might apply to either the offender or the crime.

Stivers scratched his head. "Politics? At a mitigation hearing? Never heard of that before."

Allen started, as if he'd seen a burning bush. "Well, *I* have! That's exactly the tack Clarence Darrow used with Leopold and Loeb. He knew there was no winning with the jury on the merits, so instead he raised *philosophic* objections to capital punishment before the judge – at sentencing. Those two boys, IQ geniuses out to commit the 'perfect murder' of a little boy, were saved by that ploy, and Darrow's arguments against capital punishment gained national traction in the decades that followed. Taking that approach might also explain why Fulbright didn't go for the plea bargain, wouldn't it, Sam?"

"It would at that, Counselor." She lifted her eyes from the spinning pencil. "Good to know all that cultural prep work might not have been for nothing. Besides, I have an idea as to the grounds he may argue."

"Well," Allen smiled, "you sure don't let any grass grow under your feet, do you Sam? OK, I'll bite."

Sam now tapped her temple with the pencil eraser. "They'll argue victim consent, within the context of an overreaching, culturally insensitive, insufficiently multicultural state."

"Huh?" Tom Stivers knit his brow.

But Allen, looking intently straight into Sam's coal black eyes, grinned knowingly. *I get it.*

Stivers said, "Get what? I never heard of Leopold and Loeb before."

The prosecutor and his second riveted to each other in a mind-meld. *History does matter, after all. Or does it?*

April 14
Pope County Courthouse

Three days later, the verdict being foregone, the other shoe dropped. Swaraj was found guilty of first-degree premeditated murder of the child, Roop Kumar. And just as Sam had predicted, at least as much as was clear in a superficial reading of the submitted briefs, the defense was preparing to argue for substantial mitigation of the impending sentence. After arriving together, Sam and Allen waited in the packed courtroom for the proceedings to begin, confident they'd anticipated rightly.

All rose as Thorndike entered and seated himself behind the bench, glancing with quick eye-shifts about the room. He gaveled the proceedings to order, and the broad expanse of Madison Fulbright's suited profile ascended before the seated crowd.

For the moment at least, the setting was utterly

still, even sepulchral, in anticipation of what was to come next. Boisterous activists from all sides who might have otherwise been intent on disruption had been successfully intercepted by Carl's deputies on the courthouse steps.

Homer Thorndike opened: "Are you ready to proceed, Mr. Fulbright?"

"Yes, I am, Your Honor. Thank you, Your Honor."

Allen fretted despite his preparations. Just as Sam had prophesied, his opponent had opted for a novel route to mitigation: victim consent. According to the defense brief, he was prepared to argue that Roop was not only a Hindu wife, but a devout one according to her beliefs – devout enough, evidently, to choose the ancient widow's rite of sati performed here... in Principia, Indiana, USA.

The last several days had grown even more manic, as Allen and company sequestered themselves in preparation, his office reduced once again to a riot of books, computer reprints and journal articles. All now would depend on the pitch, along with Fulbright's adroitness with unprecedented novelty, not to speak of Thorndike's toleration of it. One thing Allen knew above all else: If anyone could pull this off, it would be his old partner.

The Judge sighed, then shoved his glasses up the bridge of his nose and spoke: "I have briefs from the defense and prosecution here before me in this matter of mitigation of sentence; but as I've not attended a philosophy class in forty years, Mr. Fulbright, I must ask you to explain your concerns to me directly, as it applies to sentencing in the case of *Indiana v. Swaraj*. Are you prepared to do that, Sir?"

"I am, Your Honor. If it pleases the Court."

"It does so please," the Judge smiled wanly. "You may begin your opening remarks."

Fulbright walked from behind the defense table and placed himself squarely, if at a respectful distance, before the bench, and began:

"Mr. Swaraj has been judged guilty at trial in this matter, Your Honor. His defense was perfunctory in large part because of the inappropriateness of the trial setting to the assertion of the defendant's essential lack of guilt in this matter."

Allen leapt to his feet, intent on barking his disagreement loudly enough that the entire courtroom audience could hear it: "OB-JECTION, Your Honor. Essence notwithstanding, this says nothing as to the *mountain of evidence* against the defendant."

Thorndike peered intently at Defense Counsel. "He has a point, has he not, Sir?"

A stoic Fulbright continued: "This is not to say the defendant bears no responsibility for what happened in Stickle's glade, but *only* to suggest the incapacity of this court setting to either ascertain the degree of that responsibility or to understand the context in which the event occurred."

"*Only*, Counselor?" the Judge rejoined. "If I didn't know you better, I'd think this Court has just been insulted."

Fulbright knit his fingers together in front of him in an affectation of humility and addressed the Judge again: "Let me be clear, Your Honor. I do not intend to indict these proceedings, the prosecutor's office or Your Honor in this sense... per se; but instead to acknowledge the unprecedented character of the act in question, in this place, at this moment in time."

The Judge replied: "I'm afraid ambient discomfort hardly constitutes grounds for sentence consideration, Counselor. Then again, there appears to be clearly much more to your position than that. This brief reads like an exegesis."

"And for that evaluation," Fulbright apologized, "Please you have both my gratitude and my apology, Your Honor. Please permit me to summarize." Fulbright stepped back, bowed his head slightly and drew breath. "Defense contends that the verdict should be mitigated, if not set aside altogether, based on two major considerations." He cleared his throat audibly.

"The first is that Roop Kumar was, de facto, a married female in the traditional, Hindu, Indian sense of that phrase. She was, after all, an Indian citizen who had engaged in a sacral right of marriage according to ancient tradition. We are prepared to defend this proposition vigorously."

Fulbright now clasped his hands behind his back, addressing the Judge forthrightly. "As such, Roop felt obligated, under an equally ancient Hindu custom which many Indians continue to revere, and to which millions once subscribed, to perform sati in fulfillment of her designated wifely role insofar as the decedent, who had been widowed, perceived that role."

A gasp shot through the courtroom, prompting Thorndike to gavel his standard warning. "That will be enough, ladies and gentlemen. Those unwilling to keep their emotions to themselves will be asked to leave or be escorted from this courtroom. Please continue, Counselor."

Fulbright straightened his tie and upped the volume of his words a bit: "In India, notwithstanding legal prohibitions on child marriage, the notable lack of legal enforcement has resulted in its persistent, and hardly infrequent, practice. According to some sources, nearly one-third of all marriages in the subcontinent are of this variety. Therefore, since Roop Kumar would have been widely considered a wife among neighbors in her homeland, her designation as a child may be said to have been legally displaced by her new station.

"In that sense that she was no longer a child, the defense holds that she was entitled by the First Amendment of the United States Constitution to make her own decisions with respect to religious practice and obligation. Therefore, Your Honor, we will argue under US Code 3592, which is applicable to capital cases in federal court and so merits consideration in this one: that the victim's consent for the sati may be inferred from the rendition of events presented during the preceding trial. And, given that fact, Mr. Swaraj will expect reconsideration as to sentencing, in light of the Supremacy Clause of the United States Constitution which mandates precedence over state statutes in the event the two entities conflict."

"I am well familiar with the Supremacy Clause, Mr. Fulbright."

The hum in the crowd had resumed, yet the Judge's gavel lay strangely still, unused in Thorndike's limp left hand as he stared straight through Defense Counsel. "Her own consent? That is your argument?"

"Not our entire argument, Your Honor."

"I can't wait for the remainder," Thorndike sighed, "especially given *this* opening."

Fulbright's voice rose as he resumed: "The parts of our argument are linked, your honor, in the following sense. Since Mr. Swaraj and the decedent share a common culture with respect to such matters, the defense will argue that, notwithstanding his presence at the site of the sati, the defendant could not have regarded his participation as anything other than the fulfillment of his own role in that same ancient custom.

In short, even if convicted of murder, the defendant did not act murderously *with respect to his intent.* And since the predicate for mitigation will be established for the decedent, so, too, will the question of the defendant's intent be deemed liable for mitigation under federal judicial guidelines."

Allen was transfixed with professional admiration. Fulbright was going for a two-fer, arguing alternative mindsets for both offender and victim which would ensnare the first amendment in the bargain. In other words, if Roop genuinely believed herself a wife, and Swaraj believed her one as well, the substance of their religious belief might become germane after all. How was 'Western Civilization' to judge…?

Thorndike set his head in his hands looking down, fixated on the bench in front of him, as if to deflect any distraction that might impede his absorption of Fulbright's argument. After a lengthy pause, he sighed: "All right, Counsel. Suppose – just to *be* supposing – that I grant such grounds. By what process of Jesuitical sleight-of-hand do you propose to defend the proposition that this child should be, postmortem, transformed into a 'wife' *as recognized by the State of Indiana?*" An expression crossed his face that suggested, to Allen, incurable disbelief.

Fulbright's hands were clasped tightly now, white-knuckled, behind his back, where Allen could see. "On the grounds," he said firmly, "of the Equal Protection guarantees of the Fourteenth Amendment, Your Honor, framed within the First Amendment's guarantee against State interference in the practice of religion. Our popular understanding of marriage is in a state of transition, after all. Its context is now much more inclusive than at any time in the past. By way of contrast, the tradition from which the decedent's union descends is from a storied past that is *millennia* old."

"That hardly speaks to the illegality of the age issue now, does it, Mr. Fulbright?" said Thorndike.

"Well, Judge, we hold that the gravity of child sexual proscriptions does not apply because, as Mr. Swaraj has sworn by affidavit, the union had not been consummated at the time of the incident, and there has been no evidence offered to contravene that assertion. Moreover, given that fact, this sort of unconsummated child marriage is, without question, a custom which has a claim to religious recognition, notwithstanding the prevailing Judeo-Christian bias against it. The only difference in this case seems to be that the '*Other*'" – Fulbright carefully enunciated the word, air-quoting for effect – "is involved.

Defense Counsel looked up at the ceiling, punching his palm in unconscious emphasis. "This is a key point, Your Honor. For our Constitution, by custom, assumes a privileged position for Christians and Jews in, for example, the age and number of marriage participants, which leaves polygamists subject to legal discrimination, out in the constitutional cold so to speak. Whether that is right or wrong, in and of itself, is not for the defense to judge. But in a multicultural nation like America, the State must not be allowed to play favorites."

Fulbright now leveled his gaze straight at the judge. "If what I'm saying is valid, then all is quite simple, really: If Roop Kumar was indeed a wife, in her mind at least, then the sati may well have been a consensual act, and Mr. Swaraj should be entitled to leniency, on the grounds that *his intent* during the incident was to behave nobly by honoring her wishes, in accordance with his beliefs, thus mitigating his actions. To do otherwise would be to uphold the supremacy of the Western paradigm. Consequently, this amounts on its face to an impermissible discrimination under our founding document."

"And you are prepared to present witnesses to back up this claim?"

"Certainly, Your Honor, along with much expert opinion establishing the historical legitimacy of Roop Kumar's marriage in India. Then I shall present witnesses regarding the young lady's psychological frame-of-mind and the multicultural dimension of the defense argument against the aforementioned charge of discrimination."

Allen sighed, wondering if the judge had taken note of Roop Kumar's miraculous post-mortem maturation, via Fulbright, into a 'young lady'.

Thorndike paused for a moment, allowing his forehead to rest in the cradle of his palm. Then he started, looked up, robustly gaveling in the still-buzzing courtroom to silence. "So, if I understand this correctly, Counsel, you plan to challenge the legitimacy of generations of statute law on marriage, the status of minors *and* Constitutional precedents respecting religious freedom, is that right?"

Fulbright smiled broadly at the question and shrugged, "I believe it can be done persuasively, Judge."

"If you say so," Thorndike replied. "But then I must explain at the outset the procedure I will allow."

He cleared his throat. "I think it is no exaggeration to say that this case is *sui generis*. I can recall none even remotely like it, especially argued on these grounds, in all of American jurisprudence. Therefore, it is my intention to permit significant latitude to all sides, more than I would normally countenance, in the examination and cross-examination of witnesses. I will also expect... no... make that *demand,* civility *at all times* between counsels and witnesses, and between the counsels themselves. Is that clear?"

"Very clear, Your Honor." Fulbright ramrodded his posture.

"But this is no history seminar, Counsel. Just keep that in mind. You must carefully direct your inquiry and stay focused."

"Certainly, Judge," Fulbright said, "although we must admit that history informs all events to some extent, does it not?"

"The past is dead," Thorndike growled.

"No, it's not, Your Honor," defense counsel countered. "It's not even past."

Sam's fists clenched: 'Faulkner' she recalled.

Allen thought he heard the Bench emit a soft snort. "It's your funeral, Counselor. Proceed."

April 16
9:10 a.m.

No one can say Lata Besant doesn't dress for a part, Allen mused. Her green sari, nicely accessorized with bangles, rings, and face ornaments, she looked the quintessential Indian matron; yet the illusion was only skin-deep, as Tom Stivers had lately discovered.

As she took the oath, Professor Besant's hand scarcely brushed the proffered Bible. Slowly, with great deliberation, she stepped up to the witness chair, adjusted the drape of her garment like a Luna moth spreading its wings, then descended into the witness chair.

Madison Fulbright approached her with great deference. "Good morning, Professor," he began. "We all thank you for taking the time out of your busy schedule to be with us this morning."

She gave an Olympian nod.

The attorney turned to the jury and established eye

contact. "Professor, will you please detail your credentials for this court?"

"Yes," she replied. "I hold a BA in sociology from Yale University, an MA in psychology from Cornell, and a PhD in women's studies from Oberlin. I have published ten articles on women's issues and have addressed many seminars and forums on issues of interest to women, particularly minority immigrant women in the United States. I am also working on a long-term project in subaltern studies, dealing with matters of post-colonial trauma and neo-colonial exploitation."

Fulbright nodded. "And where are you currently employed, Professor?"

"I am the Chairperson of Women's Studies at Magdalene College."

"And do you have tenure?"

"Of course," she replied, as if surprised at the question.

Fulbright shuffled through a pile of papers on his desk. "Professor, are you acquainted with a practice known as *suttee*?"

"Yes, I am." She flashed an enigmatic smile.

"Would you explain the practice to this court?"

"The word is actually *sati* and is derived from Sanskrit. *Suttee* is a British corruption. Its general translation is 'a virtuous wife,' and it denotes the spiritual status accorded a widow who voluntarily immolates herself on the funeral pyre of her husband."

Fulbright paced steadily between the far window and the vacant jury box. "And can you tell us something about the origin of this practice – in a religious context, I mean?"

The professor cleared her throat, and the courtroom fell silent. "It symbolizes the marriage of the goddess Sati to Shiva against her father, Daksha's wishes. When he failed to invite Shiva to a great sacrifice, the mortified goddess immolated herself out of shame for the way her husband had been slighted. Shiva was so devastated by the loss of Sati, that he relinquished his position as commander of the armies of the gods, which thereby suffered defeat at the hands of demons. The gods, badly needing a remedy, resurrected Sati as Parvati, who married Shiva again, and begat Kartikeya, the great divinity of war. The practice, then, amounts to a re-creation of that sacrifice-resurrection cycle."

"By which you mean committing suicide through burning," Fulbright summarized.

"That's correct," the professor said. "But it's more complicated than that."

"How so?"

"Well," she continued, "in Hinduism, a woman represents the repository of greatest energy. That energy is called *shakti*. It is essential to a man's well-being, just as his management and channeling of it is essential to *her* happiness. They are one spirit, existentially one body, utterly interdependent and inseparable. According to tradition, when a man dies, his wife's status may be transformed in a way commensurate with such sublime intimacy. In other words, the widow may choose to accompany her husband into eternity, to reside with him in a state of eternal bliss. That is the motivation for sati."

"What if," Fulbright said, "a woman is frightened, quite understandably, by this prospect and chooses not to make this spiritual sojourn?"

The Professor looked puzzled. "Why, of course, she may decline to do so. An authentic sati requires that certain conditions be met. For instance, wives who have been unfaithful may not engage in the rite. Neither may those who are menstruating, for they are deemed impure. But most of all, for sati to be legitimate, to be sanctified, it absolutely must not be *coerced*."

"Have there been any cases of coerced sati, to your knowledge?"

"There have always been rumors to that effect from time to time; but you must remember: When the British ruled India, it was supremely in their interest to magnify such claims in order to justify their interference with Indian culture, and expand their influence, while at the same time contrasting alleged Indian 'barbarity' with their own Christian 'piety.' Suffice it to say that since India achieved its liberation from the oppression of the British Raj, there have been perhaps forty cases of alleged sati of any sort, and no successful prosecutions have resulted from these."

"Then, perhaps this case represents a real precedent here in the United States?"

The Professor frowned. "I am afraid that, yes, perhaps this is so."

"Now, Dr. Besant, we have heard testimony from the coroner that opiates were detected in the tissue of the deceased. Do you recall that testimony?"

"Certainly."

"Is this, then, indicative of coercion?" Fulbright asked.

"I don't think so, Mr. Fulbright," she smiled. "Such substances are quite common in South Asian rituals. Indeed, it would have been more remarkable if there had been *no narcotics* present."

"You mean in terms of the cultural authenticity of the rite..."

"Exactly."

Fulbright turned to his table to retrieve a folder. "Your Honor, may I present these articles attesting to the latter point in evidence?"

Thorndike nodded, and head down, pacing again, Fulbright proceeded. "Wouldn't you agree, Dr. Besant, that the average American citizen might consider this practice extreme, even cruel?"

The professor smiled and turned to the judge, as if

on cue. "That is an understandable reaction from the perspective of your average American citizen, that is to say from a *Eurocentric* vantage point."

"Why would, in your opinion, that be an inaccurate or immaterial point of view?"

"It is very simple, Counselor," she replied. "That reaction is taken from a Westerner's construction of the colonized being, or as we often label that theoretical individual, the Oriental 'other.' The attitude of colonizers toward the colonized is formed, not from the truth, but from translations of events, practices, religions, etcetera, which they do not, cannot possibly understand.

To devout Hindus—indeed, even to the sati widow herself—the act represents an achievement of transcendence from the temporal to the spiritual realm. She exists in another reality of her own making, where the ordeal is nothing alongside the eternal bliss she anticipates."

Besant again turned toward the judge. "So, what may seem a terrifying flame to us may seem a babbling brook to her. She is neither martyr nor hapless victim. She is a subjective self, exercising autonomous choices which, as a free being, it is her right to do. And this choice is viewed by many in India, as in the Asian-American community as admirable, selfless, divine even."

"And is India unique in holding this perspective?" Fulbright asked.

"Not at all," Besant said. "Western literature is replete

with similar imagery. In Alfred Noyes' poem, 'The Highwayman,' the innkeeper's daughter contrives to kill herself so that the commotion will save her lover. Not her husband, but her *lover*! One of the most enduring stories of the *Titanic* tragedy involves the decision by its women to disdain the lifeboats, in favor of remaining with their lifelong mates. Romeo and Juliet, Hamlet and Ophelia, Abelard and Heloise—the only qualitative difference lies in the details of motivation. For the net effect is the same: suicide as the ultimate expression of faithfulness and devotion. And these examples only scratch the surface. There are many more – of the sacred variety, of course."

"Do you mean religious practices that are akin to suicide?"

"Why, yes," the professor continued. "When this woman..."

"Objection, your honor," Allen said. "The witness is mischaracterizing events. The victim here was a ten-year old child, not a woman."

"Sustained," Thorndike wheezed.

Besant began again: "When this woman climbed voluntarily onto that log pile..."

"*Objection!*" Allen thundered. "The professor's 'woman' was a ten-year-old child, and the question of volition is still at issue here."

Thorndike glowered down at Lata Besant. "The

witness is directed to discontinue using those inaccurate terms. Continue, Mr. Fulbright."

Fulbright nodded at the witness, who then said, "as I was trying to say before, the sati ceremony was an expression both of earthly love and spiritual devotion. This is not unprecedented here in America, you know. Jehovah's Witnesses often refuse life-saving blood transfusions. Christian Scientists often forsake modern medicine in deference to the healing power of prayer. And sati has a much older lineage in Indian tradition than either of those practices."

Defense Counsel straightened to full height. "Would you provide other illustrations, as to how people from different cultures often misunderstand one another's customs and perspectives?"

"It is normal," Besant said, "for people to arrive at conclusions about alien subjects by employing standards with which they are comfortable, by which they were raised. But surely, people who are appalled at sati might be surprised to learn that Indian women are just as astonished that Salem once hanged witches; that Jewish, African-American and immigrant women burned to death early in this century while confined to brutal sweatshops such as the Triangle Shirtwaist factory; that they suffered unspeakable indignities at the hands of exploitative bosses and husbands; or that young girls died in their thousands in the grimy alleys of our cities from botched abortions. America's treatment of its own women has much to answer for."

"So, people who live in glass houses," Fulbright led the witness, "shouldn't throw stones?"

"That is correct," Besant nodded.

"Finally, Professor," the attorney said, "would you be so kind as to define the term 'postmodernism' for us, in terms lay persons might understand?"

"I'm certainly willing to try," Besant replied. "Postmodernism, in short, is a philosophy, a worldview, a way of interpreting people and events beyond the universes of our own knowledge. The Western world, at least since the late 18th century, was built on the concept of modernity; that is, a world in which scientific inquiry, objective fact-finding, and political philosophies were the foundation stones of a new state, freed from the fetters of either religion or social tradition. People and nations might disagree on the interpretation and universality of these facts, but not on the objective rational processes by which they were produced and upon which they could be debated."

Again, she smiled. "Postmodernism dates from the early 1940s, evolving during the 1960s from a literary device that French academics like Michel Foucault and Jacques Derrida labeled 'deconstructionism.' Deconstructionism suggests that any artistic creation or text possesses an inherent *relativity* of meaning, defined not just by the writer, but by the reader, and not just by the speaker, but the listener as well. Writer and reader, speaker and listener rather cancel one another out, leaving in their wake, not knowledge in the objectively modern sense, but merely *translation*.

"Taken in this context then, it becomes impossible really to *know anything*, at least in our modern sense of the word 'know.' To postmodernists, therefore, there can be no 'truth,' except inasmuch as it exists in the mind of the translator. Naturally, this new philosophical construct has transformed, in a revolutionary way, traditional standards of 'good' and 'evil,' 'civilized' and 'barbarous,' because the methods used to arrive at such determinations were, and in my opinion, *are* fatally flawed and therefore illegitimate."

His examination's superb, Allen thought. He stared at Fulbright, straining to detect even a hint of conscious affectation or disingenuousness. Instead, he saw utter sincerity, as if he were hanging on Besant's every word.

Fulbright then said, "And how does multiculturalism fit into this new paradigm, Professor?"

"Well, multiculturalism is the only political philosophy which makes any sense, or has any prospect for success, in heterogeneous communities. For if all is a translation, then no single community may rightly prevail over the others by anything other than oppressive means. Once this inequality between cultures has given way to a paradigm of multicultural appreciation and equity, sources of inter-communal conflict will cease to exist. Cultural autonomy, cultural comfort will be protected and optimized.

"Unfortunately, those who benefited the most under the old paradigm resist such trends fiercely. But they are on the wrong side of history, the wrong side of fate. The days of a largely homogenized European, male-dominated culture are surely numbered and – "

"Yes. Well…"

Allen suspected Defense Counsel had been thrown a bit off his stride and wanted badly to shift gears. He was out over his skis.

Fulbright said, "Then, if I may attempt to recapitulate, what you have said here today concerning the merits of this case of sati prosecution, is that Roop Kumar's voluntary—and we have been given no reason to believe otherwise—suicide, the prosecution of her martyrdom seems, in light of a postmodern interpretation, to be both arbitrary and culturally arrogant."

"I would not quarrel at all with that synopsis, Mr. Fulbright," the professor said.

Fulbright said, "Thank you so much for your valuable time, Professor. This has been most enlightening."

Spellbound by what he'd just witnessed, Allen's mind raced. As much as he'd hoped she'd be off the mark, Samantha stood as tactically vindicated.

He now had a clear view of where his old partner was headed, along with the design Fulbright wished to flesh-out. Yes, a sati had taken place. But far from having been "murdered," the girl had entered this religious sacrifice of her own free will. Nor did the defendant, Swaraj, regard his participation in sati as abetting *murder*.

America's Constitution forbade State interference in the exercise of religion. And since American statutory law was, in this context, little more than a collection of codified European biases, "translations" as Besant had put it, its executors lacked both the standing and the perspective with which to enforce their edicts *transculturally*. Therefore, inherent American justice was incapable of comprehending, let alone proscribing, the rite of sati. And given the undeniable demographic trend toward a multicultural society, practice of sati was not only morally defensible, but it was also now politically unavoidable.

This confirmation of the defense strategy would serve to crystallize Allen's own, and to stiffen his resolve. Clearly now, this case, *Indiana v. Swaraj,* would have wide-ranging implications involving matters of life and death itself.

Throughout Besant's testimony, Mark McCorkle had been scribbling and furiously passing notes to Samantha who, in turn, handed them to Allen. After pausing a few seconds to sketch an outline, its margins peppered with memory triggers, Allen rose to conduct his cross-examination, anticipating that it would end, not with a whimper, but with a bang.

He began: "As the Good Book says, Professor, "the last shall be first. So, let's start there, shall we?"

Allen walked around the prosecution desk and anchored his left hand to it, hitching his right hand to his hip. "Professor Besant, would you please finish your earlier thought, the one Mr. Fulbright seemed so eager to suppress? What was the point you were trying to make, exactly?"

"I don't know what you mean, Mr. Prosecutor," she responded tersely.

"Allow me to refresh your memory. Your Honor, would you please direct the court recorder to read back the professor's last response to defense counsel?"

Thorndike complied, directing her to read the passage aloud.

The court recorder did so, and at a certain point Allen halted the reading. "Thank you. Does that refresh your recollection, Professor?"

The witness stiffened, her face pinched. "What I meant, put quite simply, was that this country is changing and will continue to change in the coming decades. As its citizens, we may choose to embrace that change, or resist it. Those who select the latter option will be deluding themselves and living in the past, unable to jettison the cherished myths at the heart of their elitist perspective."

Allen said, "Ah, but how do we *define* culture, Professor? Isn't it defined by transmissible features: language, religion, art, and the like? You have included sexual variations as cultural. Should the definition of culture really be that expansive?"

"Objection." Defense Counsel rose. "I believe the Court is decidedly uninterested in Mr. Southworth's anthropological ruminations."

"Sustained," Thorndike grunted.

"Ok, Professor," Allen reloaded, "this word *shakti* you've spoken of: haven't you really implied that a woman's 'energy' in Hindu culture is considered intrinsically *wicked*, requiring the direction of a *man*?"

"You simply do not understand," she replied. "Nor *can* you understand Hindus and Hinduism. And your pretentious attempt to do so is patently absurd."

"Are you certain of that, Professor Besant?" The Professor glared at the Prosecutor.

Allen pivoted. "Then let's now chat about this idealized institution of child-marriage, shall we? What is the current age of consent in India, Professor?" He paced in front of the witness stand without looking up from his notes.

"It is eighteen. However, that leaves an incomplete

historical picture. Before 1891, there was no age of consent." Besant shifted her posture in the witness chair.

Allen let his clipboard drop to his side. "So, there were actually situations in which small children, even infants, were wed, is that correct?"

"Yes, but…"

"And often they were married to much older husbands, is that right?"

"In those instances," Besant said, "the union would remain unconsummated until puberty."

"You mean that such prohibitions would apply to girls like poor Roop Kumar, is that right?"

"Yes, of course."

Allen stood before the witness, staring straight at her. "Tell me, Professor. Are you… *comfortable* with such practices?"

"It is not a matter of my comfort, Mr. Southworth. It is a matter of culture, and not an issue on which ignorant Westerners should venture forth a judgment. After all, such marriages were commonplace in the West well into the 15th century. One cannot, and so indeed should not, judge the validity of another's cultural dictates."

"Dictates?"

"That's right."

Allen smiled. "So, you would feel much the same about… oh, say… cannibalism, is that right? That constitutes a cultural issue does it not?"

Professor Besant straightened her posture and smiled confidently. "That depends on the context," she began. "But I think that it is far more barbaric to mistreat a live man than to eat a dead one, Counselor."

Allen sighed somewhat theatrically. "Fair enough, Professor. But why was it, do you think, that Indian culture abandoned the tradition of child marriage?"

"The short answer is that it hasn't. By some UNICEF estimates, almost twenty per cent of Indian girls marry by the age of fifteen."

"And once again, why is that Professor? After all, you yourself testified that it is now against the law."

"It is. But that does not, in and of itself, impugn historical antecedents. Child marriage was, and is still, practiced widely in India for myriad reasons: poverty, the preservation of caste, or alliances between families. And for all practical purposes, those unions enjoy de facto recognition as such."

Allen affected bewilderment. "Well, if that's the case, then why was the age of consent changed by statute, Professor?"

"The British of course. They were determined to destroy Indian traditions and replace them with their own."

Allen bore down. "Professor, is it not so that the British were prompted to raise the age of consent in India because of political pressure brought by the 'Hindu Lady,' real name Rukhmabai? That, having been married at eleven, but living apart from her husband, she was sued eleven years later, in 1880, by a dissolute husband who commanded both her conjugal presence as well as her inherited property? Didn't that case become a *cause celebre,* attracting enormous sympathy for her both in India and in Britain itself? And didn't the British courts ultimately come down on the husband's side? Rather shoots down your theory about the British, doesn't it?"

The academic slashed back: "Leave it to the British to side with property. Besides, they backed down because of the Hindu nationalist uproar generated by the case, that's all."

Allen pressed on: "But Professor, the Age of Consent Act was passed in 1891, reversing the court's decision from eleven years before. Why weren't they fearful then? Did anything else prompt the law, perhaps?"

Allen reached to get documents from the defense table. "Have you ever heard of a young girl named Puhlomnee, Professor Besant?"

"She has nothing to do with this case, Mr. Southworth, and you know it."

"She was an eleven-year-old Bengali girl who was fatally raped on her wedding night in 1889, isn't that right?" Allen whisked away an unruly forelock. "Was not *that* the *reality* the British Raj could no longer *ignore*? What does that incident say of the venerable institution of child marriage?"

"Really, Counselor! Are you so naïve as to think that rape never occurs within the confines of Western marriage? Wouldn't that nullify equally the Western institution?"

As I've stated previously, the British are responsible for corrupting, then nullifying ancient traditions with the scratch of a quill pen. Roop Kumar was an Indian. Her marriage vows were of much more ancient provenance than your own, or the vaunted Age of Consent Act. In her mind, she was a wife and a widow. The sati followed as the deliberate consequence of those convictions."

Must admit, she's one tough broad. Try another angle.

"Are you aware, Professor, that a young woman's so-called marriage at age one was annulled recently in India?" He handed a related BBC report to the Judge. "What does that say about the legitimacy of child marriage, do you think?"

Besant's brow knit tightly. "It argues for the opposite conclusion, actually. After all, if something does not exist, it requires no annulment, does it? You are hoist by your own petard, Mr. Prosecutor."

The crowd hummed at the interchange, prompting several whacks from the gavel. Judge Thorndike looked quickly at his watch and then gestured for Allen's next question.

Allen glanced at his own watch and said, "In light of the lateness of the hour, Your Honor, I request a recess."

"Granted," the Judge bellowed. "We'll reconvene at 2:00 p.m."

Sam and Allen decided to retire to the Cock-a-Doodle-diner for lunch; the place served a mean tuna melt. She was uncharacteristically reticent on the short drive over, busy composing her critique, Allen guessed. The place had once been a bank branch and so, with a little advance notice, one could reserve a private table inside the old safe. Allen's reservation was automatic, as the staff was well-aware, and it would allow a little privacy, at least.

After their melts arrived, Allen bluntly asked, "How do I crack her?"

"Quit playing on her turf," Sam replied instantly.

"By which you mean… what?"

"I think you must reach beyond the immediate issue of child 'marriage' to address the wider implications of legitimizing it, even if obliquely." Sam picked absently at her food. "You have to make Thorndike imagine the dark future impending if..."

"So, I should turn Besant's feminism *against* her, is that right."

"I really think it's that simple. She's getting away with murder up there by draping herself in the victimhood of the 'other.' You need to show the judge just what her 'other' is."

Allen smiled and stuck a French fry into his mouth. "Well," he said, "it's not like we're unprepared. We've got the ammo. Guess it's time to let fly."

"Yep," Sam agreed. "And bugger the consequences. Don't forget Stivers' ace-in-the-hole, as your *coup de grace*."

Allen's smile broadened. He pushed his sleeve up a hairy arm: "Nothing up *my* sleeve..."

Sam flashed a hint of a smile; then it dropped, and she said, "Let's get back."

The courtroom was, if anything, even more crammed for the afternoon session. As Sam and Allen walked in, Madison Fulbright was huddled with Professor Besant, whispering. Thorndike gaveled the scene to order and ordered the witness to retake the stand, reminding her that she was still under oath.

Allen sat and took a moment, his hands on the table, his eyes riveted on the papers in front of him. Then he rose, edging around the guardrail toward the witness. "Good afternoon, Professor."

"Mr. Southworth," she nodded.

"Let's establish something at the outset, shall we?" Allen asked. "Sati is, and has always been, an aberration in Hindu society, is it not?"

"That is quite true, yes," Besant smiled.

"That the Hindu dharmas do not mandate such behavior by Hindu widows, isn't that right?"

"That is essentially correct. Sati has always been an unusual event, the practice of which should not besmirch an entire religion."

"I'm sorry, Professor," Allen interrupted. "Is it your impression that I was doing that...besmirching Hinduism?"

Besant smiled. "I suppose that I was anticipating the thrust of your line of questioning. It seems to me that the charge of cultural misogyny lies in ambush somewhere in my near future."

"Not wishing to disappoint you, Madame, is it not the case that, even today, in *some* segments of Hindu society, women count for little more than chattel?" He fingered additional documents on his desk. "That they are regarded as mere adjuncts to their husbands? Is *that* not a reason some women have, over the years, chosen death over widowhood?"

"Such reports are much overblown."

"Tell me, Professor," Allen confronted her, "what is the status of widows in contemporary Indian society?"

"I haven't the vaguest notion what you mean."

"Well, allow me to assist you," Allen offered. "Is it often *customary* in India for Hindu widows to remarry?"

"It is perfectly legal for them to do so. In fact, their right to do so is enshrined in law."

"Ah. But with all due respect, that's not what I

asked." Allen began pacing side to side. "Is it or is it not true that in India, some Hindu widows—speaking generally now—are forbidden *by custom* to remarry, and are actually deemed to be evil omens and financial burdens?" He wheeled abruptly. "Wouldn't such a woman sometimes be forced to lead an ascetic existence to *atone* for her husband's death, which she is regarded to have caused?" He ticked points off his fingers: "She may not speak to a man, must remain barefoot, sleep on the floor, is forbidden to leave the house of her in-laws and becomes, in effect, nothing more than a scullery drudge. Is that not true?"

Besant glared steadily and hissed through clenched teeth, "As I have already explained, Mr. Prosecutor, widows are legally allowed to marry and to inherit property and to go wherever they wish."

"OK," Allen said, "then let's play the postmodern game for a moment. To what agency do we owe the laws bestowing widows their putative protection?"

"Why, the government of India, of course."

"Do you mean to tell this court that Hinduism reformed *itself?*"

"Really," the Professor sighed, "this is becoming so *tedious*. You are assuming that Hinduism *needed* reforming."

Allen smiled: "Isn't it true that those very laws are *British* laws—passed decades before India's independence? Now isn't it grand that the British were ignorant of postmodernist theory, else they likely wouldn't have passed such laws? Wasn't their passage fortuitous for the women of South Asia?"

"*Objection, Your Honor!*" Fulbright thundered. "Professor Besant is the credentialed expert in this field, not the prosecutor."

"Pardon me, Your Honor." Allen assumed a more deferential posture toward the witness. He sensed Besant was feeling strained. "Dr. Besant, did you intend to challenge the statement I just posed to you?"

"Philosophically, yes, I would," she said. "You simply do not have the proper perspective from which to launch such criticisms."

"So," – Allen drew close to the witness stand and leaned in – "your issue with me is not with the *facts* as I've presented them, but solely with my *ethnic* background – my *irreducible, indelible, inescapable subjectivity as a Western male.*"

"In a manner of speaking…"

"What about *your* ethnicity, Professor?" Allen smiled blandly.

"My…"

"You're not Indian at all, are you?" Allen paused for effect. "Aren't you, in fact, actually of Portuguese/Irish heritage? Weren't you born, raised and baptized in a Catholic Church in Lowell, Massachusetts under the name, 'Gillian Wishing'?"

"I—"

"*Gillian Wishing*," Allen repeated. "Besant is a *made-up* name, is it not? You are a *convert* to Hinduism, are you not? How do you exempt yourself from the *inescapable subjectivity* of your own ethnic background?" In the corner of his eye Allen saw Madison Fulbright glower from the defense table, chin on his fists. Plainly, the Prosecutor's words were hitting their mark.

Besant suddenly seemed tentative, unsure. "I can explain that. You see…"

Dr. Lata Besant straightened her shoulders. "I have reached a state of sublime transcendence." Her eyes began filling; she found a tissue in her robes and swiped at them.

"Sublime transcendence…" Allen repeated calmly, with a slight smile.

Giggles migrated through the spectators.

Allen kept his query soft: "Rather like a sati widow? Except that you sit here before us, in a heated courtroom, reputedly eminent in your field, amply paid and tenured. Not exactly equivalent, is it?"

For the first time, Besant was speechless.

Allen pressed on relentlessly: "Now, then, am I correct in assuming that you believe accounts of coerced satis to be somehow spurious?"

"I didn't say that," she murmured. "I merely said that the British had a vested interest in exaggerating them, inflating the actual numbers of coerced satis."

"You will allow, then, that there have been more than a few coerced satis?"

"Not when one takes into account the degree of ignorance and bias on the parts of observers, who were generally agents of colonialism."

"Then," Allen said, "all the contemporaneous eye-witness accounts that exist in the historical literature – hundreds of them, from soldiers, missionaries, merchants and Westernized Indians themselves—were all lies:

"Not *lies* in the strictest sense of the word," Besant said carefully. "But such accounts were and are, by definition, misrepresentations of an alien culture."

Allen turned to the judge. "I present in evidence, Your Honor, official Government of India police reports from the 1820s, which tabulate satis in the province of Bengal during that period, reports which Governor General William Bentinck dubbed the 'dreadful list.'" Allen handed documents to the court clerk. "There are hundreds of victims reported here, Professor Besant. Is all this mere fabrication?"

Besant insisted, "They are all translations of events through an *imperialist* lens. Besides which, that was a very long time ago."

"Perhaps," Allen shrugged. "But is it not the case that a celebrated sati took place, in the open, before tens of thousands of pilgrims in Rajasthan in 1987? And that subsequent police investigation revealed it to have been *coerced*? That the eighteen-year-old bride tried to flee and was forcibly retrieved, placed on the bier and pinned to her husband's corpse?"

Besant sat stone-faced.

"Your Honor, *please*," Fulbright pleaded. "Coercion is the issue here. Defense has not acceded to Prosecutor Southworth's rendition of events in this case, let alone those in India."

Allen handed over another sheaf of documents. "Your Honor, I offer in evidence press accounts from The *Times* of London, the *New York Times*, the *Hindustan Times* and *Time Magazine*, all attesting to the facts as I have related them."

"Overruled," Thorndike growled.

Allen returned his attention to the witness. "Well, Professor Besant?"

"Yes, I have read that there was an instance of sati in 1987. But the facts as to volition are disputed."

Allen feigned confusion. "Still, the police report would tend to verify my account, would it not?"

"Possibly…"

"Professor Besant," Allen pressed in, "have you ever heard of the BJP?"

"Yes, of course. It's the ruling political party in India."

"And the Hindu Mahasabha and the RSS – have you heard of them as well?"

Besant nodded.

Allen felt his forehead perspiring now, and he drew a hand across it. "Is it not true that both of these organizations—indeed, even the BJP itself—either overtly supported the right to perform the 1987 sati to which I just alluded, or refused to condemn those who did?"

"Perhaps."

"And is it not also true that these same groups have resisted calls by opponents of sati, including many of *India's* largest feminist organizations, to forbid *chunari mahotsav*, even *commemorations* of the sati, such as that which our entire nation witnessed recently at Stickle's glade?"

"That is their right, of course."

"And would it surprise you to learn that the buyer of Stickle's glade, where the event in question occurred, was none other than the Hindu Mahasabha, acting through the Ganges Mission?"

"To the best of my knowledge, Mr. Prosecutor, foreign organizations are legally entitled to purchase property in the United States." She smiled wanly toward the Judge, seeking a life-ring."

"More to the point, Professor," Allen persisted, "where exactly do postmodern multiculturalists draw the line? May it lie perhaps along the limit separating notions of universal humanity from simple translation, especially where virtues such as compassion, justice and common sense are concerned?"

Allen shrugged his shoulders, open palms at his side. "Or *isn't* there such a limit? Are you suggesting that nothing is intrinsically out of bounds, unless of course it possesses the requisite cultural and historic pedigree?"

No reply. "Professor?" *Silence.*

"Well," Allen hammered, "what about sacrificing virgins? Crucifixion? Chattel slavery? Perhaps Jefferson Davis was justified after all in defending the right of *his* people to their 'peculiar institution,' of slavery? What about *that*, Professor? Were the rebels entitled to their 'servants,' after all, because slavery *was* a vital expression of their 'culture'? Slavery has an ancient provenance, has it not?"

Fulbright stood. "Objection, Your Honor. Mr. Southworth is browbeating this witness. And to no coherent purpose, I might add."

Allen smiled. "All right, then, just one more question, Professor Besant. *If* everything we believe is a *translation*, every interpretation must be *subjective*. There can be no objective historical truth, then, is that right?"

"Crudely put," she replied, "but close enough.

Fulbright had seen enough. "Your Honor, counsel is doing nothing more in this cross-examination than abusing the witness and tying up this court with matters in which, it has been amply demonstrated, he is woefully under-qualified."

"I'm finished with this witness, Your Honor." Allen strode to the defense desk and cast his notes dismissively on the table in front of Samantha.

"No more questions, Your Honor."

April 16
4:00 p.m.

Round two had gone to Allen, no question. Back in the prosecutor's office, Sam noted that he seemed almost giddy about his performance with Besant. *Disconcertingly so.*

Plopping his briefcase on his desk, Allen said, "Fulbright took a huge risk by placing all his eggs in *that* multicultural basket."

"Yes," said Sam, "you broke a few with that cross. The good professor is clearly unused to being contradicted."

"I don't think we'll have to worry about her any time soon," he sighed. "Exposed. A few good questions passed on by McCorkle, and there she is: an ideologue, who clearly hasn't thought some of the larger questions through. Revelation of her birth identity hasn't helped her either," he grinned. "Remind me to buy Stivers a fifth of Maker's Mark." He fumbled in his jacket for a pack of cigarettes and lit one up…victorious.

Sam glared at him soberly. "This isn't in the bag yet, Allen. Not by a long shot."

Allen chuckled. "Oh, I know that. Carver's a lot shrewder—and riskier—if I don't handle him right. Last thing we want is for the judge to feel sorry for him."

"I'm glad to hear you say that," Sam said. "Don't underestimate the sympathy guys like him are capable of evoking, even in the most unlikely hearts."

"I don't think I've overlooked that." He paused. "You know what really scares me?"

Sam sat on the edge of his desk. "What's that?"

"I'm not all that concerned about the rallies and protests and college kids out for a weekend lark; that's all show biz. I got a belly-full of it in the '60s."

"What then?"

"Backlash," he said. "Not with the locals. Hell, I think they're too shocked and confused at this point to be indignant about much. Anyway, I know these people. They don't like to make waves."

He shook his head and exhaled. "It's the lunatic fringe I'm worried about: You know the type, the super-patriot paranoids who live for this kind of controversy. Jan was right to get the kids out of this environment. *Anything* could happen."

"I see what you mean. But maybe you're fretting about nothing."

"They're already here." Allen scratched his chin and pointed out the Edwardian dormer window, to the street. "Peters gave me a heads-up this morning. There's one especially bad actor who has come with them."

"Someone you know?"

"Know *of* him." Allen nodded grimly, blowing a smoke ring. "Reverend Cornelius Feeley has arrived in town, ready to raise aloft the Good Book and do battle for the Lord."

Allen grunted and turned back to the window. "He's more than a caricature, more than simply a cadenced, faith-healing redneck; he's also educated, articulate, impassioned and obsessed—a dangerous combo."

"Bugger," she replied. "They're always the worst."

"That is, if he is what he appears to be," Allen added. "The toughest thing with guys like him is separating the authentic from the inauthentic... kind of like with this case's defense witnesses." He tapped out another cigarette despite Sam's disapproving glare and quickly blew a smoky cloud at the windowpane. "We'll just have to wait and see, I guess."

Unbidden, a bible verse popped into Allen's mind. It was from Judges 17:6. "In those days there was no King of Israel, every man did what was right in his own eyes."

"The sooner this trial is over...," Allen muttered.

**April 17
10:00 a.m.**

Next in the witness chair would be Theo Carver. Allen decided to gamble and hand the cross-examination over to Sam, a concession he'd never have considered with any other second chair. Still, despite his feelings for her and the respect he had for her skills, he felt uneasy. They huddled again in the library over strategy.

Allen said, "He's much less likely than Besant to rattle. For one thing, he's better known in the community—"

"—as a youth organizer, facilitator and counselor," Samantha picked up. "He has an instinct for public relations that's brought him a good deal of success at schmoozing Principia's most prominent citizens."

"Schmoozing? What do you mean?"

Sam's head dipped, shrouding her face with a cascade of tresses. "Well, he's always leading small processions through town commemorating black history and trumpeting 'diversity awareness.'"

Allen smiled. "And since he's never contradicted, he's probably not very used to being publicly challenged."

Sam looked up sharply. "You can't be too smug, Allen. He's great at preempting opposition *before* it happens, tossing around nuggets like justice, diversity, tolerance, inclusion, and empowerment as rhetorical shields. Who can oppose *those* things, after all?" She threw up her hands in mock frustration. "Carver's been virtually invulnerable in these parts up to now because he's a disciple of the negative proposition, that which can't be disproved. He rarely appears to lose an argument, and always seems to walk away smiling."

"Slick as hoarfrost on a wooden step," Allen nodded, rubbing his chin a little nervously.

Sam frowned. "As much as I love your cornpone witticisms, Allen, you mustn't be so dismissive because, you know, I think he really believes in his message. In fact, I'm rather counting on that."

This bit of bravado invoked an anxious pride in Allen, though he happened to know Sam's self-confidence was well-founded. Tom Stivers, following a couple of weeks in Chicago and Milwaukee over the winter, had unearthed an Achilles heel in Carver's vita as well. Sam was going in well-armed.

Sam added, "He'll be a worthy adversary and, unless we're very careful, potentially risky with the Judge. I'm afraid that misplaced guilt can sometimes be as addictive and intellectually enfeebling as crystal meth, and I don't have time to rehabilitate Thorndike."

Allen watched Sam take a last glance in the mirror. "How do I look, Counselor?

"Go get 'em."

As their footfalls echoed on the way out of the cavernous chamber, Allen immediately regretted his patronizing sendoff.

When his name was announced, Carver appeared, resplendent in his variegated headgear and billowing robe, processing regally down the aisle trailed by two massive bodyguards in dark glasses. *One thing you have to give Theo Carver,* Allen mused. *Just like Besant, he knows* how to make an entrance.

In his fist Carver clutched a wooden stick that he'd told reporters was possessed of powerful *juju* derived from the spirits of long-suffering ancestors. At first disdaining the proffered Bible, he asked instead for a copy of the *Qur'an.* Then he relented, observing to the bailiff that the latter was simply the latest, much improved incarnation of the former: "And we're all 'People of the Book.'" As he sat down, Carver projected a palpable pride and fearlessness, even behind that ever-present smile, off which all adversity seemed benignly to ricochet.

Madison Fulbright had been ambivalent about calling this witness, but old man Savarkar insisted, despite Fulbright's investigation having revealed troublesome hiccups in the activist's background. He reassured them all would be well, especially given the large file of civic accolades Carver had been awarded over the previous decade. And while Fulbright remained cynical about this witness's penchant for affectation, he knew many people found Carver an impressive, even inspiring, speaker.

So, Fulbright opted to roll the dice, daring to hope that with proper handling (and a bit of luck from Allen) he might help the Judge forget the Besant train-wreck of the day before. In so doing, he might begin a new dialogue within which to shield his client, and maybe even make some new case law in the bargain.

Savarkar's dictum had limited his options from the start, it was true. And Fulbright had definite qualms about this whole line of argument. But the old man would settle for nothing less than achieving a precedent: recognition of an entitlement to cultural autonomy or, failing that, the huge flush of publicity that would spin off the confrontation.

Whatever the old man's motivations, they were irrelevant to Fulbright, so long as Swaraj continued to follow instructions. The defense consul had already decided against putting the defendant on the stand. He was too inarticulate a lamb to throw to the lurking Southworth. In a sense, Carver would act as a stand-in for the colonial "other," in a more theatrical, and shrewd manner than Swaraj could ever convey on his own.

Besides, such questions were ultimately more political than philosophical in their resolution anyway. In the absence of a compelling rebuttal, Fulbright felt he'd already won one battle, if not the war quite yet.

He rose from the defense table, smoothed his vest, and inserted his lucky gold pen in his jacket pocket. Head half-bowed, index finger placed carefully to his lips, he approached the witness box. "Would you please summarize your educational background for us, sir?"

"I possess a BA in sociology from Marquette University in Milwaukee and a doctorate in multicultural studies from Magdalene College."

"What, exactly, do you consider your avocation to be, sir?"

Carver straightened up in the witness chair. "For the past ten years, I have been involved in the work of the Diversity League, which I founded. We act as facilitators, conducting human awareness seminars and sensitivity training; we mentor at-risk youth and provide drug education. In addition, we have established extended programs of community outreach, food drives, educational presentations, things of that nature. We serve as far afield, sometimes, as Chicago."

"And would you be so kind as to share with this court your personal mission statement, that is, what you are trying to accomplish?" Chin resting on his index finger as if deep in contemplation of the witness's every word, Fulbright turned his back to Carver.

"My mission, which is also that of the Diversity League, is to educate as well as to agitate; to promote truth and justice for all people, regardless of race or ethnicity. Demographic trends, after all, dictate that America's future is diversity and diversity is her future."

Fulbright turned back around. "Would you please expand on that?"

"Demographic trends clearly indicate that by the year 2025 only fifteen percent of new entrants into the job market will be white males. Ninety percent of new immigrants in the next fifty years will be non-European. Yet the Eurocentric power structure continues to act as if nothing will ever change."

"More specifically, sir," Fulbright faced Carver, "how do you believe this imminent transformation of the American perspective will alter the way in which this court should view such issues as Roop Kumar's marriage and her subsequent sati?"

Well,"—Carver assumed a professorial mien, leaning slightly forward—"the answer is really obvious when one pauses to examine it *dispassionately*. Many of these new immigrants are justifiably unenthusiastic about shedding their culture and customs, even controversial ones, at the door – even a 'Golden Door' – of our nation."

"Objection," Sam jumped up. "With apologies to

Emma Lazarus, the witness is assuming facts not in evidence. Sati is a cultural *aberration*, not a traditional Indian custom."

Fulbright smiled indulgently. "Your Honor, the witness is making a *general* statement regarding an immigrant's enduring connection to culture. No reference has yet been made to sati.

"He's right, Ms. Desai. Overruled."

After a pause, Carver went on: "Increasingly, new arrivals to America look upon their culture as an extension of themselves, a haven from the hostile and unfamiliar support systems available in what is, to them, a foreign land."

Carver's brow knitted with focused sincerity. "Therefore, America must learn to accommodate itself to these newcomers, not simply because it is politically practical to do so, but because it is the *right* thing to do… out of basic fairness."

"You mean," Fulbright injected, "you feel this is an historical debt that should be paid."

"Think about it," Carver continued. "Americas black, brown and yellow citizens are compelled to send their children to schools where they are indoctrinated with—and required to capitulate to—curricula which are neither diverse nor inclusive. Not only are they subjected to negative stereotypes of their own people in the process, but they have their heads crammed full of European perspectives, heroes and the like, all in the name of assimilation."

Carver pressed his palms together. "You see, the United States is not a single culture but a smorgasbord of cultures which coexist uneasily, despite all this distortion, under the fiction of an 'American Dream' – a fiction which only obscures the diverse reality of our multicultural nation. But thankfully, things are changing."

Fulbright put a finger to his chin and nodded. "Now, do you believe that these realities of which you speak make our job of assessing the legal status of foreign customs and cultures more complicated – more difficult? What exactly do you mean when you refer to America as a *multicultural* nation? Do you believe this concept is more relevant today than it used to be?"

"My apologies." Carver bowed slightly. "This country has always been multicultural, however inequitably constituted. The word 'multicultural' merely describes an adverse condition of longitudinal power, in which cultures end up ranked in a descending hierarchy of power, privilege, and influence. And it is certainly no secret as to *which* culture has been on top all along," he said. "But with the growing appreciation of diversity, society will transform itself into something latitudinally multicultural Then all peoples will share power and wealth equally, according to each other mutual freedom and respect."

The witness leaned back and folded his hands over his stomach. "Of course, there's a very large elephant in our 'living room,' you know – an inescapable truth we don't like to talk about. In the very time I've been on this stand, one hundred people have been added to the world's population, only six are white. A new majority is emerging." He paused to let that fact sink in. "And in that light, what is it really, I wonder, that motivates this prosecution? Dare I say 'insecurity'? Dare I say *'fear'*?"

"But does that mean there are no universal values across cultures? Do what have been called the 'old eternal verities' really exist?"

"Nothing is eternal," Carver replied. "And of whose 'truths' do you speak?" he air-quoted. "At one time, slavery was an eternal truth, as were the patriarchy, colonial domination and the so-called nuclear family of the nineteen-fifties."

He looked down briefly to smooth his robe, then gazed toward the ceiling. "You know, the *truth* is not carved in stone. It's more like a celestial Etch-a-Sketch— an ever-dynamic, spontaneous act of creation, thank God. Ours is no monolithic nation. It is an *association* of nations – and one that can only survive in an atmosphere of mutual *respect* and *equality*. Without these, there can be only one result: disintegration – a shaking of the toy, if you will, to erase the flawed image and begin anew." The witness smiled broadly. *"But,"* he shook a finger, "if mutual respect reigns in our society, such impulses would be bridled, and the nation's bonds assured. *That* is the guarantee of our futures together. Therefore, our strength, our unity, really does lie in our *diversity*. That phrase is not a *paradox*, but a *prescription*. We may leave the toy to its natural evolution, and this future will surely unfold."

"And, specifically, as multiculturalism applies to this case?"

"Yes," he cleared his throat. "It is very simple, really. This entire prosecution is illegitimate, because its functionaries are alien both to the event and to the cultural spirit that drove the event. They have not tried to understand the Hindu perspective on marriage or sati, nor could they have understood *had* they tried. They bring too much cultural baggage to this court; and this prevents them from acquiring a fair and respectful perspective. Now, however, since the jury has been freed from the burden of their erroneous judgment, we are most grateful for a chance to put forward our case at length to *you*, Judge." Carver nodded respectfully at Thorndike, who nervously shifted his shoulders in his chair.

Then Carver shook a finger at Fulbright. "You know, white people worship their own martyrs all the time, biblical and otherwise, whether Jesus on the cross, Esther before Haman, Nathan Hale on the gallows or Davy Crockett at the Alamo. Such martyrdom myths serve a real purpose: they reaffirm cultural values. Yet here, the State has chosen to cast a heroic and virtuous act—a manifestation of a culture far more ancient and richer than their own—as a remnant of barbarism."

Fulbright said calmly, "Why do you think the State would do that?"

"Partly out of ignorance," Carver shrugged, "partly because it puffs up the very Eurocentric culture that banned the practice in the first place; partly because it diminishes the Oriental 'other'; but mostly because it makes Mr. Southworth look like a knight in shining armor, riding to avenge a ravished damsel."

Fulbright noticed Allen wince and said, "Mr. Carver, just so the Court understands you fully, you see no criminal offense here, do you?"

"Where *is* the crime, exactly? The bride's family doesn't deem it a crime; nor does the husband's family. And, most pertinently, the sati mata herself is not distressed, having chosen the fate of her esteemed forebears of her own free will. She is honored. She is sanctified. We have assessed no crime here in this courtroom – unless, of course, we count the crime of prosecutorial arrogance."

"Objection." Sam stood. "How does defense counsel expect Your Honor to digest credible hearsay from a dead child?"

Sustained," the Judge smiled. "Indeed, His Honor possesses no such gift, Mr. Fulbright."

The crowd laughed tentatively, given the subject, and Fulbright paused till the noise subsided. Then he lowered his chin onto his chest and rumbled: "Mr. Carver, could you speak to the wider cultural ramifications of this… arrogance?"

"Surely." Carver tented his fingers and suppressed a cough. "Nothing less is at stake here than the right of the Hindu community to retain its cultural authenticity, and to continue the process of rediscovering itself within *its own context*, rather than that of the colonial oppressor. This case is a bellwether, for if citizens like Mr. Swaraj are allowed the *freedom* to practice their own religion, then America will preserve her stability, now rooted in its newly acknowledged, indispensable diversity. But if people like *the defendant,"* Carver pointed at Swaraj, "are *denied that freedom,* then our future looks bleak indeed, and much discord may lie ahead of us."

Carver paused and then said, in a voice that seemed on the verge of breaking, "This resonates with me, you see, because millions of my people were kidnapped from Africa centuries ago, deprived of their culture, their religion, their heritage, their self-respect. For many of my brothers and sisters, the consequences were catastrophic.

"This is why Afrocentrists, like me, labor tirelessly to reconnect African American youth to their motherland, in order that they may become centered, crippled no longer by the stereotypes inculcated into them. My colleagues and I work so that these youths no longer will be confined to the restricted, linear, deductive processes of European habits which their own ancestors discovered long ago were far too limiting and anti-humanist." Carver's eyes glistened with tears.

"Besides," he continued, "there is a natural connection between my mission and this case. Sati may have begun in Africa, in ancient Egypt in fact. The practice was even mentioned in the Book of the Dead. So, you see, in his way, Mr. Swaraj's claim to a cultural birthright hit very close to home for me and symbolizes the fight which people of color must wage constantly, to save both their souls and their identities."

He leaned forward again, in a softened tone. "To say that Hindus or Muslims or Navajos or Chicanos or Ibos, for that matter, lack the moral centeredness with which to judge *their own cultures* is degradation by dismissal, an attempt to assert the so-called *superiority* of one culture over *another*. The people of this country, this state and this nation need, *soulfully*, to ask themselves whether this is the kind of nation they want: a nation in which one culture may, *with impunity, disrespect all others*. In truth, this issue is destined to redefine *patriotism itself!*"

Hmm, thought Fulbright. *Carver seems on the very verge of losing it. Time to turn the heat down a mite...*

Quietly, he asked, "If Roop Kumar were miraculously

able to appear before us today, in this courtroom, what do you think she would say about these proceedings?"

"Objection, Your Honor!" Sam shouted. "Talk about *speculation*! This witness has no expertise in juvenile psychiatry, nor, it must be hoped, in the occult."

"Neither" Fulbright shot back, "would a psychiatrist have any expertise in the cultural dimensions of psychological well-being. And this defense *is* multiculturally based."

"I'll allow it," Thorndike replied crisply, holding up an open palm before Sam could speak again.

The witness relaxed and slumped slightly into his chair. "I firmly believe that she would be confused and indignant that her very private act of sacrifice had become the business of the State of Indiana." He stroked his chin. "She might wonder whether what she had been taught about religious freedom in America had been a fiction, after all. She might wonder just how far from India she would have to travel, how many generations she would have to traverse to escape the shadow of the colonialist."

"Thank you, Mr. Carver." Fulbright turned toward the Judge. "Thank you for providing an alternative, even *visionary*, perspective on these complex questions." He shot a quick glance at the activist, who he noticed was mopping his brow furiously. "I request a recess, Your Honor."

X

Sam objected and was sustained. More than ready to proceed, she had no wish to give Carver time to recuperate—that is if he was indeed as drained as he appeared to be, for it was impossible for her to divine this guy's true emotional and physical state.

Letting her adversary stew for a few moments, Sam feigned last-minute busy work at her desk and doodled caricatures of the witness on a yellow note pad. Sam and Allen had mapped out their strategy the night before. Sensing the judge's eyes were glazing over, she certainly wouldn't begin with any debate over multiculturalism.

At last, she looked up and began her cross: "Mr. Carver, what exactly might you consider your avocation to be?"

"I don't think I understand your question," Carver replied.

"Well, are you an anthropologist? A psychologist? Historian? Archeologist? Sociologist?"

Carver crossed his legs. "Well, as I told Mr. Fulbright, I essentially possess a degree in sociology and a doctorate in multicultural studies, fields which embrace aspects of many of those disciplines."

"Essentially?"

"That's right."

"Uh huh," Sam said calmly: "And you have testified

that You received a B.A. from Marquette University, is that correct?"

"That is basically correct." Carver fidgeted slightly in the witness chair.

"What do you mean when you say… '*basically*'?"

Carver hemmed. "I mean *precisely* what I said. 'Basically' is a perfectly acceptable word that stands on its own."

Sam grabbed a sheaf of documents from the prosecution table and began to riffle through them. *Thanks, Tom Stivers…* "Would it surprise you to learn, Mr. Carver, that there exists no record of your having received *any* kind of diploma from Marquette University?"

"Not really," Carver replied. "I neglected to mention that I had a dispute with their department of history, with respect to the curriculum."

"So, you did *not graduate* from Marquette…"

"I *would* have, but I didn't *choose* to, as a matter of principle" The witness inserted a finger inside his collar. "I elected not to jump through their hoops."

"Really," Sam said, in a blunt monotone. "Well, you have lied to this court, have you not?" She smiled indulgently.

"That is only the way *you* might construe it, Ms. Desai," Carver said, a corner of his mouth twitching. "

"And how else might it be construed, Mr. Carver?"

"What I mean," said Carver, "is that any analysis of an event is, ipso facto, *subjective*, derived from a perspective informed by culture. My perspective is *Afrocentric* and different from yours. Your reading of facts may not be the same as mine, and neither is intrinsically truer.

Carver was smiling through a profusion of facial sweat, Sam noticed.

She said, "So you did *lie.*"

"That is your construction of events... your *translation*" he shrugged. "The important, irreducible fact is that I possess all the requisite *knowledge* to fulfill my mission. That is all that should concern anyone."

"All right, then," Sam said, "why don't you tell us about your doctorate from Magdalene."

"What do you wish to know?"

"Dr. Carver, you have never been enrolled in graduate studies at Magdalene College, have you?"

"No. I received the degree in a public ceremony, a fact which would seem to indicate essential academic equivalence, should it not?"

"Your doctoral 'degree' was honorific, was it not?"

"I just said as much. You may deal with that reality as best you can.

Sam saw Madison Fulbright grimace. He had known about Carver's honorary degree, but assumed its conferral had been based on *some* measure of prior academic distinction? Right now, she'd bet he was thinking, *God damn Magdalene College! God damn my own gullibility!*

Having skewered the witness all she needed to on

that point, Sam instantly moved to change the subject: "Would you please expound a little more on your 'unity through diversity' theme, so that we all might understand it well?"

Carver heaved a sigh and then said: "I simply maintain that the diversity of the nation demands mutual respect between cultures, a respect and collective mutuality which, in turn, reinforces our common sense of inclusive nationhood. But for this to work, cultural integrity must not be compromised."

"And for you, cultural autonomy or integrity might also include... religion?"

"Yes."

"Or language?"

"Of course."

"And customs?"

"Absolutely."

"Then under such a societal model, Dr. Carver, might not the Southern United States that became the Civil War Confederacy have made a valid argument that some men had the right to own other men?"

"Aha!" Carver's chest swelled. "But that was the kind of *longitudinal multiculturalism* of which I spoke earlier." He nodded excitedly, glancing at Thorndike, convinced that he'd proven his point.

"Well, then," Sam countered, "you should have little

trouble coming up with a few examples of contemporary multicultural paragons: latitudinal utopias, as it were."

Carver frowned. "These models are, for the most part, theoretical and without current form—yet."

"Sort of like Communism, Dr. Carver? More readily achievable in theory than in practice, hmm?"

"*Objection!*" Fulbright thundered. "The prosecution is clearly badgering the witness, Your Honor. This case has nothing to do with Communism."

"Sustained." Thorndike scolded: "Please confine any facetiousness to your closing arguments, Ms. Desai."

Not missing a beat, Sam moved close to the witness. "All right, Dr. Carver, let's play twenty questions, shall we? I'll give you examples of places that would seem to contradict your premise that diversity promotes peace and strength, and you respond with an example that proves the rule. Are you game?"

Carver looked to the judge. "This is ridiculous..."

"*Objection!*" boomed Fulbright.

Sam said softly, "Your Honor, the jury is being asked to evaluate this crime according to an unprecedented sliding scale, premised on notions of cultural equivalence and moral relativism. I simply propose to explore whether Dr. Carver, whom the defense has offered to this court as an expert witness, can defend his proposition with some sort of comprehensible metric.

Surely, if what he says is credible, he will be able to buttress his point of view and the State will suffer the consequences."

Thorndike sat mute for a long moment. At last, he said, "I'll allow it."

"Fine," Sam said, grinning on the inside. "Dr. Carver, I'll begin, and you will answer with examples of functional, credible, multicultural nations according to the criteria of *latitudinal*, multiculturalism you have just advanced."

Carver sat stone-faced.

"Lebanon." Sam spoke loudly.

Carver said nothing.

"Bosnia."

Silence.

"Iraq."

Still nothing.

"Sudan."

"Rwanda."

"Afghanistan."

Carver finally bestirred himself. "Madame Prosecutor, you must understand that we cannot play this silly game, because you see, we harbor different interpretations of principle. Bluntly I must say that your sense of justice is not mine. Your sense of freedom is not mine. Your sense of virtue is not mine. This is, after all, my major point. When diverse peoples originate in such different spheres of principle, the *only* recipe for a just society is tolerance, respect, and inclusion. There is no alternative. If you need more help comprehending that, perhaps you should read my book, *Heritage Lost, Heritage Found.*"

"Ah, yes, your book." Sam smiled blandly. Indeed, let's discuss your book, shall we? To start with, when was this work first published, Dr. Carver?"

"Nineteen ninety-one."

And by which *house* was it published, Dr. Carver?"

"Diversity House."

"Allow me to ask you to confirm that a few of the following statements do in fact derive from the text of your work. I'll do my best to keep them in context. All you have to do is answer 'yes' or 'no' as to the accuracy of my reading."

Fulbright stood. "Your Honor, haven't we been subjected long enough to Ms. Desai's dog-and-pony show? What has any of this to do with sati or, for that matter, with the guilt or innocence of my client?"

Sam said, "It has everything to do with both, Your Honor. The defense put Dr. Carver on the stand as an expert witness in 'multicultural studies' without specifying just what he claims to be an expert in. A close examination of his book is essential, both to evaluate his credibility as an expert and derivatively, to evaluate his argument for the acceptability of sati in this country."

"Your Honor," Fulbright fumed, "my client has withstood defense's unconscionable attacks with grace and civility. How much browbeating should he be expected to endure?"

Judge Thorndike regarded defense counsel pensively. "But Ms. Desai only wants to read what is in the witness's own book. How is that browbeating?"

Fulbright said, "Your Honor must anticipate that statements within the book will be lifted out of context to assist the design of the prosecution."

"Nonetheless," Thorndike insisted, "these are the witness's own words. And if Ms. Desai takes improper liberties, you may, of course, raise objections, and I will consider each of them in turn. Now," he addressed Sam, *"let's get on with it."*

Sam smiled and whisked a shock of hair off her shoulder. "Dr. Carver, is it accurate to say that you believe, as you state in your book, that ancient black Egyptians laid the foundation for modern physics?"

The witness nodded.

"Yet you present no evidence, cite no manuscripts, and employ no footnotes to substantiate this claim."

"They are unnecessary. Those are linear, Western *crutches.*"

"I see." Sam pursed her lips slightly. "Similarly, then, you offer no evidence for your claim that black Egyptians also invented writing? Papyrus fragments, perhaps?"

Carver straightened in the witness chair. "That Africans invented writing, there is little doubt. Our own oral traditions verify that. We have yet to discover the conclusive material 'proof you seem to require." He chuckled dryly, then glanced at Fulbright, then the Judge.

Sam gazed at a far corner of the courtroom and said gently: "Do you not sense an inherent irony in the notion that your *oral* tradition verifies the invention of a *written* system?"

Carver scowled.

Sam waved aside her own digression. "Be that as it may, all of the ancient buildings of which you write—the palaces, the reservoirs and cathedrals which you assert used to exist in sub-Saharan Africa—all those happen to share the incidental quality of never having been dis-covered, is that right?"

"Something like that, yeah," Carver replied.

"Let's explore this fixation on Africa more deeply, then, shall we? Don't you claim in your book that ancient black Egyptians also developed electricity and antibiotics; performed sophisticated brain surgery; smelted steel, mastered flight. Even discovered America millennia before Columbus?"

"That is accurate," Carver replied. "We have the accounts of ancient travelers and oral tradition, of course, to anchor those claims."

"Is it not so, that you also claim that the foundations

of Western philosophy and science originated in ancient Egypt and were stolen by the Greeks? That a centuries-old conspiracy among scholars has deprived Egypt—and, by extension, Africa—of due credit for those intellectual achievements? Even that Napoleon ordered the nose of the Sphinx shot off to obscure its Negroid features?"

"That is also true," Carver stated impassively.

Sam leafed through the book and fingered a page. "Here, on page 127 of your book, Dr. Carver, you make the following statement, and I quote: 'It is abundantly clear that Aristotle and Pythagoras, among others, traveled to Egypt to plunder its ideas, successfully erasing their true origin once Aristotle's pupil, Alexander the Great, pillaged Alexandria and burned its massive library.' Do you stand by this statement?"

"Of course," Carver beamed. "It's in my book, after all."

"So it is, Dr. Carver. So it is," Sam smiled. "But tell me, please. Do you know how Alexandria came by its name?"

Carver looked bored. "Why don't you enlighten me, Ms. Desai?"

"It was named for its founder, Dr. Carver. Alexander the Great."

"So?" he shrugged.

"So, leaving aside the question of why Alexander would sack his own creation," Sam followed, "how could he have burned its library decades after his own death?"

"You're lifting everything out of context," Carver whined.

Then he snarled. "Dates in antiquity are inherently difficult to ascertain, we may all agree."

Sam flipped to a post-it note marker. "Here, on page 103, you contend that the Ten Commandments were derived from an as-yet-undiscovered African constitution, in which were also written down the world's first democratic principles and the basis of our modern judiciary, is that right?"

"That is correct. Yes!" Carver replied.

"Yet again, where is your documentation for this claim, Dr. Carver?"

Unnecessary Ms. Prosecutor."

"Sam stepped back, scribbled down several notes and then pirouetted once again toward the witness.

"OK, then," she resumed, "let us examine the potential impact of your views on your *educational* efforts, shall we? Would you please explain why you feel it is important to indoctrinate students in their culture of ethnic origin?"

Fulbright rose. "Objection to the word 'indoctrinate,' Your Honor. Argumentative."

"Sustained," Thorndike sighed. "Ms. Desai, would you strain for less provocative wording, please?"

"Yes, Your Honor. Sorry, Your Honor." Sam turned again to Carver. "I ask you once again, Dr. Carver, to explain the reasons for *instructing* students in their culture of ethnic origin."

"It is essential for the development of their cultural awareness, identity and pride. Without those qualities, students are left without models and without the self-esteem they require to perform academically. And they are left at the mercy of Eurocentric propaganda."

"I see." Sam absently tapped her thigh with her pen. "The goal, then, is essentially therapeutic – to raise student performance levels and make them feel better about themselves."

"That is correct."

"Is there any evidence that this strategy – increasing ethnic self-esteem in order to enhance performance, is effective in helping achieve the latter goal?"

"Well, I think the answer's an obvious yes, don't you?" Carver spoke now to the judge, as if to recruit him.

"Then the same should hold true for Greek students. Or, say, Italian students who study the glories that were Greece and Rome? Or that, conversely, German American students might be emotionally crippled by studies of the Nazi era?"

Carver wriggled in the witness chair. "I must assume so.

Sam paced before the jury. "Can you cite any studies that would substantiate this hypothesis, Dr. Carver?"

"Not at my fingertips, no."

"Incidentally," Sam said, "since you often refer to

'African' culture as a unitary concept, is it your contention that Europe, too, is monocultural? That is, represented by just one culture?"

"At its essence, yes."

"And what in the world might that mean?"

"It's plain enough…"

"Then Icelanders and Turks," Sam ticked off on her fingers, "Finns and Portuguese and Italians, Churchill, Hitler, Stalin, Mozart, Attila, Rembrandt and Cromwell, Goebbels and Michelangelo—all sprang from the same cultural loins?"

Carver chuckled. "As far as I'm concerned, at least the ones I've heard of did, yeah."

"And as I understand it," Sam went on, "the same would hold true for American blacks, since the Afrocentric curriculum which you teach focuses primarily on Egypt, is that right?"

"Primarily, yes."

Sam cocked her head and scratched a temple. "But Dr. Carver, the ancestors of most African Americans, didn't originate in Egypt, did they? Is it not so that there are roughly 800 different languages in Africa? There's no more homogeneity in Africa than there is in the monocultural Europe you imagine, is there?"

"It doesn't matter, Counselor. Egyptians are Africans, and their civilization was African. Black Americans are African. Where's the confusion?"

"Then I would take that to mean Egyptians are predominantly black." Sam returned to her table to retrieve some documents. "And that's important to you. Otherwise, the racial tether to which you connect students' self-esteem wouldn't exist, would it?"

Carver frowned and clasped his hands together. "Classical Egypt *was* Nubian, which is to say, black. Yes."

"Dr. Carver, have you ever heard of Frank Snowden?"

"What about him?"

"He's a distinguished classicist at Howard University who disagrees with you."

"What do you expect from Eurocentric academe," Carver snorted. "That's an ignorant and racist view."

"But he's *black*, Dr. Carver," she shot back.

"Then he's an ignorant *Tom*," Carver spat.

Sam thumbed through a sheaf of papers. "Did you know he points out that Egyptians, being Arabs, are not eligible for affirmative action? How does that square with your assertion that Egyptians are 'black'?"

"Just shows me that the man has some catching-up to do."

"I see. Then let's pursue another question. Are black Americans Africans?"

"Of course," Carver replied confidently. "They are children of Africa."

Sam handed him a document. "Would you be so kind as to read this for the court?"

Fulbright shot up, shaking his head vigorously. "Objection, Your Honor. The prosecution is digressing all over the place. This whole line of questioning is irrelevant."

"If it pleases the Court," Sam replied, "if Mr. Fulbright can elicit testimony on the relative autonomy of culture in the constitutional cosmos then, surely, I should be allowed to explore the depth of that belief. It goes to this witness's entire credibility."

Thorndike hesitated a moment, but said, "I'll allow it. Please read the document, Dr. Carver."

Carver glared at Sam, then reluctantly accepted the proffered paper and began to read. "Neither my father, nor my father's father ever saw Africa or knew its meaning or cared overly much for it. I have a fierce repugnance toward anything African… I am an American, not an African, and I resent being coupled permanently with Africa. Once and for all, let us realize that we are Americans, and that we were brought here with the earliest settlers and that the very sort of civilization from which we came made the complete absorption of Western modes and customs imperative if we were to survive at all."

Carver paused and looked up.

"Go on, Dr. Carver, if you please," Sam urged.

"'In brief, there is nothing so indigenous, so

completely "made in America" as we.'" Defiantly, Carver crumpled the paper in his fist and cast it to the floor.

Gently, Sam asked, "Do you know who wrote those words, Dr. Carver?"

"Probably that Snowden from Howard," Carver sighed dismissively. "I can't be expected to agree with everything that stupid Tom writes."

Sam's gaze followed the object. Then she pivoted and walked toward the bench, making shifting eye contact with Thorndike as she stooped to retrieve respectfully, the crumpled wad which Carver had discarded, and placed it gently on the Prosecution table. "That sentiment," she enunciated carefully, "with which you so contemptuously littered this courtroom, was written by W. E. B. Dubois, a giant, a pioneer in this nation's early civil rights movement. Would you call him a *Tom*, too?"

Carver looked to the empty jury box, sullen, unapologetically silent.

Sam paced instinctively toward the empty jury box, wagging her head as if in disgust. Then she whirled on the witness. "Would you please tell me, Sir, whether or not the following individuals from history were, in fact, black: Socrates, Cleopatra, Alexander Hamilton, Daniel Webster, Abraham Lincoln?"

Carver thrust his chin toward his persecutor. "Yes. Yes. Yes. Yes. Yes."

"But where is the evidence, Dr. Carver? Are not vast

armies of *genuine* academics arrayed against you, armed with the fruit of centuries of *legitimate* scholarship? How would a court of law operate without standards of evidence, Dr. Carver? How would we ever have resolution if all allegations, all claims—irrespective of that standard—were accorded equal standing, equal weight?"

"You might ask yourself," Carver parried, "why it is so *important* to you to prove that they were *not*, Ms. Desai."

At that moment Sam suddenly realized that her zealous questioning might well appear bullying, overreaching, compensatory. *Hold up*, she thought.

"As for your precious *evidence*," Carver smirked, "I would steer you for enlightenment in these matters to the work of Dr. Howard McCaffrey, a research scientist at Oak Ridge Laboratories, who has written extensively on these subjects."

Sensing an opening, a coy smile animated Sam's pretty face; Carver looked nervous and drained. "Are you referring to Howard McCaffrey of the Oakland Diversity Treatises Project, which is the blueprint for many Afrocentric curricula in this country? *That* Howard McCaffrey?"

"Yes, he's the one."

"Are you aware, Dr. Carver," Sam pounced, brandishing an affidavit snatched from the prosecution table, "that although *Mr.* McCaffrey works at Oak Ridge, it is in the capacity of a lab technician, not a research scientist? He has no college degree. I offer this corroborating material as evidence, Your Honor."

"We've been through this." Carver waved her off.

"I see," Sam nodded. "By the way, Dr. Carver, I am told you claim family lineage back some two-thousand-five-hundred years, to a West African royal line."

Carver nodded.

"But no corroborative documentation of that lineage is available?"

"Again, that would be redundant to oral tradition."

"And may we also assume that you consider *yourself* African?"

"My cultural affinity is African, yes. I am Afro-centered."

"Continuing on..." Sam charged ahead, "is it your contention that all cultures have been equal in their effects on mankind? I mean, except, that is, for Europe's greater perpetration of evil."

"Objection," Fulbright barked.

"Let me put it this way. Are the beneficial bequests of all cultures around the world essentially equal? Or has the Western Civilization made a case for having fashioned uniquely appealing precepts involving such things as individual rights, liberty, democratic principles and the basis of secular law?"

Clearly annoyed, Carver sighed, "Their effects are relevant only in how they affect their own people."

"Then, the Fourteenth Amendment, the Magna

Carta, the Declaration of the Rights of Man, the Bill of Rights, the Preamble to the Declaration of Independence—all of these could have arisen just as easily in an Animist, Buddhist, Muslim or Hindu culture, as a Western one?"

"Surely," Carver replied. "*If* they had been deemed *necessary*."

"Then, why weren't they so deemed? Was there no oppression of human beings elsewhere other than in Europe and here in the United States?"

"Circumstances," came the reply. "Perhaps people of color already had those things you've spoken of."

Sam suddenly realized that silence had fallen on the courtroom. Her own voice echoed in the vacuum, she noted to herself. "Fair enough. But a major tenet of your philosophy seems to be that the West imposed foreign, arbitrary, inappropriate cultural mores on foreign lands, one such being the prohibition of sati in 1829, is that right?"

"That is correct." Carver leaned forward. "The hateful legacy of Anglo-American imperialism on the rest of the globe is mankind's foulest blot."

"Really?"

"Really."

"You're sure of that?"

"That's right."

"Well, Dr. Carver," Sam said, "European *empires* are

long gone, are they not? Yet to your knowledge, how many of the former colonies have denounced Western science?"

Sam waited but received no reply. "How many have openly reinstituted the slave trade, or renounced the principles that sparked its abolition? Has the Indian Government rehabilitated sati? Are universities purging themselves of all Western thought? Are European languages being banned? Is India deconstructing its democratic system?"

Again, Sam paused.

Fulbright leapt to his feet. "Your Honor, *objection*! Counsel knows better than to badger the witness in this fashion. She is showboating."

Thorndike looked puzzled but remained mum.

Sam said, "Where, oh, where, Mr. Carver, is the mad rush of the 'other' toward its long-lost *authenticity*, as evidenced by rejection of Western innovations? And—if former colonies do not denounce such manifestations of Western influence—where lies any basis for *American citizens* to do so?"

Sam planted herself in front of Carver, arms crossed defiantly over her chest, head cocked to one side, awaiting an answer.

Fulbright supplied one: "*Objection!*"

The witness shouted, "That is a blatantly *racist* observation!"

Thorndike finally spoke out: "Sustained. Ms. Desai will refrain henceforth from any-and-all attempts to filibuster this witness and this court. Is that understood?"

Sam nodded perfunctorily, then resumed: "Now please answer this question, Dr. Carver: Couldn't the same rationale that you have applied here today to legitimize sati be employed to excuse other forms of cultural expression which might be incompatible with our current society?"

"Since I have no idea what you may be referring to," Carver dodged, "I cannot respond."

"All right then, I'll make it plainer," Sam said. "What about *female circumcision*, a practice many equate to sexual mutilation? Or *purdah*, the forced seclusion of Muslim women? How stand you on *dowry murders*?"

Carver sat silent, stone-faced.

"What about African slavery, Dr. Carver? What do the guardians of cultural autonomy have to say on that subject?"

Carver shook, as tears descended his cheeks.

Madison Fulbright rose and roared, "Your Honor, *please!* Counsel for the State is simply browbeating this witness. She is less interested in his views than in pontificating her own prejudices and ethnocentrism. These are not questions intended to elicit truth so much as they are fashioned to showcase Ms. Desai's own grandstanding. I move that her last attack be stricken from the record."

Judge Thorndike grunted, shaking his head as if to banish cobwebs. "He does have a point, Counsel," he growled at last. "That last series of questions hardly seems designed to draw a coherent response. Just how far afield do you think you should be allowed to go here? I know I said that I'd give great latitude, but this is, after all, a court of law, not some Ivy League seminar."

Sam sensed that she'd indeed gone overboard. "I'm sorry, Your Honor. I felt it was important to get at the question of moral and cultural relativism, for they are intricately connected. Perhaps I might rephrase—"

"*Perhaps*," the judge interrupted, "you might defer such lofty pretensions to your *closing*. The last question to the witness is ordered stricken. Anything else, Mr. Fulbright?"

"Not at this time, your honor, except to point out that the State's entire presentation has been contemptible!"

"Point taken, Counsel." Then Thorndike nodded to Sam to continue.

"I have no further questions for this witness, Your Honor," Sam stated firmly. Then, as she started back to the prosecution's table, she suddenly stopped and whirled about. She had to take a last shot: "Excuse me, Mr. Carver, I do have one more question. Do the precepts of your proffered multicultural utopia therefore approve the sacrifice of little girls?"

Madison Fulbright leapt to his feet, his massive arms gesticulating wildly. *"Objection! Objection! Objection!"*

"Withdrawn, Your Honor. Thank you, Mr. Carver."

Sam sat down, satisfied, and folded her hands on the broad oak table. She smiled at the foundering witness, then cast a wink at Allen.

In the back row of the courtroom, Pandit Savarkar sat pining for a cigarette, gravely concerned over the latest turn in the trial. With great deliberation, he withdrew a memo pad from his jacket, scrawled a brief message, then handed it to one of the giant bodyguards preparing to escort the shaken Theo Carver from the scene.

The impassive praetorian behind opaque lenses didn't read the folded note, slipping it furtively inside his vest. Then the guards hustled the witness—panting, sweating, tearful—down the aisle and outside the courthouse to a waiting limousine. The smoke-paned car revved, then roared out the rear entrance of the parking lot and sped away toward the Ganges Mission.

April 17
4:17 p.m.

Exhausted, Allen slumped into one of the overstuffed armchairs in the law library on the second floor of the courthouse; Sam sat straighter nearby. Through a large, semi-circular window framed by ribbons of brittle, peeling green paint, Allen gazed out over State Street and the large parking lot on the other side, now thickly populated with the denizens of the press encampment and other interested parties. A podium had been erected behind one of the lot's thick concrete retaining walls; enough people milled about it to signal an impending speech. It was only a matter of time before Cornelius Feeley got into gear, ruining what should have been Allen's exultant mood.

Sam had dismantled the credibility of Fulbright's star witness, leaving the defense case in tatters on the courthouse broadloom. But much more remained yet to be done. The prosecution had the burden of proof, after all. And—since Swaraj's guilt for coercing the girl was, at best, conjectural—now Allen probably couldn't avoid attacking the ritual itself. He'd have to supplant debates over volition with the prospect of cultural choice: *Civilization or Barbarism*. One way or another, he knew he must end up on the side of the angels, not the demons.

Fulbright, he suspected, might just quit while he was behind. He could hope to score points on Allen's rebuttal witnesses and mesmerize the judge with his closing argument. For his part, Allen had no problem with that strategy.

Sam sidled over to hand him his favorite: bourbon with ginger-ale. "How 'bout a drink, sailor?"

Allen grinned, "Actually, I ought to be buying *you* a triple after *that* performance with Carver. I've told Mark and Tom to pack it in, since Thorndike's adjourned for the day... well, till Thursday actually.

"And I'll tell you another thing, Sam," Allen moaned. "This case better end soon, or I'm going to go postal." He gulped some drink. "All the circular reasoning—it gives me vertigo.

Samantha pulled a chair around to face him, knee to knee. "I didn't expect you to sound triumphal, Allen, but we did some damage today. Sure, it's an uphill climb, but we're also battling the zeitgeist after all; don't forget that."

Suddenly feeling a tad better, he said, "C'mon, why don't we take a little break, get some air, grab dinner out of town? There's a great little place just outside Burr Oak, just across the border in Michigan that's far enough off the beaten path that we might not be recognized."

It was an animated ride; as he and Samantha breezily chewed over Carver's testimony, it seemed to him as if she was sitting closer than usual. *Wishful thinking, maybe.*

In any case, Sam was chattering away on the tactical challenge ahead: how best to employ McCorkle's dopey sincerity as foil to Carver's deflecting smugness. Allen, on the other hand, remained transfixed on the inveterate fraud of it all, reacting more from intuitive outrage than strategic instinct. But that was never good; so, strangely, while they might spar rhetorically, Allen sensed they were talking past one another.

Yet that didn't mean that they couldn't begin to relax and let the pressure slip away. Allen turned up the volume on the car stereo. "*This* is one of my all-time favorites," he said, "from my misspent youth. Do you know it? 'A Simple Twist of Fate.'"

"And *this* is where I *spent* that misspent youth," Allen gestured with a wave of the arm out the window as they ascended Bald Hill. "This is as close as you get to a mountain in this part of 'Michiana'," he said, pointing out the hump. Deep defiles crevassed the precipitous slope of the eroded moraine as they drove the serpentine stretch.

Sam said, "It almost reminds me of the Burma Road."

"Yeah, I've seen pictures."

"*I've* seen the *Road*."

"Show-off." He swatted at Sam playfully and took a corner faster than posted.

"Watch out!"

The Lexus' tires squealed, and the car barely glanced the meaty rump of a large buck, which sprawled to the pavement. The vehicle went into a spin, but at last came to a safe rest at the edge of the drop-off, facing the direction from which they'd come. Behind them, the terrified animal managed to regain its footing and clamber off.

Allen's heart stuttered with an adrenaline surge. "Jesus, Sam, are you alright? That guy came out of nowhere."

She nodded and smoothed her skirt. A car that must have been following them at some distance drove by them slowly, perhaps wondering if they needed any assistance.

"I think I'm OK." Sam peered over the cliff. "Not much room for error on this stretch, is there?"

"No, there's not," Allen said. "They really should do something about it—someone could get killed." Trembling slightly, he backed away from the precipice and onto the narrow shoulder.

Having cheated fate, they both laughed. Allen made a *very* careful U-turn and continued toward their destination. Then he saw a car stopped at an abandoned gas station just on the other side of Bald Hill, and Sam asked, "Isn't that the car that passed us back where we grazed the deer?"

"To tell you the truth, I didn't notice what it looked like." Allen glanced in his rearview mirror. "They won't get much service at *those* pumps," he noted mildly. Then, when the station was all but out of sight he said, "I guess they've figured that out; here they come behind us. Or am I being a tad paranoid?" She said nothing.

Allen still felt punchy with adrenalin when they arrived at their destination a short while later.

Sam squealed with delight, "You said it was a restaurant – you didn't tell me it was in such a lovely spot!"

A "Vacancy" sign flashed suggestively from the tasteful signpost that marked the adjoining Crossroads Inn, nestled in a grove of large beech and maple trees that arced over the highway.

Allen said, "It *is* nice, isn't it? They have a few secluded cabins, too." Absently, he looked for certain landmarks in the gathering dusk. "Carl Peters has a hunting lodge not far away…"

He reached for Sam's hand and chivalrously helped her out of the car. But still feeling woozy, it was he who stumbled at the door of the restaurant. "Steady," Sam said, reaching for his arm.

He all but fell into her embrace. "Oh, my God," he groaned, burying his face in her raven hair. "I just, just felt—unglued there for a moment."

"Always the rationalist," she said, "A brush with mortality will do that."

"No." He held her face in his gloved hands. "No, I don't care about myself; it was *you*," he said fiercely. "I—I can't lose *you*."

His lips brushed her cheek, and she turned her head – not in rebuff, he felt, but in *redirection*. "Allen, don't," she whispered. The mingling of their tears, cheek to cheek, was more intimate than any kiss could have been. "I'm not going anywhere," she said. "You can't lose me."

"Sam." Overcome with residual fear, the unrelenting pressure of the last few months, and the intensity of their intellectual interplay, he crushed her in his arms. "Sam." Completely undone, he whispered, "I can't go in there. I can't."

"Do you want me to drive us back?" she said. He shook his head.

She pushed him firmly to arms' length. "I'll get a room," she said. "You sit here." She moved him onto a bench near the entrance, away from the sweep of headlights and the eyes of approaching diners.

He sat and waited, and she returned shortly with a key.

"Come on." She led him toward a cabin, supporting his shaky frame. "I've ordered a meal from room service. You need to eat. And then sleep."

She helped him out of his overcoat and suit jacket, stripped off his tie and turned back the covers. He undressed behind the bathroom door and came our wearing a guest robe that had been hanging there. She pointed him to the bed, where he collapsed in a fetal position.

He sighed, "Just give me half-an-hour, OK? Then we'll have dinner…"

Idly, she picked up his shirt and trousers from the floor where he'd dropped them and hung them neatly in the closet.

Suddenly she was drawn to the window by the vaguest of noises—leaves rustling against the window, someone walking past an adjacent unit?—and feeling suddenly uneasy and vulnerable, she drew the drapes.

Now what?

Sam took the keys for the Lexus from Allen's coat. Still a little unsettled, she scanned the parking area for activity but saw no one. Then she went out, moved the car to a spot closer to their unit, retrieved their briefcases and re-entered the cabin. She settled into an armchair, elbows on knees, chin resting prayerfully on steepled fingers, and watched—what *was* Allen, anyway? Her colleague? Friend? A lover?—as he slept.

The Crossroads Inn, she mused. *We've indeed arrived at a crossroads. Where to go from here?* During preparations for the case and the subsequent trial, their relationship had become symbiotic. They could read each other's moods and anticipate one other's questions now. Whatever mutual attraction they shared had been transmuted into their work, where intellectual vitality became the sort of intensely creative, generative force that kept them both energized—giddily high, sometimes—through long days, late nights and close quarters.

When the food arrived, Sam tried to rouse Allen. He turned, whimpered, and twitched the way a dog will while dreaming, but didn't wake. She ate some dinner because she was starving after the rush of their day in court, and their near-miss after. Then she poured a glass of wine to calm her nerves and took out her notes from the day's trial. *No, Sam, tomorrow will be soon enough to review those...*

At last, she stood vacillating between the couch and the bed. Then, shrugging off her clothes down to her slip, she eased carefully under the covers and switched off the bedside lamp. "Oh, what the hell," she sighed, then insinuated herself into Allen's arms.

He stirred and moaned.

"Shhh, my darling," she whispered, so softly it was only a breath. *Let Fate make of this night what it will.*

PART IV

April 19
10:15 a.m.

Allen woke abruptly ten hours later, staring wide-eyed at the ceiling. It took a few seconds for his mind to recollect the circumstances, confirmed by the vision of Samantha Desai dozing contentedly next to him. Their passion during the night had occurred spontaneously, prefaced by mutual snuggling, the brush of her lips on his cheek and his aggressive response. *It was,* he mused, *like a dream.*

Of course, for some months now he'd imagined this moment, always accompanied by a healthy measure of obligatory guilt. Yet strangely, that emotion was absent now, and that made him wonder just how much he'd changed over the last few months.

Sam stirred, flopping a tawny arm across his chest; then she drifted back into deeper sleep. And looking at her beside him, Allen felt awash in good fortune. As he stared at her, gently swiping back the ebony strands that concealed her face, her eyes opened.

"Good morning, Love," he said.

"Hello, Darling." Sam half-rose to offer a long, lingering kiss, their tongues entwined, eager and restless and their lovemaking began anew.

9:30 a.m.
Pope County Courthouse

When court resumed, to no one's surprise Madison Fulbright did indeed opt to cut his losses and rest his case—thus avoiding another pointless tussle over multiculturalism. After he'd formally done so, Judge Thorndike asked, somewhat wearily, as if he already knew the answer, whether the prosecution wished to call any witnesses in rebuttal.

"The State," Allen declared, "calls Dr. Mark McCorkle to the stand, Your Honor."

Fulbright settled back for the show, more than a little relieved to rest his case. He'd touched all the bases. And the prospects were good that he could give as well as he'd got and do to Allen's rebuttal witness what had been done unto his own. And if he could just nuke today's witness, yesterday's carnage might be neutralized.

Fulbright had a dossier on McCorkle, but it wasn't much to work with. Though technically qualified as an expert, the man seemed an oddly unambitious character for an academic. McCorkle's lack of professional stature was curious; whether his inveterate goofiness was to blame, or some deeper shortcoming, he couldn't be sure. What he did know was that McCorkle knew his stuff. And Fulbright knew better than to underestimate a financial underachiever.

Allen had thought long and hard about the matter of his final expert witness. Originally, he had budgeted a substantial sum toward the procurement of some academic rock stars. Sadly, he'd found none who were willing to risk their reputations on such a controversial trial. In the end, he decided to go with McCorkle. After all, the defense had utilized local talent, so it might seem like overkill if he drew an academic carpetbagger from outside the area. That could play right into Fulbright's hands.

In any case, Mark had been the only member of Magdalene's faculty to support the prosecution, making him the only game in town. More importantly, Allen had been working with him for months and sensed that Mark would be better prepared to face down the defense attorney than any outsider could be. Allen was confident that the man's singular earnestness and straightforward manner would hold up well, no matter what was thrown at him. Sure, Mark was an odd duck, but then experts often were. He hoped the Judge would be impressed by someone willing to look him in the eye and give it to him straight.

The courtroom fell silent, save for the rustling of reporters' notepads issuing from the rear. Mark lumbered to the witness stand, rigidly erect as he raised his right hand for the bailiff. He puffed his chest out a bit as he promised to tell the truth, the whole truth and nothing but, saying "I Do" in a slow, clear voice.

He'd tried to dress up for the occasion but, in Allen's opinion, had fallen short. The standard issue houndstooth jacket was so cliche, he thought, its regulation dark brown elbow patches fraying visibly at the edges. Under the jacket, he wore a pale-yellow shirt which strained against his protruding stomach. The shirt was tucked into a pair of worn khaki pants, giving him an unpleasant, monochromatic effect of head-to-toe beige. Allen's decision not to take Samantha's dictum of contrasting his shirt to his pants seriously, now had come back to haunt him.

Allen took a deep breath. *That* shirt was clean at least. No visible coffee or ketchup stains. And, to his surprise, McCorkle's graying mop of curls did look as if it had been recently brushed. Then he noticed Samantha, who was making not-to-subtle brushing motions to her face and chin in the Professor's direction. He looked back at McCorkle, now seated in the witness chair, to see a few crumbs of what he assumed to be some remnants of a breakfast meal trapped in his beard.

Mark waved back at Sam, mistaking her subtle gesticulations.

How can such an intelligent guy be so indifferent to the impression he makes on others? Allen stood up and gave a quick once-over to his own ensemble, a dark navy, single breasted suit with a crisp white shirt, a blue and yellow paisley tie. He might not be as flamboyant as Fulbright, but he did have style.

Near the witness chair Allen set up an easel containing a whiteboard, markers, and certain materials to be used later in the testimony.

Then Allen began: "Professor McCorkle, will you please give this court a synopsis of your credentials."

"I hold a BA in History from Chicago, an MA from Northwestern and a PhD from Cambridge University."

"That's Cambridge, England, correct?" Allen asked. McCorkle wasn't one to puff up a résumé or trumpet his own accomplishments. But if ever there was a time for it, it was now. Thorndike needed to know that this was a serious historian. "Cambridge being, along with Oxford, one of the two finest universities in England, if not the world?"

"Yes, I'd say that's generally recognized in academe."

"Do you specialize in any particular period in history, Dr. McCorkle?"

"My major field of study is the history of the British Empire," McCorkle said, "with subsidiary areas of African, Middle Eastern and South Asian history."

Allen nodded. "Just so there's no confusion, that last field would represent what geographic region precisely?" Mark shifted in his chair. "Pretty much the region that was once part of the British Empire in South Asia—that is, the area of the present-day nations India, Pakistan, Sri Lanka, Myanmar and Bangladesh."

Turning toward the judge, Allen said, "Now then, Professor, this means you are credentialed in the fields of both the British Empire that once ruled the region, *and* in the modern history of the region itself."

"That is correct."

Allen handed a dossier to the judge, and Thorndike asked: "Does the Defense have any objection to these documents, Mr. Fulbright?"

Fulbright cleared his throat. "Not at this time, Your Honor."

Allen picked-up on the qualification but pressed on. He walked back to the prosecutor's table and fingered several papers lying on top of it. "Professor, I know some of what I ask you will seem redundant, but would you please explain again to the jury in simple terms what *you* understand sati to be."

"Sati as a practice," McCorkle straightened his posture, "is an ancient ritual in which a Hindu widow self-immolates on her husband's funeral pyre as a final homage and consummate act of loyalty and devotion. It is culturally associated with Hinduism, and formerly of some sects of Sikhism as well, but it is not scripturally enjoined. Neither do Hindu fundamentalists openly discourage it."

Allen cleared his throat. "Could you elaborate on that a bit, Professor?"

"Well," McCorkle began again, clearing his throat, "most Hindus regard the practice as a perversion of the Hindu texts. Neither the Vedic or any of the early Dharmasutras or Dharmasastras make mention of it. In fact," he continued, "the Rigveda explicitly states that a widow should return to her father's house after her husband's death."

"I see," Allen responded. "So, would you consider the practice of Sati more a cultural or a religious practice?"

"Oh cultural, to be sure," Mark answered immediately. Even in its heyday, over one hundred-fifty years ago, it was practiced by only a small minority of Hindus and Sikhs, usually among the upper castes, and generally only in particular areas of the Indian subcontinent: Rajasthan in the West and Bengal in the east. Some nineteenth century reporting estimates 6,000 instances of sati in Bengal from 1815 to 1824, but with a population of nearly twenty million, this was still a very rare event, at least in its classic form."

"And what exactly do you mean by—in its classic form?"

"Its classic form being the ritual in which the widow is placed or jumps upon the funeral pyre of her husband," McCorkle said calmly. "Other manifestations include the construction of small huts in which the deceased husband and widow are burnt together. In other regions, pits were dug in which the husband's remains were lowered along with other flammable materials. The widow would then jump or be pushed into the pit once the fire had started. Certainly, the classic ritual isn't the only way for a widow to kill herself, if she is determined to do so. Still, it is an extreme aberration."

Allen winced at the thought of jumping into a burning pit, "and the widow would commit this ritualistic suicide voluntarily?"

"In theory, yes."

"If there was no religious mandate to do so, then what was it that induced them to make this sacrifice?"

"It was an outgrowth of the caste system, I think," the Professor mused. "Hinduism is a faith grounded in fatalism, an acceptance of destiny and suffering, leavened with the promise of starting again: reincarnation."

"And in your expert opinion, how and why did sati attach itself to Hindu religious practice," Allen asked.

"Well," McCorkle leaned back in his chair and interlaced his fingers across his broad paunch. He was in his element now. "The origins of Sati are very obscure, but I subscribe to the theory that it began among Rajput warrior castes as a way of preventing wives from falling into the hands of their enemies, who were known to commit mass abduction and enslavement of captured women. But nothing is certain. Some say the origins of sati are more ancient. There are even accounts of it left by Alexander's Greeks, who witnessed the ritual over two millennia ago."

"Well, ten-year-old Roop Kumar was hardly at risk of abduction or mass rape in Principia, Indiana, Professor," Allen reasoned aloud. "Were there any other motivations for the practice? For example, why was this onus placed on widows?" Allen's tone was prodding.

"They have long been regarded as burdens to the family," Mark expanded. "She is, to all intents and purposes, blamed for her husband's death. And while her in-laws were charged with the widow's support, the quality of that life is minimal. In old India, widows were not allowed to remarry, nor have control of their children. They were forced to dress plainly and consigned to scullery work for the rest of their days."

"Any other inducements?" Allen asked.

"As the practice spread among the Indian castes, it became something of a cultural trend that conflated the act of sati with the idea of an elevated state, a status symbol, if you will. The widow would achieve a sort of martyrdom and the act would give her and her husband the prospect of reunion in paradise. Her family gains prestige, while her in-laws are enriched by her dowry and relief from the burden of her lifelong support."

Satisfied with his witness's performance thus far, Allen proceeded: "Professor McCorkle, you have listened to Professor Besant minimize the coercive nature of sati while Mr. Carver made the argument that Westerners are not even qualified to judge the morality of the ritual. What are your thoughts on their conclusions, respecting descriptions of sati's origins and history?"

"Let me put it this way," McCorkle said. "While some of the facts they related are accurate, their interpretation of the historical context of this practice could be construed as…" As he paused for a moment, Allen could see his eyes through smudged glasses, looking up, as if searching for the right word.

"Deceptive," he concluded. "There is no reference at all to the reaction of other cultures to sati, for instance. Neither did they consider all the other interests involved in depriving the poor widow of life. Historically, just as in this case, everyone seems to have had something very temporal to gain from the event, except for the widow herself. Professor Besant rather ignores those, I think."

"Would you please expand on that assertion, Professor?"

Bending forward slightly, McCorkle answered, "You must understand that when the British first came to India, they did so as merchants, not conquerors. In fact, for the first hundred-odd years of British rule in India, the East India Company, not the British government, ruled formally, though the latter did exercise extensive regulatory control. I tell you this, so you may understand that Englishmen were initially very *leery* about interfering in the religious affairs of their subjects, regardless of the ruling entity. It was bad for business."

The Professor straightened his glasses, then shoved them up the bridge of his nose. "Those in charge feared their profits might suffer from such intervention. And it seemed folly to court rebellion. Now, that was all well-and-good, so long as the British presence was minimal. But as more merchants, soldiers, bureaucrats and, especially, missionaries came to India, more of them stumbled across the practice of sati and were horrified by it. The cases of child brides were especially difficult for them to accept. And so, a reforming impulse sprang up which lobbied energetically for the abolition of sati. These folks recorded and left behind literally hundreds of documented accounts of sati, including some attempts by British citizens to stop the ceremonies, often at substantial risk to their own lives."

From force of habit, the Prosecutor paced in front of the vacant jury box. He asked: "So instances of widows being forced to commit this act against their will…and more to the point, child widows…are well-known to history it seems," Allen responded, turning to the room.

"And was sati the only cause over which the British interfered in native customs?"

"Oh, by no means," McCorkle said in a stronger voice. "As the British presence in India grew, they resolved to stamp out local practices they considered unacceptable. For instance, they attempted to discourage the killing of female infants, a practice that is sadly still common in much of Asia. They also suppressed brutal gangs of thugs who roamed the highways and byways of India, strangling travelers as a sacrifice to the goddess Kali—quite literally, thousands of people a year.

"And especially regarding women, the British passed laws affecting the right of widows to remarry and inherit wealth, as also to set a minimum age of consent— twelve, I believe—this happened after the death of a ten-year-old on her wedding night. These measures, too, were vigorously protested at the time by some Hindu 'traditionalists.'"

"OB-JECT-SHUN!," Fulbright bellowed, shooting to his feet. "Your Honor, the Hindu practices of the 19th century writ large are NOT on trial here. The record of British colonialists in India, while fascinating, is hardly relevant to the task placed before us today. We are talking about a man's right *now*, in the late twentieth century, to practice the religion of his culture, which Professor McCorkle has been so assiduous in besmirching. I call upon the prosecution to limit his questions to the purpose of extracting information relevant to this court, or to excuse him from the stand."

"Sustained," Thorndike agreed. "You've been skating on thin ice for a while, Mr. Southworth."

"Yes, Your Honor," Allen said. "What about today, Professor?"

"Today?" McCorkle stammered; his train of thought derailed yet again.

"Yes, Doctor, *Today*," Allen pressed. "Is sati still an established practice in the Hindu culture? Does it remain an integral part of daily Hindu life and practice?"

"By no means," he replied. "In addition to the British campaign to suppress sati on the grounds of human rights, along with the assistance of prominent Indian figures like Rammohun Roy, the so-called 'Father' of modern India, the Governor-General abolished the ritual in 1829."

"But surely if the British sought to stifle this important part of Indian culture through their domineering, imperialist, one-sided world view as the defense contends, then the Indian government MUST have taken measures to reinstate the practice after independence? Right?" Allen asked.

The Professor's face registered surprise, oblivious to

the sarcasm in Allen's tone. "Well, no," he said. "Various Indian-ruled territories began banning the practice as early as 1812, and Hindu leaders such as Swaminarayan preached against the practice by arguing that it had no Vedic standing and that only God could take a life he had given. So, you see Mr. Southworth, Hindus themselves have fought against the practice, just like British imperialists. But it wasn't until about a decade ago, forty years after the end of the British Raj, that the Indian Government enacted the Prevention of Sati Act, making it a capital offense to support, glorify, or attempt to commit sati, irrespective of the volition of the widow."

"And has this prohibition been effective?" Allen pushed.

"There have been scores of suspected cases in the last fifty years or so," McCorkle continued, "that were of the same spectacle variety we have seen here. The most spectacular contemporary case occurred in 1987; the police concluded it was coerced.

"Was anyone punished for this murder?" "No."

"Why not?"

"Several reasons," Mark began. "First, even though thousands participated in the event, no one would come forward as a witness. Shrines and celebrations of the sati, though also technically illegal, continued anyway, heedless of legal repercussions."

He began to stroke his beard, then continued.

"More important, perhaps, was the fact that the issue has melded with others as tests imposed by Hindu fundamentalists seeking dominance over other communities. They are especially strong in Rajasthan, where the sati in question took place. Leaders of such groups as the Hindu Mahasabha and the RSS refused to condemn the act or its participants."

McCorkle drew his open palm over his face. "You see, it has gotten wrapped up in a host of other issues. So-called 'authentic' Hindus now organize politically against allegedly inauthentic, Western-oriented Hindus, smearing them as colonialist relics. Once cultural difference entwines with politics, the aims become more suspect."

"So, I take this to mean you don't hold deconstruction theory in very high regard?"

"I suppose that depends on what you're after," McCorkle conceded. "If one seeks an intellectual device by which to declare victory preemptively in any argument, without even contemplating major questions of history, let alone answering them, then I suppose it is useful.

"But" he raised his voice, "if one is honestly engaged in the pursuit of knowledge *and* truth, of clues as to what lies ahead, as well as lessons with which to illuminate past mistakes, it can be mischievous. Because, at its core, deconstructionism is reductive: It posits that there is no objective truth because there are no objective universal standards by which to assess that truth."

"'No objective universal standards,'" Allen repeated, his index finger wagging in the air in the direction of the Judge.

"One civilization's as good as another, multiculturalism and deconstruction say." The witness paused to drink from his water glass. "And *yes*, not being, uh, *judgmental* so to speak, is less likely to get people mad at you. "But consider this: It's also less likely to produce a coherent standard of behavior. For to make a judgment, one must also possess a critique with which to defend it. Without grounds for critique, this becomes a wonderful environment in which misguided idealists and opportunistic hustlers may flourish. But it also would deprive ten-year-old brides of the cultural protection once afforded unquestioningly, by virtue of simple residence in this country."

"A child like Roop Kumar."

"Yes, most definitely."

Allen walked back behind the defense table, grasped the rail behind and bowed his head to the audience. "What is your candid opinion of both Theo Carver's views of this case and the prospective view of multicultural America to which that school of thought has given rise?"

"My *candid* appraisal?"

"None other."

"I respect Mr. Carver's work in the community," Mark shrugged. "But I think he does a profound disservice to it by spreading what are essentially myths disguised as history and using them to discredit both the discipline and the very means by which students and citizens must judge events that occur in the world every day."

"Hmm," Allen chuckled. "That's a mouthful, Professor. Would you please distill your rebuttal into a brief synopsis for this court?"

"I'll do my best." McCorkle inhaled deeply. "His whole emphasis on diversity is very appealing. It's designed to be so. But what does that word 'diversity' really *mean* in a cultural context?"

Allen turned, then nodded encouragement, smiling.

"If it means," Mark continued, "simply and traditionally, that people of all backgrounds are welcome in this country, to share in its freedom and prosperity, then you won't get any argument from me. But that's a lot different from looking at cultural diversity as both an *intrinsic and perpetual* condition of our political system. Because, you see, America isn't a permanent 'mosaic' any more than it's a European clone. Here, let me demonstrate."

McCorkle flicked a marker from his coat and grabbed a panel from the easel Allen had set up next to him. "For our purposes, let's allow that what I'm about to draw represents the dynamism of American culture."

He drew a circle, with two smaller circles inside it, almost like a geological representation of the Earth's crust, mantle, and core.

"Here," he pointed to the outermost circle, "are new entrants coming to America, from all over the world, bearing with them a bewildering assortment of languages, creeds, religions and so on. For many, the only thing they share in common with natives or naturalized citizens is the overall system by which their new freedoms are delimited and given form." Mark looked toward the Judge: "And that is not a contradictory concept, by the way." Thorndike nodded an acknowledgement of the point.

Pointing now to the center: "Here," he said, "is where those definitions and rules come from: our Constitution, our art, our traditions, our common law..."

"And the great mass in the middle circle?" Allen put in.

"Why, *that* is the diversity of America," Mark said earnestly, "the place where groups feel their way along, sometimes over several generations, toward the center core of American identity."

Allen said, "In what sense, then, is Mr. Carver right when he talks of the reality of American diversity?"

"He's only superficially right, because in his interpretation," McCorkle pointed again toward the middle of the circle and tapped gently for emphasis, "there is no central, abiding, definitively national core." Mark drew a box with his fingers. "Remember his Etch-a-Sketch illustration?"

"You would quarrel with his simile?"

McCorkle nodded reflexively. "Of course. This nation is no Etch-a-Sketch, to be shaken and remade episodically. It is a synthesized amalgam, enriched by the vibrancy of the diverse peoples who inhabit her. Ours is an enviable, yet at the same time, dynamic condition *protected by*," he leaned forward as if to emphasize the words, "the oldest constitutional government on Earth. And that this government is derived from Western civilization—its religions, its literature, and its philosophers—is hardly a propagandistic claim. It is an incontestable fact of history."

Allen folded his arms. "Let me play devil's advocate for a moment. Isn't it dangerous or provocative to elevate one culture over another like that, in such a diverse environment as you describe? Doesn't Mr. Carver have a point?"

McCorkle straightened his back and winced. "Look I'm not suggesting that Europe or Europeans are inherently superior—*morally* or *intellectually*. All kinds of factors induce cultural advance or stagnation, independent of one another: geography, climate, individual genius, microbes, accident and sometimes just dumb luck. *Good history* – and there really is such a thing – *should not be hubristic.*

"But fairness doesn't demand *blindness*," McCorkle said firmly. "If it were possible, for example, to place Notre Dame Cathedral alongside a thatched hut to demonstrate the respective architectural sophistication of cultures, as evidence that the one was more technologically complex than the contemporary other," he shrugged, "that would not be unreasonable.

"But to be fair, one would have to keep in mind that, if the same feat were somehow replicated for a comparison two thousand years ago, you might end up with the opposite result. It would, nonetheless, be unreasonable to draw any conclusions as to the respective morality of cultures from such a comparison."

He reached for the glass of water on the witness stand and gulped some down. Then he said: "The same cannot be said when examining respective cultural practices, however. Within America's traditional legal context, to forbid a practice such as sati might reasonably and unashamedly be defended as an act of civic virtue by Western lights. Here, it is perfectly reasonable— unless the philosophic foundation of this nation is to be scrapped—to render moral judgments on rites which are judged today as barbarous, not just by Americans, but the vast majority of South Asians, not to speak of most of the world.

"Principles either define a culture or they do not. Either a larger civilization derived from that culture is living and viable, or it is vulnerable, decaying, moribund."

"And might this be one of those defining moments, when we must choose between the two?"

"Absolutely, in my opinion," the witness said. "But since many people naturally avoid conflict, their receptiveness to many of the arguments advanced by the witnesses for the defense seems more explainable, if not excusable."

Sweat beads erupted on McCorkle's brow; he pulled out a handkerchief, quickly mopped his forehead and went on: "Not only that: One of the reasons, in my opinion, so-called Eurocentrism is under such assault is that the wrong inferences are being drawn from, and sometimes imputed to, traditional scholars."

He cleared his throat. "The way history has played itself out does not constitute evidence of racial or ethnic superiority. Nor does it speak to the rectitude of European cultures just a few decades removed from fascism and communism to which they also gave rise. No serious scholar should contend otherwise.

But America is a more refined incarnation of the

Western legacy. It possesses a synthesized culture all its own. We cannot pretend that this country, however dynamic it may be, can be reinvented, or redefined, if you will, its *core values* contorted so as to conform to the latest demographic trends, and still maintain the type of unity and success it has enjoyed up to now."

Allen affected bewilderment. "But Theo Carver has testified that we have no choice but to adapt to changing 'demographic trends,' as you call them."

McCorkle gripped the witness chair, his gripping fingers white with stress, or perhaps excitement. "In my opinion, Mr. Carver is at his most disingenuous when he attempts to undermine our national purpose. He is really scheming to pit one group against another, to the point that, eventually, our entire society will be infected with recrimination. And the fact that we need even to debate these issues at this advanced date—whether to allow a *child* to join her dead *husband* on a funeral pyre—speaks volumes about the success of the Carvers of this world."

More agitated now, Mark twirled his beard with his index finger. "Diversity already *defines* America and always has. Our diversity is inherent, integral and *permanent*. The only diversity that needs preserving in America today is *intellectual* diversity. And in that spirit, even opinions like Carver's should be protected within the context of the established legal precedents, political traditions and common law that define us as a united American culture."

He sat back in his chair. "That's it... in a very big nutshell."

"Thank you, Professor," Allen said. "Thank you very much."

"You're very welcome, Sir."

Samantha grinned approval at the two as the prosecutor rejoined her at their table. She patted Allen's hand collegially while passing him some notes and gave McCorkle a discreet thumbs-up.

Allen had accomplished precisely what he'd set out to do. He'd allowed his witness to make a reasoned and coherent case. McCorkle had placed sati in proper philosophical and historical context. *Underappreciated he might be at Magdalene, but he sure as hell isn't by this prosecution.* Allen was hugely grateful – and McCorkle's testimony hadn't cost a dime. Yet till after Fulbright had taken his shot, Allen couldn't be certain he hadn't gotten just what he'd paid for.

April 19
1:30 p.m.

Madison Fulbright had been uncharacteristically quiet during Allen's examination. He'd sat tilted back in his chair, listening, thumbs hooked in his vest, occasionally stirring to jot a short note on his legal pad. For the most part, he seemed the picture of equanimity: serene, pensive, a slight smile rippling intermittently across his face.

But Allen suspected that Fulbright's demeanor masked a silent intensity, and he harbored little doubt that his former colleague had been champing at the bit for 48 hours, awaiting the chance to strike back, to reclaim the initiative.

Fulbright looked more magisterial as he rose, impeccably attired, suave, supremely confident. For a moment, he regarded his quarry, his head slightly atilt. Then the stalking began:

"A *nutshell*," he began. "May I say, sir, that you have selected a most appropriate container for your argument." Then came the big smile.

"You've a right to your opinion, Mr. Fulbright," Mark replied stolidly.

"Mr. McCorkle. Excuse me, *Doctor* McCorkle," he corrected. "How long have you been at Magdalene College, in a professional capacity?"

"About six years," Mark replied equably.

"Six years," the attorney repeated. "And would you please tell the court what your salary was last year, *Professor*." Fulbright turned his back to the witness.

Stunned, Mark met Allen's eye.

Allen, too, was unprepared for this line of attack, but he readily seized the cue. "Objection, Your Honor!

This line of inquiry speaks neither to the witness's expertise nor to his testimony in this case."

"Excuse *me*, Your Honor," Fulbright rejoined whirling. "But the quality of an academic's testimony is directly tied to his or her standing in the field. And since a measure of one's eminence in this, as in any other, field may be at least partially a function of the market-place, Dr. McCorkle's relative professional standing is relevant."

Thorndike didn't hesitate. "I'll allow it."

"Now then, *sir*," Fulbright said. "I shall repeat the question: what was your *salary* last year?"

"I, uh, am part time and so, uh, am unsalaried." Hesitant, almost inaudible, he said, "Last year I earned about seventy-five hundred dollars."

"Excuse me, Dr. McCorkle," Fulbright cupped his ear toward the witness. "Would you please repeat your answer, so everyone may hear it?"

Mark repeated it, more loudly than Allen would have preferred.

"And tell me, Dr. McCorkle. Do you have any benefits with your employment? Dental? Medical? A retirement plan?"

McCorkle hung his head. "No, I do not."

"You don't have tenure like Dr. Besant, do you?" Fulbright drilled. Then he stepped back from the witness and regarded Mark with what looked like studied contempt. "Tell me, Professor, have you applied for work elsewhere? I mean, this hardly seems enough of a salary on which to raise a family."

"I have no family, but, yes, I have applied elsewhere," McCorkle replied, subdued. "Hundreds of times."

Allen winced; Samantha sucked in her breath. They hadn't expected Mark to say anything like this. They glanced at each other. "Christ!" Allen muttered *sotto voce.*

Fulbright cupped his ear to the audience. "Excuse me *doctor,* what was that?

Hundreds of times? *Hundreds?*"

"Probably." Mark hedged, as he pulled at his tie.

"Well, then, Professor," Fulbright gloated. "And why do you suppose no one wants you to work for them?"

Mark replied, "I… don't know, really." He shook his head. "I just don't know. I guess I don't interview very well. Or because my field's not in vogue. Or my age, or my politics. Or even my race and gender. I—I don't know."

Allen's gut roiled. *Damn! He looks like a cornered animal.*

Fulbright paced in the Judge's direction now. "Ah, I see. Your inability to find a job is a result of *discrimination* against *you,* not because you are *undistinguished, un-esteemed* in your field?"

Mark's left hand gripped the chair's arm and trembled. "I told you; I just don't know."

"That seems to be one of many things you *don't know*, Professor," Fulbright smiled.

Allen jumped up. "Your Honor, Counsel seems more intent on humiliating the witness than in eliciting testimony."

"I agree." Thorndike glowered disapprovingly at the defense attorney. "I think you've made your point, Mr. Fulbright. Please proceed."

"Very well."

"Would it be all right," McCorkle asked the Judge directly, "if I removed my jacket?"

Thorndike nodded.

Fulbright moved in. "Dr. McCorkle, it is your contention that Roop Kumar was *compelled* to commit sati, is that right."

"I believe so, yes." Mark shifted in his chair.

"Professor McCorkle, do you possess other degrees of which the court is unaware?" Fulbright spun his pen between his large fingers.

"I don't think I understand what you mean."

"Well, are you also trained as a sociologist? An anthropologist? A psychologist? A theologian, perhaps?"

"N-n-n-o..."

"Then, how in the world," Fulbright nudged, "do

you believe yourself qualified to render an opinion as to the state of mind of Roop Kumar on the morning of her death?"

McCorkle sat upright. "I base my evaluation on historical accounts of the practice and the evidence of coercion many of them contain."

"But you yourself have testified that many women who performed this rite in the past did so voluntarily. Is that not the case?"

"Objection, Your Honor. For the tenth time, Roop Kumar was no woman."

"Sustained."

Fulbright started again. "But many of the widows committed sati voluntarily, right?"

Mark nodded.

"Thank you, Professor. Then your conclusion that this was a so-called coerced *sati* would require something other than historical expertise, would it not? It would seem to require an after-the-fact psychological profile, would it not?"

Allen pounced. "Your Honor, the State of Indiana does not recognize the right of a ten-year-old to consent to such a thing. So, it is immaterial to this case."

Fulbright roared: "It has *everything* to do with this case, Your Honor, because she herself *committed to the act*. At least until the Prosecution proves otherwise."

Thorndike's brow knitted. "I'll allow it so long as the contention is confined only to the *rite*."

Fulbright looked again at the witness, hiking-up his eyebrows as he waited for a reply.

Mark said, "Perhaps it would seem so. But part of the historian's craft involves speculation on a whole spectrum of issues. History, after all, is about human beings and…"

"Ah yes," Fulbright agreed. "But we are discussing a contemporary, not an historical event, is that not so?"

"Yes, but—"

"Thank you, Professor," the Defense Counsel broke in. "And you are not licensed to render psychological evaluations, are you?"

"Of course not, but you misunderstand—"

"*Thank* you, Professor." Madison Fulbright turned away.

"Now then, would you consider yourself an admirer of the British?"

"That depends on what—"

"Are you not what one might fairly call an Anglophile?"

"Of course not!" Mark snorted, with uncharacteristic emotion.

"You admire the way in which white Englishmen snatched up half the world and its people, don't you,

Professor?" Fulbright toyed with some papers on the defense table.

"That's ridiculous!" McCorkle protested.

"*Is* it?" Fulbright laughed, almost loudly. "Haven't you written articles which veritably gush about the British dissemination of culture—civilization, as it were—to the rest of the *benighted* world?"

"Listen, Mr. Fulbright, you have completely mischaracterized my line of argument."

Fulbright's contemptuous tone seemed finally to elicit emotional resistance from McCorkle. The hammer blows of the unexpected personal attacks had intimidated him, Allen thought, that was all too clear. As comfortable as Mark might feel about his command of the subject matter, he seemed mortified by this unmasking of his professional standing. But now Defense Counsel had returned the battle to Mark's turf, where he might at least counterattack.

McCorkle said, "I do not look upon the British as paragons of virtue, but it would be silly to deny that they have had influence on the present-day world far disproportionate to their relative numbers. Great Britain was an imperialist nation, and in this sense the World should be grateful: They disseminated the fruits of the Enlightenment and the Industrial Revolution to distant lands that might otherwise never have become acquainted with concepts of democracy, individual liberty and universal humanity. They spread scientific knowledge; built roads, canals, railroads, telegraph lines and irrigation systems. They founded universities and cities like Hong Kong, Singapore, Bombay, Calcutta, New Delhi, Melbourne, Ottawa, Baltimore and Boston."

McCorkle grasped the chair arms for support, huffing and puffing so audibly in response to Fulbright's smirk, Allen was half-afraid the big man might suffer an asthma attack or worse.

Mark went on: "They ended the slave trade in places where it had been routine since antiquity. They provided a common language to regions drowning in linguistic stews. And they had the fortitude to end practices like sati and human sacrifice which they considered affronts to civilization. They brought democracy and secular law in their train. How many of us today, in this age of political conformity, would have the courage to do the same?" Fulbright placed his palms together and offered an ironic bow.

"Well, that was an eloquent speech, Professor." Allen could read his former colleague pretty well; he'd be too smart to engage in a prolonged historical debate with McCorkle. He leaned forward now, expecting Fulbright to try another tack.

Let's see," Fulbright said. "The Enlightenment, scientific knowledge, universal humanity—juxtaposed against, hmmm, slavery, linguistic stew, *sati, human*

sacrifice! Sounds a helluva lot like Anglophilia to *me!*"
He glanced at Thorndike, throwing his huge arm in the
air in mock frustration.

This time, it was McCorkle who smiled; he'd made
his point. "You have a right, of course, to your opinion, Counsel."

Fulbright changed his tone, spiraling his open palm
above his head: "Now, then, Professor, you speak so
glibly of moral absolutes, as if some worldwide consen-
sus exists, even on matters of life and death."

"Is there a question in there somewhere?" Mark
asked.

"Only this," Defense Counsel refocused, looking
grave. "How do you think Hindus might react to certain American practices such as, say, capital punishment,
sexual promiscuity, abattoirs, surrogacy or abortion?
Mightn't they regard *those* as *immoral,* even *barbarous?*"

"Yes," McCorkle replied. "And well they might."

Fulbright looked surprised. "Do you indict *American* culture as well, then?"

Mark drew himself up in the witness chair. "Not
our *traditional* culture, but aberrant strains within it
which are intrinsically at odds with its established moral
precepts. That, of course, is the risk a democracy takes
and must live with. This is not unprecedented, after all.
The reason we were able to rid ourselves of slavery is that
we could recognize the inherent fallacy, the fundamental

contradiction that made civil war inevitable. But all the relativists and multiculturalists offer are excuses for practices which were, at least up to now, unthinkable to us."

Mark spread out his arms, exposing prominent sweat-stains. "Please understand that I'm not talking about India here. If a democratic India opted for the practice, I suppose they would be entitled to it, or to fight over it, just as we fought over slavery."

Imperialism is gone, after all," he said. "Yet India still regards sati as a crime on its books, however imperfectly it may be enforced. And the United Nations Charter on Human Rights, for better or worse, originated from Western thought, largely disseminated by the British Empire and the United States."

McCorkle threw his hands up. "Yet how could any enlightening Western impulses have ever occurred without stepping on someone's cultural toes? Whether, and the degree to which, America has slipped its moorings is certainly an issue that can spark debate over the interpretation of our core beliefs. But that's much different from arguing that we have no core beliefs at all. And the fact that we, as a nation, have grown accustomed, even comfortable, with behavior that would have appalled our grandparents, says much more about contemporary life, along with its arguable misdirection, than about the integrity of an earlier moral code."

Fulbright started, as if taken aback. *But dammit,*

Allen thought, *McCorkle has opened-up a new political avenue for Fulbright to pounce on...*

Defense Counsel asked, "Would you characterize yourself a conservative then, Professor?"

"In what sense?" Mark shrugged.

"In the sense that you hate change of any sort."

McCorkle let out a quick, quiet laugh. "That's preposterous, Counselor."

"You would prefer that this country remain dominated by *white European men*, would you not?"

"My perspective on this country's history and politics has been molded by certain principles in which I believe strongly, if that's what you're asking. The fact that I am an Irish American male is irrelevant to that molding."

"You're very *protective* of those principles, aren't you?" Fulbright nodded.

"I suppose... unless they change so much as to affect our core institutions. Then I become somewhat revolutionary myself."

"*Aha!* So, you are a relativist, *after all, are you not?*"

McCorkle frowned. "Only inasmuch as my principles are consistent, relative to a *larger idea*," he said. "Multiculturalist reductionists, at their core, believe in nothing *but* mutual sovereignty—which means essentially that they are devoted to the principle of being devoted to *no* principles, at least none with any universal application to all human beings.

Remember, sir, that when the British outlawed sati, *that was a revolutionary act!*" He pointed at the attorney. "It was Hindu *conservatives* who rose to defend their traditions; but their protests were grounded in religious dogma, not humanist reason. So, whether my rising to the defense of American principles makes me a conservative or a revolutionary is for you to judge, and for me to live with."

The defense attorney strode toward the judge's bench. "Then, from your own words, those who believe that this country should respect cultural difference and rejoice in cultural diversity—whether the defendant, or Mr. Carver, Dr. Besant, or any of the good people who have rallied to their support—are not only *barbarians*, but *un-American as well!*" His last words echoed throughout the courtroom.

Amazingly, Homer Thorndike's hand lay limp on his gavel; he appeared transfixed by Fulbright's vehement exchange with the witness.

"That is *your* characterization, not mine," McCorkle answered.

Defense Counsel pivoted. "Mr. McCorkle, you have spoken disparagingly—and somewhat inconsistently, I might add—of conservative Indian political parties such as the BJP, RSS and Hindu Mahasabha, to which you've affixed my client, is that right?"

Allen glanced at the defendant, Sirkar Swaraj. *A*

courtroom newcomer entering ringside would be forgiven for failing to realize Swaraj, who was supposed to be the main attraction. Now he was almost invisible.

"I have said," McCorkle tapped the witness chair, "that such political parties are communal organizations who represent orthodox Hindus and make no bones about seeking Hindu supremacy in an otherwise diverse, democratic nation."

Fulbright scratched his head. "But now I'm confused. Isn't diversity a dirty word to you?"

"Come on!" Mark snorted.

Fulbright leaned against the defense table. "Well, let's see. Do you support or oppose affirmative action?"

Once again, McCorkle looked at Allen, who said sharply: "Your Honor, please. This badgering of my witness has gone on long enough. As broadly as the Defense Counsel might wish to cast his net, this case is not about affirmative action, nor is my witness and his views a defendant here. This foray doesn't even pass the laugh test."

Thorndike glowered. "Maintain your civility, Mr. Southworth, or I'll maintain it for you." He turned to Fulbright. "Counselor, he does seem to have a point, however infelicitously expressed."

Madison Fulbright calmly redirected his gaze to the judge. "If Your Honor will allow me, I think all I intend by this line of questioning will become clear presently.

Since this case has become intertwined with political philosophy, some license might reasonably be expected and indulged."

The judge sighed wearily. "Very well, but get to the point, *please*. No gratuitous digression, understand?"

"Perfectly, Your Honor. Thank you, Your Honor." Fulbright turned back to the witness. "Well, then, Professor. What do you say about affirmative action?"

"If you must know, I am opposed to it."

"'Curiouser and curiouser,' Professor. "You have more in common with those you denounce than you know. All of the aforementioned Hindu organizations oppose special electoral and governmental set-asides for particular groups which, incidentally, were first installed by the British governors you profess to admire so much." *Hm. Defense Counsel's done some homework, too,* Allen noted.

The witness made no reply.

"No comment, Professor?" Fulbright teased.

McCorkle rotated his large head stiffly. "That was done to maintain balance and reduce tension between various communities by reassuring them, minimizing suspicion of favoritism..."

"Sort of like multiculturalism, right?" the lawyer smirked.

"I suppose," McCorkle conceded.

"Professor, is it not the case that these so-called

universal truths you carry on about merely represent a desire on your part to superimpose Western Christendom over the world's other great civilizations? Is it not true that you disdain certain non-European components of American society? That you are not only contemptuous of them, in fact, but fearful as well?"

Mark fidgeted.

"Don't you secretly, in your heart of hearts," Fulbright pressed, "long for 1950s America, the land in which you grew up: baseball, hotdogs, apple pie and Chevrolet? An America that had its minorities under control?" He chuckled at the witness, even while glancing out of the corner of his eye at the judge. "Isn't the only real difference between Joan of Arc and Roop Kumar, at least in terms of the way in which they're perceived, the color of their respective skins?"

"You're twisting everything..."

"Haven't you better things to do, Professor, such as looking for *full-time honest work?*"

Allen leapt to his feet again. "Your Honor, these gratuitous insults do nothing to advance this inquiry and are not worthy of *the dignity of this Court!* I demand that counsel apologize for his intemperate and mean-spirited remarks."

Fulbright shot back: "I will not apologize, Your Honor, given the way my own witness was browbeaten mere days ago! If the witness' motivations are vulnerable to scrutiny, that's *his* doing, not *mine*."

Thorndike rapped his gavel so hard Allen thought it might splinter. "That may be so, Mr. Fulbright. But if you believe you can take liberties with me in the conduct of these proceedings, you are sorely mistaken. I sincerely hope you do not wish to impugn the dignity of this Court."

"Now, *proceed!" Thorndike admonished* – civilly, if possible."

"I'm finished with this... *expert* witness, Your Honor." Fulbright tossed a sheaf of notes onto his table and sat down behind it.

The judge's expression morphed into a smile. "In that case, does the prosecution wish to redirect?"

"Yes, Your Honor," Allen replied.

"Then, proceed—*please!*" Thorndike waved his gavel toward McCorkle.

Fulbright's cross had been rough on McCorkle, Allen knew. His witness had done as well as should have been expected, given Fulbright's ad hominem attack at the outset. But he'd never fully regained his footing under the unremitting assault of the defense. Allen saw little profit in revisiting the philosophic debate; that, in any case, he judged to have been a draw. So, he resolved to briefly rehabilitate his witness's *bona fides*.

Allen strode up to the witness box. "Professor McCorkle," he struggled to convey a little reassurance with his smile. "Do all full-time professors at Magdalene possess credentials superior to yours?"

"Indeed, no."

"You have an earned PhD, do you not?" "Yes."

"Isn't it true that several full-timers at the college are actually what's known as PhD/abd?" Allen turned his back to look at the judge.

"That's right."

"And Professor McCorkle, what does 'abd' mean?"

Mark sighed, "All but dissertation."

"So, while these full-timers *claim* to have PhDs, they haven't completed the major requirement for a doctorate, which is the dissertation, is that right?"

"That is correct."

He let that fact sink in a moment, then said, "Have *you* published, Professor McCorkle?"

"Extensively," Mark replied. "Four years ago, a monograph of mine on the Indian Mutiny was published – that sold out its first printing and was reviewed very favorably in many outlets, both domestic and international. I also contributed a chapter to a recent volume on the British Empire that is widely used in introductory courses on imperialism. And I have presented several papers at conferences and written scores of book reviews."

Allen cradled his chin in his right palm, and frowned, as if perplexed. "Yet Dr. Besant is tenured at Magdalene, and you are not, is that so? How do you account for that?" *Hope he knocks this one out of the park...*

Mark said, "That question would best be directed to the powers that be at the school, I suppose. I honestly try not to complain. But since Mr. Fulbright brought it up, in order to impugn my credentials, allow me to say this."

McCorkle arched his broad back. "Part-timers like me teach most of the courses the university offers, at a bare fraction of salary—with no benefits, besides—simply because we love to be in the classroom. Unfortunately, we are less esteemed, as a result, than tenured staff. Or to borrow a page from Defense Counsel, considered less *eminent*. I have no problem with having my expertise questioned. All I ask is that I be judged on my accomplishments, not my market circumstances. For there is no *market* in academe. There is only preference... and of course, tenure."

Allen nodded and smiled. "Thank you, Professor McCorkle. You are excused."

April 19
4:17 p.m.

Allen asked for and was granted a recess. It was time

to take stock, to assess the damage done by his rebuttal witness.

Mark McCorkle had proven a wash. Though initially
useful, he'd been badly shaken by Fulbright's vicious
jabs. And Allen blamed himself for that; he should have
anticipated this kind of assault on his witness's credibility.
Now he worried that, faced with a parade of "experts,"
the judge might winnow out the least credible. And while
his redirect had helped limit the extent of the damage
Fulbright had done, Allen couldn't be sure how much
was irreparable.

As Allen lingered at the prosecution table, arranging
folders and stuffing them into his briefcase, he rolled his
eyes at Sam—his fair comment on the day. She looked
worried, wagging her head at him in the direction of
Carl Peters, who was sitting two rows back in the spectators' section.

On gaining Allen's attention, Carl rose and shuffled
heavily toward the two, glancing left and right. "Jesus,
Allen," he whispered, "we got troubles." The Sheriff
hitched up his sagging trousers inelegantly, scanning in
all directions. "Today's *Dispatch* is out. And guess who's
the main attraction? *You.* And your 'second.'" Carl shot
a thumb at Samantha.

"What the hell are you talking about?" Allen asked.

Carl handed him a rolled-up newspaper. The two
men huddled, their backs turned to the front of the

courtroom, and Carl spread the paper where Sam could see it, too.

The region's premier newspaper more resembled the *National Enquirer* that afternoon than the *South Bend Dispatch*. Sprawled across the front page were three photos; it took Allen a moment to recognize himself and Sam in them... and to identify the context.

"Jesus Christ." Allen froze, jolted by an explosion of pain so intense he was certain he must be having a coronary.

The first photo was of him and Sam in an emotional embrace on the doorstep of the Crossroads Inn. The second, through the cabin window, showed Samantha apparently unbuttoning Allen's shirt. The third, captioned "The morning after?" depicted the prosecutor and his assistant leaving the cabin, arm in arm, smiling at each other.

The bold headline and subhead read:

"SATI" TRIAL ERUPTS IN SCANDAL.
Does tryst compromise Prosecution?

Scanning the article's text, Sam, gasped, then covered her mouth with her hand:

In a surprising development Wednesday, Allen South-worth, leader of the prosecution team in the so-called widow-burning case of Sirkar Swaraj has suffered a major blow to his credibility.

Compromising photographs obtained and published exclusively by the Dispatch suggest that the Prosecutor had an overnight tryst with an assisting attorney at the Crossroads Inn, a secluded hideaway just outside Burr Oak, Michigan.

While the photos do not constitute definitive proof of a sexual liaison, they leave Southworth in the compromised position of having to explain his overnight presence at the Inn on the evening of April 18. The prosecutor is married and the father of two.

Mr. Fulbright could not be reached for comment. But a spokesman for the Ganges Mission of Principia hastened to contrast the alleged behavior of Mr. Southworth with his "sanctimonious and jingoistic assault on the virtue and even the sanctity of Hinduism, Roop Kumar, and the very notion of a tolerant, diverse, multicultural America."

Allen had read enough. "Christ, Carl, is there any way Sam and I can get out of here without starting a riot?"

He felt an urgent tug at his sleeve. Struggling for her game-face, Samantha looked up. "I don't think it would be a good idea for us to leave together Allen; it would only make a bad situation worse."

The Sheriff leaned closer. "The lady's right, Allen. The national media are camped outside with their teeth bared. You'd only be providing more photos for tomor-row's editions if we hustled you both to the same car. Why don't you let Jonas take care of getting Ms. Desai the hell out of town?"

Sam glared defensively. "What do you mean by that, Sheriff?"

"Only that the press, tabloid *and* mainstream, has already staked out your apartment, Ma'am," Carl said. "So, I've taken the liberty of arranging a safe house up in Marcellus—that is, unless you object. I just thought it would be easier."

"I'm sorry, Carl," she said. "I meant nothing by it. Of course, I'll go with the deputy."

Allen's head began to spin, awhirl with calamitous visions: the destruction of his standing as prosecutor at the worst possible time; Sam's humiliation; the pros-pect of national ridicule. Then, of course, there was his family. How he hated thinking about that most of all.

Carl deadpanned, "Can't say much for your timing, Allen. Thorndike's a liberal, but he's not *that* liberal. Now we've got even more of a goddamn mess..."

Allen shook his head slowly. "I've gotta get out of here and buy some time, Carl, to figure out how to respond to this. Not too long, but I'll ask the judge for a continuance, a couple of days at least, maybe set up a news conference for the day after tomorrow..."

"That soon?" The Sheriff asked, wide-eyed.

"I think," the Prosecutor said, "that in this situation less'll be more. The longer I delay a response, the worse the hype will be." He slipped into the chair next to Sam and squeezed her hand under the defense table. "This is all my fault," he said fervently. "*All* my fault. But I'll get us out of it somehow. I'll be in touch with you tomorrow night over our next move in court. We still have a case to win."

Carl said, "You know that this was likely a set-up, don't you Allen? I thought something might be afoot when that Savarkar character stole out after Carver's testimony."

"Sure looks that way, doesn't it?" the prosecutor replied. "Somebody or some*thing* badly wants to get Swaraj out of this, after they'd gotten him into it. But I can't dwell on that now."

Sam sat staring at the table, absently twisting her necklace. Carl tapped her gently on the shoulder, hinting she should leave with Jonas. She inhaled deeply and rose as she began to pack her briefcase. Without another word, Allen disappeared with Carl down the stairwell to the basement of the court-house. There, screened by a cordon of security, he and the Sheriff exited to the parking lot.

But to their surprise, stealth was unnecessary. "Well, I'll be damned," Carl sighed. Not a single reporter was there to impede their flight. He asked one of his deputies where the mob might be. The deputy jerked his thumb toward the front of the building. "There's a knot of reporters, cameramen and microphones buzzing around something, or someone as yet obscured."

"What the hell is it?" Allen asked the burly sergeant. "All I know is," the trooper shrugged, "it's some woman. Quite a piece, too, from what I understand."

Gotta be connected to the headline somehow. "

"Carl," Allen said, "send somebody to get the details while we're still here."

He sat in the idling squad car and awaited the trooper's return, trying to distract himself by sketching an outline of his closing argument. *And since further testimony has been rendered moot by this latest development, it'll have to be brilliant...*

A tap on his window interrupted him. Allen buzzed it down.

The trooper bent down. "The Sheriff sent me." "That woman I mentioned a few minutes ago, the one talking to the reporters...They say she's your *wife*."

Allen recoiled. The pen fell from his limp hand. He simply sat, dumbstruck.

Carl Peters hurried to the car and got in, just as the swarm of reporters spotted them. "That tears it," he barked. "With all these vultures around, this is hardly the time for a family reunion. Let's get the hell out of here." "The Sheriff coughed, and the small caravan sped away along with its, now inert, devastated cargo.

April 19
6:30 p.m.
Cassopolis, Michigan

Allen had never fully appreciated what a godsend Carl Peters could be in a dicey situation.

Anticipating his need for privacy, the Sheriff whisked him away to his hunting cabin, followed by a deputy in an unmarked car to be left at Allen's disposal.

Carl's cabin was situated on a remote side road, about twenty miles east of the fateful Crossroads Inn. Allen scanned the large main room. For a guy who complained as much about his job as Carl did, he was anything but incommunicado here: The place was wired with all the requisite communications equipment—CB radio, fax, computer link—anything the Sheriff might need to stay in touch. Not that he'd neglected creature comforts, either, including a hot tub, satellite dish and a fully furnished bar.

A homely, wood-burned plaque hung over the mantle of the capacious fireplace: "Go For Burrrrr—Oak," Allen read aloud. He lifted a quizzical eyebrow at Carl.

Sheriff shook his bowed head and chuck-led ruefully. "A little joke between me and my missus. This place has been pretty much furnished by my poker winnings."

"Well, Carl," Allen said mildly, "remind me not to sit in with you and your cronies anytime soon. I seem to be shit-outta-luck."

Carl frowned but took the time to point out additional amenities, including a fully stocked fridge. Allen would want for nothing. "Thank you, Carl," he said, shaking the big man's hand. "I'm very grateful."

"You sure you'll be alright?"

"Right as rain." And he waved the men away.

But the amenities provided cold comfort once Carl and his officers left him alone... to brood. He tried to immerse himself in writing a letter of resignation to Judge Thorndike. But to quit at this stage of the trial, especially when his assistant was equally compromised, seemed inconceivable.

Then again, what choice have I got? How can I possibly argue my case to Thorndike when my face—and Sam's—are splashed all over the nation's papers? Yet a pause in the proceedings at this point would probably mean that any enthusiasm for prosecuting Swaraj aggressively would likely dissipate.

Allen stared vacantly at the legal pad...as if *it*, rather than his own missteps, was his real nemesis. He simply could not focus.

Bowing to the inevitable, he mixed a bourbon and

soda and, against his better judgment, surrendered to habit by turning on the six o'clock news. Like a moth to a flame, he was unable to resist the temptation to witness the spectacle of his own destruction, watching with the sound muted—until Jan's oddly gaunt but disarmingly pretty face flooded the screen.

All the way up to the cabin, he'd visualized the worst: the hectoring, the tears and the hare-brained reporters inquiring about Jan's "feelings." Yet there she was: well turned-out in a Kelly-green ensemble that perfectly complemented her auburn hair, but showing no tears, sobs or heaving shoulders. Rather, her aspect was one of perfect, even surreal, calm. Allen restored the sound after Jan had finished reading from a prepared statement, set her script aside, and indicated she'd take some questions. They came at her like pepper spray:

"Ms. Southworth, what prompted you to come here today?"

"After I was informed about the *Dispatch*'s early edition, I felt I had no choice but to appear before you all, to set the record straight with respect to my husband."

"Is it true you and your husband intend to divorce?"

"No, that is *not* true."

"But you don't live together any longer as man and wife, is that correct?"

"I've spent the winter in Florida with my children and my elderly parents, in part to spare the children the publicity surrounding this very high-profile case. Allen simply wanted to put us far from the media circus, to allow us to live our lives as normally as we might—with season passes to Disney World." Jan flashed a disarming smile at the crowd. "That sort of consideration is, incidentally, typical of my husband."

"But, Ms. Southworth, how do you feel about the photos in today's *Dispatch*?"

"What about them?"

"What do *they* say about your husband's consideration of *you*?"

"Typically, when Allen has a case like this, he immerses himself in it." Jan was in total control, smiling as if indulging a simple child. "The effort is unstinting, the hours murderous. He's very good at what he does and often sets strategy sessions in unusual venues and at unusual times, to capitalize on the creativity that springs from change of scene."

"So, he was 'caught'," she digitally air-quoted, "with an attractive woman who happens to be his co-counsel. So what? I have no doubt they were working on the case. It's happened before, it will happen again, I have no doubt about that."

"But what about his state of undress, Ms. Southworth?"

"Those photographs suggest nothing amiss. As far as I could see, he was missing only his tie." Jan leveled a searing stare at the impertinent inquisitor. "If that's proof of an affair, you might as well indict fifty percent of the male workforce on any given 'Casual Friday.'"

Jan threw back her head defiantly. "You people must understand something: Marriage is about trust. Without it, nothing else matters. I trust my husband implicitly and always have. It's as simple as that."

"Do you think your husband will step down as chief prosecutor in this case?"

She shook her head in defiant condescension. "Anyone, and I mean *anyone*, who thinks Allen South-worth is going to cut and run from his professional and civic obligations, and that he will be driven away by tawdry, unsubstantiated gossip, simply doesn't know the man I know. Not only will he *not* resign, but I am also confident that he's preparing his closing arguments as we speak – and what's more, he'll *win* in the end."

Jan clasped her hands before her. "May I speak to larger, more crucial issues for a moment? There is much more at stake here than personal matters, ladies and gentlemen, and I urge you all to remember that. Both the character of our society and the direction of its future are endangered by the incoherent arguments the defense has deployed to rationalize what is, in essence, *the sacrifice of a child*. And *that* is the issue on which you good people ought rightly to be focusing. To do less seems to me unconscionable."

Allen's thoughts of Samantha were now eclipsed by those of his wife—his astonishing, vivacious, brilliant wife—who'd somehow managed to pull off the most exquisite piece of public theater he'd ever seen. Not only had she salvaged what now passed for his honor – and perhaps, his case in the bargain – she'd also framed the context of his argument for him.

Quickly, he called Carl Peters and asked him to track Jan down and arrange a meeting. Then, with renewed confidence and intensity he dove into the task of composing his closing arguments.

April 21
6:30 p.m.

Allen labored through the night and on into the next day as if in monastic seclusion, breaking down, into digestible format, all the tortured arguments he'd absorbed, distilled, and concocted during the past four months.

Jan had not only removed a potentially fatal distraction from his work, but she'd also re-energized Allen's flagging resolve not to squander an unmistakable opportunity. After all, he'd never been one to miss an opportunity. And to do so now, after his wife had laid everything on the line for him, would have compounded the indiscretion he'd committed with Sam.

Roop Kumar must reclaim her place in the forefront

of his mind. Had she shrieked for mercy through the orange flame and acrid smoke that early morning in the forest? Or had salvation been her goal? Maybe it was somehow a perverse mixture of both.

Now the gravity of his task weighed upon Allen's labors again. For if his old friend and former partner succeeded in mutating the law he was obliged to serve, an ominous precedent would be set. America would be staring down the barrel of a gun. Civic mortality and disintegration loomed—not unlike Roop's fiery fate.

Allen reminded himself that these questions were far more consequential in the long run than his own failures and peccadilloes, and that these more crucial issues should be the fulcrum of his closing argument. Not even victory could erase the mess he'd unwittingly made. Nonetheless, there would be plenty of time for recrimination and restitution later, after this battle had been finally joined. *And won.*

April 22
10:30 a.m.

Despite its inapt location smack dab in the fields of rural Indiana, the Wharf had great seafood. And since Jan had spent her first ten years in New England, it had quickly become their favorite hangout in the earlier, happier days of their marriage. Here they would sit, among the ersatz nautica, feasting on lobster and steamed clams, planning their future together, their lives enriched both by mutual passion and expectation. It was late now, just before closing, as Carl had prearranged to skirt prying eyes. For her part, Jan had taken the precaution of sending her limo driver up over to Fort Wayne as a decoy, while she drove her Lexus to the restaurant.

Until just a few hours ago, those happier days had seemed irretrievable. Yet, as Allen walked in and spied his wife, a nostalgic shiver coursed delightfully up his spine.

She stood quietly, staring out the window over the river below, her chin resting in an open palm, the other arm crossed under her bosom. At first glance, Allen thought she'd never looked lovelier, draped in frosty cashmere. Yet as he approached, he realized Jan was markedly thinner – to a degree the TV cameras must have helped conceal. *These months must have been hard on her,* he thought with a pang of remorse. Strategic makeup hadn't entirely obliterated a furrow of dark circles under her eyes and inflamed capillaries on her nose. Even her hair seemed less lustrous, unusually coarse, and she'd styled it in a cap of tousled curls he'd never seen before.

As he approached, he squeezed her knobby shoulder. She jumped up, startled, and held herself awkwardly as they exchanged a stiff embrace. Starting, Allen apologized for startling her and sat down in his old familiar seat. Then he looked deeply at Jan.

He felt a broad smile spread unconsciously across

his haggard, bristly face. "Good morning, Starshine." He thought maybe use of his newlywed nickname for her might help break the ice; but he couldn't help feeling that, given the circumstances, the greeting sounded chirpy, even ludicrous.

"Hello, Allen." Jan smiled, as she arranged her napkin, businesslike. "You look terrible."

Up since Thursday, working on my closing," he explained almost giddily. "It doesn't matter much at this point. I'm on an adrenalin high and heading for the home stretch. I'm also starved. How 'bout you? Shall we dine continentally?" *Boy, my nervous nattering must be transparent to this woman who knows me so very well.*

"Not this late, thank you." She seemed not to be put off by his clumsy behavior. "I've kind of lost my appetite." He asked about the kids, who were still in Florida with her parents, then suddenly serious: "Are you all right, Jan? I mean, are you feeling, OK? You look almost too thin to me."

The transformation of her face was unnerving; any pretense of familiarity had instantly fled. "Oh, I'm just ducky, Allen, as long as I stay away from the newspapers." Her leveled gaze held no love for him; it felt decapitating. Allen bowed his head, trying to buy time…and to process her countenance.

Jan smiled grimly. "Oh, don't play that wounded contrition game with me, Darling. Wasn't it enough that you contrived excuses to stay away from home? Any particular reason why the *coup de grace* has to involve public humiliation?"

Allen's face flushed with genuine hurt. "Do you really think I planned it that way, Jan?"

"Oh, please," Jan scoffed. "A conspiracy? Is that the best you can do? I expected a little more originality than that, quite frankly. She took out her compact and dabbed powder on her face.

Allen said, "But your statement to the press, Jan – what was that all about? I thought you understood…"

"Ha! That's rich," she spat, "and so typical of you. Because it *is* all about Allen Southworth at the end of the day, isn't it? Well, my dear, you needn't fret; I'll keep up the façade, if merely to retain my own feeble sanity. I just ask in return that I not be treated like a fool."

"Listen, Jan," Allen tried recovering, "I know I screwed up, and I'm as sorry as I can be about it, but…"

"But what, Allen? Are you going to give me some jive about the changing culture and shifting mores getting the best of *you*? Who's the cultural relativist now?"

He had to admit: Her hostility stung, not to speak of her accusations of hypocrisy. "Am I a hypocrite? Fine, I'll cop to that if you want. But you know damned well that I'm basically a good husband and father. I've missed the kids, by the way…"

"Are you indeed? Faithful as well?" Her rueful chuckle sounded bitter.

"You know I am, Jan. That at my core I'm a good man. Hypocrisy is the tribute vice pays to virtue. Remember…"

"Oh, my dear, you can do better than Rochefoucauld. Or at least you'd better try."

Stupid of me. How'd I forget she was a Philosophy major?

Then, as if she'd suddenly exhausted herself, Jan sighed, "Listen, Allen, you have a very important job to do. That was also a big part of my performance today. The bad news for *us* is that my defense was, to say the least, inauthentic. The good news for you, however, is that I did it well enough, I think, to deflect those idiotic reporters. I'd take advantage of that, were I you."

For a moment Allen felt frozen in disbelief. Then he managed to blurt, "But, Jan, what does this mean for… us?"

Jan smiled tight-lipped, enigmatic, Mona Lisa-like. "I'm not quite sure how to answer now, my Dear." She gathered her things. "But we can address such questions later on. In the meantime, you'd better get yourself straight and do your job. Lord knows I've done mine. So why don't you just make sure that you win this case, so that I will not have abased myself to no purpose." She flopped her arms to her sides, sighing heavily. "We'll have plenty of time for reckoning after."

Following that cryptic aside, Jan planted a bloodless kiss on Allen's cheek, turned and strode out of the restaurant, skittering waiters clearing her path, leaving his ego floundering in her wake.

April 23
8:00 a.m.

It was an arduous undertaking, but Allen managed to redress the imbalance between his intellectual readiness and his situational scruffiness.

After taking a few quiet minutes more to review his notes, he sat out on his balcony absently watching the traffic woosh by in the morning rain. Then he headed back to Principia.

During the drive to the courthouse Allen listened to an audio tape of Henry Fonda performing as Clarence Darrow, more to prep for what he knew would be Fulbright's eloquent presentation than to polish his own delivery. Yet as he listened to Fonda's superb rendition, certain parallels between *Indiana v. Swaraj* and Darrow's signature case, the infamous Scopes "Monkey" trial of the 1920s, came to mind. Then, it had been biblical literalism in the dock; here, it was multiculturalism.

Then, Scopes had become a mere pawn, talked into violating the prohibition against teaching evolution in the schools, so that the ACLU and Clarence Darrow could make their larger political and cultural appeal to an insatiable public.

Darrow's career had always been staked on the defense, William Jennings Bryan's legacy on the prosecution. The Monkey trial is remembered for many things, but hardly at all for Mr. Scopes. Like Swaraj, he'd been dispensable to the larger drama, a useful pawn—a different sort of human sacrifice, this time to obscurity. Forever after, he would be a mere asterisk to the larger courtroom drama over the teaching of evolution in the schools. That had been nothing short of a cage-match, pitching reason against dogma, very much like the present contest.

Allen knew that at least he had the facts of the matter largely on his side. That is, unless the defense succeeded in casting doubt as to the very existence of objective fact in the Judge's mind. What troubled Allen most was that he'd been cornered into assuming the role of prosecutor-cum-philosopher – ironic, since he'd always avoided philosophy as too abstract, intangible, detached from everyday existence.

That was yesterday. He now realized that those same abstractions both defined the cerebral processes, *and* delimited thought's acceptable boundaries. Those boundaries, he appreciated, commanded the debate he and his friend Fulbright would conduct a short time later. Still, he couldn't shake the uncomfortable suspicion that he'd been lured into a snare by Fulbright's tactical baubles, like the fly to the spider's parlor. Now he was forced into a battle of philosophic ideas: one in which he was less practiced, less at his ease.

But now he was left with the daunting task of rendering these complex questions of political and religious philosophy into language that would be not only intelligible to the judge and a national audience, but convincing as well.

To evade the courthouse circus, Allen drove the borrowed unmarked car to the Sheriff's department. From there he'd hitch a prearranged ride with Carl Peters. The Sheriff was waiting in the parking lot, kibbitzing with Jonas. Their smiles disappeared when they saw Allen drive up and swing briskly from the sedan.

"Hey," Carl chuckled, now with a roguish grin. "You clean up pretty good."

"You'll never know *how* good," Allen smiled. He opened the trunk and retrieved files. "What's the word from the courthouse?"

"Everything's on schedule, as far as I can tell. Apparently, Fulbright's gonna run the gauntlet of reporters waiting in front of the door. Hoping to get on the tube, I suppose. Anyhow, it's a great diversion for us."

"Maybe," Allen sighed. "Not that he really needs more exposure at this point. Not that *any* of us needs it either," he added. "What about Ms. Desai?" *Damn my need to keep feigning formality in front of these two.*

"She's already at the courthouse." Carl tapped out a cigarette. "I delivered her there at about six this morning. She didn't look good, Allen."

"None of us does at this point," Allen replied lamely, snapping his briefcase shut. "Shall we depart, gentlemen?"

Jonas opened the door for Allen, then eased his massive frame into the driver's seat. Carl landed heavily on the passenger's side, snuffing his smoke while fingering his shirt pocket for a Tums.

Allen said nothing more on their short drive, merely scribbled some last-minute tactical inspirations on his legal pad, doubting he'd ever employ them. As in all the big trial moments of his career, an odd, inscrutable dynamic had overtaken him, preprogramming toward a stream-of-consciousness state.

It had always been like this. It was too near the event to prepare further, but his brain was busy, organizing thoughts, polishing phrases, choreographing the gestures that would define the performance. It was all there, though he couldn't yet envision it and wouldn't be able to do so, strangely enough, until its extemporaneous composition and delivery. Allen's subconscious knew the outcome long before his conscious mind did.

April 23
8:40 a.m.

Madison Fulbright was already in the courtroom. He preferred to use these last few moments before proceedings began to acclimate himself to the arena. Hoping to clear his mind, he fidgeted with his lucky pen, twiddling it with his thumb and forefinger. Win or lose, this case had been a kick—at once the most stimulating and most frustrating he'd known. He'd never been in the habit of giving any ground to the opposition, let alone the avalanche of concessions he'd made in the last several days. Nor had he ever been reduced to relying overmuch on witnesses and arguments peripheral to the material facts. And he bridled instinctively at having been instructed in his craft by the Machiavellian Savarkar.

And yet, what a gift from the media gods this case has become! The issues are so transcendent, so incendiary, so damned topical. And it suited perfectly his innate love of the abstract. The law afforded him a good living. But the tedium of his profession would have been unbearable were it not for the occasional spectacle.

Fulbright was ambivalent at best about the cause for which he now labored; and he tried not to dwell on the little girl at all, lest he delude himself into thinking that the exotic underpinnings of her kind of death were just beyond his capacity to understand. Besides, rendering moral judgments wasn't his job here; making that task more difficult *was*.

He had enjoyed fencing with Allen. And as much as he regretted seeing his old friend's personal life splashed over the newspapers, scandal involving a rival did have its compensations. Defense counsel would seem untarnished, even burnished by contrast. And anything that might distract his opponent from the task at hand would be heartily, if discreetly, welcomed.

One last act remained to be played out. The score might be technically even so far, but Fulbright was confident that the trial's laurel wreath was his for the taking. Allen's legal talent was considerable; his inquisitorial skills perhaps the best Fulbright had ever seen. But closings were less about substance than the timbre of one's voice, the enunciation of lyrical phrases, sometimes alliteratively strung together to assist memory with bullet points articulated in devastating succession.

Then again, he'd better be careful not to patronize old Thorndike too much; that could all too easily backfire.

A clamor from the courthouse anteroom was like a slap, startling Fulbright momentarily. Deputies equipped with metal detectors were admitting spectators one by one, and the raucous street noise crashing in—reporters, cameramen jockeying for position, demonstrators regaling onlookers—made further reflection impossible.

Then, Samantha Desai strode in, head down, clearly preoccupied. Fulbright had watched her closely during the trial, uncertain as to what her story was. But for all her savvy, her erudition, her sophistication, one feature was unmistaken; she was irreducibly mysterious. Whatever the truth of the tabloid exposé, Allen Southworth was one lucky son-of-a-bitch; he'd give the Prosecutor that.

Then Allen entered, a little stiffly, Fulbright thought. It had to have been 72 hours of the worst sort of stress imaginable for him but, oddly, he looked none the worse for the wear. He managed a polite but stilted greeting to his co-counsel. But Samantha's gaze was averted, riveted to the table, her posture rigid as a manikin's. Then she folded her hands and turned to Allen, who was busily scratching notes to himself. *Pretending not to notice her discomfort,* Fulbright figured.

Sensing his scrutiny; she looked up and offered Defense Counsel a pained smile.

"You okay?" Fulbright faintly heard Allen ask his assistant.

She nodded, but without conviction.

Fulbright looked sideways, but spied Allen, under cover of the prosecution table, squeeze her hand, then give her a thumbs-up, visible enough for public consumption.

The courtroom filled quickly. Then buzzing conversations stilled with the words, "All rise." Homer Thorndike wearily trudged his way behind the bench as the bailiff proclaimed the court in session. Then the judge perched his bifocals on the end of his Roman nose and stared at the defense table. "Is the defense prepared to make its closing statement, Mr. Fulbright?" *His tone suggests it better be,* Allen thought.

"Yes, Your Honor," said Fulbright. "Then, proceed, please."

Allen cradled his head on his fingertips and tried to read the old jurist, who was leaning back in his chair, elbows on the rests, index fingers touching his lips in attentive anticipation. *What,* the prosecutor wondered, *does he imagine his role should be at this point? Surely, he's never seen a case like this one in all his years as a judge. So much has changed in the country since he first rose to the bench.*

One thing seemed sure: The old man was up against it now. Whatever his verdict, this Gordian knot might ultimately be left for nine Supreme Court justices to untie or to cleave. A virtual acquittal would seem to risk an unthinkable precedent. Yet an unmitigated sentence might also leave a wound on the body politic that would likely never heal.

Madison Fulbright stepped from behind the defense table to a spot halfway between his table and the judge. Flipping his spectacles onto his nose from their perch atop his vast brow, his hand grasped the lapels of his jacket, and he regarded his assembled audience with a disarming smile. This professional ballet had gone unchanged for years: He'd choreographed each gesture and movement meticulously for maximum impact, designed to evince simultaneous feelings of admiration, comfort, and accessibility, even for an effective audience of one.

He inhaled deeply and began: "Good morning, Your Honor. First of all, I'd like to apologize for putting you through this ordeal. Had the State not overreached, this entire procedure might well have been unnecessary. And if Mr. Southworth had not prejudged this matter, we all might have been saved the expense, you the inconvenience, and my client the anguish of this awful trial."

Fulbright withdrew his pocket watch, checked the time, and then continued.

"Ignorance is a regrettable thing," he began, "for a condition of one's unknowing may lead, as in this instance, to the misunderstanding or misinterpretation of a sacred religious ritual into a criminal act. Now, the

State suspects much about what went on last November in Stickle's Glade. But what does it actually *know* as incontrovertible fact?"

He paced slowly from side to side, to and from his initial position before the Judge. "It knows, largely because the defense has stipulated as much, that Roop Kumar expired on the cremation site of her dead husband, and that her father-in-law witnessed the sati ceremony. And that, Your Honor, is *all* the State *knows*. The rest of their *story*—and I choose my words carefully—is at best conjecture, and at worst, the most cruel and vicious type of slander.

The prosecution contended they would have witnesses to coercion of this young woman, yet they have presented only one—and that was a witness discredited for the caprice of his memory and the weakness of his spine, who, incomprehensibly, could identify *only* my client, Mr. Swaraj. Not a word of those who allegedly *pursued* Roop Kumar, those who *threw* her into the flames and *held* her there; not a word of any of the other participants in this supposed atrocity.

Oh, the prosecution says, 'But it's Swaraj, and Swaraj alone, who's responsible for this dastardly deed!"

Yet how, one might ask, is it possible for one man, single-handedly, *to throw a terrified woman into an inferno* without becoming himself engulfed? And if he had help, would not those individuals be just as conspicuous in a witness's memory as my client supposedly is?"

Fulbright paced purposefully before the bench. "Well then, the prosecutor charges,"—he stopped in front of Allen's table—"what about the opiates found in the tissues of Ms. Kumar? Yet we have presented ample evidence that drugs of this sort are commonplace in the rituals of South Asia. Indeed, it would have been a remarkable and suspicious sign of inauthenticity had the authorities *not* found such substances in her blood. "Similarly," he said, ratcheting up his volume, "the prosecution construes the presence of bamboo staves as proof that the deceased was pinned to the fire. Yet we have also presented evidence that bamboo is the fuel of choice in such rites. The bamboo once again argues, not for criminal intent, but for the genuineness, the authenticity of the rite."

Fulbright reached for his handkerchief and dabbed his sweating brow. "How, then, to account for the State's zeal in prosecuting my client, a man already grieving for his son and daughter-in-law. Is it ignorance? Disrespect? Bigotry? *Fear*?"

He stood in the center of the floor, hands folded together at his waist. "Maybe it's a little of each, Your Honor." He nodded and paused for a moment, as if reconsidering his own answer.

At last he said, "But let us not be too harsh. I fully

understand the outrage felt by my learned colleague about this event. The difference is," he said, his volume rising, "I can distinguish my *feelings* from my knowledge – or lack of it. American democracy is based, not on *feelings*, but on the pursuit of *truth*, and the *wisdom* from which truth descends.

"*But*," he held up his palm like a traffic cop, "and it's a *BIG 'BUT'*: *that* is not to conclude that there is one, all-purpose, universal, *All-American* truth to which we must, in perpetuity, defer. Implicit in the First Amendment to our Constitution is the principle of *religious diversity*—enshrined and preserved from adulteration or mischief at the hands of the State. The First Amendment states unequivocally that 'Congress shall make no law respecting an establishment of religion.'"

Fulbright continued to pace the room, while glancing frequently at the Judge. "Other nations are chronically wracked by violent communal confrontations, each party insisting on interference in the religious practices of the other. Not so here…until now."

He paused, then recommenced: "In America, citizens and lawmakers are often constrained from interfering in religious practices. Otherwise, convents might well be closed for both confining women and then subjecting them to material deprivation. Louisiana snake charmers would be forbidden from endangering themselves and others in their quest for spiritual rapture. Christian Scientists would be forced into hospitals and subjected to procedures that they consider damning to their faith.

Jehovah's Witnesses might be subjected to persecution for refusing to salute the American flag, and Quakers for their refusal to fight on its behalf. Native Americans would be forbidden to use peyote in their ancient ceremonies, despite the dictates of tribal tradition."

Religion, Your Honor, is a personal matter – a *very* personal matter. Individual routes to salvation are as varied as they are colorful. That is as it should be. The desire for redemption has ancient roots; it is deeply held, and desperately sought after.

For some Hindu widows, the one sure route to redemption—until outlawed by alien masters—lay for centuries in sati, ritual suicide. That this religious practice shocks us, that it even astonishes us, says nothing about its appeal to *certain Hindus*, who may be just as dumbfounded by our consumption of animal flesh, our cultural obsession with pornography or our single-minded pursuit of material possessions. That is *their* perception, *their* reality; ours is ours.

But—" Fulbright pointed to the defendant, who stared back without expression. "Mr. Swaraj is a citizen of the United States, possessed of all the constitutional guarantees this status confers. The fact that his religious belief is less palatable to you, or to Mr. Southworth, does not mean that it is illegitimate, or that Mr. Swaraj is less entitled to the same protections Christians enjoy.

And the same might be said for Roop Kumar herself," he added quietly. "In the absence of evidence to the contrary, in light of the testimony of Dr. Besant that Westerners are only capable of poor translations of other cultures, does not Roop Kumar deserve the benefit of the doubt here?"

Fulbright shrugged, palms up: "After all, her community reveres her. Her family worships her. None, I repeat, *none* of them has come forward to denounce Mr. Swaraj or to contradict his version of events. In their minds, her selfless act speaks to enduring principles honored by all cultures: virtue, piety, devotion, and fidelity. Why are we unable to respect these, without necessarily agreeing with or admiring their every manifestation?"

Fulbright coughed, then exhaled loudly. "Lastly, I wish to address the issue of multiculturalism, which the prosecution regards as the supposed source of all evil here in the United States. Whether Mr. Southworth likes it or not"—he addressed the judge full-faced—"and I'd bet the farm he does *not* – America *is* being *transformed* by the cultural diversity of its population.

And that is as it should be. Since this must be a nation in perpetual demographic and cultural flux, and since religion is an undeniable characteristic of culture, it will never survive absent religious toleration. That impulse is, after all, what drew Congregationalist dissenters to Plymouth Rock in the first instance; it's what drew oppressed Irish Catholics from their famine-ravaged land to help build the transcontinental railroad; what attracted persecuted Jews from a pathologically anti-Semitic Europe. Why, this is an impulse that, by all rights, should evoke *celebration*, not suspicion; *praise*, not pejoratives; *reaffirmation*, not retreat.

"Yet apparently," Fulbright sighed, "the prosecuting attorney sees, in this Hindu family's pain, a threat to Christian dominion over our land. So, he seeks to disparage all cultures that presume to coexist with Eurocentric Christian America. He sees them as somehow dangerous, heretical, even barbarous.

But our cultural norms may either stabilize social forces or stitch a straitjacket. And you *know* what happens to people in straitjackets. Whatever those 'norms,' they must be mutually agreed upon in order to be said to exist at all. Short of that, they cannot be imposed for long upon an increasingly diverse and contrary population without running the risk of engendering communal strife, even civil war."

Fulbright paused for a long moment. Then: "The solution, Your Honor, lies in enshrining diversity as normative; mutual respect and toleration as the rule."

He went on: "Now, I harbor little doubt that you

will hear much from my distinguished colleague on the subject of universal truth and fundamental constitutional principle. I trust Your Honor won't be taken in by it all. Constitutional principles, history shows us, are malleable—that is, able to conform to evolving political will. The Founding Fathers are long dead. So, too, is their homogenous universe, with its blindness toward inconvenient contradictions like chattel slavery, Native American genocide and patriarchal oppression. Those men were hardly paragons, and neither are we."

He cast a sidelong, slightly accusatory, glance toward his old colleague who, head down, was frantically scribbling notes on the large pad in front of him. "Yet, we find ourselves here to judge a practice and culture about which most of us know next to nothing. In a nation in which over one-half of all marriages fail, how do we presume to judge a Hindu widow's conception of matrimonial fidelity, devotion, and honor? In a nation rife with single-parent households, amidst rampant proliferation of the most grotesque and demeaning pornography, serial infidelity, blatant teenage sexuality and epidemic illegitimacy, what right have we to cast judgment on the propriety of this young woman's marriage?"

He thumped his fist into his palm repeatedly now. "In a nation performing over a million abortions every year, what metric have we by which to calibrate the sincerity of Roop Kumar's devotional sacrifice? Had she less power over her fate than an unborn child?"

Defense Counsel pivoted on his heel. "Questions like these, of course, provoke howls of anguish from the State. Yet how can cultural relativism endanger the moral fiber of a nation, truth be told, whose moral fiber already has been unraveling for a long time, its threads pulled by the very illogical conformity that White, Christian America seeks to impose? And when sincere, genuine apostles of cross-cultural understanding like Professor Besant, or Theo Carver, attempt to explain the narrow-mindedness of this view, and to bridge the chasm of cultural misunderstanding, how do people like the good prosecutor respond?"

He pointed to Allen. "They viciously assail them and subject their characters to *personal vilification and ridicule.*

"The *real difference* between such social prophets and prosecutors like Mr. Southworth is simply this: Where he sees evil, they see ignorance; where he sees danger, they see opportunity; where he sees murder, they see *fidelity.*"

Fulbright knew when a closing was going well; and he could sense it was now.

He said, "There is a special strain of arrogance at work here, Judge. The ancient Greeks called it hubris, or excessive pride. It is the hubris of the very same White Eurocentric culture that enslaved most of the globe, massacred the Native American, the South Asian and the African. Even the Australian aborigine wasn't isolated enough Down Under to elude destruction. To those peoples, the Western culture of greed, of material obsession and spiritual emptiness, is a culture of violence and death."

Fulbright clasped his hands behind his back and peered intently, yet at the same time, wistfully, out the window and onto the street. "I wonder sometimes: Are white men in this country really *proud* of a slave-built Monticello? Of that fateful meadow along the Little Big Horn? Of the powdery ash of Hiroshima? Of the Lorraine Motel in Memphis? I doubt it. Yet we sense precious little remorse manifested here. All *we* get is *hubris*...

That great apostle of nonviolence, Mahatma Gandhi, was once asked his opinion of Western civilization. After thinking for a moment, he is said to have replied, 'I'm all for it. Maybe they should try it sometime.'"

Tentative laughter rippled through the audience; Fulbright let it subside, then said quietly, "Your Honor, my client is a simple man. He is not vengeful. He does not seek to hold Western imperialism to account, or to request atonement in repayment of an insurmountable debt, for which there is no excuse, and from which there is no escape. No," Fulbright shook his head, "Sirkar Swaraj merely asks to be let alone, to reflect, to honor, and to grieve."

A pause.

"Does he ask too much? Must the price of freedom, in an America dominated by Eurocentrism, be to endure the dishonoring of his daughter-in-law's heroic act, and the denunciation of his forebears? His traditions? His culture?"

Fulbright held an open palm toward his client, inviting the Judge's scrutiny of the man. "You might as well ask Sirkar Swaraj to cut off his hand or desecrate a family shrine."

I leave it to you, Judge. We may move forward or else risk going back. American society may continue to grow and flourish with the blessings true diversity confers or instead choose the poison over the remedy. It is indeed that simple, in the end. Thank you so much for the generous gifts of your time and attention." Then he turned and strode wearily back to his chair.

Allen wasn't surprised at Madison Fulbright's deft performance and fluid eloquence. He'd seen it all before, in dozens of previous incarnations. He never failed to impress; this was Fulbright's stage—even if, in Allen's mind, he had performed in a theater of the absurd.

All through Defense Counsel's presentation, clever ripostes had leapt to Allen's mind, witticisms he might employ in his upcoming joust with his former protégé. Yet an uncharacteristic prudence gave him pause. This trial had become enough of a farce. The last thing he needed to do was to overplay his hand.

With all the drama the case had generated, all the unwelcome distractions and unexpected pitfalls, certain stark facts remained, Allen knew. The reality of Roop Kumar's devaluation and death could not simply be shunted aside to advance the utopian fantasy that was intercultural harmony. *Can't believe the degree to which I let myself get trapped in this box. This shouldn't even be close.*

Samantha offered the slimmest of encouraging smiles. He thanked her with a grateful wink so discreet it seemed but a twitch.

Remaining seated, his hands clasped tightly before him, Allen raised his eyes toward the judge, trying to divine his mood. *What, precisely, is his reaction to Fulbright's tour de force?* That Defense Counsel had made a deep impression, Allen could little doubt. Yet now Thorndike just peered down: impassive, unreadable.

At last Allen rose and walked to the window on the opposite wall. There he stood for a few moments, contemplating the mid-morning sky, gathering his thoughts.

The courtroom grew still.

The prosecutor brushed his right hand through his hair, then turned, hands clasped behind him, ambled toward the empty jury box and then abruptly turned to the judge, in whose countenance he saw nothing welcoming.

Then he began his summation, just as a preacher might.

"Occasionally," he pointed to the window he'd just looked through, "one must take the time to drink in a morning sky—simply to be reassured by the reliability of its wonder, its sublime constancy. Most people find comfort in the relative predictability of the natural world; I certainly do.

Perhaps that's why this case has affected me like no other. Perhaps it's because I've suddenly grown uncertain as to the nature of our universe or, more particularly, the rationality of its most divine product," Allen spread his arms as if to embrace the crowd—"us."

Allen gazed at the judge. "To hear Defense Counsel tell it, what we have here isn't a murder trial at all. Instead, it is a gigantic misunderstanding, owing to the incapacity of the State—*that's me Judge!*—to comprehend the complexity of the wider world and the wealth of the gifts offered up to the State of Indiana, even to the United States of America, by cultural *Diversity*."

Allen glanced reflexively at the jury box, then at the judge.

"Since Mr. Fulbright seems so transfixed on 'incontrovertible facts,' let me recite a few. One: This little girl – not 'young woman' – was, whether that union was physically consummated or not, forced to 'marry' (Allen air-quoted) a twenty-four-year-old adult.

"Two: This little girl was deliberately drugged with opium by the defendant, or with the defendant's connivance.

"Three: This little girl was brought to a funeral bier and compelled under the influence of opium to sit upon it—with a dead man's head in her lap.

"Four: This little girl was forced to watch as the funeral edifice was set ablaze amid the chants of a fevered crowd.

"Five: Smelling the fire's smoke, feeling its heat, sensing her peril, this little girl attempted to escape.

"Six: Participants in this 'sacred rite,' (air-quoting again) the defendant among them, pinned this little girl to a corpse as the flames licked at her garments, singeing her tender flesh.

"Seven: This little girl lost consciousness, at least we pray she did, from inhalation of the smoke as fire consumed her tiny body, soon charred into a second corpse."

As Allen leaned against the prosecution table now, he could see that his recitation of bare facts had affected the judge, whose hands appeared to be trembling slightly. "Now, is it any wonder the State has a problem smiling on the likes of *that*?"

The prosecutor placed a hand on his brow and pressed on: "To hear Defense Counsel tell it, this case somehow has more to do with my own prejudices than with a murder. Apparently, rather than seeking justice for such an unconscionable act, I am instead more obsessed with molding the character of our national culture along lines that comport with those most obsessive, he seems to believe, of all my concerns: my gender and my race.

It seems to him that I'm even intent on dragging the American Constitution into this, and in such a way that it will elevate European white males to a position forever triumphant and enthroned.

Now, at first blush, it would seem that the Defense Counsel has masterfully made his case, for the principles he evokes in its support are very important ones. Indeed, they would seem to go to the heart of what it means to be an American, wouldn't they? Who, after all, could be against tolerance, freedom, and religious liberty? What right-thinking American would *not* oppose bigotry and oppression? Who among us would deny that America is the product of a vast assortment of cultures, drawn to this land by an equally bewildering assortment of motives? This is *diversity*, right? That's *always* good, right? That's what this country's all about, right?" Allen gazed at his audience, before again turning and walking toward the window.

Pensive for a moment; he then turned again toward the Judge. "But there are several difficulties, Your Honor, with this depiction of the facts, and with the principles that underlie them. Defense Counsel's argument is specious, diversionary, and *fundamentally* dishonest."

He reached for a water glass on the prosecution table, took a sip and then resumed. "Let us consider the last portion of Mr. Fulbright's closing first, shall we? Think of this world and what you read about it every day in the newspaper or hear about it on the television news. Much of that reporting relates unrest, civil war and communal hatred."

Allen began counting on his fingers: "India, Bosnia, the Sudan, Afghanistan, Lebanon, Iraq, Rwanda. Then he held up a fist. What all these have in common, Your Honor, is the very characteristic Defense Counsel and his intellectual confederates seem to prize so highly— cultural diversity. Please understand that by this phrase I do not refer to constellations of ethnic restaurants, costumes, folklore, and music and festivals, but instead to the deep chasms of mistrust that make separate groups, dare we call them tribes, of people: those that can render an entire nation, in the lexicon of pop psychologists, 'dysfunctional.'"

He paced again. "I'm talking about issues that really matter to people: the languages they use, the deities they worship, their heroes and their villains, the traditions they cherish—all those things that make it so difficult for them to coalesce into the types of broader civilizations in which, given a perfect world, all would feel themselves to be *one*, despite their cultural differences.

"So, you see Your Honor, Defense Counsel has neglected to relate the most important part of the history lesson, the reason multiple millions from those very nations have found their way to the United States: because they sought a place where equality of opportunity was at least aspired to; where the maladaptive cultural baggage of the old world might be left abandoned at the docks; where the individual may transcend institutions of the old country enshrining gender, race, class, faith or caste.

In the United States, it is *individual* freedom that provides the confidence with which to *welcome* diversity – *not the tribe's freedom to embed it*. Here, principles built upon the rights of the *individual* blaze the path with which to surmount the artificial walls separating one group of people from another, walls which are often built from nothing more substantial than mindless prejudice, clan affiliation or random genetics."

Allen approached the bench again. "Let me illustrate for you exactly what I mean, Your Honor. You may have noticed, and been a bit confused by the oscillation of this triangular debate about customs between America, the British Empire, and the subcontinent of Inda, because this case is, after all, about an Indian custom banned by the British long ago, a prohibition that persists in an independent India to this day.

The British Empire is what catalyzed Western expansion into less developed regions of the globe. And since American political antecedents are British, the United States—at least to the multiculturalist—is merely the next incarnation of that expansive, repressive Empire in particular, and Western hegemony in general.

Of course, many of our people – here and around the world – do have well-founded grievances that stem from *genuine* persecution. Yet misery may also derive from *perceived* grievance, delusion, and occasionally—as in the case before you—from political opportunism.

Throughout this trial, Your Honor, you've been subjected to a blizzard of buzzwords employed by the defense in order to claim victimization: Eurocentric, white, male, Western, imperialist, patriarchal and many others. Any suggestion that the world might logically impute a legacy of greater freedom and achievement to the so-called 'Western world' invariably draws fire from those who discern in such an assessment a calculated insult.

"But in the cleansing light of truth, available for all to read for themselves in genuine scholarship, what are we to do? Does it matter at all that the Western world, of which the United States is undoubtedly a part and with which it shares Mr. Fulbright's villainization, was the *first* rather than the last region on Earth to abolish slavery? Does it matter at all that the transatlantic and Indian Ocean slave trades were abolished, for the most part, by the exertions of the British Royal Navy? Does it matter that America fought its bloodiest war against part of itself—*over slavery?*"

Allen rubbed his neck and looked at the floor. "Your Honor, as uncomfortable as it may be for some to accept, hard facts remain. We are a Western people philosophically, and we must remain so if we are to continue as a nation our parents and grandparents, not to speak of our Founders, might recognize. Our children must be infused with attendant principles, for only then will they guarantee a political context within which true diversity may not only survive, but flourish. In fact, those principles are its shield and buckler. Without them, this country would be just another grisly headline, an ethnic stew of peoples lacking any rubric under which to unite, to meld peaceably into a common citizenry, to set guide-lines and rules of conduct that apply to the government as well as to themselves.

After all," he enunciated, "it is important for us to remember that ours is the only nation in world history that was *invented*.

I understand fully that notions of objective moral standards seem somewhat quaint by the contemporary measure of such things. But I am an unrepentant traditionalist where such truths are concerned and can apologize only for the shortcomings of those who try to live by them, not for those truths themselves.

If you examine international law today, for instance, as it is manifest in the United Nations charter, what will you find?" He pointed to the pages of an open book on his desk. "You will discover paeans to liberty, democracy and individual rights and freedoms, which, while they originated in the West, now dominate the globe *intellectually*. Chinese dissidents erect a facsimile of the Statue of Liberty in Tiananmen Square. India flourishes as the largest democracy on the planet. Barbarous practices once regarded as integral to the cultural landscape as the common cuisine are now discredited and denounced, if not yet eradicated: among these slavery, serfdom, autocracy, human sacrifice, child marriage and—yes— sati. In the name of the cultural 'other,' is Mr. Fulbright prepared to renounce this trend merely because it originated in the 'malevolent West', or because it was imposed in myriad climes by the British Empire?"

Allen spread his arms wide. "Of course, he isn't. He knows that little Roop Kumar, whom you'll note Defense Counsel has repeatedly referred to as a woman, not a child, was *not* a victim of European tormentors or British ghosts. That is the point, after all, isn't it? The principles on which this nation was founded, the majestic *ideas* by which we govern ourselves, are supposed to prevent such an act as sati. Isn't intellectual diversity, the marketplace of ideas among *free* people, which long ago reached the conclusion to eradicate such practices, the only kind of diversity that really matters? For, in truth, sati is less an idea, than an antiquated scrap of history, a discarded remnant that must remain ever discarded.

Yet Defense Counsel's definition of 'freedom,' at least for little Roop Kumar, seems indistinguishable from that formless, skeptical dough of *license*, absent the leavening ingredient of healthy standards of liberty. Without this leavening, license seems to be all that freedom means: unbridled, unfettered, unabashed, and in the end Hobbesian anarchy—the sort of absence of restraint that excuses even a little girl's ritual destruction. Iniquitous practices like sati are difficult to banish with mere laws; they must be thoroughly discredited, excised, pulled up root and branch and cast away from the public mind.

The idea that such an interpretation of 'freedom' as Mr. Fulbright has purveyed it, is what drew immigrants to this country is preposterous. Contrary to his assertions, this country has chosen *not* to allow religion to infringe, carte blanche, on basic civil and individual rights, or even on institutions deemed vital to civil order and fundamental law – otherwise polygamy would still be permitted to Mormons; human sacrifice to Native Americans; life-saving blood transfusions would be denied to the children of Jehovah's Witnesses. Why, even slavery might still exist as an institution sanctioned by Southern clergymen citing the Biblical fate of Ham and his descendants, forever to be hewers of wood and drawers of water.

Your Honor, we must remind Defense Counsel that freedom and liberty do not confer unlimited license; that they must be tempered by responsible *limitations*. Yes, setting those limits, especially in these increasingly fervid times, may be an uncomfortable, even an unpleasant, exercise. And to do so will necessitate acknowledging that America was built on a foundation chiseled from a Judeo-Christian quarry. Moral codes have never simply descended out of the ether. Historically, they have derived from man's search for divinity, his contemplation of the infinite and profound belief in his or her own progress." Allen held his palms together, as if in supplication. "Religion has provided the limits by which societies have been defined since the dawn of time. And in America, it was the Christianity of its people that provided such a definition. The Supreme Court has declared these limits operative for, and I quote, 'acts recognized by the general consent of the Christian world in modern times.'

Does this mean we have a Christian theocracy in this country? Of course not. Does it mean we must impose Christian beliefs on non-Christians? Of course not.

Your Honor, if we repudiate this view, if religious 'freedom' is reinterpreted as license, if adherence to even these supple limits melts away – " he paused again "—then all bets will be off. Remember, the philosopher Nietzsche's most famous aphorism was *not* a declaration, but an observation: '*If* God is dead, then *all is permissible.*'"

He stared at the Judge unblinking, as if straining to ensure that the gravity of the quotation had sunk in. "Unpleasant as it may seem, since ours is a *Western* nation at its core, we must be prepared to acknowledge and reaffirm the legitimacy of our philosophic custom, which permits not only differentiation between cultural practices, but active discouragement of those customs repellent to the society in which we live – not out of a desire to elevate one race of people or one particular culture above others, but because those ideas define *American* precepts as to what constitutes a right under

American Constitutional Law: that no citizen may be denied life, liberty or property without due process of law—even if *religion decrees* denial of those. This is what has made American culture so exceptional, so enduring, as well as so emulated."

As if bearing a ponderous burden, Allen allowed his shoulders to slump wearily. "You know, if it were not so sad, the multiculturalist contention that America has no synthesized culture of its own would be laughable. Why, Americana—our cinema and pop art, basketball, Elvis, the Blues and Broadway—is everywhere taking the world by storm. One may argue whether these manifestations are uplifting or not, but *not* that they don't *exist*."

He took a few steps to regroup and then went on: "The larger, and more important, point is that the philosophic bequest of the West to the rest of the world, the preeminence of 'Reason' upon which our American culture and this entire prosecution is based, is no more the property of the West than numbers belong to Arabs, algebra to ancient Babylonians, or printing to the Chinese. All these things are the collective achievements of the community of man. Each generation stands, as Newton noted, on the shoulders of the giants preceding it."

Allen paused and rubbed his palms together in

thought. "In the end, though, we are left with the essentials of this case, which Mr. Fulbright so blithely dismissed at the beginning of his address. This much we know:

An underage ten-year-old girl, identified as Roop Kumar, was found dead on the funeral pyre of her dead *husband*—and I use that word advisedly, for I need not remind you that such a union would not have been recognized by the State of Indiana. Mr. Swaraj acknowledges that he was there. And he was seen by an eyewitness to throw the terrified child back into the flames. That all the other perpetrators cannot be identified and apprehended does not diminish *his* guilt one bit. In fact, his refusal to name those who assisted him only *magnifies* his culpability.

Most significantly of all, perhaps, Mr. Swaraj had motive, in the form of the dowry that he was allowed by custom to retain following the death of his *daughter-in-law*. And that he claimed that dowry mere hours after the event is hardly reassuring for the defense."

Allen paced more slowly and deliberately now before the bench, as if arguing with objective dispassion only: "But this case, at its core, doesn't come down to the victim's state of mind, or even whether her death was a murder or a suicide. Given her age, it cannot matter. Mr. Swaraj was responsible for her. In the State of Indiana, a child under the age of sixteen may not marry, drink alcohol, drive a car, drop out of school, vote in an election, be tried as an adult, or engage in sexual intercourse. Why do we have such laws? Because society—*that's us, Your Honor!*—has determined that a child *is not yet a responsible, autonomous being.*

In light of all this, are we prepared to say any child may now decide to immolate herself while, by their silence, adults who witness the immolation lend tacit approval to a decision that the State of Indiana has previously held the child hadn't even the autonomy to make? Especially if the child who supposedly 'decided' was shepherded to her place of death by an eager crowd,—and was drugged, insufficiently, as it happened, to quell her pain and terror?

Once Roop Kumar awakened to the fatal danger she faced, she struggled to escape with the desperation of a cornered animal. But it was hopeless; in the end, she was pinned to the corpse of a man she barely knew and held there until her shrieks subsided, her tiny form grown limp and smoldering. And all this," he swept his right arm broadly in the direction of the defendant, "brought to pass by the man who was supposed to *protect* her from all *harm*, not to speak of grim *death*."

Allen now strode again to the window and gazed out at the warm sunshine. Then he turned one last time face the one man he was trying so desperately to persuade. "Your Honor, I humbly ask this: What kind of country do you want our grandchildren to inherit? It has not been, and notwithstanding one's cultural or religious predisposition, God willing, *it will never be* an American custom to burn widows, particularly tiny child widows. Yet the matter is in your hands now.

Will we remain a nation which has been the envy of the world and true to its past? Or a nation that has lost the ability to discern good from evil, the moral from the immoral, civilization from barbarism. You must now summon the courage to stand for the acknowledged truths that the laws of our civilization have bequeathed to us... and sentence the defendant to the full measure of punishment required by Indiana law."

Allen bowed humbly. "Thank you, Your Honor."

The courtroom erupted in cries and shouts. Swaraj's supporters and Carver's followers in attendance rose to denounce the prosecutor's words, hurling epithets like brickbats: "Hypocrite! Adulterer! Imperialist!"

Homer Thorndike bellowed for order from the bench, whacking his gavel down as the demonstration continued for almost five minutes. At last, on the Judge's orders, bailiffs removed the worst offenders from the courtroom. Still, through it all, the Judge appeared rock-steady, determined, if a bit startled. Once order restored, he adjourned the proceedings, and the principals filed out.

Now the chaos migrated out to the street, where disruptive attendees crashed into counter-protesters waving flags and belting out cacophonous renderings of "God Bless America." Reporters scurried off to their mobile units to ready remotes on the closing arguments for the six o'clock news.

Madison Fulbright departed the courtroom characteristically and marched boldly through the front door. Reporters scrummed around Fulbright's towering form. One might think, looking at him, that the jury had already returned to announce an acquittal. But his demeanor was standard operating post-trial procedure for him.

"Mr. Fulbright, how do you feel?

"Why, I feel fine. Just *fine,*" he beamed.

"How do you think it went today?"

"I believe we made our case persuasively and I'm certain Judge Thorndike's decision will reflect that fact."

"What about your client? How does he feel?"

"Mr. Swaraj is in good spirits, confident in the fairness and good judgment of the judge, and the fine folks of this town and of this country."

"Is it true your client has been approached about a possible book and movie deal?"

"I can't comment on that, either to confirm or deny."

With that, Fulbright begged off, pleading the exertions of a long day, and made his way to his Porsche. Once inside, insulated from the din, he took the measure of the contest. He had to give it to Allen. He'd spoken, as an old law school professor used to put it, "off the cuff and from the gut," with elegance and precision. On most points, he'd given as well as he'd got.

Fulbright wished, ruefully, for another bite at the apple, a final rebuttal. But that was every defense attorney's fantasy.

He'd done as well as any other lawyer might under the circumstances, what with the strategy that'd been shoved down his throat. Sure, there were those who would have been better prepared for the philosophic angle, but they probably would have put the judge to sleep. What Fulbright lacked in scholarly heft, he'd had to make up with style, pure panache. And in a contest of style, he knew he was second to none.

All would depend on the mood of the judge: how closely he'd listened and whether he'd be moved primarily by cold logic or the dulcet tones of righteous, passionate benignity.

As the furor subsided in the courtroom, Allen spoke quietly with Carl Peters. Carl had stayed nearby to see personally to the safety of the prosecution team. At last Allen nodded to the Sheriff, indicating he wanted a moment alone with Samantha.

Crossing the room, he glanced tentatively at Sam. Ostensibly packing her briefcase, she seemed rigid now, as she'd been throughout his presentation, hands trembling, shivering with tension. His heart twisted, defeated by the necessity to treat her kindly, ethically and responsibly. *A no-win situation...*

The sexual element had been the very least of what he'd shared with Sam. *No point denying it, not even to Jan.* Even if he'd managed to convince his wife that he *hadn't* made love to Sam that night, he couldn't have denied that he *had* shared something extraordinary with her. Jan might forgive a circumstantial affair, but could she forgive something *real*, a relationship that had demanded both passion *and* restraint?

Jan couldn't recover from such knowledge; she'd know she couldn't share that with him; if she knew it, their marriage would be well and truly finished.

It is true, he thought, *what they say: You can't have too much love in your life – real love, generous love, rather than the ersatz, mawkish, pop culture variety.* Ironic really, because what he'd shared with Sam had not eclipsed the renewed devotion he now felt for his wife. It had, perhaps, even made that devotion possible—by demanding mature and moral responses of him.

"Sam." He took her hand tenderly.

"Your closing was superb, Allen," she said. "It really was."

Whatever the outcome, it was over. After having worked so hard to gain the conviction of an Indian, Sam had felt a little treasonous, sitting there with so many activists now arrayed against her. Logic and emotion battled in her soul. To have invested so much of her intellectual capital in this case—only to be rendered ineffectual: the wages of sin...and of scandal.

She couldn't begin to calculate how much the last few days had cost her, spiritually and emotionally. She was surprised, since she'd come into the case with no expectations and had worked willingly with Allen, even while striving to maintain propriety. She knew that there was no further place for them to go—only beyond herself, to rise above petty personal concerns, to sacrifice her own needs to the remaining demands of the case.

She asked him now: "Where will you wait for the verdict?"

"I don't know," he replied, raking his hair with

both hands. "I'll tell you this, Sam, if after everything that's gone down, I manage to win this case, I'll owe it all to you."

She could tell his voice was stanching a tremor. "You not only divined *their* strategy; you defined *ours*. I'd have been embarrassed badly here without your help."

"It would seem," she corrected, "that you've been embarrassed here *with* my help." She glanced at the insinuating photographs on the front page of the creased and folded *Post* visible in her open briefcase.

"You and I know the truth. I'm sorry it's played out the way it has." Allen's face twisted. "You understand why it was pointless to try explaining myself to the masses."

"Of course." She nodded briskly to cover the lump in her throat. *What now? Allow myself to be immolated in the backdraft of this case?* Her reputation, her professional credibility, even Allen himself had been swept away from her. Or perhaps not.

Nothing had changed, really, despite the rumormongers' clucking. Whatever they had of each other was tied, inextricably, to *Indiana v. Swaraj*. Whenever Sam might review the case in the future—and she was certain she *would*, often—she'd have the satisfaction of knowing they'd given it their best shot.

She touched his shoulder in one last, generous impulse and said, "We put everything into it, Allen—mind, heart, and soul. We lost nothing of ourselves in the giving and discovered a good deal in the sharing." Then, she smiled. "You can't lose that."

The sounds of voices and footsteps at the rear exit brought them back to their present need to exit safely. They put several feet between them as Carl Peters and a deputy entered the now-empty courtroom.

The deputy said, "There's a Miz Stark waiting to speak with you, Mr. Southworth; I'll take you to her."

"M-Miz Stark...?" Allen stammered.

"Go on, Allen," Sam said. "I'll meet you back here when the Judge settles things. That is, *if* he settles things."

"Got your cell?" Allen asked.

She aimed it at him as if it were a six-gun. "Got it."

He started for the back stairs; she hung back a moment after he'd gone.

Peters broke her reverie. "Why don't you and I go someplace and have a beer? Loosen up a little bit while this thing sorts itself out."

The Sheriff's genuinely compassionate, Dutch-uncle countenance had just the stabilizing effect she needed to restore a little perspective. "You're on, Carl," she said gratefully. "Thanks."

The deputy directed Allen to an unmarked car. A woman's head could be seen through the tinted glass. "Jan?"

Suddenly euphoric, Allen bounded ahead and opened the door without looking inside. "When did you start using your maiden name again, *Ms. Stark?*"

He slid into the back seat – but his wife wasn't there; it was his sister-in-law. "Betsy?" he said.

Allen," she almost whispered. "I trust all went well at the courthouse."

"We'll know for sure soon, but I have a good feeling. Where's Jan?"

Her face sagged. "She's down at Heartland, Allen."

Allen saw her swallow hard and her eyes mist. "She was supposed to tell you when she saw you at The Wharf. Damn it, Allen, she *promised* she'd tell you!"

"Tell me what? *What*, Betts?"

"Jan's got cancer, Allen. Breast cancer. She was diagnosed just before Thanksgiving."

Thanksgiving. November. Christ. "Just as—"

"Yes," Betsy nodded, "just as this thing was gearing up. She didn't want to be a distraction to you. Believe it or not, she felt that letting you know she'd gotten sick would let you down when you needed her most."

"Jesus." Allen squeezed his eyes shut. His pulse raced, and his mouth grew suddenly dry as he searched within himself for a response, any *useful* response to the awful news. *Do something... have to do something... something has to be done...* "Has she been treated?"

"She's had a mastectomy and a full course of chemo

over the winter. I was there most of the time, too, help-ing Mom and Dad look after the kids. *And* Jan."

"Christ." Allen's mind raced as pieces of the puzzle fell into place. Jan's gauntness, the dark circles around her eyes, the odd quality of her hair—obviously, in hind-sight, a wig. The stiff way she'd suffered his embrace. She'd always paid the bills, so she'd kept any medical notices under his radar, especially during this case…

He muttered, "I should have been there, should have been informed." *She tried to tell me months ago, Carl said she'd come to the office, but Sam was there. I shut her out.* "But it's under control," he wished aloud, as if asser-tion could equal fact. "She's in remission…?"

Betsy shook her head.

"Then, *what?*" He almost burst out a sob. "Why has she been admitted to Heartland… now?"

"For another course of chemo, a stronger cocktail," Betsy frowned. She lifted her hands limply. "She thought she felt well enough to be up here for the end of the case, but she's had a bad reaction to it."

The deputy got into the car and slid behind the wheel. Allen suddenly felt a strange composure. He leaned over the front seat and said, "Heartland, please, and hurry."

It was a good thing the drive to Heartland was short and the traffic was light—and that Allen wasn't at the wheel. He felt so numbly dazed by the time they arrived;

he was half-afraid he might have to be admitted himself. Betsy steered him to the oncology floor and Jan's room. The sight that greeted him wasn't reassuring. A cluster of white coats was gathered around a bed; he hoped against all reason that it held anyone other than his wife.

One white-coated woman turned toward him. "Mr. Southworth?"

Allen could only nod.

"May I speak to you in the hall?" She introduced herself as Dr. Francine Castro. "I'm the oncologist on Jan's case."

Her wanting to talk to him was chilling, reminding him of his mother's death three years before. The doctor touched his arm gently; he recoiled. But fully alert now, he had to brace himself for whatever was to come.

Dr. Castro led him to a small conference room; Betsy stayed with Jan. "You need to know some things before you see your wife. First, believe me, she's resting comfortably..."

"We can talk in here," the doctor motioned.

Allen went in silently and sat down. The doctor said, "May I ask what you've been told about Jan's condition?" He recapitulated what few details Betsy had provided. "I didn't know; I wasn't told ..."

"Mr. Southworth," Dr. Castro said, "I want you to listen closely to what I have to tell you about Jan, all right?"

Allen nodded.

"Her condition is grave. She's had an unanticipated negative reaction to the chemotherapy. We've been coordinating with her Florida oncologist, but we didn't expect this reaction."

"Unanticipated!" *What a word!*

"This protocol always takes a toll on a patient, but I honestly expected Jan would weather it. But her heart is weak, and her kidneys are starting to fail now. And the tumors have grown very aggressive. She's just worn out, I'm afraid. We've been trying to manage her pain, but she resists—largely because she's been waiting to speak with you."

"*Unanticipated!*" Allen repeated, anger mixing with his fear. He'd left a lucrative partnership specializing in malpractice; the specialty was still in his blood; and his blood rose. He got up unsteadily. *"Do you know who I am?"*

"Mr. Southworth, this isn't helpful—"

"I'll conduct my own investigation into this... *unanticipated* reaction? And if I find any evidence of neglect or malpractice, I'll—"

Suddenly crestfallen, Allen collapsed heavily back into the chair, his shoulders convulsing with grief. This *was all his fault. He* had caused this. "I'm sorry. I'm sorry," he mumbled again.

"Come," the doctor said, firmly but gently. "Your wife wants to see you."

He allowed Dr. Castro to walk him back to Jan's room. Each step filled him with dread and ponderous foreboding that made the short distance seem like a mile. When he saw Jan, lying amid the labyrinth of plastic tubes sustaining her tenuous life (or prolonging her agony) he broke down completely. Under the hospital gown, she was so thin. And without the wig she was almost bald; only a few downy wisps sprouted from her skull. He only now realized what an exhausting deception her breakfast performance had been. Such courage.

Dr. Castro placed her hand on Jan's forehead and stroked softly. "Jan," she said, in a hushed voice Allen could barely hear. "Jan, your husband is here. Allen's here to see you."

The doctor stepped aside, and Allen replaced her. "Jan, I'm here, Honey." His voice quaked badly. He lifted Jan's swollen hand, caressed it and pressed it to his lips. She showed no signs of knowing he was there. "I'll never leave you, Jan. I'll never leave you again…"

He stared helplessly at the doctor, who said, "She might regain consciousness later," she said. "We're doing everything we can."

"What can *I* do?" he asked, mentally trying to think of medical options that might be more effective, or at least more active: *What* can *I do? What can I* do? A tiny shift in intonation, he'd learned in law school, could dramatically skew meaning and interpretation…

Betsy came to his side. "Talk to her, Allen. Hold her hand. Just… *be here.*"

"I don't know how to do that. I've *never* done that," he painfully realized aloud. "I've *never* been there for her." He threw up his hands as if imploring heaven. A terrible self-indictment, it seemed more than he could bear.

"Tell her about the trial and your closing," Betsy said hoarsely. "You'll think of something. You're the great Allen Southworth; pretend she's your judge."

And jury…?

5:30 p.m.
B&L Tavern Roseland, Indiana

Sam was enjoying yet another night out with the Sheriff. At this moment, a night on the town with someone as down-to-earth as Carl Peters was the perfect prescription for her. Disdaining the company of the pretentious for the hoi polloi, the pair went to the B&L Bar and Grill out on Route 6, where they gabbed like schoolgirls over thick, deliciously greasy burgers, massive onion rings and serial pitchers of beer.

For the first time since the trial began, Sam was able to gain impressions about it from someone besides Allen or Mark McCorkle. Generally determined to keep his mouth shut about trials as they proceeded, Carl was at last ready to share his thoughts.

"The case was too closely fought," she said. "We can't expect a ruling any time soon." To the good, a prolonged decision would mean the judge was grappling hard with the complex arguments to reach a decision."

The Sheriff said, "It was like a high-stakes poker game. I expect it'll take at least three days."

"I'll see your three days and raise you," Sam grinned. "Make it three months."

Carl grimaced. "You know, I don't think the entire trial should've been allowed to go beyond the material facts of the case. I know Principia: keep it simple. Shaky or no, those facts pointed to a murder—and that's where the matter should've ended." He shook his head. "Too much philosophical mumbo-jumbo, and I bet the Judge feels the same."

Sam found it difficult to disagree. By allowing the argument to digress into matters of cultural relativism and the like, Allen had given the impression of a de facto admission that his case was weak, that hard facts were missing, that the circumstantial evidence wasn't compelling enough. The Defense had selected the battleground.

"On the other hand," she countered, "as I see it Fulbright forced the issue, leaving Allen no choice but to refute. To have caved to Besant and Carver on the stand would have been risky as well; they might've assumed command of the whole case."

"That's exactly what the defense was hoping for," Carl said. "Sometimes a shift of focus is all that stands between a life sentence and a never-ending cause. Allen took their bait."

A telling point, she had to admit. All three of them— Allen, Mark and she herself – had become so energized by, so immersed in the cerebral challenge Fulbright presented, perhaps they'd taken their eye off the ball. Yet again, how else could they have chosen? The Mahasabha had clearly come to their community to stir the political pot. And Theo Carver was unlikely to have gone gently into that good night in any case, nor would he now. To follow Carl's prescription would have presented too great a risk of descent into an interminable nightmare of postmodern license.

"Where does it end?" Carl asked.

Sam nodded. In those cases, ordinary jurors usually preferred commonsensical compassion over the tortured pleas of philosophers and theologians. Still, what if, by accepting the philosophic challenge too eagerly, she and Allen had recklessly—if unintentionally—played right into their hands?

"We've opened Pandora's box," she shuddered, "liberating cultural demons of which ordinary citizens are ignorant. Not all cultural differences are bridgeable, you know. This might be only the beginning of very ugly times."

Whether or not they agreed on every point, Carl and Sam welcomed the blessed release of the evening. As the night wore on and they emptied pitchers, they drew together in a comradely, even therapeutic way. The tensions of the investigation and trial slowly dissipated. If the suspense persisted, their ability to affect the outcome had not. At least the matter was now out of their hands.

Not long after, they left the B&L, and Carl drove Sam back to the safe house (a rather dingy housekeeping motel Carl had chosen for the size of its rooms and the security of its location). His phone went off as they pulled up in front. He listened briefly, then hung up and sat silent.

"Allen?" Sam asked.

"No," Carl sighed. "That was Jonas. Jan Southworth's seriously ill. Cancer. Doesn't look good. Allen's with her now."

Samantha reeled back against the car seat. "Can you take me to him?"

Carl looked at her with tough love in his eyes.

She then held up her palm. "No, you're right. I don't suppose that's the best idea I've ever had."

Carl said, "Will you be alright?"

With effort, she pulled the corners of her mouth into a quaking smile. "Thank you, Carl. I'm exhausted. And thanks for tonight; it was just what the doctor ordered."

He saw Sam safely to the room, checked it over perfunctorily and said good night.

Alone, Sam's mind flooded with thoughts of Allen. Her heart ached for him, and the dark, stale kitsch of the motel setting only accentuated her sense of isolation The room stank of cigarettes; there were burn holes in the carpet and the pressed-wood end tables. Sam undressed, jumped into the shower and began to scrub vigorously with the heavily scented bar soap. She was sick of it all. *Sick of it! Sick of all the smoke… and the mirrors.*

April 24
3:30 a.m.

Allen's suit coat hung crookedly over the back of the bed-side hospital chair. His sleeves were rolled to the elbow; he'd stuffed his tie into a trouser pocket. His shirt had come un-tucked and was blousing up around his suspenders. That morning's professional shave felt scratchy against his hand; his fresh haircut had flown awry; the massage he'd gotten before the trial was a memory of self-indulgence.

Betsy had tried to bring him food, but he was too nauseated with shame and fatigue to eat; now she sat silently on the other side of Jan's bed. Allen felt desperate for a drink, and just as desperate not to leave Jan's side for a moment.

He'd interviewed the doctors and taken notes—not to prepare for a lawsuit, but to wrap his mind around facts, figures and prognosis. He'd spoken with the airlines and his in-laws. They were to fly out of Orlando with his children on the first flight into Chicago. He'd then booked a limo to shuttle them to Principia—faster than a layover for a connecting flight to South Bend. He'd arranged with the Sheriff's Department to have his own car delivered to the hospital parking lot.

Details. Action. It was the only kind of control he knew and understood.

Now that the ordeal of the hearing was over; he couldn't speak of it.

"Jan," he said to his still-unconscious wife, "I found a copy of *Kids are Worth It* at the nursing station. Barbara Coloroso's one smart lady." He started reading aloud from it...

Chapters and chapters later, he'd read himself hoarse, but still he read on, as if Jan's life somehow depended on his ability to keep his vigil from falling silent.

At last, he slumped back in the chair. "Christ," he sighed, "I've been a lousy husband—and no raging success as a dad, either. I'll make it up to you, Jan; I'll make it up, I swear..."

Then he became aware that Jan had opened her eyes and turned her head to look directly into his tortured face, silently conveying more love than he'd ever seen in her before. She opened her mouth, clearly trying to speak. Allen took her hand and bent his ear to her lips. He *felt* her words rather than hearing the syllables, and once she'd breathed them out, he wasn't quite sure what they'd been. He looked desperately at Betsy. "What did she say? Did you hear?"

Then he felt Jan's tortured, withered hand grow limp in his. Her eyes closed as she let out a single, soft breath. *Gone...*

"What did she say?" he asked Betsy again. He wasn't sure he had them right; he couldn't swear to them in a court of law. "Was it, 'Make me proud?' Or 'You *made* me proud?'"

"Allen, it doesn't matter," Betsy's voice choked. "She loved you."

"Oh, but it *does* matter!" Jan *was* his judge and jury; she'd rendered her decision. One verb form or the other, it changed everything. Past tense meant he'd succeeded; she'd acquitted him. "*Make* me proud is imperative; it means I *haven't* made her proud, not yet!" To have left the job undone was the worst sort of failure; that would deserve conviction, a life sentence. "*I need to know.*" Past his limit, beyond empathy or consolation he muttered, "There's a difference; I need to *know...*"

April 25
8:30 a.m.

Sam's cell phone rang while she was eating a late breakfast at a local IHOP: The judge was ready; court would
reconvene at 10:00 to hear his ruling.

Carl phoned shortly after. "Heard from Allen by
any chance?"

"No."

Awkwardly, he continued: "Mrs. Southworth passed
away during the night."

Sam felt like she'd been kicked in the gut.

Carl said, "I tried to track Allen down at Heartland,
but he's gone, probably to organize things for the kids.
I've got an APB out on him," he sighed. "We need him
at the table for the decision."

"Compassionate leave, surely!" Sam said. "You'll
stand in?"

"Of course."

"Hold it a minute, call on another line… No shit,
Jonas? Hardly a surprise, I guess. Thanks."

"OK, I'm back, Sam. Listen: Thorndike has postponed *everything*… till fall at the earliest, likely the end
of October."

"How appropriate," Sam offered. "Just in time for
Halloween.

August 28
Near Plymouth, Indiana

Judge Thorndike always enjoyed the sound his foot-falls made on the long, wrap-around porch of his country home: the rhythm, the solidity of them. He especially relished their cadence this August morning as he watched a crimson disc peek over the Eastern horizon. His golden retriever, Jupiter, frolicked in the yard meanwhile, enjoying his morning constitutional, the climax of which was invariably signaled by a lusty roll in whatever piece of putrefying matter he'd most recently trotted home. That's why Jupiter spent most of his time outside.

The Judge's modest mansion was his refuge, some-what isolated at the end of a gravel road that bordered a state forest; he had no visible neighbors. The surround-ing immensity of the corn fields this time of year lent his place a distinct coziness that somehow offset its remote-ness, at least for him. The Judge settled into his rocking chair, his back nicely buttressed with the cushions so lovingly sewn by his recently departed wife. Along with all the other everyday reminders, they always made him think of her. Yet as he watched Jupiter roll in his varmint grease, Thorndike knew well enough that he was stalling, looking for an excuse not to sit down with the Swaraj sentencing file. The case had tied his cerebral synapses into knots, impeding his progress toward resolution and leaving him unable to escape the sensation that none of the options facing him were good ones.

In one sense, deciding this matter should be simple: the victim was a minor after all, and Swaraj had responsibility for her. Instead of protecting her, the defendant had participated, passively or not, in the ritual resulting in Roop Kumar's death. That Swaraj bore a measure of *responsibility* was not at issue; the degree of his *culpability*, however, was. And to ascertain that, Thorndike had to wrestle with the nature and status of the victim herself, socially, legally, and perhaps most hazardously of all, culturally.

Had Roop really been married, in any legal sense of that word? How about in a more expansive, global, extra-legal sense? And did the answer to that question even matter in the end, when mitigation was the issue at hand, and not the comparatively simpler matter of guilt or innocence?

Yet what vexed the Judge most was that he was being called upon to divine first, the presence of volition in the little girl's mind, and second, the pertinence of that answer to existing law. Had she really, even in delusion, desired her own death? Was an over-the-hill jurist like him well-enough equipped philosophically to chance an answer? That was a tougher nut altogether.

Of course, Thorndike had heard of multiculturalism before the case came along, but he hadn't been precisely sure what it was, beyond some vague notions of tolerance and liberality, especially as it involved immigrants and their divergent customs. The multi-cultural movement also seemed to transmigrate across a universe of aggrieved interest groups, within which varied constellations connected to subcultures undreamt of fifty years before, all brimming with indignation at any perceived slight or manifestation of disrespect. In his somewhat cursory research Thorndike had even run across demands on the internet regarding prohibitions on lascivious "street expression", and resistance mounted against the city of San Francisco by its local "S&M Community." This merely confirmed the jurist's suspicion that, disqualified by demographic, he was the wrong judge for this case.

But the Judge's training and life-long liberal instincts tended always to evoke sympathy within him for the excluded and the disenfranchised. After all, he reminded himself, so much of American jurisprudence was devoted to the pursuit of rights.

Diversity seemed to guarantee the social felicity necessary to progress--American as well as global. Diversity would bring new ideas, new perspectives and therefore, new strength to the American idea. The ideal of diversity would infuse the "pursuit of happiness" with real populist meaning, after all.

Then again, he thought, it was such a diabolically

supple word, that it could prove a stalking horse for anarchy in the minds of some, guaranteed to melt those few surviving bonds of civilization that still bound Americans to one another, as it worked its way through the body politic. Southworth had made that point tellingly. Far from spreading felicity around the world, violence, hatred, and political discord were all that deep-seated cultural diversity had ever seemed to bring. And truth be told, Thorndike's own Henry Ford-like dismissal of history as "over" in that earlier colloquy with Fulbright at the beginning of the sentencing phase, merely masked his own life-long interest in the subject; for the Judge believed all other fields eventually ended up in that one. History is what provides perspective and analogy, as well as any human claim to prophecy based upon objective reason alone. Of all fields open to enquiring minds, therein lay wisdom.

And as a dyed-in-the-wool progressive, Thorndike believed that the evolution of human societies, from their earliest beginnings, progressed inexorably from the simple to the complex, from diversity to synthesis, from diffusion to cohesion, rather than the other way around. And if that were so, wasn't the emphasis on diversity merely a mad dash in the *wrong* direction, culturally speaking? Wasn't this civilizational *devolution* instead?

Yes, immigrants hailed from diverse backgrounds, but the country had always had guardrails, rules-of-the-game if one liked, in which those core differences were eventually subsumed and assimilated. Were we to ditch all that now, and roll dice that might cough-up cultural chaos?

Then again, who'd *written* those rules in the first place? And why had one culture presumed the prescriptive right to dictate its own to others, especially given recent demographic trends? Mustn't the American government respect the sentiments of its increasingly diverse population? Otherwise, what did "democracy" even mean?

The day had gone gray with leaden clouds drifting in from the north. Jupiter was off varmint-hunting again. The Judge's coffee, neglected during his rumination, languished cold in his cup. Wearily, Homer Thorndike rose and headed for his law library. *Time to work.*

9:00 a.m.
Pope County Courthouse October 22

Judge Thorndike gaveled his courtroom to order over the dense, expectant audience and took a swig of water. He'd already postponed this hearing weeks longer than he'd felt he ought to have done; the long delay reflected the rival jurists within him, battling for his conscience and what would pass for his legacy. Now the day of decision had finally, fatefully arrived.

"Good morning, ladies and gentlemen," he began. He nodded at both defense and prosecution tables, then abruptly noticed: "I see that the Prosecutor seems to be absent from these proceedings. Is there an explanation for this?" Thorndike's surprise was feigned, of course. He'd been made well-aware of Southworth's decline in the intervening months, in the wake of his wife's death.

Samantha stepped forward deferentially. "I am sorry to report, Your Honor, that Mr. Southworth continues to wrestle with personal issues in the aftermath of his wife's death. At present, he is unavailable for this proceeding."

The Judge pursed his lips. "Then are you prepared to represent the State of Indiana in his stead?"

"I am, Your Honor."

"And you, Mr. Fulbright?"

The Defense Counsel stepped forward and barked, "The defense stands ready, Your Honor."

Homer Thorndike cleared his throat and took a deep breath. "I must begin by saying that I have never been placed in a more uncomfortable position in my career than I have in this case. The incident which took the life of little Roop Kumar and for which Sirkar Swaraj has been convicted is, by my lights, ineffably horrific. Having said that, I feel compelled to note, once again for the record, that this case also seems to me *sui generis,* insofar as the law respecting sentence mitigation is concerned."

He seemed to take notice of Samantha squirming in her seat, then proceeded:

"It rather goes without saying that the defendant was fatally neglectful in his role as the little girl's guardian. That is the most charitable conclusion one can reach based on the evidence presented here. After all, he has been identified as having attended the ritual. And while his active participation in the act of immolating Roop Kumar has been challenged, his tacit consent may, at the very least, be inferred from his attendance and failure to intervene. And although consent in such a situation seems on its face morally despicable, it is not necessarily dispositive to the question of his active participation in the event. I have determined that Mr. Swaraj was complicit and, as the very fact of his conviction implies, culpable in the child's death."

Judge Thorndike saw Fulbright's fingers were clasped before him; he'd bowed his head as if in supplication. He smiled within himself, then continued:

"Yet it is this issue of complicity that troubles me the most, simply because of complications that necessarily intrude from the issue of the multicultural context which has been the subject of such vigorous debate in this case. So, I will now address these.

To begin with, federal guidelines governing mitigation of Class A felonies clearly specify that account may be taken of the victim's state of mind, even the possibility of the victim's consent to the act. Speaking broadly, this provision would seem to apply most commonly to cases of assisted suicide, in which the victim had clearly taken steps to facilitate the ultimate act that resulted in death. Yet the most persuasive arguments in these cases involve an appeal to *common* suffering, and to the empathy we are prone to feel for those in the throes of it."

The Judge felt his hands trembling slightly, as did the papers they clutched. He tried to steady both: "Such fellow feeling certainly applies here as well. But our sympathy is directed instead toward the pain Roop Kumar unnecessarily endured in that fire, a conflagration which ended a young, healthy life rather than marginally prolonging a moribund one. Such would seem to compound our horror at the defendant's action rather than mitigating his guilt in any way.

"However," he said, "I cannot escape the fact that this sati event is inextricably bound up with culture and religion, albeit a religion that seems exotic and incomprehensible to most of the citizens of our State. This is not the same thing as saying that murder can ever be condoned or excused under the cloak of religion."

Thorndike cleared his throat and then went on: "Still, this is a *mitigation proceeding, not a trial to determine guilt or innocence.* As such, the *degree* of culpability in the defendant is the issue, assessment of which would seem to rest, to a large extent, both with the defendant's state of mind, and even with that of the victim, Roop Kumar, herself. Does the fact that she was, in the eyes of the state, a minor and therefore legally incapable of reaching a decision involving her own life or death, in effect, nullify her exercise of the religious beliefs that impelled the sati? If so, then there is no issue of mitigation to settle here."

Fulbright raised his head and extended his long arms, clutching the edge of the table before him.

Then, again, the Judge uttered that fateful qualifier: "*However*," prompting an audible buzz in the courtroom, "evidence has been presented which seems to fortify the position that this sacrificial rite is often perceived as an act of praiseworthy martyrdom by its participants, however misconceived this concept may be by our lights. There seem to have been, in India, no small number of such child widow-brides popularly acknowledged to be praiseworthy martyrs by the general public, whatever else Indian law has had to say on the subject."

Thorndike turned the final page of his decision and read: "Therefore, it may not be unreasonable to assume that Mr. Swaraj, who had arranged the marriage of Roop Kumar to his son, regarded her truly at the time of the sati not just as a daughter-in-law and a widow, but as a widow who was engaged in a noble act."

Thorndike looked up and saw that Samantha Desai's face had fallen into a mask of what looked like near despair. He went on: "And since sati has an ancient history in India, both licit and illicit, it is not *unreasonable* to assume, in a multicultural context, that Roop Kumar was prepared to engage, even if against her own interest, in a willing decision to sacrifice her own life. And if this is true, then surely the defendant may, in his role as her husband's father, likewise fall within the ambit of that cultural rationale.

"This, then, it seems to me, speaks directly to the defendant's state of mind. In fact, it draws a direct line to the issue of *motive* in the crime for which he has been tried and found guilty. And, in that context, the linkage between the decedent's *perceived* role in her own demise, and her father-in-law's *perception of ritual propriety in this instance*, would seem to this Court to satisfy the conditions allowing for mitigation as set forward by the federal guidelines."

The audience's rumbling reaction suggested profound discomfort with the ruling Thorndike was about to give, yet he pressed on:

"Therefore, I have decided that the defendant be sentenced to incarceration for a period of three to five years – said sentence to be limited to time served and the balance suspended. In addition, the defendant will be subject to three years probationary supervision."

Then, with what he hoped would sound like MacArthur-like finality, he brought down his gavel and raised his voice against the mounting din: "These proceedings *are closed*."

Immediately after Thorndike uttered his last syllable, he saw Swaraj collapse into his chair as if felled by a pistol shot.

Then a deep cadenced hum arose from the gallery, and Thorndike brought his gavel down again. He felt his face flush, and his voice trembled, "*Order! Order in this court!* I will have *order here or else!*"

"God be *praised!*" a man wailed. Others began to chant eerily: "*Sati mata ki, sati mata ki…*"

"I *mean* it!" Thorndike stood up, striving to elevate his voice over the din, but to no avail.

More in the crowd took up the chant: "*Sati mata ki, sati mata ki.*" Others put handkerchiefs to their faces and sniffled quietly in the verdict's wake.

"*That's it!*" the Judge thundered. "I hereby order the officers at arms to clear this courtroom forthwith! This court is adjourned." And he shattered yet another gavel to bits on the bench, its shards scattering to the floor below, where febrile spectators scrambled over one another for the cherished relics.

Instantly, the streets outside the courtroom descended into bedlam: Ecstatic Hindu celebrants charged out, proclaiming vindication. Reporters and cameramen found themselves caught in a vise between emerging spectators and sympathetic supporters in the street clamoring to join them. Within the milling throng, placards bobbed, cymbals clanged, flutes and trumpets lent raucous dis-harmony to a scene unprecedented in the history of this small town, now transformed in an instant into a national metaphor, a bucolic talisman.

October 22
11:12 a.m.

For what seemed like hours, Samantha sat at the prosecution table, cradling her head in her hands. The verdict had shaken her: every tenet of ethics she'd ever held, every conviction she'd ever espoused, every assumption she'd ever made regarding the inexorable march of modernity and reason, now lay in tatters. That this judge had swallowed Fulbright's argument simply defied belief...

She felt a gentle touch on her shoulder. Carl Peters said, "I'm sorry to pester you at a time like this, Sam, but have you heard anything from Allen? We still can't find him... anywhere."

She shook her head. "This makes no sense, Carl. It's just not like him to disappear for this long without telling anyone. Betsy Stark has the kids. She must know where he is. There must be some explanation, even beyond his grief...that is if he's still alive."

Carl turned rigid, staggered for a moment. He'd long harbored the same thought.

Sam felt as if she'd been sucker punched. After all

they'd gone through, now this. She fretted about his hearing Thorndike's decision second-hand. *Will he survive this day?* She couldn't banish that nagging query.

"Listen Carl," she said, in urgent but hushed tones, "you've *got* to find him. I'm afraid he'll be capable of anything in his state of mind – that is, if he hasn't already done the worst."

The Sheriff rubbed the back of his neck, speechless.

"Please, Carl, you can salvage this awful day if you just find him. Please!"

"Don't worry Sam," Carl nodded, "I'll find him. I have a sense about these things, and I think I know Allen; he's no quitter. But I have to ask: have you got any idea where he might be – some *private* place, maybe… meaning no offense, of course, Ma'am."

Sam immediately thought of Bald Hill and told the Sheriff, who nodded in recognition, then left quickly. Then she slumped into her chair again and tried to catch her breath.

She couldn't help feeling an enormous sense of failure. She should have been with him, to support him when he needed it most: to help with the kids, make casseroles or cakes for the wake, *something*. Any real friend would have been there. That is, if he'd even desired that… Sam wished she could have miraculously read his mind.

At last Sam steeled herself and went outside. The detritus of this *cause celebre* wasn't pretty: Hundreds of people sporting banners and signs still milled about, by turns celebrating, condemning or commiserating about the verdict. A legion of reporters was taking it all in, doubtless to exploit the juxtaposition of the case's notoriety with its Bedford Falls-like, All-America setting. Several rushed up to Sam, but they were mostly asking about Allen. Everyone wondered where he'd gone. She no-commented them off.

This isn't the way it was supposed to come out, she thought. *How could the judge have winked at this atrocity? Can America even make any claim now to be civilized?*

Then she heard a voice close to her right ear. *Allen.*

"Think they're gonna fete us – or hang us?" he grinned.

Her first impulse was to hug him, then instantly she thought better of it. He looked thoroughly drained, and at the same time, exhilarated by something. *He's sleep-deprived or suffering from post-traumatic shock,* was Sam's best guess. He looked a mess, hair askew, five o'clock shadow, stained shirt only partially concealed by the jacket he'd slung over his shoulder. *That's Crown Royal on his breath,* she thought, *but it's old...*

She wondered how he'd managed to slip to her side in the crowd without being noticed; but now they saw him beside her, and he shuffled toward a bank of microphones that had been prepared for after-trial post-sentencing interviews?

Some in the crowd – reporters, students, Ganges

Mission Hindus, representatives of the Diversity League and curious townspeople – appeared overtly hostile as they jostled for position. Oddly, aside from representatives from a local Right-to-Life chapter, there was not a women's group to be found. Across the street, Madison Fulbright looked over, leaning against his Porsche, sporting a shit-eating grin. *Of the victor over the vanquished,* Sam thought. Then, just as quickly, the smirk vanished when he spotted Allen. Guilt perhaps, she mused.

As he neared the mics, Allen's mind raced with images from the past few hours, during which he'd contemplated the passage between life and death. Even before Jan's death, he'd convicted himself of his own willful neglect of her. And for what had seemed an eternity those past few months, he'd looked for ways to inflict well-deserved punishment on himself. Myriad alternatives had leapt to mind: swallowing pills, crashing his car, swallowing the 38-caliber pistol Carl had given him in the cabin. He'd even driven up to Bald Hill to watch the sunrise and finger the weapon as he gazed over the valley below.

But then, as he watched dawn peek over the horizon, Allen sensed the death impulse receding. An unexpected serenity reasserted itself from unfamiliar recesses in his mind, abetted perhaps by the inescapable realization that his death would only make things worse. Most importantly, his kids needed him now more than ever.

He'd have to leave the maelstrom he'd created for himself and reclaim what was left of his family.

Now as he ascended toward the dais, a reporter blew-up Allen's reverie with unexpected deference. Taken aback for a moment, he looked behind him for Sam. She was nowhere in sight.

The reporter asked: "May we have your reaction to Judge Thorndike's decision, Mr. Prosecutor?"

Allen leaned wearily forward into the battery of mics and fell into a moment's forethought, absently massaging the back of his neck. He'd had little time to digest the result he'd heard reported on the radio as he drove toward town. He hadn't even contemplated tactically what his response would – or should – be.

Yet not really knowing what he would say, but somehow confident in his ability to say it well, Allen began: "To say I'm disappointed with the Judge's ruling would be to vastly understate my feelings.

"Occasionally, as much as it may dismay some of us, our legal system fails. Our history is punctuated with horrid examples: Dred Scott, Lizzie Borden, the Scottsboro Boys, Emmett Till, OJ Simpson. In my opinion, the suspended sentence of Sirkar Swaraj will take its place among these as a notorious miscarriage of justice."

A young woman followed up: "Then why do you think the Judge didn't see it your way?"

Allen leveled a steely gaze at her. "Well now, that's

a great question, to which I can offer only an intuitive response. In my opinion, the spirit of our times places a false, coerced, enforced political orthodoxy above candid discussion of anything that threatens to offend that perspective. That sort of climate, in turn, fosters intimidation, self-doubt, fear and an unattractive temptation to chip away at the principles which I believe have made this country the envy of the world."

Allen swiped at an unruly strand of hair that hung limply across his face. He was glad to hear himself speak well, off-the-cuff, relaxed, and from his heart. "American success, at its core, is really multi-*ethnic,* not multicul-*tural.* To pretend otherwise is to perpetuate a dangerous illusion that may well spell the end of this great experiment. I was under the impression that Judge Thorndike, presumably infused with the same values and principles with which I was raised, would be immune to such a specious hokum. I guess I was wrong.

However," he said sternly, "make no mistake about the 'message' conveyed by today's ruling: which is that the principles of the Western Enlightenment must now defer to a hodgepodge of practices and traditions that bear no relation to this country's foundations or, in my opinion, to its prospects for future success. Rather than being the last best hope of Earth, as Lincoln called us, we stand in danger of balkanization, perpetually sniping at one another with the same caliber of irrepressible conflict that so haunted the Great Emancipator.

It was my job to prevent this from happening. I failed, and I apologize profoundly for my shortcomings. That's all."

Then, ignoring forests of hands and a chorus of shouts, Allen stepped down to the street and purposefully strode into the courthouse. To his surprise and gratitude, the crowd chose not to pursue him.

Entering his office, Allen saw a sealed envelope lying on the floor, apparently slipped under the door. It was addressed to him, in what he immediately recognized was Sam's hand. Wearily, he plopped down into his swivel chair, opened the envelope, unfolded the enclosed note and read:

Dear Allen,

I lack the words to express how sorry I feel at Jan's passing.

The courage she showed toward the end revealed so much about her character, her fidelity and her love for you. I can only hope that the time will not be long coming when your tears are transformed by fond memories into knowing smiles of healing acceptance.

I'm so sorry I couldn't stay to tell you about these things in person. By now I'm sure you must be processing the awful ruling, and likely probably blame yourself even more than I blame myself.

Given the circumstances, I can see no future for "us," at least not until a great deal of time has passed, and the wounds of love and of battle have healed.

That battle has just begun for you Allen, whether you want to fight it or not. I believe the stakes are simply too high, and your profile's too large to forsake the fight now.

Please be consoled by the knowledge that I will be with you in spirit, every step of the way you take. For now, I can do no more, at least until I've sorted out my own mind; the line for me, between intense admiration and love, is just too fine.

And besides, I neither want nor would be able to compete for your heart with Jan's unconquerable spirit, at least not yet.

Much, much love, Allen. Always,

Sam

EPILOGUE

June 22
8:37 p.m.

Some months later, after a measure of calm had returned, Principia basked in the early sun of the summer solstice, on a warm evening of surpassing loveliness. Atop a ridge bisecting Prospect Hill Cemetery, a lone figure strode toward a black granite tombstone. There he halted respectfully and removed his hat.

Ever since the verdict had been announced, the outcome of the Swaraj case had sparked a firestorm across the country—pitting ethnic, sexual and political identity groups against one another, emboldening extremists on all sides, shattering venerable political alliances. Allen and Madison Fulbright hadn't spoken since the trial and Allen's subsequent resignation as prosecuting attorney. He just couldn't stay on, especially after his prolonged absence, and his indelible association with this trial. Everyone had an opinion, it now seemed: he was either loathed or lionized. Oddly, it was only Allen himself who felt shame.

In the end, he thought, *who knows where the blame really rests for this whole infernal mess?* Thorndike had blown it, but Allen couldn't help but feel the judge had been intellectually ambushed. As had he. His mind also wandered to the spectral Savarkar, who hovered like an incubus over his recollection. He must have been the puppeteer in the drama, although Allen couldn't be sure how or why. Oddly, or perhaps not, he simply disappeared, likely back to India, immediately following the trial. Carver hung around, sweating to rehabilitate his damaged reputation as best he might. His 'movement' would go on, perhaps with more popular energy than ever.

Allen had been to the cemetery several times since Jan's funeral, the largest attended in Principia's history, at least if Greg Conkling, the local funeral director, could be believed. Allen had come this evening for the same reasons impelling every visit, to talk unashamedly, to grieve, even to compose imaginary banter with his mate, lover, and friend.

Guilt lingered though, especially since life had been good for Allen since Thorndike's ruling. He'd been offered more work than ever before and had been invited to Chicago and Milwaukee as a consultant for high-profile cases in the emerging culture wars. As in his own big case, they'd involved the ritual abuse of girls and women: genital circumcision, honor killings, child brides, polygamy and the like.

Viscerally, Allen sensed that an inflection point was at hand, that national calamity lay somewhere over a clouding horizon, sounding a fire-bell in the premature night of this new century. He'd even been approached by an agent to pen a memoir of the sati trial and sell movie rights to the story of the case with which he and Fulbright were now—like Darrow and Bryan with the Scopes "Monkey" trial—forever linked.

But to milk that tragedy for personal gain? It just didn't seem right to Allen that he should.

Unhurried, he now unbuttoned his leather trench coat and reached inside for an envelope. He removed a piece of paper from it. Then slowly, deliberately, he lit one corner with a disposable lighter. He held it at some peril in his fingertips, watching the flame dance and leap as the paper curled and blackened.

A check was burning, a big-dollar one that had been hand-delivered by messenger that afternoon – an advance on that proffered memoir, if only he would just expose his soul yet again about the case. *Maybe someday,* he thought, *but not yet.*

A brisk wind gust lifted part of the burning check's ashes into a vortex and scattered them to a particulate oblivion. Allen pinched the last remaining fragment of the check, and then let it blow away. *Not very lawyerly of me,* he smiled to himself.

For a moment, he stood, eyes closed, a friendly zephyr whispering in his ear. Then Allen began the short walk down the slope and through the iron gates to town.

His Town.

The End

ABOUT THE AUTHOR

DR. BRUCE WESTRATE is a scholar and historian specializing in the British Empire, Modern Middle East, Modern Africa, and South Asia. Currently, he serves as Master Teaching Chair in the Humanities at an elite private prep school in Dallas, Texas. Born and raised in rural southwest lower Michigan, he holds a B.A., M.A. and Ph.D. in History from the University of Michigan at Ann Arbor and remains an avid Michigan football fan. Dr. Westrate is the author of **The Arab Bureau** (Penn State Press, 1992), the definitive work on the subject, currently in its thirtieth year in print, often cited and widely praised in such outlets as *Journal of Military History*, **Oxford History of the British Empire**, and *Middle East Journal*. In addition to book reviews, columns and commentary for the *National Review*,

Westrate also contributed a chapter on the British abolition of sati in India to the compendium *Rediscovering the British Empire* (Krieger, 2003) which served, in part, as inspiration for this novel. Westrate lives in Dallas, Texas with his wife of over 40 years. They have two children and continue to split their time between Texas and Michigan.

www.ingramcontent.com/pod-product-compliance
Lightning Source LLC
Chambersburg PA
CBHW030842030726
47495CB00005B/1329